Pr

"charming" with "skillful prose and compelling characterization ... a book you won't want to miss"

Writer's Digest Book Awards

"Really classic, soul-moving stuff. It is unforgettable... The romance was described exquisitely -- gorgeous, living-eternally writing! ... you have created a masterpiece ... I absolutely could not put it down."

Marilyn Savage Gray, author of *The Real Shakespeare*

"LK Hunsaker has a compassionate voice and an artistic eye. This is a realistic, warmly emotional novel and an engaging, satisfying read."

CRR Reviews

"One thing you always do sooooo well is incorporate all the senses of your characters. I love that so much about your writing. Not only are we in their thoughts, but we are remembering, smelling, seeing, touching right along with them."

Cheryl Pierson, author of *Fire Eyes*

"In the style of most great storytellers, Ms. Hunsaker has created a cast of characters that captivated me, had me on the edge of my seat, not even wanting to close my eyes at 4 am. Though I am known for not wanting to stop reading in the middle of the story, I can scarcely recall a time that I have become so engrossed in the lives of the characters so totally. "

dee and Dee Dish ... About Books

"The writing is excellent. Very evocative and searing."

Keena Kincaid, author of *Anam Cara*

Novels by LK Hunsaker

Finishing Touches (2003)

Rehearsal: A Different Drummer (2006)

Rehearsal: The Highest Aim (2008)

dedication

This one is dedicated to my Uncle Les.
artist, musician, educator
philosopher
We still have much to learn from you.

With Love,
Loraine

acknowledgements

There are always so many to thank with the release of each new book, I hardly know where to begin. As always, a huge amount of appreciation goes out to Rulon, Liz, & Eric, my husband and children, for their ongoing support. And to my extended family and friends who I tend to neglect while in the midst of character and story creation. Thanks for not throwing up your hands and walking away.

I would like to thank Vicki Blankenship for use of her song lyrics as this novel's music epilogue. It's amazing how someone else's words can echo my own thoughts so well. And you did it in only a few lines!

Thank you to my critique partner, A.L. Marquardt. Yes, why was I telling readers that it was his face she found instead of ... an elbow?

Thank you to Paul Bucalo who read the rough almost-final draft and pointed out little things that made a big difference in the actual-final book. You could have slept more in between reading instead of giving yourself a headache, though.

To Kathi, Ami, and Sara Hawkins, my business partner, a burgeoning young writer, and a yanked-in reader who is hard to yank in. Thanks for the draft read and editing assistance! Nice to know the ARC was exciting enough that it's bedraggled by now. Beautiful website. ;-)

To Kris Dawson and the other folks at RoadieJobs.com – keep rockin' on the road and moving the music out to us.

Thank you to Mercer County, PA Commissioner Kenneth Ammann for assistance in getting just the right 'ledge' photo to use on my cover.

And to Ines of InesCreations.com for use of her gorgeous photo of the moon! Need a photo or design help? Tell Ines I sent you.

Finally, to Dr. Dee Preston-Dillon of Cultureplay.com for fueling my psychology passion and sharing your knowledge of and love for the cultural, artistic, spiritual, wide-open view of the science of the mind. I'm tremendously glad our paths entwined.

In Memory of Michael Jackson:
You were one of those in it for the passion of the art. Rest in peace.

Off The Moon

a novel

LK Hunsaker

ISBN 978-0-9825299-0-4

Library of Congress Control Number: 2009935123

I've Waited For You lyrics ©2008 Vicki Blankenship from "Blue Flame Trance" 2009. Spotted Kiva Productions. All rights reserved. Reprinted by permission.

Cover art: LK Hunsaker
Photo of Moon ©2009 InesCreations.com Used with permission.

elucidate publishing

elucidate publishing
staff@elucidatepublishing.net
PO Box 1262, Hermitage PA 16137
(we prefer email!)

Printed in the United States of America

This novel is also available in electronic format, ISBN 978-0-9825299-1-1

Part One

"Who knows if the moon is watching
o'er poetic souls tonight
while blindly they go wandering
amidst the pale gray light
A harbinger, the owl flies
it pays the dark no heed
and poet souls see only flight
no danger in its wings..."

(from **If The Moon Knows**, ©2000 Ryan Reynauld)

"C'mon Reynauld, you're already in fryin' water. Where're ya going?"

Ryan veered around his bodyguard, dodged an ugly silver car doing a bad job of parallel parking, and jogged across the street. Daws would stay on his heels even if he was late, and Mac could wait. What choice did he have? Ryan paid for his time.

X ⟋ He stopped in the middle of the sidewalk to peer up at the office building. The height made him cringe. It wasn't even one of Manhattan's taller buildings. Seven stories. Tall enough.

"What is up with you today?" Daws stopped at his side. "You're edgy as hell and you've seen this building a thousand times. What is so fascinating?"

"Not sure. Maybe nothing." He strode a wide angle around a couple of girls heading his way as they eyed him, pushed through the glass doors, and slid between a crowd of business suits and briefcases. It reminded him of a mud-covered pig rooting through tight-assed penguins. Grinning at the thought, he decided to hold it in his mind to use later.

Daws cut him off. "The paycheck is *that* way."

"And what are you going to do? Throw me over your shoulder and make me go? Come on, lighten up. I'll only be a minute." He feigned anger at the body blockade. "Either get out of my way or come with me. There's something I gotta do."

"Something you can't do across the street where you're supposed to be?"

With an eye on where the girls he'd avoided were descending and joining forces with a few more, Ryan shifted out of their vision as much as possible. "Not unless you can pick this building up and move it over there. Might get kinda messy, though."

Daws crossed his arms in front of his chest. "I'm not one of your flattering fans who thinks you're hysterical. You're holding everyone up and no matter who you are, their time matters..."

Ryan ignored the rant and ducked around to sprint toward the elevator. He called for someone to hold it when it started to close. Stares answered and relief showed on a suit's face just before the door clenched tight. "Great. Guess we do the stairs."

"Let it go, Reynauld. I promise if you're good and play nice, I'll bring you back after work."

"Funny. We're getting a crowd, you know. The more we delay, the more there'll be and I'm not giving in." Ryan noted the glower and did his best not to smile while near-sprinting toward the stairwell. He took the first couple of flights two steps at a time as he called to Daws he'd meet him at the top, and slowed part way up the third. What was he doing? Why did he have to check it out when he was already late? But then, when wasn't he late? Why today? He shrugged. Why not today? It woke him up the night before. There was no sense letting it nag him instead of walking up and looking.

At the seventh floor, he pushed aside the yellow no trespassing tape and turned the door handle. It worked. The hallway he crept into looked like any other hallway, except no one was in it. A deserted office building floor after nine in the morning was a strange thing, but no stranger than the building owner marking the floor off with no explanation. It had gone unused for months. No code violations. No events Ryan ever heard about. It was simply closed. His writer's brain couldn't accept there wasn't a reason. No one else seemed to care, remarking only that the owner was eccentric and did such things from time to time. It wasn't good enough. There was a reason.

Ryan walked down the hallway and peered through open doors. There was nothing in the offices but a few scattered desks and chairs. A good place to write. Quiet. Non-distracting. Maybe that was why he'd been drawn to it. He could find the owner, or have someone find the owner for him, and ask about using it. Not using it exactly, but *not* using it, since the guy wanted it *not* used. Writing music, sitting by himself, wasn't using it – only occupying a bit of its space. There was plenty.

Nearly at the end of the hallway, he turned at a door slam.

"Are you happy yet, moron?" Daws gestered with his phone. "Enrico says there's not only a couple or three girls down there, but a whole damn army of them descending. Can we escape out of here before I have to call in the crew?"

"So we'll wait 'em out." He ran his fingers along the white wall trim. No dust. And no dusty smell. The silvery blue carpet looked new but without the new carpet scent.

"You're shittin' me, right? Wait 'em out? And that's worked real well in the past."

"Yeah, okay." With a deep breath and a thought that Daws would've been more occupied if Ryan had arranged an actual army of girls, he headed back.

And he stopped.

"This way. Let's go."

Taking three steps back, Ryan looked into the empty office he'd just passed. Nothing. He thought he'd seen something, but there was nothing. At his guard's taunt, he continued forward. But the window was open. Why? At the next open door, he peered inside. The window was closed. So was the next one.

"Hang on a second." He returned to the room. The window was open. There were no bars, nothing. And no one there.

"What are you doing now?"

"Something's out there." Ryan drifted closer. The seventh floor. He could see people in the windows across the road, shadows floating around in the building where he was supposed to be.

"Reynauld, if you saw something out that window, it damn well better have been a bird or I'm calling the nuthouse like I should have umpteen times before."

"Maybe it was a bird." Of course. He *was* a moron. What else would he have seen? Too many shots. It was nothing but way too many damn shots the night before. Still, he wasn't sure. And he couldn't look. "Do something for me. Look out the window." He frowned at Daws crossing his arms in front of his chest. "I'll go, no hassle, no stalling ... just look out the window for me."

"Not interested. I've seen pigeons and I'm not a big fan of the dirty creatures."

Ryan gave up. Seven floors were too much to look out over. His stomach twinged already from standing halfway across the room from the open window.

At the door, he paused. He had to know.

With a knot in his throat, he hurried over before Daws could stop him and before he lost his nerve, and touched the frame. A cool breeze slapped at his face. Spring air. Normally he loved it, but this time it made him shiver. Or it was nerves. Daws muttered in the background about leaving his ass there. Ryan knew he wouldn't, not for long. He would be back.

Gritting his teeth, he stepped closer, prepared for the flapping of pigeons. There were no birds. But there were shoes. To his right, on the wide window ledge, a pair of old tennis shoes were perched, their heels against the window and toes pointed forward ... out. His stomach turned while his eyes followed the shoes up to baggy jeans, a faded sweatshirt covering most of the fingers underneath, and a diminutive face with long straight hair sweeping across it with the breeze. Startled eyes caught his: round greenish-brown eyes. A girl. Young, emaciated. Afraid.

What did he do now? Yell for Daws to get the police? It would scare her more and that was probably the last thing that would help. If anything would help. Maybe nothing would. Maybe this would be the life-changing event his brother told him would eventually happen to make him be an adult. Maybe he was destined to live forever with watching a young girl end her life. But not if he could stop it. No amount of venting through songs would ever help him deal with that.

He forced his voice not to shake as he had practiced a bazillion times at the start of his career. "Is the view nice up here? Myself, I prefer the ocean view. You know, 'cause if I fall in the ocean, I can swim. I've yet to learn how to fly, though. But hey, to each his own, right?" He got nothing but a stare. "I bet it's cool to watch everyone down there scurry like ants. I don't have the nerve to look myself. Heights aren't my thing. But hey, describe it for me. I'm visual. I'll get it from what you say."

Her eyes remained on his, wary. She said nothing.

"How about if you come this way more so I can hear you better? I haven't heard a word yet."

When he reached a hand toward her, she slid farther from him. He pulled it down. "Hey, it's okay. I'll listen harder. I'm Ryan. I'm supposed to be at work across the street but decided to check out your place first. Glad I did. I don't often get to meet anyone who goes to extremes to be alone as much as I do. It's quiet out here, huh? Well, not so much since I'm annoying you and you can tell me to go away if you want. I know how it is." Complaining to himself about sounding so stupid, Ryan heard Daws return and tried to wave him away.

"Had enough air yet? I should leave you to deal with that crowd alone. It'd serve you right. What in the hell are you looking at?" Daws stuck his head out.

The girl pulled away more.

"No, it's okay. He'll leave. One of us is bad enough, right?" Ryan shoved the guard back and found her leaning to try to see inside. "Come in. It's okay."

She leaned back against the dirty brick wall. Hair blew into her face and out again.

Ryan studied her features and decided she had to still be in her teens, although it was hard to tell as thin as she was, much too thin to be healthy, and pale. Where were her parents? Other family? Friends? Someone. There had to be someone who wondered where she was, someone who was supposed to be caring for her. He had to gain her trust, at least somewhat. How?

His mind drifted to his favorite thing other than music. "Do you like boats?" She held the stare. "I love boats, and I can tell you the view from a boat drifting out on a quiet lake is like nothing else. Isn't it? Especially when the sun begins to set and even better when it begins to rise. It's been forever since I saw it. How about we go check it out? Weatherman says it's supposed to be gorgeous the next few days. Want to get up before dawn and watch the sun rise over the river? I know a great spot where we won't be bothered."

Her face relaxed.

"I can pick you up from wherever you want and you can bring a friend or two along. I know it would be crazy to accept a blind date from some idiot who just happened to show up on your window ledge, but if you invite someone, it's cool, right? Daws'll be there. He's nearly everywhere I am, although I can ditch him if you'd rather. He's not as grouchy as he looks. Well, he is grouchy, but he's a sweet grouchy. Don't tell him I said that." He waited while she stared. "What do you think? I can try to arrange a boat. Do you like boats?"

"I've never been on one." The voice was nearly a whisper – soft, shy, and still afraid.

"No? Wow, then you're missing something. I bet you'll love it. Can I take you? Not just you, but you and whoever you want to bring. A brother or something is fine, too. Whoever."

As she watched him, the fear drained but something else filled her eyes. Sadness. Longing. She was entirely too desperate. Stupid thought. Of course she was desperate. Why else would she be up there? He wasn't letting her go. She was coming back in. Whatever he had to do, she was coming back in.

Noise within the room turned his head and Ryan nearly panicked at the sight of Daws and several uniformed policemen. They would scare her for sure, and she was just starting to calm. One of them asked him to move. The girl flinched at the strange voice, backed up again.

"Wait." Ryan pushed himself up onto the ledge and told the officer to stay where he was, away from them. He ignored a moron comment from Daws. Ignoring his stomach wasn't so easy. Damn, he hated heights. He hated looking down over one staircase. This ... this was suicide. He was going to lose it.

"What are you doing?" The girl's eyes drew him in.

He shrugged, very carefully. And he fought the sickness that welled within while he rose to standing position, his fingers clamped onto the window frame. "Thought I'd see your view first since I'm trying to share mine. Gotta say..." Managing to breathe took most of his concentration. "I like mine better. Your turn?"

"Go in."

She was worried about him. It gave him a glimmer of hope.

The officer told them both to come inside and they'd get help. Ryan considered asking for a barf bag but decided he couldn't let himself barf. It would throw his already overly shaky balance. "So?" He forced his eyes on the girl. "How about we go see the water now? From a boat. A small boat. Or a large one if you'd rather. I can deal with water below me."

He wasn't sure she'd be able to hear his voice over his heartbeat. He also wasn't sure his heartbeat wouldn't get strong enough to bump him right over the edge. He was becoming horribly sure he was not going to live through this. Maybe the heart attack would kill him before he had to hit the pavement. Which would be worse?

"Go in."

"Not without you. It's your turn. Come share my view now."

She looked toward the window where the officer poked his head through, saying they would get help, everything would be fine. Ryan considered throwing the moron comment at him, but he was doing his job. What else could he say?

"Hey." Trying to act less idiotic than he felt, he hoped he could convey with his eyes half what the girl could. "We're having a chat here. Can you give us a minute?"

The officer hesitated and was pulled back by someone not in uniform.

Without moving any part other than his neck, he returned to her eyes. "See? Just us again. So you have a name?"

She stared.

"Yeah, I know, I'm a stranger, and probably stranger than most, but really I'm okay. Ask that grouchy guy in there who calls himself my friend. He'll vouch for me. Maybe. Depends on the day … and you know, maybe today he wouldn't. But uh, I do have friends who would. Wanna meet them?" She was thinking he was insane. It was in her eyes.

Noise from below, down at street level, caught his ear. He didn't dare look. She did, though.

"Being watched, are we?"

She glanced over, and back down.

"Anything for a show. Ignore them. Ready to go in with me?"

Her eyes remained below, toward the voices yelling 'jump' and others preaching in one way or another. Vultures, all of them. Ryan couldn't imagine a life so pathetic they'd use this as entertainment. What was she thinking?

"Ryan, is it?"

A strange voice pulled his attention and his heart flopped at his movement. "What? I'm kinda busy."

"It's not working. You need to come back in and let us handle it."

Questioning the guy in a business suit with a glance, he saw Daws standing close, telling him to come back in. Except he couldn't. He was in this too far. A shiver scared the hell out of him and he gripped the window tighter. He told the guy to back off when he grabbed his wrist.

"Go in." Her voice was calm, the eyes more so. He was losing her.

"Not without you."

"I won't go back. I won't let them take me back."

Take her back? The police. She'd done it before, or tried to do it before. A big help they were, apparently. She looked down at the crowd.

The crowd. If there was one thing Ryan knew how to do it was to work a crowd. "What if I promise not to let them?" Her eyes returned.

"What if I promise they won't bother you or take you anywhere?"

She waited, wanting to believe him maybe.

"If I can fix it so they won't, will you come in with me?"

"You can't."

"No?" He grinned. *Can't* wasn't something he acknowledged. Those he worked with called it ego. He called it what got him as far as he had come. "Daws." Carefully turning back to the window, he found his friend close by. "So we got a good crowd down there yet?"

"What?"

"How big is it? You know I'm not about to look. Photographers? Newspapers?"

A quick warning flashed in his eyes, but he played along. "A crowd. Hell yes, there's a damn crowd. They caught wind of who you are and the place is packed for blocks."

"Hey, a guy has to keep his name in the papers, right?"

"Reynauld..."

"Trust me." The words were barely mouthed, meant only for his guard. He forced his attention away from the window and toward the girl. It took all the acting skill he'd learned for his job to tell himself he was on stage, overlooking a crowd only a few feet away. He was behind a microphone. She was a fan. He let her round eyes and long lashes become his focal point. A fan. And a microphone.

He heard his voice shake at the beginning, but he steadied it as he sang one of his songs, one in development he didn't like yet. *Behind a microphone on stage.* He raised the level, wondered if they could possibly hear him seven stories down. His voice carried well. He couldn't count the times his mom told him to lower his voice when he jabbered in excitement. When he was younger. He learned to control it as he grew. Voice lessons to sharpen and strengthen it helped that. Still, he doubted they heard him seven stories down.

The thought jolted him back to where he was and he stopped.

"You're a singer."

He nearly laughed at her question. Anyway, it sounded like a question. "More or less." Her confusion intrigued him. She had no idea who he was, even with Daws using his last name. "You don't follow music much, do you?"

She stared. Relaxed. Standing seven stories up, backed against a brick wall, she was relaxed enough to ask if he was a singer.

Talking about music helped relax him, enough his heart beat slowed a touch and his stomach calmed. Maybe he would get out of it without plunging its contents into the crowd. Great headline that would make. Even better if he followed it down. He had to pull from that thought.

"Yes. I'm a singer. Songwriter. Guitarist. A touch of piano. Jack of all music trades. Not all. I haven't learned much production yet. The one I was just trying to sing is mine. It's bad. But it's mine."

"Are you done yet?" Daws. Annoyed. Maybe even scared.

Ryan didn't look back. "Don't know. Think I need a microphone. Doubt they'll hear me down there. Shoulda thought of that." He kept his eyes on her.

"They can hear you in here and they're waiting with handcuffs. This has to be your stupidest stunt yet."

Handcuffs. Wonderful. Good headline, though.

"Go in. They'll arrest you." Her eyes widened.

"If they do, he'll bail me out. And I'll tell them it was all my idea. They won't bother you."

"No." She looked toward the edge, down.

"Hey. Don't. Really, it's fine. It's promo. No big deal. Likely help sales. You know, like the Beatles and their rooftop concert. Got them arrested, too. Great stunt."

She returned her stare.

He started singing again. Louder. When he came to the end of the words he'd written, he paused, and made up more.

"Let's *go*, Reynauld." Daws had definite fear in his voice this time. "You come in now and we only get a fine."

"Hell no. Jail time is better publicity." He sang louder. Ryan had no idea where the words came from, but they revolved around her, and they kept her attention.

He stopped. Her eyes held him in. Every part of him wanted to reach out and grab her, pull her back inside. Daws talked to him, told him he'd have a hard time finishing the album in jail, making up words like Ryan was. They wouldn't leave him there. They'd get him out.

"Are you okay?" Her voice was too calm.

"Yeah, I always get sick-looking when I'm on a ledge. Weakness on my part, I guess. Gotta give you credit. Don't suppose you'd come in now?"

She shook her head. "They'll take me back."

His stomach turned. Fear. For her. "No. I won't let them. Promise." He had a definite feeling she wanted to believe him. But she didn't.

He turned to be sure his guard had the window clear. He didn't see anyone else but kept his voice low, in case. "Tell them we're coming in. Make sure ... make sure they know it was my idea. She's ... an actress. Stunt person. Make sure they know I hired her."

Ryan thought he might not listen this time. Daws followed him through a lot of stupid stunts, but his expression said this was too far. Except he knew this one wasn't a stunt.

"Don't move." His eyes held a fierce warning.

"Don't worry." Ryan put all his focus on trying to breathe as his guard disappeared. A few seconds. He knew it was only a few seconds, but it felt like eternity before Ryan saw his face again.

"We're gonna get one huge-ass fine, but they're leaving."

"Good."

"Good. Yeah, I'm sure the label's gonna think it's good."

"They will when it helps to shove my face all over again. Things have been slow. Are they gone?"

Daws looked back and nodded. "Except a couple making sure you come back inside so they don't have to go scrape your sorry ass off the pavement."

The imagery hurt his stomach. With a shallow breath, he turned back to the girl. "It's fine. They think you were part of my act." He offered his hand.

She shook her head.

"I promise. They won't take you anywhere. I'll give you a lift wherever you want to go, or we can sit inside and chat, or go find a boat. Although the boat thing might be better tomorrow when my heart starts working again and I'm not so nauseous." He raised his hand an inch higher.

"I can't."

"Sure you can. Hell, if I can stand out here during a heart attack and fake a publicity stunt, you can edge back this way with me. I think you're gonna have to 'cause otherwise I'm not gonna be able to move."

"I can't be alone anymore."

He studied her face. Her eyes were calm, yet so deeply bothered, hurt. Ryan had never been the emotional type. Everything always brushed over him, at least that anyone could see. But this ... this girl, in clothes too big and hair whipping across her face, standing against the building as though fighting its support and wanting it all at once ... nearly brought tears to his eyes. She couldn't be alone. "What if I promise you won't be?"

She was wholly unimpressed by his words. He had to wonder how many promises she had seen already broken.

"What's your name?" At her hesitation, he tried harder. "Please. Just tell me your name."

She glanced down and back to his gaze. "Kaitlyn."

A cool breeze rustled her hair and smacked at his face. A pigeon swooping by made him cringe. But he kept her eyes. "Kaitlyn, I promise you. I promise I won't let you be alone again. Please, come in with me. I know you have no reason to trust me, but what do you have to lose? I promise."

Ryan knew Daws was behind him, making plans to try to catch him if the heart attack finished him off and he fell, or if he moved and slipped. At this point, he wasn't sure it wouldn't be preferable to get it over with than to fight the sickness in his stomach and pain in his chest, and the feeling he would fail and have the image of the girl in his head forever.

She took his fingers. Shyly, shaking, her fingers slid into his while she watched his face.

He swallowed hard to keep himself in control. The fingers were cold, bony, so small he was afraid to grip them. But she accepted. "Thank you. Can you help me get off here now? I seriously don't think I can move."

With more hesitation, she inched toward him, and squeezed his hand. "It's cold."

"Not inside." Ryan slid his feet closer to the window. How he got in, he wasn't sure, but her hand was still in his and Daws was apologizing to the remaining officers. They left after a glance at the girl said they didn't quite believe the story.

"Want to introduce me to your friend?"

His friend. Ryan supposed she was now, or would need to be. Her eyes were more wary than they were on the ledge. And she looked even smaller. "Kaitlyn, meet Daws. Fred Dawson. My bodyguard."

Daws stepped forward and reached for her hand. She retreated, hiding halfway behind Ryan, still gripping his fingers.

He turned to her. "Hey, it's all right. I know he's kinda huge and scary looking, but he's safe. I trust him with my life. Literally." His heartbeat began to calm with her gaze. "You're safe, Kaitlyn. And I promise you won't be alone anymore. I understand more than you realize." Her eyes were doubtful but maybe he would explain in time. Maybe he could eventually tell her that even with the crowds trying to grab him and girls throwing themselves at him all because of the image, that most of the time, he felt utterly alone within his guarded shell. Without Daws, and his family, he couldn't imagine dealing with it.

She wrapped around him, the tiny arms barely noticeable as they pressed his side, her face against his neck.

Ryan set his arms around her back, carefully and slowly, so he wouldn't scare or hurt her. He had never dealt with someone so frail. Or with anyone who needed him nearly as much.

Tension drained and filled his stomach. "I'll be right back." He saw fear when he pulled from her arms. "It's fine, I just.... I need the men's room, but I'll be back. Daws will be here." Her eyes widened. "Kaitlyn." She flinched when he touched her face. "Hey, I promise it's all right. Give me three minutes and I'll take you out of here and we'll go somewhere to chat. Okay?"

She didn't argue and he couldn't wait for better than that. Ryan rushed from the room and hoped to hell the plumbing on the unused floor still worked. Finding a door and pushing in, he leaned over the closest bowl and released the nausea.

Daws told Ryan to stay put until he could provide a fake departure and lure fans to follow or leave. His guard had called in part of the security team. Two of them stood at the doorway of the office. It made Kaitlyn nervous so he took her to a far wall and sat on the floor against it.

"It could be a while. Might as well sit with me."

She looked back toward the door and over at the window.

If necessary, if she headed toward the window, he would get there fast enough to stop her. If he had to, he'd call a guard over for help, although Ryan imagined it wouldn't be hard to stop her. Even if he wasn't bodyguard-size.

She shivered.

"Here." Getting up again, he removed his jeans jacket and held it for her. "Too hot for me now with my blood pumping like it is. Go ahead." She didn't move, so he wrapped it over her shoulders. He couldn't help wonder why she would hug him as she had one minute and cringe at his nearness the next.

"So do you listen to any kind of music?" Ryan kept an eye on her, but lowered back to the floor. "Let me guess." He tilted his head as though he could actually figure out what she listened to by studying her. "Heavy metal, right? Guns N' Roses?" No reaction. He tried again. "Hip Hop?" Humor didn't work. He shrugged. "Beethoven? Or ... Go Gos? Goo Goo Dolls? There has to be something you listen to."

She grasped the edges of the jacket with opposite hands and pulled it tighter.

"Sure you don't wanna sit?"

With another glance at the door, she backed up against a desk and lowered slowly, half facing the door, half facing him. Far enough she could get up and away if he so much as moved. She looked like she might jump if he did.

She wouldn't *go with them again*. The police. He wanted to ask her about it, about where she meant. Some kind of mental facility, he guessed. From what he'd heard off-hand about the places, Ryan could well understand her fear. She wasn't crazy.

"So, is there somewhere I can take you? Someone who'll want to know where you are?"

She shook her head.

"Where are you staying?"

Her head dropped onto her arms wrapped around her knees. He could barely see her face, her eyes closing. The girl was exhausted.

Ryan decided to take her home, to his loft. He had an extra room. Music equipment would have to be moved and stuff he hadn't bothered to put away would have to be taken off the bed. And it was a mess. His housekeeper wouldn't be there for a couple more days. He supposed he would have to add a day or two to her schedule as bad as he was about cleaning up after himself. Kaitlyn would think he was a pig. Just as well she knew the truth, he figured.

"Let's go." Daws stood in the doorway. Kaitlyn's head jerked up at his voice.

Ryan pushed to his feet and offered her a hand. He was surprised she took it and was careful not to squeeze her fingers too hard. Her eyes touched his, questioning.

"It'll be fine." He half expected her to bolt back to the window and grasped her arm when she stepped that direction.

"I have a bag." She looked toward a desk against the wall.

He didn't release her, not sure it wasn't a ploy. But he walked with her, and she leaned down to pull a faded brown miniature book bag from beneath the desk. It wasn't big enough to hold clothes. Had she left it with a note inside? There had to be something in it that mattered with the way she gripped it against her body.

She stayed on the side opposite Daws and pressed into Ryan when one of his guards got close. The path was clear and Daws rushed them into the hired car. He gave the driver directions to circle a couple of blocks, then stop across the street in case they were still being watched.

"Take us to the loft." Ryan pushed on his shoulder.

"Hell no. All of this just to try to get you to work, you're damn well going, even if you are two hours late."

"This isn't the time. It'll wait."

"Not with the kind of money they're putting into this thing, it won't."

Ryan leaned forward. "You work for me. I make the calls."

Daws turned in his seat, a large hand helping him stay faced backward. "There won't be cause to work for you anymore if you keep this shit up. And I may work for you, but I'm the closest you've got to a friend in this business. Don't think all those leeches you have over partying all the time are going to stick around if you lose all this." He glanced at Kaitlyn and turned back around. "You're going to work."

Daws was right, but then, what did Ryan care if any of them stuck around? Still, he was paying a hell of a lot for studio time.

What was he supposed to do about Kaitlyn? He couldn't imagine she would want to sit at the studio while they put down new tracks and went back over bits of edits to re-recorded what they didn't like. It was boring to watch. Often, it was boring to do, especially since they edited the hell out of everything. She didn't need to be surrounded by strangers, either. She needed to be ... somewhere comfortable, and warm. Somewhere she could unwind.

But he had to work. Girls didn't come before that. Ever. Not even one he didn't mean to find.

With his guard's guarantee he would tell no one it was anything other than a publicity stunt, Ryan led her into the building. He offered to call someone to pick her up and take her to the loft while he worked, but Kaitlyn shook her head.

"Damn it, Reynauld. What got into you pulling a stunt like that? Daws, why didn't you throw his ass over your shoulder and drag him in here?" Ginny grazed Kaitlyn with the look she gave any of the girls who attached themselves to him.

"Good morning." Ryan threw an arm around his manager. "Thought I'd give the day a jump start, so to speak. You missed me, right? Or you were afraid you might miss me?"

"Reynauld, I am fifty years old and I divorced a man five times cuter than you are with more money than you have only because he annoyed me one time too many. Why I'm still putting up with you, I don't know, but don't give me any of your mouth today. I've already had to sweet talk Mac into not going off to Bermuda with what we're paying him, for unused studio time, by the way. You better have a damn good explanation and it better not be...." She eyed Kaitlyn again. "Aren't you young to hang out with him? Trying to get your parents to sue us for..."

"Ginny, stop there. It's not like that."

"No? And yet you're two hours late because you and your little *friend* here decided to be cute and..."

"And hey, it's promo. My name is all over the papers again. Gotta be worth a bit of lost studio time."

"Hm. We'll talk more later. In private. Get moving." Strong fingers tried to shove him toward the studio. "Sweetheart, can I call you a cab? He has work to do."

"She's staying with me." Ryan went back to her. "There are chairs outside where I'll be working. You can sit with Daws..."

"No spectators. Send her to your place if you want. Daws will find someone..."

"Not this time. She stays with me or I take her home."

Virginia Gray, a woman he was rarely able to argue with, looked between him and Kaitlyn, noting her clothes, studying her face.

She stepped backward.

Ryan caught her hand. "Hey, it's all right. They're not used to me bringing anyone in, but..."

She backed away more when a couple of his musicians approached, laughing.

"Damn man, she's been fuming. It's amazing she hasn't knocked you flat already." Ned moved his gaze around Ryan to Kaitlyn. "Uh, since you were late anyway, you coulda taken her to her own place for clothes instead of making her wear yours."

"Stop there." Ryan moved closer to the girl and kept his voice low while Daws backed everyone away. "Ignore them. You're all right here. They talk a lot, but they're okay. No one's gonna bother you." Her eyes darted toward the exit. He wasn't about to let her go. "I have to get to work. Come with me."

He had to half pull her toward the studio, ignoring Ginny's glare. With an apology to Mac for being late and a quick introduction, Ryan pulled a chair in front of the window where she would be able to see him ... where he would be able to see her. "If you need anything, tell Daws. He'll make sure you get it." He glanced at his friend. Daws would know Ryan expected him to keep an eye on her.

Ryan threw out each of his musicians' names although he didn't expect she would care enough to remember them all. Ryan didn't always remember their first names. He was glad he did at the moment. Even if they were staring, wondering why in the hell he had a girl there, and why he bothered to introduce her.

"Have a seat." He held the chair, but she held her stance, close to him, back nearly against the wall. He wasn't going to be able to leave her. "Or..." He grabbed the back of the chair and tilted his head toward where he was going to be. "Come on in with me. You'll have to be careful about when you talk or anything but I don't suppose that'll be much of an issue for you."

"Whoa." Ginny stepped in front. "Too far, Reynauld. There's no reason she can't sit right here, or back at your place if you trust that..."

"I'm not asking permission and anyone who has a problem with it can keep it to themselves." Ryan didn't care how shocked they were. He was frustrated enough talking to someone who wouldn't answer. "If you want me here today, you're gonna have to stop bitching about everything I'm doing." He felt his stomach tighten at the stares. But he wouldn't back down. Not this time.

In near silence, he caught Kaitlyn's eyes, relaxed his own expression, and took her behind the glass, setting the chair close to the door where it wouldn't be in the way. She stayed on her feet while the musicians filed in behind and took their places to tune their instruments. And she didn't sit in the chair. She lowered to the floor beneath the window, pulling her knees up, her back resting against the wall. Ryan couldn't fathom why she preferred the floor but he wouldn't argue. At least she seemed okay there.

A couple of hours in, they took a quick break. Mac said to make it a short one since they were behind schedule and Ryan offered Kaitlyn a hand to help her to her feet.

"So how'd you get him to bring you in?" Ned stopped beside them, too thoroughly amused, by the look on his face.

"We only have a few minutes." Ryan swerved around him.

"Okay, so I can walk and talk at the same time. Where'd you meet her? Hell, you haven't been anywhere I haven't recently. Unless I missed something." Ned followed out the studio door to the hallway.

"It's been a long morning. Can this wait?" Ryan didn't bother to get an answer. He stopped at the restrooms. "Back in a sec. Yours is there."

"Hey, maybe she wants to follow you into the john, also." The bassist snickered. "Okay with me. She might want a good view of a real man." He winked at her.

Ryan shoved him against the wall. "Knock it the hell *off*."

"What in the fuck is wrong with you?" The bassist shrugged away with a push against his shoulders. "Damn. We always harass the hell out of your girls. When did you start giving a shit? And when did you start bringing them here?"

"She's not my *girl*. Knock it off."

"Whatever. You're the boss." With a sideways glance, Sam pushed through the door.

Kaitlyn caught his eyes and disappeared into the ladies' room. Damn. He'd only meant to.... Disappeared. She was alone behind the door. His stomach knotted and he debated going in. The stall she was using would be closed and Ryan didn't figure anyone else was in there. Except it would freak her out even more.

He told himself to unwind, to give it a couple of minutes, and he went into the men's room. He didn't acknowledge the bassist's look.

She wasn't in the hall when he came out. Girls took longer. Ryan knew they did. He would give it another minute.

Still, she didn't come out. He paced and pondered whether to knock, to play it safe or give her space. And he told Ned to go on ahead, he'd be there in a minute.

A girl who walked past threw a grin.

"Hey. Could you do me a favor?"

A small pivot and she sauntered up to him, casting her eyes down his body and up again. "You're Ryan Reynauld, aren't you? I heard you were working here. You're taller than you look on stage."

"Not saying much, is it?"

She smiled, the bright red lips parting to reveal perfect white teeth. He smelled roses as she stepped closer. "Funny, I didn't expect anything remotely like humility to come from you. Based on what I've heard."

He knew without a doubt this girl would go find a closet somewhere with him if he asked. "And yet you're standing here talking to me."

"I like men who know what they want."

He would sure as hell consider asking if he hadn't already been so late, and if he wasn't worried about Kaitlyn. "Uh huh. Well, I'd owe you big time if..."

"Anything."

Damn. Maybe she'd be around later. "Uh, this is gonna sound weird, but ... there's a girl in there who doesn't feel well. I just wanna be sure she's okay. Would you mind ... don't tell her I asked you to check, just..."

"Morning sickness or did you break up with her?"

He brushed off the implication. "Neither."

"Sure. Not much of a favor, but if you think of anything else, I'll be back out in a minute." Swiveling her hips, the tight jeans showing every move and curve, she edged into the toilet.

Ryan paced more. Another minute passed. Daws came out of the studio and asked what he was doing. "Just a sec." His guard remained in the hall.

The girl came back out. "Is she off or something? 'Cause she's just standing against the wall. I tried to talk to her but she didn't answer..."

"Anyone else in there?"

"Just her. Is she a nut case? Should I call someone?"

"No. Thank you. If you give that guy down there your address, he'll have something sent as..."

"Tell you what. I'll give him my phone number instead. In case you want it for anything." She winked. "Good luck."

Ryan called Kaitlyn's name as he entered. The girl was right. She stood against a wall, holding her bag. "Is this view better than the studio?" He crept closer. "I mean, at least you don't have my ugly mug in your face, or you didn't have, but ... come on, Kaitlyn. I gotta get back to work."

She didn't budge.

"Did I scare you? I won't hurt you. You don't have to be afraid of me."

She shook her head.

Daring to move in front of her, he touched her fingers and eased into a light grip of her hand. "So come on back. I'll try to finish quick."

"I should leave. I'm too much trouble."

His breath caught. "No." He ran his thumb over her cold hand. "You're no trouble. It's fine." Too much trouble. Who had she been too much trouble for? Her family? "I'll tell them I need to leave. If you don't want to be here, I'll tell them I'm done for the day. But come out of here. We'll ... get something to eat. I'm starving. Maybe not a good subject for the toilet, but..."

The door opened. "Reynauld, quit making an ass of yourself and..."

He looked over at Ginny. "Not now."

"And I expected you to be at least half undressed. Glad you're not. Let's go. Break's over."

"Damn, would you watch what you say?" He started to tell her he was leaving, but Kaitlyn moved ... away from the wall. "Need me to take you home?"

Her eyes jumped to Ginny's and returned. Her head shook.

"You're okay with going back in the studio?"

She started toward the door and paused until Ginny backed out of the room.

The stares told him he would have to come up with an explanation of some sort. They would have to be answered. She returned to her position on the floor, still refusing the chair. Ryan sighed and decided to think about later. He had to work.

Her eyes remained on him; at least they were whenever he checked. The studio was warmer than he liked, and it annoyed him until he thought about the iciness of her fingers. She needed warmth. He wanted to go over and see if they were thawed. He wanted to ask if she had things somewhere. Something other than the little bag still tucked against her side. Clothes, maybe. Something not as old and baggy as what she was wearing. He wanted to ask again where she was living, who she lived with. There had to be someone, somewhere.

"Reynauld?"

He looked through the window at his producer.

"You missed your cue. Are you all right? You look ill."

Amidst heckling from his band about altitude sickness, Ryan shook his head. "Nah, I'm fine. Let's get this done."

"Try staying with us, then."

He forced his thoughts as far from the girl and the window as possible, and tuned into the music playing through his headset. He closed his eyes to try to think of nothing but the sound. And he lost the words. The music stopped. With an apology, Ryan told Mac to start again. He hit the cue, got the words, wasn't happy with his tone but figured his producer could fix it ... and Kaitlyn shivered. Why did she shiver? It was warm.... He fumbled the words and the music again stopped. "*Damn.*" Pulling off the headphones, he pushed a hand through his hair. "Mac, I'm sorry. This isn't gonna work today."

"Yeah, I was getting that. Go home. We'll start early tomorrow."

He set the phones on the stand. "I'll work through lunch and dinner if I need."

"I know you will." Mac gave him a half grin.

Ryan went to Kaitlyn and offered a hand. Her fingers were still icy. His drummer started to comment and Ryan threw a silent warning to force his silence.

"Can I talk to you a minute before you go?" Mac glanced at Kaitlyn. He wanted the conversation private.

Ryan told her he'd be back in a sec, leaving her close to Daws, and followed to the water dispenser. "I know. This is costing me money..."

"Who is she?"

"Why?" He wasn't sure how to answer.

"I hope to hell you haven't caught anything from her. 'Cause she looks..."

"No." Ryan could see he didn't believe him. "I haven't been close enough to catch anything more than I would catch from you."

Mac nodded. "Good. You might want to keep it that way."

"It's not like that." He saw the bassist try to talk to her. She stepped back, eyeing him. "I gotta go."

"Reynauld." Fingers gripped his arm. "Be careful."

"Always." He grinned and went back to Kaitlyn while she first evaded the bassist and then moved away from Daws as he backed Sam off.

She was a child, a frightened child. All he could think about was why? Why had she been pushed to such an extreme? Attention, maybe. He'd heard of girls making half-hearted attempts for the attention they weren't getting. But her eyes said differently. He had never in his life seen such honest sincerity in a gaze as he did in hers. It was a look well beyond her age as he guessed it.

"Ready to go?" He stepped between her and the others. He wanted to tell her it was okay, that he wouldn't let anyone bother her, but he didn't want to make it an issue in front of his musicians. "I'm starving. What do you like? I'm not picky, so we can stop and get anything." Ryan paused to let her answer. She didn't. She was keeping an eye on those around, still without directly looking at anyone. "We can decide on the way. Let's get out of here."

She drew in when he touched her back to guide her in the right direction, but he left his hand there. He wanted the contact.

She wouldn't say what food she preferred, or anything else, from the passenger seat of his current rental car. Renting threw off fans who tried to watch for him and he enjoyed the different experience of each vehicle. Daws pushed him to have a driver so he wouldn't be out on his own, but he couldn't deal with that much restriction. He liked to drive. Now and then, he drove down places he hadn't been just to find his way back, and to be alone. It was about the only time he was ever alone. Somehow, someone always knew when he was home and decided to drop by. Mostly, it didn't matter. Now and then, he shoved them out the door. They knew to expect it.

What was he going to do with Kaitlyn? A young girl staying at his place would look bad, for both of them. That kind of publicity, he didn't need. She maybe wasn't of age yet, and that could especially be bad, but he couldn't put her out with nowhere to go just because it didn't look good to have her there. He would have to find a place for her.

His brother's, maybe. Will's wife could look after her. Ryan would call later and get their reaction. Tracy and Will were always taking in stray animals, or at least taking them into the backyard and caring for them until they could find someone to adopt them. He wondered if the last mutt Will picked up was still there. Hopefully not. The thing scared him, although most animals didn't. That one, some kind of Rottweiler mix they thought, didn't like humans, or other animals. Will expected it was abused but thought he could turn it into a decent pet. Ryan had his doubts.

If they would take that animal under their care, they would never refuse Kaitlyn. And she would flourish with Tracy's devotion and his mom's fondness for cooking.

She still wouldn't suggest a type of food, so Ryan decided to stop at his favorite Chinese takeout. It was usually fairly empty. Their business was good but almost no one stayed to eat.

Pulling in front, he went around to open her door and again touched her back. She looked at him but didn't tense as much. Car sounds and exhaust fumes gave way to a jingle of bells against the door and the savory sweet aroma of whatever was sizzling in the kitchen. His stomach growled.

"One Ryan special." The owner smiled after calling back to his cooks. "And for the lady?" He asked her directly.

"Everything's good here." Ryan tried to see which huge food image on the wall above the counter she focused on. He couldn't tell. "Trust me to order for you?" Getting a light nod, he added something different than his, not spicy, then guided her to a chair, held it and sat across from her. "Is this all right?"

She caught his eyes.

The continual non-answering bugged him and he put his focus on the window, watching city life pass around them. An old white TransAm zoomed by and made him think about adding one to his collection. He wouldn't want it in the city, though. The starting and stopping and brake-riding would be too hard on it. He could use it only when he drove to his brother's but it wasn't especially a good long-ride car, either. He'd rented them now and then, newer versions. Fun, yes, but not what he needed, at least not now.

Silence annoyed him more than not getting answers and he talked about his work just to fill the air. He didn't bother with questions.

When he lost something to talk about, Ryan gave up, hoping the food would be done any second so they could leave.

"Are you going to turn me in?"

Not sure he heard her right, her voice a whisper over the kitchen sounds, he leaned closer. "If I were going to, I would have already." Her expression was again doubtful. "Kaitlyn, you're safe now. I don't know what you're running from exactly, or trying to escape, but if you need anything ... if you need help, say so. I have a lot of friends in a lot of places. I can help you take care of whatever you need."

"Why?"

He raised his eyebrows, unsure what she was asking.

"People have said they wanted to help. They always wanted something else, not to help. I don't … I can't…"

Ryan moved to the chair next to her. "I don't want anything from you." He took her fingers when she pulled back. "Look, this is going to sound very arrogant, I'm sure, but there is nothing I need from you, and I don't mean that the way it sounds, but I have a lot of people who help me when I need it. If I want something, I can get it. My life is my music and not really much else. I don't know how to make you believe I'm telling you the truth because obviously a lot of people haven't, but I don't want anything from you."

She stood and headed for the door.

"Kaitlyn." Ryan followed and took her arm. "Where are you going?"

"I'm in your way."

Stunned, he shook his head. "No. You're not in my way." He heard the owner say their food was ready but kept his attention on her, on how to convince her. Quite a task that would be since he couldn't quite convince himself.

The bell rattled and she moved farther from people coming in – loud young guys who scanned her. Ryan pretended to scratch his forehead to hide his face. One of them spoke to her and she backed up.

"Let's go." He went to pick up their order. As he paid, he heard a laugh about what she wore, that it was a shame to cover up her figure with her big brother's clothes. He didn't dare say anything. They'd recognize his voice.

Plastic bag in one hand, he grasped her fingers with the other. "Are you coming with me?" She nodded and stuck close until he shut the car door behind her.

He started the engine, appreciative of its soft purr. "Do you have things somewhere you need to stop and get?"

She clutched her little bag in front of her stomach. "I don't have anything else."

He couldn't even respond. How would she have nothing but that? She had to have something somewhere. "Okay. Are you all right with going to my place for now?" At her silence, Ryan gave up and pulled away from the curb. She would have to be okay with it, he supposed. He had no idea what else to do.

2

"Sorry, it's kind of a disaster area." Ryan pushed stuff to the side of the table to make space to eat. "Kaitlyn? Are you hungry?"

From where she stood close to the door, the girl looked lost. He decided to let her settle in on her own time while he pulled warm containers from paper bags and went to the kitchen to grab colas, keeping an eye on her enough to be sure she didn't leave.

He set her Chicken Lo Mein in front of the chair beside his. Maybe the smell would entice her. The General Tsao Chicken they always made extra spicy for him wafted its scent up to his nostrils. His stomach growled, but he tried to remember his manners. "The bathroom is through there if you want it." He nodded toward the far end of the loft that led to the more private areas – the only private areas. Most of it was wide open. "Make yourself at home. There are towels and stuff in the linen closet. Grab what you need and if you need something you don't see, let me know. Are you going to be insulted if I start in? I'm starving."

With a bare shake of the head, she edged toward where he motioned.

Ryan cringed when she got close to the corner where he wouldn't be able to see her, and pushed out of his chair to catch up. "Hey." He touched her arm and she swiveled toward him. "No, it's okay. You're okay, right? I mean ... you'll be back out in a minute?"

"Yes."

He frowned. The yes wasn't very persuasive. "If I trust you're being honest, will you think about trusting that I'm not going to bother you? That's going to be kind of important. We're going to have to have some kind of trust."

"I need to wash my hands."

Ryan expected it was at least somewhat of an agreement. "Okay. Take your time, but if I get nervous, I'm going to knock and make sure everything's all right."

"I'm starving, too."

With a deep breath, he backed away. Starving. Except she maybe meant it literally. She looked like she could be. If she didn't eat much of the Lo Mein, he would try something else next time. He wanted her to eat well. And he wanted to call Will, but not while she would walk back in and hear him. Tonight, he needed to be available to her. Tomorrow, he would start sorting things out.

She returned within a couple of minutes and took the chair next to him, picking up the fork. "Thank you."

Ryan gave her a grin she didn't see. Her face tilted down, her profile in perfect view other than her light brown hair dangling along her cheek. It wasn't much different in color than his, though a finer texture and somewhat stringy. Maybe not clean. She'd smelled of grass and dirt when she held him. "You're welcome."

He cleaned partly as a distraction after the near-silent late lunch and she tried to help but he took her to the living room and switched on the television. She wouldn't take the remote. Flipping it to music videos since he had no idea what she might want, he left it on the arm of her chair and went back to clean the kitchen better than he usually did. There were plenty of leftovers they could use for dinner. The *Ryan special* consisted of three different dishes that always allowed him leftovers, and Kaitlyn barely ate. He offered to share any or all of his. She didn't accept.

With nothing left to do in the kitchen, Ryan headed to the couch. Her legs were curled up in front, twisted to recline against the arm of the big stuffed chair. Her own arms were stuffed between her legs and her stomach. Did she always sit that way or was she cold? It felt warm enough for him, but then, he had a racetrack metabolism for reasons he couldn't figure for as non-muscular as he was.

She accepted the blanket he offered and wrapped it over her legs and up to her shoulders.

Drained from the morning's adventure, Ryan thought about calling Will to get his brother's advice. He couldn't quite make himself leave her there again while he was elsewhere, though, so he claimed the remote and flopped on the couch, alternating between the videos he wanted to watch and switching to see what else he could find.

When he was convinced she was interested enough in the music for it to hold her attention, he went to clear off the bed in the guest room, looking inside plastic bags to remind himself what he'd thrown in there. Most was stuff he'd been given during the last tour that hadn't already been donated to a children's hospital somewhere: teddy bears with hearts and phone numbers attached, a T-shirt or two boasting the name of a town or school, a pair of ... why did he still have thrown-on-the-stage panties? He never took them ... oh, the wolf design ... he'd thought it was funny ... from the girl with a matching tattoo in a place he never should have seen from stage, and toy wolves of all kinds. Ever since that article came out about how he was fascinated by wolves as a kid, he'd been given the damn things at nearly every show. Most went to hospitals and shelters, but a few he reserved for Will's kids and a few he kept. Very few.

Shoving it all in the already-crowded closet, he pulled back the brown comforter and covered the bed with fresh sheets. She had no clothes with her. He sure didn't have ... well, he didn't expect she'd be interested in the wolf panties ... and otherwise, he had nothing that would fit her. Figuring she'd have to make do, he went to his own room and grabbed a T-shirt and his smallest pair of sweatpants.

She was still watching videos when he returned and plopped on the couch. "If you want a shower, go ahead any time. There are clean clothes on the bed, first door to your left, that might work well enough for tonight. And there's bath gel a friend left here if you don't want to smell like Irish Spring. Best I can do as far as girl stuff right now."

She accepted immediately and he cringed when she closed the door.

What would he do about the next day? He couldn't take her to the studio in the same thing she'd been wearing. There would be too many comments. Maybe they would stop at a store and find something that fit, something that looked like a girl. The kids in the restaurant had checked her out in front of him. *Big brother's clothes.* Did they think she was his sister? That could work. He could say she was related. There wouldn't be issues with her staying at his place that way. Except he couldn't say she was his sister. Too many of them knew he had only a brother and a sister-in-law. But a cousin maybe. It would also stop any rude remarks. They wouldn't dare make comments about his family.

Grabbing the phone while he listened for the bathroom door, Ryan dialed Daws and asked him to spread the suggestion she was his cousin. He didn't want to say it directly. If the truth came out later, he didn't want to be on record saying she was related.

Daws didn't argue the cousin issue. "What are you doing with her tomorrow?"

"Taking her with. What else? Don't think I wanna leave her here alone."

"No shit, you don't. She may take off with everything you have."

Ryan hadn't even considered it. "Well, I'd rather that than the actual reason I don't want her alone. She's in the shower now and it's making me nervous as hell."

"Want us to come over?"

"No. She's afraid of you, I think. I want her to unwind and settle in."

"Yeah well, be careful and sleep light. She could be mental."

"She's not. I'll see you at the studio."

"Hell you will. I'm picking your ass up in the morning. Be ready."

Ryan heard a click on the other end and hung up. When he walked over to the bathroom door and didn't hear water running, or noise of any kind, his stomach twinged and he forced himself to knock. No answer. "Kaitlyn? Is everything okay?" Still nothing, and he knocked again then started to reach for the handle, hoping she hadn't locked it.

It turned and she was there, hair wet and streaming down her back, his T-shirt huge on her tiny frame, the sweats gathered into a bunch at her ankles and brushing the floor. "Guess it's good I'm not bigger, huh?" He didn't get an answer and it didn't bother him. Returning to their previous positions, Kaitlyn picked up the blanket and wrapped into the oversized chair. A hummingbird in a hawk's nest. She didn't fit in his loft any better than in his clothes.

She barely ate when he heated the leftovers, and Ryan always had the urge to snack while he settled in at night, so he got up to see what he could find. Dumping chips in a bowl for her, he preferred to remain the pig he was and eat directly from the bag, likely till they were gone. He couldn't offer a beer or much else of what he had. There were tea bags, though. Tracy left them last time she and Will visited. She said it would help him relax. He had yet to know whether it would since he hadn't bothered to open the box.

With little belief it would work, Ryan shoved two mugs of water in the microwave and leaned back against the counter to wait. Had it only been that morning he found her? Why was he pulled to the building today of all days? Many times he'd wondered about it, about why the top floor was closed. Always before he managed to push it out of his thoughts. He was damn glad he hadn't been able to this time.

At the first beep, Ryan shoved the button to open the door, and with a deep sigh, he grabbed the mugs. Unable to carry everything, he took the chips out first, handed her the bowl and went back for the mugs. He tugged on the strings for a few seconds, inhaling the warm herbal scent before giving up his hiding spot.

"My sister-in-law says this is good for relaxation. Haven't tried yet, but thought we could."

She didn't take it, her eyes wary.

"It's just tea. Chamomile if I'm saying that right. I'm not much of a tea drinker. A good whiskey shot is more my line, but ... well, I guess I better not offer that."

Her fingers touched his when she accepted. And her body slumped into the chair while she sipped the tea and indulged in a few chips. Already, she seemed nearly a different person than earlier in the day. Maybe she would be all right. Maybe it wouldn't be long before he could call Will and make his request.

He couldn't sleep. He kept seeing the vision of Kaitlyn lying on the pillow and cuddling into the blankets like she hadn't had any in so long she'd forgotten what it felt like. Grabbing a shot of the whiskey he couldn't offer her, Ryan went to the main room, switched on the television, and lowered the volume. He wouldn't have been able to tell anyone what he was watching. His thoughts were on her.

With a start, he realized he'd fallen asleep on the couch, propped at one end with his head against its back. He wasn't alone. Kaitlyn was on the other side of the couch, scrunched against its arm, wrapped in the blanket, eyes closed. Ryan forced himself off the couch and went to her.

She jumped when he touched her shoulder, arms flying up into a protective posture.

"It's okay. Kaitlyn, it's okay." He caught her eyes in the near-dark of the television's glow and sat next to her. "Why are you out here? Is the bed uncomfortable? You can have mine."

She shook her head. And she didn't need to answer. He knew why she was there.

Ryan stood again and offered his hand. "Come on."

She stared.

"It's all right."

With a moment's pause, she accepted. He took her to the guest room and pulled the sheets back. Why she'd remade the bed in the middle of the night, he didn't know, but she slid under the covers with his gesture and didn't object when he joined her. Ryan was careful not to make actual contact although it was a small double. He possibly should have taken her to his room where the king size bed would give them more individual space. Somehow, that felt more wrong, though.

<center>~~~</center>

"I'm *coming*." Ryan trudged to the door and checked the peephole. With a yawn, he opened it for Daws and his girlfriend.

"Fall asleep on the couch again?" Daws glanced at the wrinkled T-shirt and sweats.

Ryan left him to close the door. "Hey Deanna. Why'd you let him drag you over here?" He grabbed the blanket Kaitlyn used the night before, moved it out of the way, and wondered if she'd slept through the doorbell and him getting up to answer.

"I hear you have a visitor who might need a few things."

Ryan threw Daws a look.

"He tells me everything. Don't worry, sweetie, I won't tell another soul. I just thought she might need something to wear until I can take her shopping. Freddy says she's smaller than I am but I found a few things that might work and some girl things I know you won't have, or at least I hope you won't have." Deanna held up a bag.

"You're an angel. What are you doing still stuck to him?"

"Enjoying the torture, both ways. So is she still here? And did you sleep at all last night?"

"Yes, and no. I uh ... woke up a few times to make sure.... She seems to have slept well."

"That's good. Is she all right, hon? He told me what you did. You're the angel. That poor thing. Did she say why?"

"I didn't ask. Thought I wouldn't push since she's barely talking to me so far." He stretched his neck.

Daws interrupted. "Get changed. Half an hour and we're outta here. After yesterday's stunt, you're not going to be late today."

"Relax." Deanna hushed him and turned back to Ryan. "Is she awake? Should I take these to her?"

"Uh, no, better let me. I don't want her to wake up to a stranger." He accepted the bag and nodded at Deanna's offer to stay at the apartment with her for the day if Kaitlyn didn't want to go to the studio. Then he went back and knocked at the slightly opened door. No answer. He nudged it farther and she looked over from where she was sitting, the comforter wrapped up around her.

"Good morning. Sleep okay?" He moved closer and held up the bag. "A friend brought a few things for you to borrow." Noting the grip she had on the comforter, pulled up like a sort of shield, he sat on the opposite side of the bed. "I have to be at the studio all day and I'll have to leave soon. Deanna ... she's Daws's live-in and a real sweetheart ... the one who brought this stuff, she said she'd stay here with you today if you want. Or you can go in with me. It's your choice. It's kinda boring sitting around the studio all day but if you want...." He hesitated, hoping she would go with him. He would never keep his mind on work otherwise.

"Do you want me there?" Her voice was light, cautious.

"If you want. It's up to you." He waited, and her eyes said she wanted a better answer. "Yes, I want you there."

She nodded and got out of bed, standing still until he gave her privacy.

Ryan refused to listen when Daws argued against taking her until Deanna said she would go and sit with Kaitlyn at least part of the day.

"Works for me and I'll love you forever for it." Ryan lowered his voice when the bedroom door squeaked. Someday he would take care of that. "She's uh ... pretty scared about something, so I expect you to knock out anyone who even thinks about bothering her."

"Oh, and I can just hope someone does. I'd love to be able to do that today."

Chuckling, Ryan turned at his guard's comment about it fitting well enough.

Kaitlyn stopped at the living room entrance. The sweater hung on her, sleeves pushed up so they wouldn't encompass her hands, and the jeans were baggy and rolled at the bottom. It looked more like a style choice than like big brother's clothes, though. She appeared older, or maybe she was only less tired. Her hair still fell straight and covered part of her face and the tops of her shoulders, but it was fuller since her shower the night before, giving a more healthy appearance.

Deanna wasn't bothered that her greeting wasn't answered. She chatted about the studio and how boring it got after the first ten minutes and that she and Kaitlyn could go wander the city a while in between if she was interested.

The girl didn't answer, but she also didn't refuse Deanna's company, at least not out loud. She did back away from Daws when he tried to hand her a cup of the coffee he'd started as soon as he entered the loft.

"You were grouchy yesterday and scared her, didn't you?" Deanna threw her boyfriend a teasing grin and took his arm. "Don't worry, hon. He only talks big. I'm the scary one of the two of us, nevermind his job."

"Yeah, no kidding." Ryan took the cup and offered it himself, relieved she accepted. "I'm a hell of a lot more scared of her than of him."

"Ryan Reynauld, what on earth makes you think you have reason to be afraid? You know I let you get away with anything. And you're the only one."

"Uh huh. I'm not pressing that issue, though, I can tell you." He focused on Kaitlyn, trying to keep her drawn into the conversation. "I'd hire this woman as a guard if she was willing." As soon as it came out, he wondered if he should have said it. "Although, she's a hell of a marketing consultant so it'd be a shame to pull her from that."

Kaitlyn watched him while she sipped the coffee she held in both hands.

"Anyway, are you hungry? I've got some microwave stuff in the freezer we can throw in before we go. Daws is going to yell about how late it is in another minute, but we've got time for a couple of those frozen eggs and bacon things wrapped in crust..."

"*Ryan*. Are you kidding?" Deanna nudged his arm. "Heck of an impression you're making. Cook for the girl. You can do real eggs."

"Are you going to keep your boyfriend from jumping my ass if I'm two minutes past the half hour?"

"I'll jump his if he jumps yours. Eat. You're always too skinny."

"Nah, you're just always comparing me to the boulder, here." He gave his head a tilt toward his guard. "You want eggs while I'm being forced to cook?"

"He already made me breakfast. Eggs, ham, toast. Puts you to shame, doesn't he?"

"Usually. Thanks for the reminder."

With a glance at his watch, Daws threw the look that said he was forcing patience. "If you're going to eat, get to it and stop jabbing or we'll never get out of here."

Ryan led Kaitlyn away from the squabbling couple and pulled out a kitchen chair for her.

"You don't need to." She touched his eyes.

"It's going to be a long day. You should eat first." He saw an objection. "And I'm starving."

Rubbing the back of his neck, Ryan could've hugged Mac when he said it was time to go home. He was beat. And Kaitlyn looked it, too.

She agreed to sit in the control room with Deanna most of the time, until late in the day when she hinted about being inside the sound room with him instead. At least Ryan figured the way she clung to his side at the end of a short break was a hint. She again sat on the floor, her legs pulled up in front, arms wrapped around. It annoyed him, as though she was trying to make herself invisible.

It also bothered him that she hadn't said a word to anyone through the day. During lunch, Deanna said he should get a professional to talk with her. Daws agreed, stressing she shouldn't stay at Ryan's, that committing her would be for her own safety. Ryan didn't agree, with either option. He couldn't risk suggesting professional help yet. She had to trust him first.

When he took her side, Ryan saw her eyes follow. He wasn't one to be bothered by stares; hell, as much as he was stared at, it couldn't matter anymore, but somehow, hers did. "Ready to get outta here?" Without an answer, not even a nod, he set a hand on her arm and ignored both her light flinch at his touch and his musicians throwing each other glances at her silence.

In the secured parking garage, at the space reserved for Daws beside Ryan's currently unused space, his stomach told him it was past time to eat. Maybe he would actually cook for her instead of stopping for take-out, even though he was exhausted.

He held the door of his guard's '87 Monte Carlo while Kaitlyn slid into the back and then got in beside her, leaving the front for Deanna. He'd stopped complaining about being squashed into the back of the thing long ago whenever Deanna was with them. She wasn't very often, and at least the T-tops were off so it didn't feel too closed in. Neither he nor Kaitlyn was big enough to require more space than the car allowed.

The thing always smelled strongly of leather from its immaculately maintained seats. Daws didn't hire someone to take care of his car as Ryan did. As far as he knew, playing with it was the only hobby his guard had.

"So what do you like to eat?" Ryan relaxed against the head rest and considered grabbing one of her hands just so they wouldn't again be nervously folded on her lap. "I've got nothing at the loft, but I can arrange something."

She didn't answer, but Deanna bitched about him ordering out again.

"I meant I'd have groceries delivered. You know, *real food* as you call it. What about ... steaks would be quick. Do you eat steak?"

Kaitlyn gave him her eyes only.

"You mean you're actually cooking for the girl?" Deanna pivoted in her seat. "Wow, you better know that's an honor, Kaitlyn. The best he usually does for his company is a catered meal. The boy is really lazy when it comes to stuff around the house. Not that he doesn't deserve to be since he works his tail off on the job, but..."

"All right. Thank you." Ryan tried to shut her off. "She's seen my place already and I'm sure she's figured out I'm a lazy slob. You don't have to rub it in."

"Yeah, so what's with your housekeeper? Are you ready to find one who actually cleans yet? Because, you know, Ryan, paying the woman for what she does is kind of ridiculous."

He shrugged. "I trust her not to bother anything if I'm not there. That's not so easy to find."

"A lot of good it does when you have to do what you're paying her for."

"She's old, Anna. She does what she can. What? You want me to cut off her only source of income other than the pathetic social security she gets? Can't do it."

"Hm, I think she could do more if she wanted. She's playing you since she knows you won't fire her."

"Whatever. Anyway..." He turned back to Kaitlyn. "Steaks all right? The potatoes'll have to be boxed 'cause it takes too long the other way. You'll eat steak and potatoes, right?" Getting a nod he barely noticed, Ryan grabbed his cell and hit his sixth speed dial number. They would get it to his place fast. He tipped well and they all knew he did.

As he ordered, he asked Daws and Deanna if they wanted to stay – a courtesy only, and he knew Daws would agree. He didn't trust the girl. He didn't want her in Ryan's loft. He would likely hang about even more than usual while she was there. Ryan supposed it was good. He had no idea what to do with her and since she barely spoke, he felt like he was talking to himself. Not that he didn't.

~~~

Across the room, Ryan sipped his beer and thought about how Kaitlyn still said nothing to anyone but him. She'd been there a couple of days since he found her, and she'd gone to the studio with him both days. Deanna dropped in to see if she wanted to wander the city and Kaitlyn did nothing but watch her, acknowledging the question but refusing to answer. It was making his musicians edgy. He never had girls there.

Even with the cousin rumor, they didn't know why he would suddenly change his own policy.

"Why are you being so quiet?" Deanna nudged his arm.

He looked back to Kaitlyn wrapped into the chair she'd claimed, away from where Daws was talking to Ned and his current girl. The drummer hadn't been invited, but then, he generally wasn't. If Ryan didn't like him so well, he would object to Ned dropping by with his girls of the moment to impress them by hanging out with 'Riveting Ryan Reynauld' at his place. No matter how often Ryan asked Ned to stop introducing him that way, ever since that one damn journalist gave him the title, Ned was intent on driving him crazy with it.

"Ryan?" Deanna stepped in front of him. "You're worried about her."

"Of course I'm worried. Hell, she tried...." He shrugged. "Maybe she wouldn't have actually but you never know, and..."

"And you barely know her. Freddy can't figure out why you took her in. I'm not sure, either. Everyone knows you're a full-out arrogant ass who hardly notices anyone around you unless they have something you want, so we're in a shock with this. We can't figure why you suddenly care about someone you don't even know. If she was older, and ... built or something, I wouldn't be so surprised."

Ryan grabbed a long swallow of his beer. If anyone else had said that to him, he'd go off. Even if it was true. Deanna could always say what she thought and knew she could. Only she and Dani got away with it, although Dani would never in the world be so condescending. And not even Daws pushed him quite that far.

He didn't see the need to defend himself to his guard's girlfriend as he watched Kaitlyn study Daws, Ned, and the girl-of-the-moment standing a ways from her, joking in between drinking. Ned and the girl held beer bottles and Daws had his big plastic mug Ryan knew held ice water. To keep his system clean and his brain on its toes, he said.

Deanna grabbed his arm when he started to move away. "Ryan, be careful. You don't know what this child's had to deal with and you're not qualified to know how to handle it. Your songs show you have an understanding of people, yes, but this ... is not something you can know about. Don't act like you can."

"Maybe I don't need to know. Maybe I only need to give a shit." Setting a hand on her shoulder while moving around, Ryan went in to grab the chips and returned to pull an ottoman next to Kaitlyn, close enough to set the bowl between them. She was starting to eat better at each meal, but still, she didn't eat a lot. Chips weren't the best thing to offer as nutritional support, he supposed, but it's what he had.

She did say a few words to him in reply to his chatter until Ned plopped down on the arm of her chair. She tried to fly out of it, away from the drummer, and knocked the bowl of chips to the floor.

Ryan grasped her hand to keep her from going far and shoved Ned back. "What in the hell are you doing?"

Ned's gaze flicked between him and Kaitlyn. "Just being friendly. I always get to know your dates, at least as much as you do."

With a glare, Ryan crouched to stop her from cleaning the mess. "Kaitlyn, I'll get it."

"It was my fault. I'm sorry." She shoveled handfuls of chips into the bowl.

"No, it wasn't. And it doesn't matter." He grasped her hands and stood, forcing her to rise with him. "The floor's had much worse on it than that, I can guarantee you, and it's just a floor. Not a big deal."

Her whole manner looked like she would bolt if he released her. Deanna tried to set an arm around her back, telling her Ryan wasn't picky enough about his loft to ever worry that much about it, but Kaitlyn moved away, as far as she could while still in his grasp.

"Relax, it's fine." He moved closer and studied her reaction, expecting her to back up again. She didn't, even when he released one hand and brought his fingers to her face. He touched her cheek and she scrunched her eyes.

"Kaitlyn, it's all right. You're safe here." He heard Daws suggest to Ned it was time to go, and to the girl with him that staying quiet would be a good idea. Ryan couldn't worry about what she might say. He couldn't stop it if his guard's warning didn't work. If she did talk, it would blow over like everything did. Eventually.

"You don't have to go." Ryan looked over at his drummer. "It's fine. I have a few movies I haven't seen yet. We can put one in."

Ned looked unsure but Deanna caught on and encouraged them to sit down, offering to refill drinks. Ryan didn't want them to leave that way. He wanted things to settle, to unwind first. He wanted Kaitlyn to see that it would.

She did sit when he encouraged her but kept looking at the chips on the floor until Ned found the broom. He joked that Ryan's rats would be unhappy he was taking food from them. Her eyes widened.

"I don't have rats. No mice, either. Can't stand the things and if I ever see any trace of them, exterminator will be here next day."

"Yeah, it's surprising you don't." Ned swept up the last of them into the dustpan.

"Hey, you don't like it you don't have to be here. And I've seen your place. Why do you think I won't even go there?"

"Just clutter. And you don't go there because it belongs to one of your lowly backup musicians. Can't have that. Riveting Ryan's gotta have people come to him." Ned threw a grin. The girl with him looked startled.

"Uh huh, and why do you bring your girls here?"

"Okay." He threw his hands in the air. "I give. What are we watching?"

Ryan kept an eye on her through *X-Men* and couldn't help wishing for the telepathic power. It would be easier to know how to deal with the girl if he had any idea what she was thinking. At least she appeared to be engrossed in the movie. But she was still wrapped within herself, the blanket he now kept on her chair pulled around her shoulders. She looked far too much within herself.

With the excuse of grabbing something from the kitchen, he got up, asked if she needed anything, saw the expected light shake of her head, and lowered onto the floor halfway in front of her chair, his back against one edge. He couldn't see her that way, but at least she knew he was right there.

At the movie's end, Daws suggested it was time for them all to clear out. Deanna told Kaitlyn to call if she needed anything, with the number she'd written down beside the phone, and gave Ryan a quick hug.

He stepped into the hallway with his drummer as they left. "Hey, sorry about earlier."

Ned eyed him and told his date he'd catch up in a minute, waiting until she moved toward the elevator. "I don't know what's with that girl, but I think the sleazy, mouthy chicks would be safer. And I don't believe for a minute she's related to you like it's going around she is. Give that crap to everyone else if you want, but not to me."

"I didn't say she was."

"Yeah but I know the game. And I know you. Just be careful or you're gonna get into more than you can handle." He shrugged. "Get some sleep, Reynauld. You look like you need it."

"Go get laid, Ned. You look like you need that more." Ryan shoved him toward the girl waiting. Cute girl, not shy. Definitely not related.

He was glad to get everyone out ... everyone except Kaitlyn. Ned didn't believe she was related. Why didn't he? They weren't close enough? She didn't talk to him enough? Or could he see Ryan was trying too hard to get her to talk to him?

Reclaiming the ottoman, he tried to judge her reaction. Ned barely touched her, if he had touched her at all. He didn't try anything. Other than having more than enough to drink, he at least showed a few manners, as normal. He was one of the least exhausting people who hung around.

"I'm sorry." Her eyes touched his. "I don't want to be trouble to you. I should go."

"Go where, Kaitlyn?" He paused, listening to her silence. "What happened?" She pulled back. It was too soon, he supposed.

Taking a chance, he found her fingers and moved closer. "What are you so afraid of?" He peered into the round eyes. "Not of me. At least, you don't seem afraid of me. Why not me when everyone else makes you jump when they get close?"

"You wanted my life when I didn't. It's yours now."

Ryan fumbled for some kind of reaction. She couldn't be serious. Although her unswerving gaze and calm resignation said she was. It didn't make sense. She only relaxed around him after he assured her he didn't want anything from her. It was his? He didn't think so.

With a deep breath, he leaned in. "Katie." He hadn't meant to shorten her name but it seemed to fit better, and her reaction to it meant something. "I will accept ... but only to the extent it means you won't try anything again, because it does matter to me." He ducked his head closer. "You matter to me."

Ryan didn't expect an answer. She didn't argue and that was good enough. He wanted to know more ... everything, but he would be patient even if that wasn't his strong point. "It's late." He stood and offered a hand. "We should both try to sleep tonight."

~~~

"Hey, I have to ask you for a favor and it's a huge favor."

Will paused on the other end of the line. "Okay, what is it?"

"No *'this time'* this time? I can hear it in your voice."

"What do you need, Ry?"

Pulling an ankle atop the other leg, Ryan fidgeted with the frayed hem of his jeans. "Well, like I said, it's big and it will mainly involve Tracy, so you'll have to talk to her and get back to me."

"It involves Tracy? Not likely, and I'm not giving her the phone since she's never been able to say no to you, although she says no to me easily enough."

Ryan chuckled. "What can I say? I'm more charming. It's a curse."

"Right. What do you want?"

With a glance toward the hallway, he hoped Katie would stay in the shower more than her two minute norm. "I uh ... want to bring a friend over."

"No way. No more of your girlfriends in front of my kids. I told you..."

"She's not a girlfriend."

"Uh huh. *She* ... and not a girlfriend? Come on."

"Deanna's a friend and not a girlfriend. So is Dani. I do have them."

"Deanna's too mature for you and Daws would kill you if you tried anything. And I think Dani might be shaky ground for that argument."

"All right. Look, I don't have much time."

"Why?"

"It's kind of a long story, but ... she's young, Will. Teen maybe..."

"*Ryan* ... I swear...

"Hell, calm down. I told you, she's not a girlfriend. I haven't touched her. It's not like that." Waiting for his brother to stop pacing, since Ryan knew he was, he looked back toward the hall. "She needs a safe place to stay. She hasn't got anywhere else, and staying here ... well, hell, you know a kid has no business staying here..."

"Wait." His muffled voice let Ryan know he'd partly covered the receiver with his hand and was talking to someone else. "Let's start again. Who is this girl and why is she at your place?"

"Because she had nowhere else to go." He got silence. "Her name's Kaitlyn and she's very quiet, bony as hell though I've been trying to work on that, and insanely shy. But her eyes.... Will, she has no one else and nowhere to go. I uh, kind of ran into her on the way to work the other day and ... she was pretty desperate to find help. What was I supposed to do? Leave her?"

"Call the authorities. If this girl is a teen, she's likely a runaway and you're going to get yourself publicity you don't want ... maybe jail time. Call the authorities."

"I can't."

"And why can't you?"

"Because I promised I wouldn't. She wouldn't come with me if I hadn't."

More silence. "You know, between every stray animal getting dumped on us and you taking in stray girls..."

"Yeah, and I do that every other day." Ryan pushed fingers through his hair. "Come on, Will. She's not a runaway. She says there's no one..."

"And you believe that."

"Yes. I believe her. And she trusts me. Apparently, she trusts no one else, but she trusts me."

"Just how unstable is she?"

"Thank you. Forget it." He heard the bathroom door open and hung up. What had he expected? It was too much to ask. Will was tired of bailing him out, although it had been a long time since he'd had to. But it was too much to ask, and it wasn't fair to Katie, since ... but all he'd promised was that she wouldn't be alone. He hadn't promised to keep her with him forever. He couldn't. Not with his job – the travel and the fans and the time he needed alone whenever he could get it so he could work unbothered. He couldn't be responsible...

Her eyes touched his when she rounded the corner.

He had to be. Every time he looked at her, he could see the fight within. He couldn't dump her on anyone else. He couldn't risk her not understanding. He would never be able to live with himself if she ... he couldn't even think about it. Over the few days she'd been there, he'd started caring too damn much.

The phone's ring interrupted whatever he was going to make himself say and he let it ring three times before he grabbed it. "Yeah?"

"What's going on?" Will at least sounded concerned.

"I told you, forget it." Ryan tried to keep his voice neutral so she wouldn't know he was irritated, more with himself than with his brother.

"All right, I deserved to be hung up on. You made your point, but I'm asking..."

"I can't do this now."

"Don't hang up." Silence. "She's listening?"

"Yeah. And I told you, forget it."

"Call me back later tonight when you're free to talk."

"Why?"

"Because I'm worried about you. This seems..."

"Don't be. I gotta go. I'm starving and there has to be something in this place to eat. Give everyone my love." Barely waiting for a response, he hung up again. "So. I think I have chicken of some kind in there. Maybe ... stir fry? Do I have vegetables?" Heading toward the kitchen to answer his own question, he wasn't at all surprised when she followed. Eventually, he figured it would get annoying to have her so often insist on being in whatever room he was in. Except she did it so subtly and quietly, if he'd wanted to not notice her presence, it would be easy enough not to. So far, he enjoyed the company ... unusual company who didn't insist on his attention.

"I'll cook."

Ryan looked over at her. "No, that's okay. You're company."

"No."

He raised his eyebrows. No, she wasn't company? Company was temporary. She wasn't expecting it to be temporary. It made him think again about insisting Will and Tracy give it a try. This girl couldn't be dependent on him, not only on him. Now and then was fine. Permanent ... permanent was not going to work.

"I know how to cook."

"Okay. If you're sure. You're not too tired?"

"I don't do anything to be tired."

Ryan wondered if that was a pointed remark. She'd tried now and then to help clean up and he always insisted she not bother, reminding her he paid for cleaning help. Granted, it was iffy help, but Ryan trusted the woman. In his business, he knew what hell it could be to find someone who would work for him only for the money and not for who he was – who would be safe to leave in the loft alone.

If Kaitlyn wanted to cook, Ryan wouldn't argue. He backed away to let her have space but couldn't make himself leave the kitchen. He got caught up in watching her. She was precise, and quick, with knowledge of ingredients and how they should go together. He didn't want to stand around and stare, so he went to grab his guitar, lowered onto a chair, and worked on music for words that came to him.

~~~

The clothes she picked out made a huge difference in her appearance. Kaitlyn had a simple, casual style with no frills but it looked nicer on her than he'd imagined. They fit well – not baggy, but not showy, still managing to highlight how cute her figure actually was, even still too thin. Ryan was glad Kaitlyn allowed Deanna to take her shopping even if she didn't speak to her. He had to go, and he had to push her to get more than two outfits plus something to sleep in. Finally tired of her refusal, he gave in after the two pairs of khakis, capris that were Deanna's idea, and a pair of sweats for around the loft, plus a few tops and a jacket. It was a start. He would insist they go again before Ryan took her to meet his family.

He wasn't sure yet when that would be other than before he had to tour. He hoped she would be comfortable there and that Tracy might offer to at least let her stay while he was on the road. Any other time, he could deal with having her around. As afraid as she was of people, Ryan couldn't imagine having her out there.

"Are you listening to me?"

Ryan pulled his eyes from Katie and looked at Ned. "What?"

"That new song. Where did it come from?"

"What do you mean?"

"I mean – and everyone else is thinking it, too – that it's about your new friend you're trying to pass off as only a friend."

"She is only a friend." He rolled his eyes at the disbelief. "Damn, Ned, she's a kid. Even I'm not that sleazy."

"Is she? Has she told you how old she is yet?"

"I haven't asked, but she's tiny..."

"Yeah, so maybe she has tiny parents. Doesn't mean anything. I don't think she's all that young. She doesn't act it, although it's hard to tell since she never talks."

"She talks to me."

"Thought about just asking her age, then?"

"What in the hell difference does it make? She needed a place to stay. That's it."

"Okay."

Ryan walked away from his drummer. It wasn't any of his damn business. And she was young. How young didn't much matter. Even if she wasn't, she had enough issues without him adding to them by being a sleazeball. There were other girls who would be fine with it.

They thought the song was about her. It wasn't. It was about him.

That was none of their business, either.

There was too much noise in the loft, too many people. Kaitlyn seemed okay and Deanna was always close if he wasn't. No one bothered her. They wouldn't dare with Ryan and his bodyguard's girlfriend keeping an eye on her, and everyone knew they were.

He wondered how to clear them out without more comments about how strange he was being, how long it had been since he let one of the girls always floating around catch his attention, and how little he was drinking. The doorbell made him grimace. With a glance at Katie, he went to answer. Anyone else would let whoever it was in. Ryan wanted fewer people there, not more.

He didn't bother to open it far enough to find out who it was. "Party's ending. Try next time."

"Is it? Doesn't sound that way." Will blocked it with a hand.

"What are you doing here?"

"You didn't call back the other day, or since."

"You coulda called. I would've answered."

"You're evasive on the phone. Harder to be in person. Is the girl still around?"

"Yeah." He backed up and closed the door. "You drove to New York because of my call?"

"It sounded like I should."

"Look, I told you, I'm not doing anything with her. You can relax."

"Good. Still, I'd like to meet this young girl you're not doing anything with who had you so rattled."

Ryan's bassist shoved against his arm and threw a greeting at Will, then stumbled away with the stench of alcohol following. "All right, but I warned you she doesn't talk much. Don't be freaked out if she doesn't answer you."

Will's eyes were in the distance, across the room. "You weren't exaggerating. Does she need a doctor?"

"She looks better than she did a week ago." Ashamed of being glad he got the reaction he wanted, Ryan set a hand on his brother's arm. "Come on, I'll introduce you."

They got stopped by a couple more guys who remembered Will and Ryan saw the one he'd been watching the closest move toward Kaitlyn. Deanna wasn't there.

"Hey, didn't know you were coming down." Ned stepped in his path and offered Will a hand.

"Last minute. How are things?"

"Could be worse. Glad you're here. You oughtta have your brother play the song he just wrote. We've been trying to talk him into it."

"Later." Ryan tried to swerve around him.

"Hell, pull the guitar out now. The party's getting kinda slow."

"Then leave." He saw her jump, pull away and walk backward into another musician, backing again when offered a smile and a steady hand. Something cold and sticky spilled on his arm when he pushed through to get to her.

As soon as he took her side, she wrapped around him, not quite as tight as the first day when they were finally off the ledge, but close.

"Katie, it's all right. I'm sending them all home now. They've been here too long. I'm sick of them, too." He spoke into her ear and saw Will watching. "Are you okay?" With a light nod against his shoulder, she released him. "Give me a few minutes and I'll them out." He found her eyes. "My brother just got here. Come meet him."

Will studied her while she averted her gaze. Like a concerned father. Maybe he would offer. Maybe he would be able to see her as a kid who needed his help and offer without being asked.

"Tracy insisted I tell you to come visit soon." Will, to his credit, didn't show what he had to be thinking. "She wanted to come with me, but the kids have too much going on right now between dance and soccer practice and school. On top of subbing five year olds this week."

"And you left her with it to come down here?"

"Mom will help make the runs, but we couldn't leave it all on her."

Ryan couldn't help the visual that popped into his head. "Yeah, I can see Mom trying to teach kindergarten."

"Right. Detention maybe. I could see that sooner." Will thanked Daws for the cola he offered with a greeting before walking away again.

With a grin, Ryan glanced at Katie's expression. It was funny how most of her face never showed anything she was thinking, but her eyes showed everything. "Mom's ex-military. Kind of a drill sergeant type although she wasn't that. I can tell you we didn't cross her." The thought frightened Katie. It was in her eyes.

Will saw it, too. "Except she's also a pushover at times. The way she gives in to the kids is crazy. They both have her wrapped around their pinkies. Makes it hard for us to say no when she keeps saying yes."

Ryan touched Kaitlyn's fingers. "So just say yes. They're sweet kids. They deserve yes."

"Uh huh, and you think they'd still be sweet kids if we always did? Wait till you have a few and you'll think again."

"Me?" Ryan laughed. "I can't see that." He felt Katie tense and leaned closer. "What do you think? Feel like taking a weekend trip soon? Up by Will's is where I prefer to go boating. Less crowded than down here. I still owe you a boat ride, if you remember."

Still saying nothing, she didn't have to. He could see gratitude ... that he remembered, maybe? Had she expected he forgot? Or that he had lied about the boat only to get her to go inside? "Sorry it's taken so long. I'll arrange the time away as soon as I can get it. This album is still a mess right now. I have to stay until it's not such a mess."

"That's a damn understatement." Ned pushed in beside Will. "At this point, it might be easier to scrap it and start again."

"I thought you liked the songs."

"Sure, but I don't like what's being done with them. It's too much … just too much. We've gotten too far from where we started. Simplicity, you know. Straight-forward. Natural. That's what drew people in."

"Yeah." Ryan pondered the words that echoed what he'd been thinking for some time. "But tell Mac that."

"Maybe I will." He walked away again.

"Good luck."

Will grinned. "Trying to make you sound more civilized, are they?"

"Trying to make me more commercial. Damn, I hate commercial music, but that's what it's coming out as, even more than last time."

"It's what sells."

"Maybe, but it's not my music when they do that. Every album is less mine until I'm thinking of finding a different career."

Will raised his eyebrows. "I see that happening like I see Mom teaching kindergarten."

"I guess. It's not like I *can* do anything else. Never could before."

"You could." His brother set a hand on his shoulder. "You could do anything you wanted, Ry, but this is who you are. Don't let them interfere with that, even if you have to go back to singing at bars."

"Right, and begging off you?"

"As I said before, those who can't do art should at least be willing to support it. Just call me Theo, but leave the ears intact."

He had to chuckle at the Van Gogh reference but Ryan had no intention of living off his brother again. He would find an in-between somewhere first. But it was getting too loud in the loft and he'd told Katie he would make them leave, so he pulled Deanna over to chat and keep watch, and made the rounds saying he wanted time to visit with Will. Luckily, it didn't take long. And he had the chance to tell the guy who had scared her to stay away from her, with Daws close enough to hear him and back it up with a look.

3

"Relax, Kaitlyn. I wouldn't bring you here if I didn't think you'd be all right."

In the driveway outside his brother's house, Ryan switched off the BMW's engine. He enjoyed driving one of his own cars again, which he rarely did other than on trips, most often to Will's. The M3 Coupe was nice for the three hour drive, better than the Esprit that only had two seats. It was also less showy, not quite as stylized, and dark green instead of silver with metallic flake. He was sure some of Will's neighbors knew the car, but he wasn't bothered much in Bennington. He generally got either friendly greetings or unfriendly avoidance and either was fine with him.

Unlatching his seatbelt, he took Katie's hand. "I want my family to be yours." At her confusion, he continued. "I did promise you would never be alone. You are part of my family now, and don't worry, they'll be glad to have you." He saw movement on the porch and found his niece and nephew flying toward the car. "Get ready. Here they come." He jumped out before they could get to his door.

"Uncle Ryan!" Little arms wrapped around his waist while even smaller arms encircled one leg. He hugged Matthew, tousling his hair, and picked up the three-year-old with blonde curls hanging down her face. "My sweet Bella. You're getting too big too fast." She smiled that huge, bright smile and squeezed his neck.

"That means you need to come around more often, doesn't it?" Tracy, who had wandered out behind them, gave him a grin and looked over at the other side of the car. "This must be Kaitlyn. It's nice to meet you, honey. Come on inside. These three may be out here playing around a while."

Ryan kept an eye on Katie while Matt talked about the basketball hoop he'd gotten for his birthday. She didn't move. "Hold on a minute, okay bud? I'll be right back to go look at it." Trying to set his niece down, he changed his mind when she gripped his neck tighter. Matt followed to the other side of the car.

"Kaitlyn, this is Tracy, my sister-in-law." He set his free hand on her back. Tracy did no more than give her a light grin. Will apparently warned her. "This is Matthew. He just turned seven." He threw a nod at the boy. "And this is Isabelle. We call her Bella, and she's kind of a leech as you can see. Miss Bella, this is Kaitlyn. Say hello."

"Hi! I'm Bella." She extended her smile.

"I told her that."

"I'm four years old."

Ryan tilted his head at her. "No, you're three and almost four."

"I'm almost four. Matt is my brother. He's seven now."

"I told her that, too." He knocked lightly on her head. "Hello? Anyone in there?"

"You're silly, Uncle Ryan." With a return knock on his head, the child looked again at Kaitlyn. "What's your name?"

"Miss Bella, I told you her name. Kaitlyn, remember?"

"I wasn't talking to you."

"Really? Fine, go on then." He set her down.

"I was kidding, Uncle Ryan."

He tried not to look as amused as he was.

"That's her new favorite saying." Tracy grabbed the child's hand. "You weren't kidding. You were being rude. Go on now and tell Grandma they're here."

With a pout, the girl went back to the house. Matt took off in a jog toward the backyard.

Tracy gave Ryan a long hug. "It's great to see you again. It's been a long time."

"I know. I can't believe how big they're getting. I kept meaning to get up here." He checked Kaitlyn's reaction. She stood close, fingers wrung together. A breeze swept at her wispy bangs and made her blink when they brushed too far into her face. The loose, thin sweatshirt she tended to wear even on nice days hid much of her frame but her eyes took in her surroundings: Will's yard and his two-story brick house, neighbors passing in cars and sitting on front porches, teens on bicycles yelling to each other. It reminded him of the way Daws scoured the area whenever Ryan was out in public.

"If I know Mom, she's in the kitchen preparing for company."

"Of course. I hope you're both hungry. We'll have leftovers forever otherwise." Tracy grinned between studying the girl. "Will should be home soon. He couldn't get out of going to the office for a short time today." She nodded toward her son returning with basketball in hand. "He's been talking about playing with you since he got the thing. Driving us crazy. We considered mailing him to you in a big box."

Ryan shrugged at his nephew's laugh. "Well then, guess I better not make him keep waiting." He touched Katie's arm. "Want to watch him beat me at kid's basketball?" Not bothering to expect an answer, he took her hand and promised Tracy they wouldn't stay out long.

His lungs expanded more deeply than normal while they ambled to the back of the house, as they did every time he was at Will's. The difference between the small town Vermont air and the stifled, exhaust-laden New York City air made him half consider finding a place well outside the city for times he didn't need to be right there. Or even a weekend place in the city's suburbs where he could unwind and open windows and find fresher air.

He offered Katie one of the lawn chairs scattered around Will's yard, but she settled in the deep green grass and wrapped her legs in front of her. By the beginning of June, the grass was at its deepest shade of healthy green and Ryan couldn't fault her for wanting to enjoy the softness and coolness of it contrasted to the warm summer sun. She'd looked around as they walked, noting, in all probability, the perfection of Will and Tracy's yard, with the grass always neat and without weeds. Hostas grew around the base of the few tree trunks within the yard, and small flower gardens bordered the porch and house. A couple of birdhouses hung on tree limbs. She also looked over at one corner of the yard where the swing set and sandbox took dominance, along with a low trampoline Matt had finally talked his parents into getting. He'd wanted one of the big ones but Tracy wouldn't have it, worried about them falling off and breaking their necks. Never mind how Ryan kept trying to help Matt by saying it was his favorite thing to do in high school gym class, other than baseball.

The dog was still there, too, in the far corner of the yard inside a chain-link fenced area and also on a heavy chain. It alternately barked and growled until Tracy stepped out and yelled at it to stop, then went into occasional low growling mode. Katie jumped at the first bark, since she hadn't seen it under shade of a large tree, but now kept looking over as she watched Matt embarrass Ryan at a game of PIG. Of course Ryan was shooting from his knees to make it "fair" but basketball was never his sport.

Bella ran out the back door full steam, her hands full of Barbie dolls and stuff to go with them, and plopped onto Katie's lap. Ryan kept an eye out to be sure it was all right and although it startled her, she seemed okay. The child rambled constantly, making up stories to go with the way her dolls were dressed and where they were going. Katie would be fine there when he toured. Bella would pull her in and the others would eventually help her feel secure.

"Uncle Ryan, it's your turn."

Accepting the ball thrust at him, he realized he'd been staring at her ... and realized what had bothered him during the three hour drive to Will's. It was the idea of her getting closer to his family than she was to him. Making him ... jealous. He was out of his mind. She was a kid and he didn't have the capability to let her be so dependent. It would be better for her at Will's. She would have family and stability instead of a bunch of single guys getting drunk and rushing from one hotel to the next and in and out of venues with girls hanging all over, and as much as she insisted on helping at his place, he knew she would help Tracy as she could. It would be best all the way around. Still...

"You have to shoot from here." Matt's voice brought him back to the game.

After ceremoniously being crowned the PIG for the second time in a row, which was maybe a little too true, Ryan suggested they go in so he could see Grandma before she got mad about being ignored.

"I'll tell her it was my fault."

Ryan rubbed his head. "I'll play again later, okay?"

"Okay." Matt took the ball and waited.

He went to the girls and told Bella to gather her dolls, offering Katie a hand. When she took his side, he spoke close to her ear. "I hope she wasn't bothering you. If she does, give me a sign and I'll distract her."

"It's okay." She kept hold of his fingers while they started to walk.

"Is she your girlfriend?" Matt teased with a smile.

"She's my friend. And your mom would jump on you if she heard you ask, so you better be careful."

"I have a girlfriend."

"Do you? Aren't you kind of young for that?"

"I can't take her out 'cause I can't drive, but we have lunch together at school and she always sits by me."

"Well, I guess that's all right. You're being a gentleman, I hope."

"I'm not a man, Uncle Ryan. I'm seven."

"Well, if you're man enough to have a girlfriend, you're man enough to be a gentleman, and you better be or I'll come to school and sit in between you."

He laughed. "I'm a gentleman, but don't tell Mom I have a girlfriend. She doesn't know."

"You don't think you should tell her?"

"I tell her I have a friend and she's a girl. I don't say she's a girlfriend, either." Smiling again, he looked at Kaitlyn then ran ahead into the house with Bella jogging along behind.

"Don't listen to him. He's at that age where girls have to be either 'icky' or a girlfriend. Nothing in between."

"He's sweet."

"Yeah, he's a mini Will. Just like his dad as a kid. Bella ... I get blamed for her a lot. Too many of my qualities. She drives them nuts."

"She's sweet, too." A tinge of sadness reflected in her voice.

He stopped her before they got to the door. "Are you all right? If this bothers you too much, let me know. I can take you to a hotel instead of staying here, or we can take a drive or something."

"You're staying here?"

He waited, confused by the question.

"If you're here, it's okay."

If he's there. Was she reading his thoughts? She couldn't. He had never said anything to make her think he was considering leaving her there, during the tour, or maybe more than that. And he wouldn't, unless she agreed. "I'm here, Katie. I won't leave you anywhere you don't want to be. I promise."

With a careful squeeze of her hand, he continued toward the house and looked back when the dog began to bark and jump up on the fence. "It's tied." He meant to sound like he was reassuring Kaitlyn, but he thought it was more to reassure himself. It was tied within the fence so it couldn't actually jump over if it decided to. Still, Ryan stepped up the pace and got inside.

"That dog needs to go." He looked through the screen door to where it was still throwing a fit about him walking into his brother's house.

"Where would she go?"

Ryan caught Kaitlyn's eyes and kicked himself. He hadn't thought of the similarity. But it was a dog, and a vicious dog from the way it barked and growled. There was a big difference. Katie would never hurt anyone. She wasn't dangerous, other than to herself. "Somewhere without little kids it could maul, preferably."

"She's tied."

"Yeah, but I'm not so sure it couldn't get untied if provoked. That's a strong dog, and anything that wants freedom badly enough can get it."

She held his gaze. "No. Not always."

Ryan caught his breath. Not always? Had she tried? Was she allowing him to question her more, opening herself, at least a touch? He wasn't sure what to start asking.

"How was your drive?" Will's voice interrupted.

She closed again. Ryan felt it. "Fine." He looked back at the dog still barking to give himself time to recover his thoughts. *Not always.*

"You weren't trying to play with him, were you?"

"Oh, hell no. We were coming in from shooting hoops with Matt. I wouldn't go near that thing."

"I'm trying to find him a home."

"It's a her."

Ryan looked at Kaitlyn. Was she talking to Will? She wasn't looking at him. She was looking at the dog. "A her?"

"Yes, it's a her." Will shrugged. "I keep calling it him. Mom said you haven't been in to see her yet. Asking for trouble already?"

"It's Matt's fault."

"Right." He started toward the kitchen.

Taking Katie's hand again, Ryan kept his voice low. "Don't worry. They'll find her a good home."

Her eyes touched his, but only for a second.

Ryan wondered if he insulted her. She couldn't think it was the same, that he thought it was as easy to move a human from house to house as it was to move a dog. But then, didn't he? That's what he meant to do. Did she know?

She was more wary when meeting his mom than when she'd met Tracy. Of course, his mom had the kind of presence that was "there" and sometimes overpowering. He figured Tracy had warned her since she would generally be insulted about not getting a reply. She always insisted on an answer or at least an acknowledgement.

"I have the guest room fixed for you." His mom at least acted uninsulted. "It's next to where Ryan will be, so pound on the wall if you need anything. Let me show you upstairs and you can freshen for lunch. Three hours isn't a horrible ride, unless he still drives the way he used to. Still, I always need a few minutes to unwind after a car trip. Come, I'll give you a quick tour and the boys can go out and get the luggage I'm sure he's left in the car."

Katie pulled back when she touched her arm.

"I'll give her the tour." Ryan handed his keys to Will at the offer for him and Matt to grab the bags.

He led her out of the kitchen through the dining room and into the living room. "Katie, don't worry if she's kind of abrupt. She can roar like a lion, let me tell you, but she's a lamb inside. I think you'll get along okay."

"She lives here?"

"Yes, ever since ... well, when they moved here, Will didn't figure she needed a separate place he'd have to help take care of. Not that he would mind, but she likes the company and helps with the kids and such. All the bedrooms are upstairs. He figures he'll convert the den – it's around the corner there – into a room for her when the stairs get too hard."

Kaitlyn paused at the bottom of the winding oak staircase when he started up the first step.

"I know, I don't like these a lot, either." He looked over at her confusion. "But you don't mind heights so it's not the stairs, right?"

She didn't answer, but she did walk up with him. Ryan didn't mind her silence as much anymore, in general. It was peaceful compared to what he was used to, but he did mind not having any idea what she was thinking except for rare occasions when he could read her eyes. *Not always.* Someone couldn't always find freedom when they wanted it. At least it was a start. It was the most she'd said about herself since they met. And it wasn't specifically about herself. She could've meant in general. He didn't think she did, though. Her words were so few he knew she didn't use them lightly, or as banter, as most did. As he did.

At the top, he gave her a brief overview of whose rooms were where, and took her to the guest room. His mom had placed a basket of "gifts" on the dresser: soaps of different scents, small shampoo bottles, toothbrush and toothpaste, a candle tin, and an assortment of candies and mints.

Katie looked at it curiously.

"She always does this, in case you forgot anything you might need. It's a welcome gift, I guess." He let her know the dresser was empty and ready to use, showed her where the extra blankets were kept in the cedar chest at the end of the bed, and said she could come over to his room if she needed anything instead of banging on the wall, which was a joke but he wasn't sure she realized it was. "In case you do come over, it's Matt's room so don't think I chose all the Spiderman stuff all over the place. I usually stay in here when I visit. They kinda keep it for me." He glanced at the brown and dark rose striped comforter. "I didn't choose this, either, in case you're wondering. She wanted it versatile for whoever stays."

"Did I insult her?" Katie's voice was soft, concerned.

"Tracy?"

She shook her head.

Ryan set a hand on her arm, nearly where his mom had tried a few minutes before. She didn't jump from him. "Mom. No, it's okay. She's just very forward. A lot of people have trouble getting used to her, but once you do...."

"I didn't mean to be rude."

Noise outside the guest room door prevented a reply.

"Take that to your room for your uncle." Will chuckled at the boy hauling the suitcase. "He insisted on carrying the biggest one. Trying to prove himself to me already." He set Katie's bag inside the door. "Kaitlyn, be sure to let us know if there's anything you need. Tracy has everything under the sun in this house somewhere. Make yourself at home." He gave his attention to Ryan. "Lunch is ready when you are. It'll hold, so take your time." Will brushed off thanks and ushered the boy back out of the room.

Ryan closed the door to prevent further interruption and cringed when she walked to the window and peered out. He moved up behind her, setting a hand on her back. She didn't pull away. "Don't worry about anyone else, Katie. Don't let their reactions bother you because it doesn't matter. I'm only concerned about you being comfortable, so if you're not, we'll leave. Just tell me."

"You want to leave me here."

His heart nearly stopped. She knew his intentions.

Moving his hands to her shoulders and turning her to face him, he leaned down to try to find her eyes. "Katie, don't misunderstand." She kept them pulled away. "Okay, yes, I've thought about asking you, in time, if you would be comfortable staying here. I didn't plan to drop you off and run or anything." She showed no reaction. "I wouldn't do that. And I won't leave you where you don't want to be. I just ... I'm afraid of you staying with me very long. Those guys I hang around with ... some of them are okay, but it's not a place for ... for anyone your age." She still didn't react. "I like having you around. I enjoy your company. But the life I lead, there are always people everywhere, and before long I'll have to tour to promote the new album and it'll be worse and I couldn't live with myself if anything happened to you."

She raised her eyes. "I don't want you hurt because of me."

"That's not ... I'm not worried about me. I..."

She wrapped around him, not clinging like the last two times, but softly. In the bedroom with the door closed. And his head told him not to let her to get so close, but he couldn't push her away. She had to know he wouldn't.

"Let's go out on the boat after lunch. Only the two of us, to give you time...." Maybe that wasn't a good idea, either. He should make it a family thing, or at least invite the kids.

She nodded against his chest and released him.

Walking her back downstairs, Ryan was more confused than he ever remembered being during his twenty-three years. She hadn't refused to stay at Will's. He supposed that was a good sign. It could all depend on the next few days before they returned to New York.

Katie kept her eyes on the water, transfixed, as though she'd never seen a lake. She took in everything, turning her head up when seagulls called out and back toward a couple of jet skies making waves. Tracy had convinced her to wear a bathing suit so they could get in the water if they decided or in case water was thrown at them from a passing jet ski. She covered it with a short-sleeved button shirt and loose shorts. Ryan couldn't help appreciating that she looked more like a girl with each passing day. A touch of color now highlighted her pale skin and the harsh edges were softer. He hoped to add to both while in Vermont.

He led her up the wet wooden boards that led to the dock and she gripped the side rail at the ramp's movement. Ryan touched her back. "It's supposed to do that. Just the waves."

She looked over the edge.

"You haven't been around the water much, I guess."

Kaitlyn shook her head and stared down at trout circling, waiting for food they often received from passersby.

"I hope you don't get seasick."

Catching his glance, she didn't look concerned, only curious.

"The boat isn't very big. It's a pontoon ... good for fishing or floating around enjoying the view."

"Hey Ryan. Back home again for a while?"

He turned to the familiar voice. "Only a few days. Had to get out of the city, you know."

"Missed the old girl, didn't you? We all know as long as she's here, you'll be back now and then."

"True enough." He threw the dock manager a grin and introduced Katie, excusing himself fast enough not to be drawn into conversation where she would be expected to answer.

More relaxed than she ever was around his coworkers, Katie continued studying her surroundings, checking each new noise, the different boats docked and floating within their roofed confines, the boaters coming and going. Ryan rushed in and out of the office to grab his keys and was assured it was taken care of well in his absence, then grabbed Katie's hand to lead her down to his rented slot. "Here she is. Nothing spectacular but we've spent many, many hours together."

With an affectionate rub along the smooth fiberglass, he stepped in and dropped their supplies – a cooler with drinks and snacks, the waterproof bag of towels and sun block, and a couple of CDs he wanted to share with her – onto one of the seats. "Ready?" He grabbed the dock rail with one hand to keep the boat steady and offered the other to his passenger, satisfied more than he knew why when she didn't hesitate.

As he always did first thing, Ryan raised one of the seats to find the storage compartment and took out two life vests. He set his on the seat and held the smaller one. "I keep them close by just in case, but you can go ahead and put it on if you want." Getting a shake of the head, he wondered whether he should let her refuse. "Can you swim at all?"

"Yes."

"But you haven't been around water?"

"Not open water."

"Oh." Feeling like the moron Daws said he was, he decided not to push the life vest. Turning over a pontoon would be a rarity. "Sit anywhere you want and we'll get underway." Not surprised when she chose the seat closest to his own, Ryan pushed Daws and work and the city out of his mind and surrendered to the smell of the lake and the hum of his engine. When he retired, he would be out there every day it was even close to warm enough. And maybe he would travel down south during winter like the birds did and rent one there at least occasionally.

He watched her while he pulled out of the dock area and urged the boat slowly ahead, out to the open water where she'd never been. Taking it slower than normal, although he always obeyed lake etiquette and kept it slow in no wake areas, Ryan wished he could see her eyes. Her head was turned in the direction he steered the boat, showing him only the side of her face and her light brown hair tossing behind her. For a moment, it reminded him of the ledge, with her hair whipping across her pallid skin. But he shoved the thought aside. That scene no longer existed. It was his turn to share his view. And he was glad he was sharing it alone.

The kids had asked to go. He nearly gave in but Tracy refused their request because of plans she had for them. Ryan knew it was an excuse, that she could see he wanted it to be only him and Kaitlyn.

They hadn't left right after lunch, but sat around and visited with his family for some time ... longer than he wanted, maybe not as long as he should have. She didn't join the conversation, but she paid attention. The moment they got into his car alone, she took a deep breath and her face became softer.

He wanted to see her eyes now that they were in the midst of the lake, past the no wake zone, so he idled the engine and went over to her. "What do you think? No seasickness yet, right? You shouldn't here, since there's land..." Catching her eyes, he couldn't continue. They were different than ever before, more than calm. Happy? There was at least a reflection of some kind of enjoyment, if he didn't misinterpret.

Ryan lowered to her side and hoped she would say something, anything, to explain the look.

"Yes."

He frowned. Had he missed something? "Yes, what?"

"Your view is better."

Trying with all he had not to swoop her up and hold onto her, Ryan couldn't do more than nod. "Want to go out farther?"

She nodded back.

He kept her out later than he planned. As they cruised Lake Parin, he rambled about things to see in the area such as the Battle Monument that he'd been to often but refused the elevator ride to the top, and Hildene, Robert Todd Lincoln's home. She appeared interested in both but his mention of Robert Frost's gravesite and house had her full attention. He would have to take her.

Allowing the boat to drift, he took her side. He'd asked earlier if she wanted to swim, and she didn't but she did reveal that she'd learned to swim as a child and it appeared a good memory. She watched fish alongside the boat and answered that she'd never gone fishing. She did eat fish if offered. And she wasn't particular about food, not admitting to a favorite if she had one.

With the sun ready to descend, Ryan retrieved the sweatshirt he'd brought for her and wrapped it over her shoulders. "Katie?" He grasped her fingers, only enough to allow her to pull them back if she wanted. "What happened to your family? Where are they?"

Her eyes lowered but she didn't pull away. The breeze again played with her hair, the plain brown straight hair that was untamed, unstyled.

"They're gone."

"Gone? Recently?"

She shook her head. "I was young."

"Then where did you grow up?"

Turning to look over the water, she caught the view of the sun heading down behind clouds. Its pinkish orange light reflected on her face. "Different places."

He couldn't ask more. Different places. Foster homes, he guessed. Why more than one? Why no adoption? She was so sweet, unassuming ... she couldn't have been trouble for anyone. Why would they not take her in permanently once they were lucky enough to have found her?

She looked back at him. "Thank you."

"For what?"

Her eyes found the sunset again, and she squeezed his fingers tighter.

Ryan hated to break the spell, to start the engine and head back to the dock, but he didn't want it to get too dark. His family would worry, although when by himself, he often sat just outside the wake area until all hours before he gave up and headed back to shore. He couldn't with Katie. Not yet.

Plopping atop his bed, he watched the curtains flap in the breeze of the open window and focused on the scent of newly cut grass. But he saw her face. She hadn't looked quite so young out there on the boat, staring out at the descending sun. There was a wisdom in her expressions he couldn't imagine understanding, a sad wisdom born from going through too much too soon.

He hoped she would sleep well in his brother's house. She went to bed a while before he finally gave in; otherwise, he would check on her and make sure she was comfortable and didn't need anything. Still in the T-shirt and shorts he'd worn out on the boat, he could smell the lake on himself and considered showering. She had. Before she joined him in the living room to chat with his family when they returned, she'd asked him about being in anyone's way if she showered. How two minute showers would be in anyone's way, Ryan couldn't imagine, but he, as always, told her to take her time. When she sat next to him, she smelled of something soft and floral: one of the soaps his mom left in the basket, he supposed.

With a sigh, he decided to wait until morning to shower. The lake smell reminded him of their afternoon together, when she opened up to him, even as little as she had. The breeze was cool and he tried to at least make himself get under the comforter instead of lying on top of it, but he was wiped out. He hadn't done anything physical enough to be so tired, but worrying about her constantly drained him. Except he was now less worried so the sudden fatigue didn't make sense. She liked his view better. Ryan hoped to hell she meant more by that than the actual view.

Eyes closed, he heard a rapping. The second time he heard it, he realized it was on his door. "Yeah?" Silence. "Come in, it's open." He expected anyone except ... Katie. She stopped at the door. Bolting upright, he stared. "Everything okay?"

"Did I wake you?"

"No, but I figured you were long asleep." He wondered why she wasn't. When she didn't explain and didn't move, he got up and went to her. "What is it?"

Only her eyes spoke. The nightlight glow from the hall shadowed her face but her eyes weren't hidden. They waited ... for him to understand without being told.

He took her hand. "Come on. You need to sleep. It's late." Ryan took her back to the guest room. If anyone walked in for some reason, he would have to explain as well as he could. It was a strange house. She was uncomfortable being alone there. He promised she never would be.

Pulling back the bedding, Ryan held it for her and crawled in after. And he apologized for the way he smelled.

Her arm was against his; she lay facing him. Close. "It's nice. Like the water." She sounded nearly asleep.

Her slight arm movement reflected her breathing, and he turned his head to watch her. Eyes closed and strands of hair dangling over her face, she looked young again, but not so scared. "Katie." He wasn't sure she heard him but finished anyway. "I can't tell you how much I'm glad you enjoyed the view."

Her fingers slipped on top of his.

~~~

Assured it wouldn't bother her to go out on the boat again the next day, Ryan accepted when the kids begged to go, only after their parents agreed to go as well. He wasn't sure his mom would, since she wasn't as crazy about it, but he was glad she gave in so she and Kaitlyn would have more chance to get to know each other.

Bella and Matthew bounced around in their swim suits and life vests while he and Will took turns behind the wheel. Bella badgered Kaitlyn constantly although Tracy kept pulling her away, and finally they decided to stop close to the shore where jet skis wouldn't be around. With the pontoon anchored and floating, he and Will debated who would stay on deck first while the rest enjoyed the water.

"I'll stay with the boat." His mom broke up the debate. "You know I'm not going down in there and I can drive this thing if I need. I've been driving much longer than either of you."

With a shrug at his brother, Ryan went to Katie with his smallest adult sized vest. "We don't get in without them."

She shook her head.

"You're not going in?" He sat next to her. "I'll stay beside you and this vest won't let you go under."

"I'm not afraid of water." Her voice was soft. And she didn't explain.

"Okay. I'll stay up here with you."

"No." She stopped him from undoing his own vest. "It's okay." Kaitlyn got up and went to the back of the pontoon to prop herself up on the seat where she could look down at the kids already splashing and laughing. Her bare knees up and wrapped by her hands, she again had a shirt over the swimsuit Deanna helped her pick out during the second shopping trip. She was shy. Too shy to be so uncovered in front of his family.

Ryan asked his mom to keep an eye on her and not push her to talk, then threw Katie a wink and jumped off from atop the stairs, close enough to splash Matt but far enough not to risk landing on him.

Through the afternoon, he spent more time out of the water than in, teasing his mom by wrapping wet arms around her shoulders until she shoved him away, plopping beside Kaitlyn and leaning close to see if she'd push him back, also, to keep from getting wet, and returning to the water when she started to get to him. She didn't push him back. She caught his eyes and held them. When he was in the water and when he wasn't. She constantly caught his eyes.

Why it mattered to him, he couldn't fathom. Girls were always staring. It was part of the job. Even if he was a homely ass and too small to have a decent build. They stared. A lot. And screamed. And grabbed at him. And he thought it was hilarious considering the huge nobody he was while growing up. If not for Will, he would've been knocked around more than he had been. His fault, he supposed. He'd always been too much of a smartass. Will kept telling him. Whatever. It worked for him.

But Katie's stares weren't like the girls at shows. She didn't even seem to realize who he was, or care. She had to know with as much as she'd already seen. It didn't matter to her. She was looking deeper – too much deeper. He didn't like it.

Ryan pulled his head back to where he was, picked Matt up under his arms, and tossed him back in the water. When Tracy called his name from the boat, he found her holding his phone. "No way. Tell them I'll call back."

"It's Dani."

"Seriously? Damn, it's been forever..."

"Are you coming or you want to call back?"

"No. Don't hang up. Who knows when I'll catch her again."

With strong strokes, he reached the ladder, gripped the railing and hurried up the metal stairs, barely drying his head and hands before taking it. "Hey, what's up, sexy?" He ignored his mom's raised eyebrows and walked farther from her. "Nah, not at the moment, but it could be. We're out on the boat. Come on over and bring that incredibly skimpy bikini you have." His voice as low as possible, he laughed at her response. "Yeah well, you know you're always invited. So what's been keeping you so busy you're don't take my calls?"

Catching up on her latest, in brief outline form, Ryan heard someone call her name in the background. Typical Dani, never stopping for more than three seconds at a time, she cut it short with a promise she'd call back soon and returned the invitation. Maybe he would take her up on it, with Katie. Dani was great with people. Maybe Kaitlyn would open to her more.

"Is everything okay with her?" Will watched his expression when he hung up.

"Yeah. Maybe. Think she wanted to talk more but as always…"

"Got interrupted."

"I'll call back later." He turned toward Bella throwing a fit about something for the second time. She was getting tired. "About time to head back, it looks like."

"We can try to get her to nap. Hate to cut down on your time out here when you have it."

"No, it's all right. I'm afraid Kaitlyn's going to burn, anyway, even with the sun block."

After a shower, Ryan grabbed his guitar and messed with a tune that came to mind while swimming. No words, just a melody. He couldn't stay up in his room long. She would wonder where he was. So he jotted a few notes and headed downstairs with it still buzzing his head. He hated thinking of melody first. It was easier to fit a melody to words than the other way around. Dani disagreed. Music seemed to pull words out of her. He'd always found it amazing to watch her write.

Finding everyone in the kitchen except Kaitlyn, he asked where she was.

"Thought she was with you. Heard you playing." Will got up as Ryan turned to go find her.

He went upstairs to check her room and the open window made him cringe until he realized the screen was there. The dog was barking. She wouldn't. Ryan jogged down the stairs and through the house to the back door. He came up behind Will.

"Don't." His brother grabbed his arm to keep him from bursting out after her. She sat just outside the dog's fence and the bark turned into a growl.

"Ry, she's already upset. Don't go over there."

"Like I'm going to let that thing break his chain and..."

"Look." Will nodded toward them.

Tracy and his mom were behind them at the door. He wouldn't stay inside. He had to be closer than that, to ... to do *something* if necessary. Stepping out quietly, he noted the dog calm, with only occasional growls. Katie didn't look at it directly but turned so the dog knew she was attempting contact.

Ryan took a few slow steps closer. The dog caught his movement, jumped toward him, and started barking again. He had to force himself to breath. "Katie." She looked over at him. "What are you doing?"

Silent amidst the barking, she remained still.

"Come away from him."

"Her."

"Okay, her. Come away from her. She doesn't want us here."

Her eyes questioned him, but she didn't move. Giving in, Ryan crept closer, keeping a side view of the furious dog, and crouched next to her. "Why are you doing this?"

Fading sunlight reflected gently on her skin. "I didn't want you on the ledge, but you stayed."

The ledge. She was comparing herself to the dog? It wasn't the same. This animal was quite able to take care of itself. It was strong, and large, intimidating ... and furious. It was like a criminal that had to be locked up for everyone else's protection. It wasn't the same.

It calmed again, though. Planted near the fence, it stopped growling and sat still. Only the eyes moved when Ryan glanced over.

His stomach turned when Katie moved closer to the fence.

"Don't." He caught her arm. The dog stood up again. "Please. You're scaring the hell out of me as it is. Don't go where he can reach you."

"She."

"She." He glanced back at the dog. "Sorry."

They sat for some time, not speaking, or moving. The dog sat again and eventually lay down, its eyes on them. Ryan tried to find the big dipper amidst the speckles in the dusk. His dad had spent many hours teaching him the constellations during camping "trips," which most often meant weekends of sleeping in a tent in the yard and building a small campfire. Now and then, he would take the boys to an actual campground to fish and go boating, and to give his wife well-deserved time off.

"That's the little dipper." Ryan moved his finger around as though he could actually touch each constellation, explaining what he pointed toward and telling her how he learned their names. He expected his family had given up watching and they were actually alone.

The big dipper appeared after a few clouds moved past, but he didn't point it out. He stopped.

"Where is your father?"

"He died when I was fourteen." Ryan pointed out the Milky Way.

"How?"

He took a deep breath. "He was a pilot. Army. The copter went down in a training accident. Mechanical error and bad weather."

Ryan felt her eyes, not able to meet them. He didn't want a response. No response ever helped anything. This time, he appreciated her silence that seemed more respectful than anything anyone ever said.

He knew they should go in. Coolness descended and he felt a dusting of dew. The air smelled of night. He loved noting the difference, the dark dampness that changed the scent of the air. He couldn't sit out in the grass at his place. The little grass around his building was across the street, in the median with traffic on both sides. Sitting out there at night would be suicide if any of his fans happened to notice. At least it would be mayhem enough it wouldn't be worth it.

Katie shifted and leaned in against him.

Turning to look at her, he didn't see that she was bothered or that she needed anything. He felt, this time, it was for him, not for her, and he wrapped an arm around her shoulder. "You're cold."

"It's okay."

"We should go in."

"No."

With a light squeeze, Ryan pulled her closer, trying to share his warmth. He studied the stars and thought about her eyes, how they followed him. He should have turned the conversation to her parents. She was probably as glad he didn't. It would wait. Asking about his dad was another step. A small step, but a step. He would let it be enough for the moment.

When he felt her shiver, he stood and offered his hand.

His mom brought them hot tea and asked Kaitlyn if she'd been trained to deal with animals.

"No." Her voice was quiet, but she answered.

"Well, you might be good at it. You sure let Chewy know who was in charge." She threw Ryan a grin.

4

Ryan unlocked the door to his loft and a weight descended – unusual after a visit to his family. He normally felt relief at being back in his own place, resuming his own life, although the short break was always helpful. This time, he'd wanted to stay longer, to keep Katie there longer. Each time they were out together alone, he learned more, in small pieces. There had been several foster homes. Most hadn't liked how quiet she was, convinced she was either stupid or mentally impaired. She was vague about the others, obviously not fond of them.

She followed into the loft. She always refused to go into a door first.

"Okay, tell me the truth now." He closed the door and touched her arm. "Were they okay? Did they annoy the hell out of you? And you can say yes, because they annoy the hell out of me quite often."

"No."

"No?" He hoped for more.

"If you need to ... it's okay." She held his eyes while he pondered her meaning. "You would visit?"

It was an agreement to move into Will's if he decided, allowing him to let go of her. His stomach turned, but he managed a light nod.

Katie touched the side of her face to his, only for a second, then walked away, back to shower, he supposed.

He stood motionless. It was good. He would call Will and let him know, that if it was okay, he would return before long and ... and what? Drop her off like a stray animal? How could he? Was she expecting it because it had happened to her so often? How could he be the next? But it would be better for her. An actual family ... a house where there were regular home-cooked meals and kids and a yard ... it would be better for her. His mom would take her under her wing. Kaitlyn had responded to her already. It wouldn't be long before she was talking to his mom as much as she did to him. She needed a parent, stability ... anything except the kind of gypsy life his work provided. It would be better.

Still, how could he?

With a quick gasp that pulled him from his thoughts, at least partly, he grabbed his bag and took it to his room. She had only gone in to him the first night at Wills. Otherwise, she stayed in her own room and looked as though she was sleeping. She would adjust well. Bella would make sure she had plenty of company. His mom would grow to love having her. Ryan was sure of it. She didn't have girls of her own. She called Tracy her daughter instead of her daughter-in-law, but Kaitlyn could be more her own daughter. Couldn't she? Tracy had her mom still. She was fully independent; even before she met Will she was fully independent. It wasn't the same as taking someone in who truly needed a parent, a mother. It would work well for both.

Staring at his bed, Ryan told himself to knock it the hell off. He couldn't be so possessive. So he was the one who brought her in off the ledge. It was coincidence. The point was to let her continue to live and to help her want to. As far as he could see, it worked. She didn't show signs of wanting to find another ledge.

He'd call Will tomorrow and they could start talking about when. His brother wouldn't refuse now that they'd met and accepted her.

He was hungry. Wondering what he had in the loft that was still edible, Ryan shuffled to the kitchen and panned through the fridge and cabinets. This and that ... nothing that held his interest. He still had single serving frozen stuff. After a few days at Will's with Tracy and his mom cooking, however, it would be pretty lame. Maybe that was good. It would show her how much better it would be at Will's than there in the bachelor's loft with morons drifting through as they pleased.

"I'll cook."

He turned at her voice. Her hair was dry. "I figured you were in the shower."

"I unpacked."

"Already?" He chuckled. "It takes me forever to do that, though you'd think I'd be used to it, right? I hate it, the putting in and pulling back out and stuffing in drawers. I keep saying I'll leave one set of stuff in bags and another in the loft so I don't ever have to pack or unpack." Ryan knew he was rambling but it covered his thoughts. "I suppose they'd get kind of nasty sitting in bags all the time, though."

She moved from the doorway and walked around him to get to the refrigerator. It took only a few seconds to find what she wanted.

"Can I help?" He felt ridiculous standing in his own kitchen not knowing what to do.

She shook her head.

As a habit to keep his hands occupied, he grabbed his acoustic and sat on the couch to play with it. He found words. Stars ... comets ... water. The images all flashed around together in his thoughts and he grabbed a nearby notebook to save phrases. Birds ... and windows. Birds and windows. Writing it at the top, he picked up the guitar again and started a melody.

As the big dipper had when the clouds moved, Katie appeared before him all at once, in a distant chair, one leg up and wrapped by her arms. Birds and windows. She looked like a little sparrow, tiny and rather plain, but full of life hidden within.

"It's ready." Her voice broke through. "I didn't want to interrupt."

Ryan stared a moment longer, then set the instrument down and went to take her hands, pulling her gently to her feet. "I uh..." He searched for words. "Are you all right around all of this? The band and crew floating in and out of here and going in to work with me or staying with Deanna and ... well, you haven't had much dealings with fans yet and they can get insane, but..." He knew he was worse than rambling. He made no sense. "Katie, you know I think it would be better for you at Will's than it is here. You wouldn't be alone. I would make sure. And there's space and a yard and ... and I know it would be better." He watched her eyes that refused to reflect her thoughts. "But ... if you're okay here ... if all of this won't overwhelm you..." He stopped, unsure it was fair to ask. Would she would be glad she wasn't being dumped or feel trapped there because he wanted it.

"I won't be in your way."

He frowned. Did that mean she wanted to stay and she wouldn't interfere with his work, or that she wanted to go to Will's and be out of his way?

She started toward the kitchen.

Ryan kept her hands. "I like having you here."

"Okay." Katie pulled away and went to take the dish from the oven. The scent of sausage and potatoes filled the small kitchen and he grabbed the plates.

~~~

"I guess they didn't want to keep a teen runaway, either?"

Ryan looked over at Daws, wondering where he'd been all morning, and shoved him farther away from where Katie was sitting. "She's not a runaway. I told you."

"I thought you were going up there to dump her with your family before it becomes an issue."

"What is your problem with her? She's not bothering you. Hell, she doesn't bother anyone. So *don't* keep talking about her like a stray animal. You're pissing me off." Ryan knew Ned was close enough to hear but it didn't matter.

"Hey." Daws set a hand on his shoulder. "I have nothing against her. I'm glad you were out of your mind enough..." He noted others around too close and lowered his voice, pulling him back even more. "I'm glad you were there at the right time. She seems like a sweet kid, but Reynauld, she's a kid and you're not, and you're going to end up in one hell of a mess if you keep playing hero to this girl."

"They think she's related. Who's gonna bother worrying about it other than you?"

Daws studied Ryan's face. "What's really going on with her? Did you ask them or did you back out? Or did she refuse?"

"She didn't refuse. She said it was okay if it was what I wanted."

"So?"

He took a deep breath with a glance over to make sure no one was bothering her. Her eyes were focused on a book Deanna gave her to help keep her from getting too bored.

"Reynauld? Did you ask them?"

"No."

"Why in the hell not? She didn't get along with them?"

"Yes, actually, she did well there. She even spoke to Mom. Only once, and only one word, but still..."

"So why didn't you ask?"

He looked over again. One leg was pulled onto the chair crossed in front of her while the other wrapped over it and led her toes to the floor, like a ballerina in tennis shoes. Her hair, always down and natural, partly concealed her face. He knew she paid more attention to her surroundings than she looked like she was.

"How old is she?"

The question pulled his focus back. "Why?"

"Do you know?"

"Haven't asked. Older than I first thought, though, I think."

Daws stepped closer. "Don't do this."

"Don't do what, Daws? Give a hand to someone who needs it? Hell, I've been given a hand more times than I can count. You don't think at least once I can return the favor, or at least pass it on?"

"That's not what I meant. Don't fall for this girl. She's too young. And she has ... some major issues going on. You can't become one of them."

Ryan walked away, over to Katie. Fall for her? He was only keeping her from falling, literally. That was it. What was so complicated? She happened to be female. Okay. He would've done the same for a young male who needed help so desperately. No one would say anything about that.

He couldn't help grin at the way she ignored, or seemed to ignore, everyone else around, but raised her head when he approached. "Hey, I wanna get out of here for a while. You want to come grab lunch with me?"

Closing her book without using a marker, she unwrapped her legs and stood.

"You'll lose your place that way."

"I know the page."

"Good memory for numbers? I can't remember them for anything. Hell, I have days I can't remember my phone number."

"You remember chords."

"Different." Ryan could see she didn't get how it was, and he couldn't explain, but apparently it was different. He let Mac know they were taking a break and despite objections, he guided her out the door and toward the building's cafeteria where they weren't likely to be too bothered.

He changed his mind. He wanted to be outside. "How about we do something else today?" At her silence, Ryan veered the opposite direction toward the building's guarded entrance and enjoyed the jaunt to Antique Café. He kept his head down enough to not draw attention and managed to get them there without notice.

The host greeted them with a friendly *how are you today* and a *right this way*. The man knew where Ryan liked to sit.

Patio seating allowed a light breeze to help him relax as it cooled the mid-Manhattan air. The gentle commotion of locals and tourists walking past reminded him of the boat and Katie sitting on the back of it watching the kids play in the water. If he had any artistic talent, he would sketch that image, as clear as it was in his mind and with as much joy as it brought him. She was at home there. He could sense it.

For the first time, he noticed a guy try to get her attention, flirting. She either didn't see him or refused to acknowledge him. Either way, Ryan was just as glad. She wasn't ready for that. She needed more time. Would she talk to him if he came over and flirted more openly? He probably wouldn't while Ryan was there with her, but if she was alone? She had changed. The shyness still flooded her, but the combination of his convenience food habit and his family's full-meal cooking had added enough weight to make her look closer to healthy. The days out on the boat gave her a touch more color even through the strong sun block. And her eyes were shinier, still fearful at times, but less so.

"Katie?" He leaned forward on his elbows to bridge part of the distance the small table demanded. "Is there anything you've ever wanted to do that you haven't been able to do?"

She took a sip of her tea, her green-brown eyes peering into his.

"Are you interested in travel? Seeing other countries? Or is there a concert you've wished you could attend? Or anything like that?"

She lowered her eyes to where she gripped her glass and played with the condensation along its side.

Filling silence, he told her of how he wanted to go by ship all the way to Europe. He'd been to Europe, doing concerts, but hadn't seen much of it because of his schedule. After taking the time to get there, he would run around to different countries and see everything he wanted to see, then take the slow journey home again. Even if it took a few months.

"Sound crazy?"

Her eyes touched his at the word.

"There is something." Ryan watched her, noted the argument within whether to tell him, and took her hand. "You know anything you tell me is safe. I won't repeat it. What is it that you want?"

Shaking her head, she withdrew ... and he saw a camera directed at them. "Let's go." He helped her up and skirted around the man into the building. His publicist would yell if those pictures got out. Maybe it was only a fan. He could hope.

He stayed inside long enough to see if the man would follow them in and found a couple of girls he recognized. Away from where Kaitlyn could hear, he told them about the photographer and asked if one of them would check to see if he had gone. In return, he didn't refuse when they asked to walk back with him, only until he got to the building.

It wasn't a fan. A fan either would have stayed until he had come out again or followed him inside to try to get closer. They were only talking. There was nothing steamy or solicitous about whatever photos he'd gotten, so possibly the editor wouldn't want them. Ryan hoped.

Kaitlyn remained distant through the day, not bothering to pick up her book, but watching things around her, watching him with an expression he didn't understand. He pushed too much, tried too hard to get her to open more. Maybe he pushed her away again. His concentration waned the later it got, the more he worried about what he had done.

"Okay, the mics are off and no one else can hear us." His guitarist motioned toward the light. "We all want to know what the hell is wrong with you recently." Trey nodded toward the rest of the band, Ryan's regulars. He was particular about who played with him, sometimes too particular, but they worked well together. He also insisted on using the same musicians in studio as on the road, which tended to be even harder to find. They had to have no more of a life away from music than he did.

"Reynauld, what's up? Ever since that cousin or whatever came to town, you're not anywhere near being *Riveting* Ryan Reynauld. You're more like ... Irritable Ryan Reynauld. Can you send her back to her family or wherever she came from and let's get going again? We've got an album to finish..."

Ryan shoved a hand against the guitarist's chest, pushing him and grabbing his shirt all at once. "*Don't* say that again. *I'm* her family now, got it? You expect me to apologize for not partying with you guys all the time now? I got better things to do that are a damn sight more important than getting drunk and picking up girls...." He gave in to the others backing him away.

"All right." He looked at the floor and regained his composure. "Look, this goes nowhere, and if I see it in the press, you're all fired and

I won't bother to try to find out who leaked it."

"Have any of us ever leaked anything? Come on, Ry." Ned was closest, the only one who had the nerve to still stand next to him.

"Okay. I know you wouldn't. It's been a long few weeks." He didn't dare look out at Katie. She would know he was talking about her if he did. "Her family is gone. I'm all she has. So give me a break, here, because you know I know nothing about taking care of anyone. It's not like I've ever done it."

Silence penetrated the room: silence he was becoming sick of and comforted by at the same time.

"We didn't know, man. You never tell us anything." The guitarist sounded both apologetic and accusing.

"Fine. Just give me a break. On stage, I'll be what I need to be. Otherwise, I won't promise anything. If you want to walk, that's up to you, but she's not going anywhere. At least not until tour and then I don't know."

"We're not walking." Ned tapped his chest. "But after five years, you could let us in on the important stuff. We give up a hell of a lot for you, to work the way you want to work. Trey just let his girlfriend walk out instead of bailing on you for the tour coming up..."

"What?" Ryan looked back at the guitarist.

He shrugged. "It's about the music. About what we're doing here. Can't be with someone who can't deal with it."

The words plummeted Ryan back to his past, to when his father was still alive and away so often and someone asked his mom how she put up with him always being gone. *Someone has to support what he's doing. He chose me because I'm strong enough to deal with it.* And Ryan dealt with it, with the moving every two or three years away from friends, by not letting anyone too far in. It was easier.

A knock on the window forced his return to the present. Deanna, waving at him to come out of the studio.

Ryan's heart thumped. Katie. She'd seen it and it scared her. Rushing to the door, he calmed when he saw her behind Deanna's shoulder. She still sat quietly. Unruffled. "What is it?"

"Relax. You always get this excited when a sexy woman comes to kidnap you and your band?"

"What?"

"You're done for the day and I don't care what time it is. I have new furniture and want to show it off." She looked around him to the others and raised her voice. "You're all coming to our place for dinner. No excuses. Let's go. Pack it up." She leaned into Ryan's ear. "You need a good shit-kickin' party. It's been too long."

"Careful. You're showing your hillbilly roots."

"Country. Not hillbilly. It's not the same."

"Okay." He pulled back from a pinch to the inside of his arm, and looked over toward Katie. "I don't know, Anna. Something's been bothering her today…"

"She'll be fine. It'll only be you two, Freddy and me, and your band, with girlfriends if they want to invite them, and a couple of my friends who I'll get huge brownie points from by letting them hang out with you. No more." She saw his hesitation. "Ryan, maybe it'll be good for her, too."

Maybe it would. "Let me ask her."

"Already did. She didn't say no."

"Anna, that doesn't mean…"

"Yes, it does. She's going to have to learn to say no if she means no. That's very important for a woman to be able to do." Her face grew serious. "You can't do this on your own if you're going to insist on doing this. You need a woman's help. So does she, no offense."

Nodding, he gave in. "You are an angel, and the only one apparently supporting me in this."

"No, Freddy does, too. He shows it different, but he does support you."

Katie didn't cling to him as much as she had last time. Maybe Deanna was right. Maybe she needed to be forced to find out it was all right to socialize. He would worry less if she was less bothered. The tour … he hoped she could handle the tour. He would have to have her out in crowds before then to see if she could.

Watching her across the room as she listened to whatever Deanna and one of the band girlfriends chatted about, Ryan thought maybe she wasn't more comfortable. Maybe she was annoyed at his aggression toward the guitarist. She hadn't said anything to him since. She'd barely said anything to him since lunch.

"Hey, handsome. Haven't seen you recently."

He recognized the girl who slid her hand around his waist and up his back but couldn't place her name. She'd come in with the bassist and another girl.

"I heard you'd be here and I practically forced Sam to let me come with. How are you?" Fingertips caressed his back.

"Good. Uh…"

"You don't remember me."

"Yeah."

"Really?" She grinned and moved her body against him. "What's my name then, tiger?'

Ryan swallowed a gulp of beer, trying to remember where he'd seen her. If he could place her in the right location…

"Jamie. Remember? Jameson, actually, and you found it funny that a woman would be called Jameson."

"Did I?" Her perfume ... he recognized the perfume. It was too heavy and too ... just too heavy. "You're here with Sam."

"No." She nodded toward his bassist and the other girl. "She's here with Sam. He brought me to keep you company."

"Did he?"

She moved her face in close to his. "What's wrong, tiger? You seem distracted."

"Yeah, well ... you're slightly distracting."

Her fingers slid down and ran along the top of his jeans. "Slightly? You don't remember me."

"I suppose I should." He used his beer as an excuse to pull back an inch, from her breasts pressed to his chest.

"And I suppose I should be offended." She didn't look at all offended as she moved back in.

Ryan knew he was being watched. Sam brought her as a test, he supposed. To see if Kaitlyn was really a cousin or friend or something. "I wouldn't blame you."

"You are so precious." Her hand moved down the outside of his hip, down to his thigh.

He wouldn't have to fake attraction. How he didn't remember this one with the low-cut filled-out blouse and skin-tight jeans making her look fully available, Ryan couldn't imagine. Although that description fit a lot of the girls he'd been with. But Katie was there. He couldn't take ... what was her name? Damn. Whatever her name was, he couldn't take her to the apartment with Katie there. And regardless of the arousal factor, he didn't want to take her home. The thought made him back up, away.

"Did I do something wrong?"

"No. Sorry, I ... it's not a good time." He felt his stomach protest. The thought of Katie seeing the girl hang on him, seeing him let her hang on him, hurt his stomach. Excusing himself, he found the bathroom and locked himself in. Damn. What was he doing? And why shouldn't he? Katie ... was a child. It didn't matter if he dated, or whatever. Still, he couldn't take a girl to the loft with her there. That would be more wrong than he could make himself overlook. Which was why Will's place would be better for her. He was a sleazeball. What could he say? He was single, unattached, as he liked it. It was his business. He wasn't using those girls more than they were using him. It was their choice. They made the moves...

But he couldn't.

Ryan turned on the faucet, splashed his face, and gripped the sink, letting cold water drip from his chin. He couldn't.

With a deep breath, he dried and went back out to ... to talk to anyone else first, before he could face her.

She was still with Deanna, only partly listening to the conversation. Her eyes kept finding the huge picture window that overlooked the city.

Ryan went to the kitchen to find anything but alcohol. His damn stomach. He was such a wimp. He couldn't guess why a girl would even bother to offer more than once.

Grabbing the 7-Up, he dumped ice in a glass and poured it in, waited to let the foam settle, and topped it off.

"Want this?" Ned pushed a bottle of vodka at him. "You're gonna have to drink some of that out of there first."

"Nah, I'm fine."

"Serious? Plain soda? Feeling okay?"

"I'm fine." He returned to the main room. She wasn't with Deanna. She was at the balcony door, going out.

His body tense, Ryan followed as quickly as he could around those in the way. He hadn't seen anyone else go out, although the soft yellow light was on to welcome those who were interested. The rest of them had seen the city at night often enough, he supposed.

Katie stood at the rail, her fingers wrapped around the metal bar, eyes cast toward the street.

He set his glass on a little table and approached as well as he could while he stayed close to the back wall. She didn't notice. Or, she didn't acknowledge him. Trying not to let his heart pound, Ryan inched closer, behind her enough to let her block the view, but getting close enough to grab her if he thought she needed to be grabbed.

"Where do you think they're going?" Her voice was light, partially caught up by the night sounds, tires on pavement, shadowed laughter in the distance.

"Who?" How did she know it was him when she didn't look? It was dark. Her peripheral vision wouldn't have made him out that clearly.

"All of them. In the cars. On the street."

"Hadn't thought about it."

Turning, she met his gaze. "You don't wonder about how others live? What they do?"

"Sure. In general. I'd have a hard time writing otherwise."

"Why do you?"

"Why do I what?" He wanted to be next to her. He didn't want to be closer to the edge.

"Write. About people."

He frowned at the question. "What else would I write about? I have to have songs and I don't like to use other people's songs. So I write them."

After a moment, she turned back.

Sensing it wasn't the answer she wanted, or that it sounded too shallow, Ryan got annoyed. She knew he hated heights, yet she remained up there at the edge. Was she trying to make him worry? Getting even? He didn't think he had that coming, regardless of how misdirected his anger had been earlier or how many girls hit on him. He'd tried everything he could think of. If she wouldn't talk to him, what did she expect? "Want me to leave you alone?"

Her head turned, a question on her face.

"I didn't mean ... not alone, alone ... I mean I can go back inside if..."

She walked up to him, stopping only inches away, her eyes piercing through. And she stood there, waiting, for something. He wished to hell he knew what she was waiting for. She saw too much in him, expected too much. If she expected him to be more than just a singer, she was bound to be pretty damn disappointed. That's all he was. He had never wished to be more than that and he didn't plan to start wishing for more.

Her eyes dropped.

"Kaitlyn." He had to clear his voice to keep it working. "I'm sorry I lost my temper earlier, that you had to see it. I wouldn't ... you know you don't have to worry about me, right? I would never..."

"I'm upsetting you. This is too hard for you."

"No." He could see she didn't believe him and took her arms. "Look at me." He waited, not long. "Katie, look at me. Please." She finally gave him a partial gaze and he leaned his head toward hers. "I'm only upset when I think I'm not helping you in the way you need. I don't know what to do for you. And I'm trying. I'm not sure what you expect..."

"Nothing." She started to say more, then paused. "I don't want you bothered by me. You don't need to worry..."

"Well I do, and there's nothing you're going to say to stop that."

She looked away, toward the city, the railing.

He raised a hand to her face to get her attention without pleading for it again. She jumped and he pulled it back. "I did scare you. You're worried now. You don't have to be."

She shook her head.

"I would never hurt you." At her silence, he tried to decide how to win her trust again. He was an idiot. He should have known better than to show any kind of violence anywhere around her. He wasn't a violent person. He never had been, other than his temper, but it wasn't a violent temper. It was defensive. There was a difference.

"Reynauld." Daws stuck his head out the balcony door.

"Not now."

"Give me one minute, would ya?"

"*Not* now." Ryan walked over and tried to close the door.

"Hey." Daws grabbed his arm. "This doesn't look good." He nodded toward Katie, his voice low.

"I don't give a shit. We're trying to talk. Everyone can mind their own damn business." Yanking his arm away, he managed to get the door shut and went back to her. She was staring. "I'm sorry. The guy thinks he's my damn parent or something."

"I'm interfering. He knows."

"I don't care what he knows, or thinks he knows." Ryan moved closer, cautiously. "You're not interfering. And I'm not bothered by you. I'm bothered by whatever scares you. Talk to me, Katie. Let me help." Her eyes fell. He had to ask. Even if she pulled away again, he had to ask. "Has someone hurt you?"

She tensed and stepped back.

He had to force himself not to ask who it was so he could go find him. Maybe he would ... later. When she trusted him more, he would find out who. With a bare grasp of control of his anger, he focused on her, on calming her enough to talk. But maybe it wasn't the place. Maybe it would be better to wait until they were back in the loft.

"Do you want to go? We can get out of here. It's late anyway." Silence. With a deep breath, he moved closer again. "Kaitlyn." Another step closer and she didn't pull back. "Don't jump. It's all right." Raising his hand, Ryan inched it up to her face and allowed his fingers to brush her cheek. She had to know it was all right, that she could trust him. He felt her tense. She didn't look at him, but she also didn't pull away.

"Promise me something." Now, he knew he was pushing, but he had to do it. "I made a promise to you, and I'll keep it for as long as you want me to keep it. Maybe longer." He grinned but she didn't see. "Promise me you won't...." He grabbed a breath and tried to continue without emotion. "If something I do bothers you, or if there's something you need I'm not doing, say so. If you want to be somewhere else, say that. Just promise me that you won't...." He couldn't even say it.

She found his eyes. "It belongs to you. I can't."

Belongs to you. She hadn't said that in some time. He'd hoped it was only a slip, an emotional temporary response. Starting to argue, he was afraid to. She meant he was preventing it. Nothing else, only that she'd put her life in his hands.

Unsure what to say, he slid his fingers back into her hair, the way his mom did to him when he was particularly upset as a child. The warm palm wrapped alongside his head did wonders to help him feel better. Maybe it would work for her, also. Or for him, the opposite way around.

Without her hair alongside her face and topping her shoulder, Ryan could see the whole profile he had only glimpses of when the wind caught the strands and pushed them around. Even her facial structure was tiny. He wondered if both of her parents had been, also, and considered asking, but he didn't want to add extra emotion. There had been enough for one day.

She was still tense, but not as much, and he tried to give her a brotherly gaze that said he would always look out for her and always be there as she needed. He could be her ... no, he couldn't. A sudden feeling he didn't want to have started to evolve and he took a deep breath, moving his hand farther down her hair and away from her face, retreating. A glow of soft yellow light fell on her ear and caught his eye. A scar? Moving the hair more, he touched it, above it, and she pulled away from him. The hair covered it again. She didn't have earrings as most girls her age had. She had a scar, a large one, starting where the earring would be.

"Did one of them get caught?" He tried to keep it light. "I've heard of that happening. Do you wear big hoops? Those things always look scary to me. I can't see how girls wear them."

She didn't look at him.

"Still have the other one?" He started to move the hair away from her other ear but she backed up. "Katie. Don't run from me."

Her eyes shot up to his, then dropped again.

He stepped back. "How about if we call it a day? I'll have to stay a few minutes when I go back in so it won't be too rude, but ... stay out here if you'd rather and I'll come back." With her silence, he left her on the balcony.

Daws was apparently waiting, or blocking people from bothering them. "You left her out there?"

"It's fine."

"Is it?"

With a glance, Ryan side-stepped him and went to talk to the guitarist. He made amends by joking with him and his date, wondering if it was the old girlfriend giving Trey another chance or a new one. He didn't bother to ask. His thoughts were on Kaitlyn. She was terrified. And he wanted to know why.

With his attention on the window overlooking the balcony, he saw her come back in. Ryan stayed where he was and she came over and took his side. Apparently, she wasn't too upset with him.

Trey tried to speak to her. She acknowledged she heard him without actually looking into his face but didn't answer. Ryan answered for her, as he was getting used to doing. He realized he had never seen her look directly into anyone else's face. She always almost looked at them, but not quite.

Ned and his current date joined the conversation, and Deanna, and a friend of hers whose name Ryan forgot and the girl who'd hit on him. And he just wanted to be home, with Kaitlyn and no one else. Suddenly, he was exhausted. She agreed when he asked if she was ready.

They didn't speak on the way and it was okay with him. He was tired of talking ... of trying to get her to talk.

Ryan went to shower after making sure she didn't want to go first, and stood under the cool water for too long, trying not to think. Although he usually took cool showers during the summer, it made him edgy and he turned it warmer, allowing it to caress his muscles, his neck that was more tense than usual, his scalp. When it ran over and tickled his ears, he thought again about the scar. How long would it take her to tell him? Maybe he should take her back to Vermont and out on the boat. It seemed to relax her. It would sure as hell relax him, more than the shower was.

Shoving it off, he dried and dressed and returned ready to apologize for taking so long. She wasn't in the living room, or the kitchen. He walked back to the hall. Her door was mostly closed; a soft light glowed from its edges.

He didn't get an answer to his knock, but went in anyway, and she shoved something under her pillow. "Sorry. I ... are you okay?"

She nodded.

He knew he should leave but ignored the light thump on his head from his conscience and ambled over to sit beside her. "If I said too much, asked too much ... I ... I'm only concerned. You know..."

"It's okay."

"Is it?" He watched her eyes. They were back to normal, not frightened as they'd been on the balcony. "Then why won't you answer me?" When her eyes dropped, he sighed, told her good night, and went back to plop on his own bed.

He couldn't figure her out. Yeah, so guys always said that about girls, but it was different. She was different. Or maybe she wasn't so much. He'd never bothered to try to understand girls more than anything they volunteered to let him know. It had always been enough. As soon as it didn't work for either or both, Ryan found it easy to say thanks and see ya. Except for the one, but it was long ago and no longer mattered.

Pushing her slowly dissolving image from his brain, he went back to Katie's growing image. She maybe wasn't quite as young as he thought at first. Her size threw him, he thought. She wasn't the size of most grown adults. Still, her face had a maturity.... he pulled himself away from that thought, also. It didn't matter how old she was. As long as no one accused him of anything he wasn't doing, it wasn't an issue. But why did she keep telling him it belonged to him, that her life belonged to him for rescuing her, and then keep pulling away? Protecting herself. Why would she protect herself from him if she honestly felt she belonged to him in some way? The two things were contradictory, weren't they? Her pulling away was a good thing. Wanting to protect herself showed...

She appeared at his door.

He knew he should sit up, to ask what she needed, but his words, and apparently the ability to move, were lost. No, she didn't belong to him. He belonged to her. He was at her mercy, fully, and she had no idea.

Kaitlyn came over, hesitated, and sat on the edge of his bed. Even without touching him, her presence was overwhelming.

He had to get up. Ryan knew he had to get up, to move away. She was too close, in his bedroom, on his bed, and he had to get up.

She raised her hand and pushed the hair behind the ear he asked about, the one he hadn't seen, turning her head so he could. There was a matching scar.

His stomach churned and he pulled himself up to get closer. When he touched her ear, her eyes closed. "Does it hurt? It looks healed."

"No. It looks ugly."

Ugly. It wasn't a word Ryan could ever come up with about her in any way. "What happened?"

She managed to keep control although he could see the fight within. And she squeezed his fingers. "One of my foster parents.... Most were okay. They tried. It was my fault because I wouldn't talk to them." She took another breath. "I had earrings ... from my dad, before ... they were small hoops and I had to talk him into it because he was afraid they would get caught...." Her fingers got tighter. "But I wanted them because they made me look more like a girl. Because I don't, really."

"Are you kidding?" Ryan touched her chin. "Of course you do. You couldn't even look masculine if you put on a beard and mustache. Katie, you look very much like a girl."

She stared like he was trying to convince her she was ten feet tall.

"You're beautiful. Anyone who told you differently is out of his mind."

Her eyes showed confusion. Ryan figured she was trying to decide if he believed his words or was pandering to her. There was no reason for him to pander. He didn't want anything from her. He couldn't say he'd never exaggerated a girl's beauty before, but he wasn't this time and he had no reason. She was beautiful, and completely feminine, and ... and he lowered his hand from her face. It was touching her face that did it, that made him start with those thoughts he couldn't have. He would have to stop.

"So." He had to return to the conversation in order to distract himself. "Did they get caught like he said?"

She shook her head. "After ... a long time at the shelter, with no one wanting me because I was too old, an older couple came. They wanted house help. It was a farm. There were boys for farming but no girls to help inside. They didn't say that."

"The boys could have helped inside. Hell, Will and I did enough of it. Not that you can tell by how badly I keep my own place." What she said finally registered. "Wait, you mean they took you in just to be free help?" Her eyes answered. "They can't do that. Not like I know much about the foster system, but couldn't you report them?"

The return expression told him he was being naïve. Report them. A young girl who didn't speak to people. "Okay, stupid question." He shifted, bringing himself closer. "What happened, Katie?"

"He said they ... the earrings ... looked like ... a tramp, that it was unholy and I had to take them off." Her fingers tightened. "I said they weren't. My father gave them to me and I couldn't. He said I didn't have a father. And I started to walk away." Shaking even through the grip she had on his hand, she pushed herself to continue. "He pulled them out, yelled that I was never to back talk him again, never argue ... never mention my father that I didn't have anymore."

Ryan breathed harder with a surge of anger and raised his other hand to her ear, brushing back the hair. Maybe he could find someone who could fix it, make it less noticeable, if she wanted to try. He wouldn't suggest it now. He couldn't let her think he agreed it was ugly. It wasn't, but it had to be an ugly reminder every time she saw her ears. He supposed that was why her hair was always straight down.

"Katie, it was child abuse. You could have had him arrested."

"He said it was me, that I was crazy and I did it and they couldn't control me. He made his boys say so, too. They were scared of him."

Ryan pulled her in and held her against his shoulder. When the time was right, he would ask her who it was, where this man was. And he would make sure it was taken care of, that there would be no other foster children ever in his custody. For the moment, he simply held her. She gripped him tightly for such small hands and arms.

When she started to relax, he moved and she tensed again, gripping harder.

"Come on." He moved a bit more, slowly, until she allowed the release. Then he pulled the blankets back from the bed and waited for her to crawl in. Wrapping them both, he guarded her in his arms when she snuggled in against his side.

~~~

Ryan generally loved press parties. He loved the crowd and the music and the food ... and he loved the attention. He loved to walk through knowing eyes were on him, that there were a ton of girls around he could pick up if he chose. They tried. During times Daws watched over Kaitlyn so he could do his job and mingle, he had a few offers. One even offered in front of her. He brushed that one off fast. The others he enjoyed flirting with before letting them know he wasn't taking them home.

He couldn't.

Regardless of how frustrated he was with the album, and how much he wouldn't mind some girl going home with him to get it out of his head for a while, he couldn't take anyone to the loft and he couldn't send Kaitlyn back alone.

Talking with some press big wig, giving him a possible maybe for a private interview with his publicist's okay, Ryan looked over to check on her. Ned was there. At her side, his drink in hand, he offered her the same. Daws stepped in and took the glass. Ned shrugged at whatever Daws said to him.

"If Patricia agrees, we're on?"

"Sure." Ryan answered the guy without thinking. "Excuse me." Stopped by some bleach-blonde chick taller than he was, Ryan tried to remember his surroundings and the cameras and maintained his polite thanks-but-no-thanks demeanor. He was nearly to Kaitlyn, too close to her to risk flirting back even if it was for looks as Patricia suggested. The woman didn't take the hint well, running a hand up his chest and leaning in, her cleavage tilting to a better view.

"I'm here with someone, all right? Back off." He took her hand away.

"Mr. Reynauld, Patricia asked me to be here and look like I'm with you. I'm one of her clients. It'll look good for both of us." She spoke into his ear. "So don't worry. I don't want you, either. Just act like you want me and I'll come around now and then. I won't go home with you. It'll only look like I might, or at least that you're willing."

Publicity. Counteracting the rumors about whether he was getting serious about Kaitlyn, that she wasn't related. He saw the flash from a camera. Felt the girl move back in ... and saw Katie notice.

"*Damn.* Okay, knock it off. Go find someone you do want." He didn't care who saw him add distance. "And it's damn well not going to look like you might go home with me. You can tell Patricia that, or I will. Makes no difference to me." Getting free of her, he headed over to Katie, to explain, except she wasn't there. Neither was Daws.

Ned gave him a curious look. "Lover's quarrel already?"

"Where'd Kaitlyn go?"

"Away from your new girlfriend. Why'd you ditch her? You're supposed to be..."

"Forget her. What in the hell were you trying to give Kaitlyn?"

"A drink." He shrugged. "Mild. Only a touch of gin. Thought it'd help her relax."

"Are you crazy?"

"Why? Hell, she looks old enough tonight, whether or not she is. No one's gonna bother her. She looks really good tonight, too, huh? Wow, I was surprised when she came in."

She looked old enough. Too flustered to banter with his drummer, Ryan walked away to find where she was. Yes, she looked incredible in the dark green dress and low, strappy heels Deanna helped her find for the party. She'd pulled part of her hair back so it wasn't all hanging straight but left enough down to cover her ears.

And she did look incredible.

He was stopped too often. So much for attention. He'd had enough for tonight.

"Reynauld, come with me."

He turned to Daws. "Where is she?"

"With Ginny. And you're supposed to stay away from her."

"She saw me..."

"Yes. I told her what it was about. But..."

"But what?" Alarms scattered through his brain.

"Let's walk." He gestured toward journalists too close by and led Ryan out of the main room into the hotel foyer. People floated around there, also, but only a few and they were easy to avoid.

Daws closed in. "Tell me why it's bothers her to see you with other women."

"She's bothered? Damn, where is she? I have to..."

"*Reynauld.*" Daws grabbed his arm. "*Why* is she bothered? Tell me you are not letting her think..."

"Hell, how do I know? I'm not letting her think anything. I'm not *doing* anything."

"You're sure?"

Ryan clenched his teeth and waited out a surge of anger that would make him say too much.

"Okay. Maybe it's only the crowd. I'll have Enrico take her home and out of it..."

"The hell you will. She won't go with him. She barely knows him. And she's not leaving without me."

Daws stared as Ryan realized what he'd said, how possessive it sounded.

He grabbed a deep breath. "Fine. You take her home if she'll go with you. She might, with you, but you'll have to stay until I get there. You can't just drop her off and leave."

"You want *me* to take her?"

"No, I want to take her myself, but this is kinda important. And Ginny would have my head if I left so early."

"My job is to protect *your* ass. I have a team for ... your visitors. Enrico is my right hand. Trustworthy."

"Daws. Either you take her or I do. Or she stays and I'll have her walk around with me so I know she's okay. No one else takes her anywhere. Ever. Until it's her choice." Ryan knew his guard wanted to argue. He was insulted maybe, but it wasn't meant as an insult. Ryan could take care of himself a whole hell of a lot better than Kaitlyn could.

Her safety was top priority. He wanted his most trusted guard, his friend, to stay with her.

Half shoving him, Daws took him back to a far corner of the huge banquet room where Kaitlyn was surrounded by people. Ginny was nearby, half turned away, leaving her too much on her own. Someone tried to talk to her. Kaitlyn did her best not to pull back; he could see it in how tense she was, in her face.

She didn't wrap around him as he took her side but it appeared an effort not to. And he had to be careful what he said.

"You look tired." She didn't, actually. But he couldn't say how scared she looked. "I'm going to be here a while. These things last forever. But Daws will take you home." Ryan caught Ginny glance from him to Daws. They could both be mad. It didn't matter. His focus stayed on Kaitlyn. "I'll walk out with you."

His manager moved in and gripped his arm. "Daws can walk her out without your help. There's someone I want you to meet."

"He'll wait." Ryan pulled from her grasp.

Careful not to take Kaitlyn's hand, not to touch her as they made their way through the crowd, he stopped as needed to make it look like they were only wandering. A small amount of flirting with girls who approached combined with the distance he kept wouldn't look like he was encouraging her or hitting on her. Kaitlyn's early departure while he stayed, although it was the last thing he wanted, would counter the rumors. If she would go. He wasn't entirely sure.

Ryan waited with her while the car was brought to the front and tried to explain. It sounded lame even to him, because it was. Still, he couldn't get around it. Her protection came over his, but his job had to stay his priority over his personal life.

She agreed to go, or at least she didn't argue. If she had, even only with a word, he would have given in, taken her back with him and kept her on his arm. She didn't want to be there. It was all over her from the moment they arrived. Too much too soon. He shouldn't have brought her. But he hated every minute he'd have to stay without her.

She was asleep in the big chair, back in her house clothes and wrapped in the blanket, by the time he returned to the loft just after two o'clock.

He shucked off his tie and unbuttoned the top of his shirt as Daws pulled up from the couch. "Was she okay?"

His friend grabbed his jacket, asked Enrico if everything had gone well, and walked out.

Ryan figured he had a right to be angry but what else could he do? Katie never would have left with Enrico, or maybe she would have if he'd asked her to, but ... but he should have insisted she stay instead. He wanted her there. He wanted her on his arm, at his side. She did look incredible and she'd tried hard to fit in, for his sake. Even fast asleep curled into the chair, she looked incredible.

He sank onto his couch and studied her. She deserved better. Will was right. So was Daws. Ryan should have found someone better to help her through whatever she was dealing with. They all knew he would let her down, and he had. There was no way he'd ask her to tour with him, not even the short tour that was only to get his face out there again while he finished the album. State fairs. Big events. Private shows. Nothing like the long country-spanning auditorium tours. She could handle it. But he couldn't. He would mess it up again, let her down too far. It would be better to take her to Will's.

5

How Deanna convinced Kaitlyn to go to her yoga class, Ryan wasn't sure. The morning after the press party when he slept in to catch up, he'd found Deanna, without Daws, in his loft and Katie was getting ready. It was girls only. He couldn't go, not even to make sure she was all right. But it was good. He would leave her at Will's soon and any step in her doing something without him would make that easier.

Since then, Kaitlyn had agreed to go out with her again, twice. Ryan knew she must talk to Deanna but hadn't yet heard her do so. Getting home before she did tonight had made him nervous, set him on edge until she came in. They were "out" Deanna said. "Girl stuff."

He should have started dinner but instead he'd paced and tried to watch videos. He hardly noticed them. Enrico had accompanied him home from the studio instead of Daws. Otherwise, Ryan would have called Deanna to see where in the hell they were. He didn't want to get his guard on the phone as long as he was still acting childish about being sent home with Kaitlyn.

Katie noticed his irritability and avoided him. She took a bag to her room while Deanna dropped a couple more off in the kitchen, and went in to start dinner. Ryan dropped onto the couch, threw Deanna a curt farewell, and didn't answer when she told him he better be pleasant or she'd come right back and pick Kaitlyn up.

Finally, he pushed himself off the couch and went in to at least see if she'd tell him about her day. A pungent scent hit his nerves. Ryan peered over the bowl where Kaitlyn dumped a wet stringy green lump. "Tell me that isn't spinach."

She looked at him, pausing her movement.

"I don't eat spinach."

"Why?" She grabbed a big spoon and started to stir it into ... cottage cheese?

"It's disgusting."

She grabbed pepper to add, then salt.

"What is this gonna be?"

"Lasagna."

"With spinach?"

"Spinach lasagna."

"You're kidding, right? Deanna set you up to this? It's not bad enough she has to try to force-feed me green stuff and wheat germ whatever at her place, but she had to push you to do it here?"

She caught his eyes. "I wanted to make it. It's not okay?"

He felt like an ass. She wanted to. "Yeah." Trying to decide how to eat his words that tasted even worse than the wet spinach smelled, he touched her arm. "I'm sorry. I'm a huge baby when it comes to food. I like almost anything in the world, except ... broccoli, celery, Brussels sprouts – especially Brussels sprouts – and spinach. Peas I can tolerate. Lettuce when it's slathered with dressing. Not much else that's green, though."

Studying him a second, she turned back to the bowl and added another herb. "You'll like this."

Ryan wasn't sure whether to complain or laugh. It was an argument. She'd actually argued instead of giving in. Possibly, she'd spent a little too much time with Deanna. But it was beautiful. He would have to at least try it, force enough down to not insult her.

At the phone's ring, he ambled into the other room to grab it. "Yeah, what?"

"Damn nice way to answer the phone. Don't want to talk to me?"

"Hey Dani. Sorry. My mind was..."

"Bad time? Did I interrupt a song in progress? You can call back. You know I don't care."

He flopped on the couch. "No, it's fine."

"Fine? If you don't want to talk to me, Reynauld..."

"Don't get your panties in a bunch. I only meant..."

"Don't talk to *me* that way, asshole. If you're in a mood, I can deal with that, but..."

"No. I'm sorry." He rubbed his head and grabbed a deep breath.

"What's going on?"

"Long story. Don't want to go into it now. What's up with you?"

A pause told him she was considering whether to let it go. "Well, I wondered if you had time to come around in the next week or so. I want your opinion on a couple of things."

"So ask. Or if it's music, sing it."

"That's not going to work. In other words, you can't."

"I'm off for tour in a few days. Really wish I could though. Will it hold?" He stood again and went to the kitchen doorway. He loved to watch Kaitlyn cook. She was so efficient...

"Guess it will. Or I'll have to decide on my own."

"You will, anyway. You only want me to agree." Ryan grinned at his friend, the way he could imagine her reaction, and met Katie's glance.

"Not this time. Hey, ask Ginny to send me your schedule. Maybe I'll catch up with you somewhere out there."

"Sure you will, but okay."

"Damn, you're being bitchy. Guess this was the wrong time to call."

"No." He pulled away from the doorframe and headed out of Katie's hearing range. "Sorry. I'm ... kind of preoccupied."

"Ryan." Her voice lowered. Apparently, there were others around. "I saw the pictures of you and some girl and the talk about her age. Of course I know most of those stories are trash and I don't pay any attention, but ... is there something I should know?"

There would be no skirting around Dani if he said too much. Ryan knew that more than he knew most anything else in the world.

"Still there?"

He grabbed another breath. "Yeah. And ... ignore the stories as usual." He couldn't quite admit that parts of them were true. Not yet. "I'd love to catch up with you soon."

"Me too. It's been too long."

"Hey, if you have to have me out there now, if it's urgent, say so and I'll see what I can do."

"Nah, it'll wait. Focus on your tour and we'll get in touch later. Gotta go. Have a good one, Ry, and take care out there. You know how much that matters to me."

"Thanks. Same here." Waiting for the click, he sighed and closed his end of the connection. Damn, he hated to say no to her. She rarely asked him for anything, especially not to visit. He would take a day before tour if not for having to go to Vermont. He couldn't do both.

"It'll be forty minutes. Deanna thought you would be later."

At Kaitlyn's voice, he realized he was still staring at the phone. "I was getting on their nerves so they sent me home. Not very thoughtful, was it? To send me back to you like this?"

She tilted her head. "I'm glad you're early."

His breath caught and he allowed himself to actually look at her as she stood in the doorway between the kitchen and living area. The summer weather had her in capris with a feminine blouse, a light peach-colored gauzy thing, and sandals that showed her toes. Her toe nails were painted to match her fingers, and her blouse. He wondered if she was still trying to convince others she looked like a girl. Or maybe she was trying to convince herself. He sure didn't need convincing.

He dropped the phone onto the table. "Wanna watch a movie? I don't think anyone's coming over tonight."

She nodded and brushed beside him to find her chair, slipping out of her sandals to pull her bare feet up on the cushion. Her scent lingered in her trail: a fresh, earthy smell. Not perfume, he didn't think. It wasn't floral. And it wasn't obnoxious. It was soft ... and stimulating. Had she picked it out herself?

"Do you want me to put one in?"

He looked toward her voice. "Oh, no, I'm up." He'd been standing and staring again. Something wasn't right with Dani. He could hear it in her voice. And he'd been a real ass.

With a frown, he grabbed a movie Deanna brought over so Katie would have something besides "macho stud flicks" to watch. He didn't bother to see what it was as he pulled it from the case and shoved it into the player. She wanted him to visit. Said she'd try to catch a show. It had been ages since she'd been to a show. Why now?

Fingers touched his arm. "Are you okay?"

"Yes. Sorry." He took her hand and led her to the couch. She could sit in the chair another time. He wanted the company tonight.

Barely into his hunk of lasagna, Ryan needed no force to continue. "This can't be spinach."

"You like it?" She paused her own fork.

"It's good. And damn I hate to admit that after I threw such a fit."

"It depends how it's cooked."

"Well..." He shoved in another bite, the scent of cheese reaching his nose before getting it in his mouth. "You should be a chef if you can get me to enjoy this." After another bite, he wondered and had to ask. "Where'd you learn to cook?"

Katie reached for her glass of water and took a quick swallow. "I've read recipes and cookbooks. It was ... there were no other books in one of the foster homes. The same one...." Her voice trailed off and she touched her ear.

Ryan veered away from the subject. "You love to read." He didn't get an answer and didn't expect one. "I don't have much here, either. We'll have to go book shopping."

"You don't need to. Deanna let me borrow a few."

He took her hand across the table. "You don't need to borrow stuff from Deanna. Let me know what you want and I'll get it, or go with you to get it. There is so little you admit to enjoying. Don't be surprised when I jump on anything I know you'll like."

After a touch of silence, she reclaimed her hand and picked up her fork. "Tracy has a lot already."

"Yes, but..." Tracy. She meant she wouldn't be there, in the loft, much longer. He didn't want the reminder. "They have an incredible library close by. A big old-look brick building that's connected now to the original library. When she takes the kids, make sure to find whatever you want, too. You should be able to find most anything there but if there's something you can't, tell me when I call and I'll find it."

She nodded and continued eating.

He nearly lost his appetite. Maybe she didn't want to go to Will's. Maybe.... No. The tour would be too hard on her. She would be fine with his brother's family. Ryan wasn't at all sure he would be fine with leaving her there, though.

~~~

She was packed, using one of his bags he hadn't in some time. It sat beside the door in the guest room and glared at him when he knocked. This time, she didn't hide the little notebook she was writing in, although she did close it. From the bed, where her legs were crossed with feet tucked underneath, Kaitlyn waited for him to explain the interruption. Her face was calmer; constantly, it was becoming more calm. When he'd picked her up at Deanna's after yoga the night before, she was sitting with the other women as they chatted – not chatting herself that he could tell, but at least sitting with them instead of across the room as normal. It made him feel better about leaving her with Will and Tracy. It also made him jealous about the way Deanna apparently helped her relax around others more than he had managed.

When he didn't explain himself, she set her notebook aside, leaving it on the bed instead of tucking it safely back into her little bag, and came over to him. Standing close. Still waiting.

And he still didn't know what to say or why he'd bothered her. He did, actually. He wanted to ask her to come out and watch a movie or something. Just be out there with him since he had to take her up to Vermont in the morning.

The doorbell made him sigh. "I didn't expect anyone tonight." Her look seemed to say she couldn't imagine why he was surprised. "I'll get rid of them and be right back. I wanted ... well, hold on a sec."

She grasped his hand as he turned and walked with him to the door, releasing it only after he checked and told her it was his drummer. He felt her back away a few steps while he opened it, barely.

"Hey Ry..."

"Ned, we have to get up and out early tomorrow..."

"Yeah and I'm not staying. Is Kaitlyn around?"

"Why?"

"I have something for her."

"You have what for her?" Ryan felt her warmth against his arm that was still holding the door mostly closed.

"I'd rather give it to her, or at least try." He raised his eyebrows at Ryan's hesitation. "Come on, man. Are you really still worried about me? Have I given you any reason?"

A soft hand slid across his back and Katie moved to his other side where she could see Ned.

"Hey. Wasn't sure I'd get through your bodyguard." He raised a CD to show her. "It's a demo of some of the new songs. I wrestled it away from Mac. Thought you might want to take it with you tomorrow. Some not horrible drum parts on there if you can hear them through his gruff voice. Top secret, though, until it's released, so it's only for you."

Kaitlyn glanced at Ryan, waiting for his reaction, he supposed, or his permission.

He wasn't sure what to say or why Ned had made the effort. His way of supporting Ryan, maybe? Or was he flirting? Thinking back, he had to admit the drummer had made quite an effort to get her to talk to him, or at least to allow him to talk without moving away. Why? The other guys kept their distance.

"I think she's waiting for you to say it's okay for her to have it, Ry."

He looked back at Ned, also the only one to use his first name, and the shortened version of it, at that. "Yeah. That was nice. Should've thought of it myself." He didn't move to intercept. She would have to take it from the drummer. He wanted to know if she would.

"Thank you." Kaitlyn accepted, her voice soft.

Ned smiled at her, too much like the proverbial cat that ate the canary. "You're welcome."

She dropped her eyes to the front of the CD where the song names were listed.

"Well, I'll get out of here." Ned took a step backward. "Have a good trip to Vermont. Tell Will I said hello and he should come to a show."

"I'll walk out with you." Unlocking the door, Ryan told her he'd be right back and closed it behind him. "So. What was that about?"

Ned shrugged. "Figured it might be hard on her to be away from you for a while and it might be comforting to at least have your music."

"That's it?"

"Damn, Ry. What else do you think?"

He stared, waiting.

With a chuckle and shake of the head, Ned tapped his arm. "Drive safe." And he headed to the elevator.

What else did he think? Nothing. He was being a jealous moron. No. Protective. He was being protective. A bodyguard, like the drummer said.

Inside, he found Katie on the couch, her eyes questioning him.

"You know, you'll have to have something to play that on." He went back to the guest room and shuffled through the closet to find a small radio/CD player he hadn't used in forever, and earphones, nice ones that blocked out surrounding noise that he did use often. It didn't match Ned's thoughtfulness, but it was something. Rubbing his head as an objection to his own thoughts, he shook it off and went back to her. "Take these with. You can play it whenever you want that way." He set them on the coffee table. And then didn't know what to do with himself.

She got up and went to the kitchen. This time he followed and leaned back against the doorway as she filled two mugs with water and put them in the microwave, taking tea bags from the drawer beside it.

Chamomile. For relaxation. While they heated, she pulled celery from the fridge and peanut butter from the pantry, paused to grab the steaming mugs and drop in the tea bags, then filled the celery. It was green stuff. She'd been finding ways to make him eat it. This was one of the better ones.

When she started to put everything away again, Ryan went to help and took the mugs, letting her carry the small plate of healthier-than-chips snack out to the couch. He was glad she sat next to him instead of in the chair, even if it was so they could both reach the plate.

With the movie returned to its case, Ryan switched off the television. He had to let her get to bed so they could be up and out early, before anyone was awake enough to pay attention. He didn't want the press or fans to know she would be at Will's, without him. His publicist had sent out ripples of information about him going to Cape Cod for a couple of days to recharge himself for the tour in hopes of throwing them off track. Ryan hoped it would work.

He offered his hand to help her up. But her closeness, and her eyes again studying him, made him back away. "I think that old player still works. If not, or if not well enough, let Will know and I'll have him pick up something better..."

She touched his arm. "It's okay."

He didn't believe for anything she meant the player. She knew he was worried. "Katie..." He couldn't voice the worry. It would make it too real. "Sleep well tonight." He figured one of them should.

She nodded and went to the guest room.

Ryan slumped onto the couch. He was an idiot. She would be fine. She would be better off with Will and Tracy than with him. With the kids distracting and entertaining her. With his mom hovering. Ryan had the idea last time they were there his mom wanted to be a mother to Kaitlyn, that she could see the need. It would be good for her. For both of them.

He sat with his hands clasped atop his head, his eyes on the ceiling, listening to the silence of the loft. It was already emptier. Not that he would be there long without her. He would be on the road. But, if she got too comfortable at Will's and decided it would be better to stay, he would have what he'd wanted – her safety and comfort and his freedom to work and play as he wished. Yet, the loft would be incredibly empty.

Letting his eyes close, he shoved it from his head, bringing in chords and lyrics and auditoriums filled with screaming fans and girls waiting around the hotel and ... a soft presence startled him.

He sat up. "What's wrong?"

"Will you be back?"

"What?" He stood beside her.

"It's okay. I ... I only want to know."

"Know what? The tour is temporary."

"Yes." She peered into his eyes, much too deeply into his eyes.

"Yes." He raised a hand to her face and brushed fingers back into her hair. "Katie, yes. I'll be there as soon as tour is over. And if you want to come back here with me, I'll be glad to have you. If you don't ... it's up to you. Whatever you want. Whatever's more comfortable."

"You'll change your mind. When you don't have to deal with me, you'll see it's too hard for you..."

"No." His fingers moved farther back to cup her head. "I won't." He knew he wouldn't. He knew it wouldn't be okay with him if she decided to stay with Will. He knew ... and he wanted her to know. "Katie." His voice was softer than he meant. "I'll be back. I promise. And if you need me, you have my cell number. Call. I can't always answer but I'll call back." She looked wary. He moved closer. "I am not leaving you. Okay? I need you to understand that I'm not leaving you. I would rather keep you with me, but I can't. Not for this. It would be ... I would be too afraid for you. And you'll be okay there. Right?"

She nodded, lightly, keeping his eyes.

"I promise. There are so many views I still want to show you. So many..." Ryan's body tightened, longing. He wanted ... and he couldn't. He couldn't allow himself to get closer and he couldn't pull back.

She touched his hair. Her eyes moved from where she played with the longer strands behind his ear to his face. Her fingers moved from his neck to his shoulder.

Ryan stiffened more, restrained himself more...

Until he didn't. He moved his lips against hers, cautiously, lightly. She didn't pull away. She returned the kiss.

But he couldn't. And he pulled back. "I shouldn't have..."

Her gorgeous, trusting hazel eyes held his. Asked him to return. To give in. And he couldn't fight what he felt. They all knew. They'd seen it, regardless of how he kept denying it. He'd fallen for her.

Against everything he'd ever been taught screaming at him to back away, he kissed her again. When she moved into it, accepting his kiss, his closeness, his arm encircling her waist, he made it deeper while he told himself he shouldn't. Her hand sliding down his chest made it impossible to convince himself he shouldn't. She didn't object.

But she was young. And too afraid.

He eased back, breathless, trying to decide what to say.

Katie wrapped her arms all the way around his back and rested her head on his shoulder.

Ryan held her there, unsure, confused, content ... frightened. What had he done? She was young. And there was so much she was dealing with. She didn't need this. But it felt right. She was comfortable in his arms, like no other girl had ever been. And she felt calm, peaceful.

He had to know just how dangerous this was before he let himself think about anything else. "Kaitlyn." He felt her cuddle closer and nearly changed his mind. Maybe it was less dangerous than he thought. "I know this is bad timing, and ... I hope you understand why I have to ask, but I have to know, and I have an idea but it keeps changing and ... I have to know." He stroked her head. "How old are you?"

"Nineteen."

He pulled back to find her face.

"Since last month."

Nineteen. Young ... too young for him, although not particularly dangerous. Legal, at least. She didn't look that old. But maybe it was her size, as Ned suggested. At times she did. Still, she was ... maybe too young. He was twenty-three closing in on twenty-four. Maybe in another year. It wouldn't be such a big deal then...

She slipped out of his grasp and went to her room when he didn't stop her.

Nineteen. Hell. Barely. Not even on the twenty edge of nineteen. He couldn't. Even if she was legal so Daws and Ginny wouldn't have to have a shit-fit. She didn't need that, anyway. Even if he'd been out on his own in the music world with plenty of female companionship when he was nineteen and thought he was old enough. She needed stability, help to work through her issues. The last thing she needed was his instability, his self-centeredness, his constant travel and ... and leaving her with his family. Or maybe she did need that. She was a kid. She needed a parent, not ... not what had been crossing his mind.

A deep, shaky breath pushed him toward his room, but he stopped at her door, to tell her ... what? After standing there for some time, he went and plopped on top of his bed. What he wanted was to go back to her room, to tell her it didn't matter, that ... that it didn't matter. He wanted to kiss her again. He couldn't, for fear it would lead too far.

Neither mentioned it on the drive to Will's, or at any point while they were there. She didn't treat him differently and he tried not to think about it. It was just one of those things. It was late. They were tired. He hadn't had a date in ... since just before meeting her. He needed to get back out on the road, back to his life and less in hers. His whole existence had been wrapped around her. It was too much, too much togetherness, too much emotion ... too much. They needed the break from each other. When he got back to see her, they would realize it meant nothing.

His family treated her as young as he had originally thought she was. They hovered, reassuring her how glad they were to have her stay. She still didn't talk to them, though. How she could live there for a month when she didn't dare talk to any of them, he didn't know. The one time she answered his mom was fine, but it wasn't enough. He had to know she would tell them if she needed anything.

Around the fire pit in the backyard after a day of picnicking and fireworks the night before Ryan had to leave, the conversation was animated, led by the kids often but also by friends of Will and Tracy who were there a lot. They decided it would be best for Kaitlyn to meet the neighbors while Ryan was still around and the Fourth of July celebration created the right opportunity. Never mind Ryan didn't want to share her so much on his last night there. Still, she sat close to him on the blanket in the park, her face intent and glorious with the reflection of explosions so bright they sometimes made her squint. She'd rarely seen them and never so well. During their family ritual of stopping activity for a moment of silence for his dad, and for all lost while serving their country, Ryan couldn't help but see her study him, the pain of his family's loss in her eyes.

When Will walked back into the house to refill drinks, Ryan followed to help, or at least with the excuse of helping. In the quiet of the dim kitchen, he tried to decide how best to say what he needed without saying too much.

"She'll be fine." Will took the glasses from him to set in the sink.

"There's something I need to ask you to do and it's going to sound overbearing and crazy, but I have to ask it anyway."

"Wouldn't be the first time." His brother threw a grin.

Ryan decided to plunge forward and let it come out as it did. "You can't leave her alone. And I mean, not you personally, but all together. One of you has to be here, or take her with wherever you go. I know it sounds high maintenance, but you can't leave her here alone, or anywhere else – definitely don't leave her anywhere else alone."

"Why?"

"I promised she wouldn't be."

He raised his eyebrows. "Ry, not being alone in general isn't the same as never having a minute to yourself. You don't expect us to follow her with every step she takes?"

"No, but ... I do mean more than not letting her alone in general. I mean if she's at the house, someone else needs to be here."

"Why?" At the silence, he tried again. "Ryan, if you're leaving this girl in my house with my wife and kids, I need to know why she can't be here alone. You can't ask me to..."

"She's not dangerous. I wouldn't have even thought of suggesting it if... Will, it's her I'm worried about."

His brother leaned back against the counter. "How exactly did you meet? And don't say you ran into her. How did you run into her? You run into girls all the time. Hell, they follow your heels and your cars and your buses and ... why this one? What makes you think she's not a fan acting out a part just to be around you?"

"She's not. She didn't want anything to do with me."

"How do you know? Some of them have done some very smart things to get to you."

Ryan told Will everything – except the kiss, he wouldn't say that – and waited through no reaction. "I don't want you to tell anyone else, not even Tracy. Of course it's unfair not to tell her. And I know you tell her everything, even stuff about me I'd rather you didn't. But I don't care about that. I don't want anyone else to know about Kaitlyn. I want her to try to live a normal life without the stigma, without everyone knowing."

"She should have professional help."

"Yeah, I've been told, and it's not like I haven't thought about it. But I think she's been there already, and I don't think it was any help. I can't do that to her again."

"They aren't all the same."

"She won't see it that way." Turning, he faced his brother head-on. "If you can't promise me she won't be alone, I'll take her with me instead. I can't deal with being out there if I have to worry about..."

"Ryan, we'll take care of her. I think on tour is the last place she needs to be. It gets hard enough for you and you're pretty mentally stable most of the time."

"Thanks."

He grinned, and regained the seriousness. "But, after this, if she doesn't show improvement, you need to consider getting her to talk to a professional."

"Yeah, but I'm trying hard to avoid that, and she has gotten better."

"Has she? She still won't say more than a word or two to any of us. That's going to be a challenge."

"She will." Ryan wasn't sure if he was trying to convince himself or his brother. "If she needs to, if I'm not here to jump in as I have been, she will."

Will didn't look convinced. "The other thing is ... my kids are here. What happens if she decides to try again? That's not something I want them to have to see or..."

"She won't. She promised me she wouldn't. And she would never do that to your kids. I know that beyond all doubt. As long as she doesn't feel too alone, she'll be all right. Just make sure someone is always here for her. If it gets to be too much, call me and I'll come get her, or have Daws come get her..."

"Okay." He pushed away from the counter and walked over to set his hand on Ryan's shoulder. "We better rejoin the party before they come look for us."

"Is she up?" Ryan stopped pacing when Tracy came back from checking on Kaitlyn. He'd slept in too late after staying up with Will too long. He had to go.

"Yes. But..." Tracy hesitated. "She's not coming down."

"What?"

"I don't know. When I asked, she shook her head and went back to her book."

"She doesn't want the goodbye." His mom came over. "This will be hard for her at first since she barely knows us." She stopped Ryan when he started toward the stairs. "Maybe you should let her do it her way. Let her be for now and call when you get back to the city."

"I'm not leaving without..." Ryan considered his mom's words. Except she didn't know about the kiss, and that Ryan had been more distant since. Or that Kaitlyn had been. "I have to talk to her a minute." Brushing objections aside, he took the steps two at a time and knocked on her door, entering without permission.

Her eyes raised to his.

"I have to go." He noted no emotion whatsoever on her face. Maybe it didn't matter to her like he thought it would, like he hoped it would. She sat on the bed, her legs crossed, the book in her lap. "I'll give you a call tonight before we leave." Still, nothing. "Take care, Kaitlyn."

He walked out her door and got nearly to the stairs, then stopped. He couldn't leave like that. Even if she didn't want more, if she didn't want an emotional goodbye, he couldn't act like ... like he hadn't kissed her. Like it hadn't meant anything. He had. And it did.

Ryan clenched his eyes a moment and went back. She was still sitting but not reading. The book was cast to her side. Her eyes had been on the door when he entered.

"I'm sorry." He forced his feet toward her, lowered onto the bed, not facing her but close enough their legs nearly touched. "I uh ... I want you to know that ... I don't mean to be distant, to act like.... I'm not sure how to handle this so as always I'm just not handling it. I've been ignoring it, and it's not fair to you. But I'm not sure right now what is fair to you so it's easier..."

She moved in and wrapped around him from his side, head against his shoulder.

Ryan sat silently, arms over hers. He had to go. He was late already and would have no time to get himself together. Still, he held her. And then he turned to face her. "I don't want to leave you. I've never in my life had this much trouble leaving anyone. Ever. I keep telling myself it's because I'm worried, and I guess I am, but it's not ... Katie, I'm so used to your company I'm not sure how to do without it anymore."

Her hand raised and soft fingers touched his face.

Afraid to break the moment, Ryan stayed as still as possible, enjoying her comfort with him, the natural ease with which she stroked his skin. She didn't speak and he didn't care that she didn't. When she moved her face closer, he found her lips. He kept it light and short. He didn't want things more complicated than they were. He only wanted her to know it did mean something. "I have to go. Ginny will yell."

"It's okay." She met his eyes. "I promise."

He gave her a grin and stood, fingers still knotted in hers. "You'll tell someone if you need anything?"

"I'll tell you, when you call."

Ryan was at a loss to answer. He would have to call regularly. Maybe that's what she meant. "Take care, Katie. Don't let Bella cling too much." With another grin, he made himself walk out of the room and down the stairs.

"Everything all right?"

He tried to look as casual as usual and gave Tracy a hug. "Yeah." He couldn't say more than that. "Thank you."

"Oh, no thanks needed. We're glad to have her."

Ryan gave the kids his goodbyes since they were still in pajamas and not allowed outside, and grabbed his bag. Will and his mom followed. Throwing the bag in the trunk, he gave his mom a hug.

She set her hands alongside his face. "You be careful. I know you're a pro by now but I still worry."

"And it won't do me any good to tell you not to."

Will waited until his mom returned to the front porch where she would watch Ryan leave, again. "Make sure you check in often the first few days. I don't care if you have to take your cell on stage with you to call, but make the time."

"Guaranteed."

He gave him a half hug. "And don't get too annoyed with Daws. He's looking out for your best interest. He's a good man, Ry. Let him be."

"And he'll be pissed if I don't get going." He turned and opened his door. "Take care, Will. And take care of her for me."

"Guaranteed."

With the purr of the car's engine, Ryan felt the weight of leaving her suddenly press on his whole being. He had to force himself to drive away.

At a nearly empty stretch of Route 7 before he got close to Albany, Ryan picked up his cell and dialed Will's number.

"Forget something?"

"Hey, you told me to call often."

"I didn't mean every half hour."

Ryan grinned at the sarcasm. "You didn't specify."

"Did you want something or just being an annoying ass?"

"Both. Put Katie on the phone."

"Already?"

"Humor me."

"Hang on. She's still upstairs."

Ryan heard the kids' voices in the distance and then a knock. He wondered if she would answer.

"Here she is."

He waited a second. "Katie?"

"Yes."

"Hey, I just wanted to know if you'd actually talk over the phone. I didn't think to ask before I left. Guess it's all right?"

"Yes."

"Good. Is Will still right there?"

"Yes."

"Okay."

"Do you want him back?"

Ryan smiled at the question. "In a sec. I wanted to know if you would say more than yes if someone was around."

Silence.

"Sorry, I wasn't trying to be offensive."

"You weren't. It's okay."

"Good." He fought for more to say to her but decided not to push it too far. "I'll call again soon. Maybe not in the next half hour, but ... before I leave tonight, like I said. Is that too soon?"

"I'll be here."

He took a deep breath. "I feel much better. Thank you." No answer, and he didn't expect one. "Will still there?"

Silence again, then his brother's voice.

"Thanks. I owe you big time, you know."

"No, you don't. Get off my phone now and keep your eyes on the road."

"They are." Hanging up, Ryan went over the conversation in his mind. He was actually surprised she said as much as she did. It was a good sign. Will had to have been in her room, alone with her, and she sounded like it didn't matter, like she already knew she could trust him. It was a very good sign.

6

He called Ginny to let her know he was back in the city. She could call Daws if she wished. Ryan didn't want to talk to him. He also didn't want to go back to the loft. Not yet.

Instead, he pivoted the M3 down Broadway, found an open spot along the road after some circling, and sat looking at the building across the corner. The one where he'd met her. He could see the bottom of the ledge where she'd stood ... where they'd stood. And shivered.

With a glance around to see if anyone was paying attention to him, he couldn't tell if they were and got out, locking the vehicle with the key fob while he watched traffic. A Thai restaurant oozed curried air and Ryan considered a take-out order. He decided against it. His stomach was tense. When he did eat, he would have to make it mild.

He waited for a red 2001 Mustang to go past – with another fleeting thought of how he liked the newest model better than the past few years – and dodged through the street before the next car got close. Swerving parked vehicles along the curb, Ryan stepped up onto the sidewalk. Then he stopped. Stared at the building. He knew someone in the studio now to his back could very well spot him out there when he should have been home packing to go, but they were behind windows. They wouldn't be able to stop him before he reached his destination.

And he wasn't sure why he felt the need to revisit the spot today ... to go up to the window where they'd met.

He scratched the top of his head as he went through the door, a weak attempt to hide his face. Again the only one in old jeans while the rest were in suits, Ryan realized not pulling attention was a useless thought. He could only hope none of his fans were in the lobby.

The ring of his phone made him cringe and he pulled it from his back pocket to check the number and stop the noise. Daws. He couldn't answer. Even when his face didn't give him away in a crowd, his voice did. Deanna said it was distinctive. Ryan thought it was grating. But it worked well enough for his records. He'd call back after a while, after he got there.

Heading to the elevator, he changed his mind. He'd used the stairs that day. He wanted to again. Besides, it would burn off some of his pent up energy. Daws would yell if he knew. Trapped in a stairwell was a hard thing to escape. Experience. But Ryan liked stairs. He liked the strain of his muscles stretching as he took two at a time. He liked the way he felt when he extended so much physical energy. It cleared his head.

He slowed when he got to the fourth flight. He had to turn around. He couldn't go up there. He had to go ready himself to leave. Daws would yell. Ginny would yell. Katie's presence would be too strong up there. The reminder.

Stopped at the landing beside a door that would lead to a hallway and the elevator down, Ryan leaned back against the cool cement wall. Up or down. Why was he even there? She was safe, at Will's. His mom would become a mom to her. Katie would allow it. She needed it. Much more than she needed Ryan hitting on her. He was such an idiot.

Starting back down the steps, he paused. And turned. He didn't need any damn elevator. He needed to climb stairs. Even if he accomplished no more than that, at least it would work his leg muscles that had been too ignored recently. The green stuff. Maybe the green stuff Katie fed him was having an effect. He was tired of sitting so much, standing behind a microphone so often. He wanted to move, to push himself physically as he used to. He was in track in high school. A damn good runner and better at the hurdles. The physical hurdles were so much easier than the mental ones. His small physique was helpful during hurdle leaping. His quickness was helpful when he'd been too much of a smartass and pissed off larger, stronger classmates.

Why in the hell was he thinking about school? He hadn't let his mind go there in ... nearly since he graduated. It embarrassed the hell out of him to be announced as one of the top of his class. He'd barely done his homework and only enough so his mom wouldn't yell. He brushed through it like he brushed through everything but his music. Still, he came out as number ten. The class was small, so it wasn't any big honor, but everyone made it sound like it was. Will being Valedictorian of his class was an honor. He'd worked for it. On top of looking out for Ryan. If Ryan had known he was going to end up on the fucking top ten by skating through, he would have forgotten to turn in a worksheet or two in order to prevent it. It would've been less embarrassing to not be recognized at all than it was to be number ten in contrast with Will's number one. Whatever. It was a long time ago. Likely, he was the only one who cared about it still either way.

The yellow tape line was still there. Opening the door to the ninth floor hallway, he stared at it. Why? Why was the floor blocked off? He would have to find someone and ask before it drove him nuts. He slid underneath, as he had last time, as he figured she must have. Or did she take the elevator? As fragile as she was, Ryan hoped she'd taken the elevator. He was winded and trying to catch his breath after climbing the stairs. Although, she likely didn't run up half of them as he had. She would have taken the stairs since no one else did. She would've gone unnoticed that way.

Trudging down the hall toward the window, Ryan looked into empty offices he passed. Still no dust. No paraphernalia sitting around. But there were bars. On the windows. He stopped looking at the rooms and looked only at each window. They all had bars, including Katie's window. And it was closed.

Ryan stood at the doorway looking at the window and the vertical bars outside it. The owner had to have heard of her attempt/their stunt. It probably scared him about the risk of a lawsuit. Now they all had bars. He wondered what Katie would think if she knew.

He couldn't go over that far. Instead, he crept to where she'd sat against the desk and lowered to sit in her place. What had school been like for her? Did she join activities? Probably not. Did she have friends? There had to have been someone she talked to at lunch or before classes, waiting on the bell to ring. There had to have been someone. Maybe he could find out. Call her up and talk to her.

His phone made him jump. Daws. With a sigh, he answered.

"Where in the hell *are* you?"

"I'm in town. I'll be at the loft soon." He kept his eyes on the window where a pigeon fluttered past.

"In town. Ginny said you've *been* in town for an hour. Where?"

"I'm fine. I'll be there soon."

"Tell me where in the hell you are before I have to send out patrols. Are you alone?"

Ryan couldn't help a grin. Alone. Yes. But much less than he usually was.

"Reynauld. Where are you?"

"I'm ... hell Daws, I only wanted a few minutes of peace. Is that too damn much to ask?" He hung up. Ignored the next ring.

Alone. The word rang in his ears. He always thought he knew what *alone* felt like, even in the midst of the constant crowds. He was alone even there, with no one close enough to him to make him feel not alone. He'd felt alone in his loft when it was quiet other than the television or his guitar. He'd felt alone in bed at night on the nights he was actually alone, and even when he wasn't. He thought he understood her when she said she couldn't be alone anymore.

He hadn't.

Since leaving her at Will's the whole true weight of *alone* set in. He was less alone than ever, in a way, because her presence was always with him. But he was more alone because she wasn't there. The longing to have her at his side, especially now while he thought about nearly losing her, about the possibility that it could happen again, was nearly more than he could handle. She was *that* alone. It was different. But who made her feel that way?

Her family, he supposed. But she said that was a long time ago. A boyfriend? Had she been left by someone she loved? Was it that kind of alone she felt? Would she ever feel that way about him?

He dropped his head back against the metal desk with a thunk. He had to go. Ryan knew he would hold things up, that it would make things harder on everyone if he didn't leave now and stay on schedule. He couldn't. He wanted to go back to Vermont. He needed to ask her.

Eyes closed, he took deep breaths to pull himself together, thinking of the yoga he'd watched the end of a couple of times when he picked her up, grounding himself, or attempting to by releasing the tension down through his body and into the floor. The thin office gray carpet. The cool metal against his back. The bit of sun finding its way through the window and bars to touch his skin. His mind returned to the boat, to Katie sitting on the back of it, looking out over the water. What did she see when she looked out there? He saw water, and trees in the distance, fish swimming below, algae clumps floating just under the surface, waves rowing back and forth and making a kind of music of their own. He saw memories of his dad fishing and picking them up under their arms to throw them back in the water. What memories did she see? She hadn't been on the open water before, but there had to be something she thought about behind her stares.

"Are we cancelling?"

Ryan looked over at Daws's voice in the doorway. "How in the hell did you find me here?"

"What are you doing?" He stood, arms crossed in front of his chest. When Ryan didn't answer, he dropped his arms and walked closer. "Did she get upset about being left?"

"No."

"Then what in the hell is wrong with you? You're throwing off the schedule. Ginny's going into panic mode."

"Sorry." He looked back at the window, at the bars.

"Maybe she's not the one who needs a shrink. Maybe you do."

He didn't answer.

Daws came over and crouched in front of him. "Ryan. What's going on?"

The use of his first name surprised him. Daws never used his first name. It was too personal. He shrugged. "Maybe I just want to know why. She won't tell me. You know how I hate mysteries and puzzles. I want to know why."

"I'm working on that."

"What?" Ryan finally looked at him.

"If you keep going with this, if it catches more wind in the press, there will have to be answers. I'm trying to find them before the questions come."

"We don't talk about her to the press. At all. It's not their damn business."

"Since when does that matter? Someone will look into it. You know that as well as I do. If there's anything to find, I want to find it first. And don't bother to argue. Your protection is my job." He stood. "Let's go before Ginny decides she can't put up with your ass anymore and ditches you for someone easier to take."

"And before you do, right?" Ryan shoved himself to his feet and started toward the door.

Daws grabbed his arm. "If I was gonna do that, moron, I would have long ago. It's not like I haven't had better offers."

Ryan nodded. "Then maybe you're the moron for not taking one of them." He pulled out of the grasp and headed toward the elevator. Daws wouldn't want to do the stairs. Neither did he. Not going down.

7

"She's asleep. It's late, Ryan."

"Yeah. Sorry. It's been one of those days. I tried to call earlier…"

"Out on date with your new love interest?" Tracy's voice teased.

"What?" He plopped onto the hotel sofa.

"The girl all over the papers. Publicity stunt or someone we should know about?"

"What girl?"

"Ryan, it's everywhere. They're saying she's your newest … well, interest, to put it politely."

He sat up, scratching his head. "Felicia?"

"Felicia. So?"

"She's … no one." He stood again, restless.

"Nice, Ryan. Girls like to be called that. Here's your brother."

"Tracy…"

"You couldn't call at a normal hour?" Will sounded half asleep.

"No. Sorry I woke you. What does she mean it's everywhere? About Felicia? Did Katie…?"

"She means it's everywhere, and since she's annoyed, I can guess what you said about it."

"Will." Ryan sat again. "It's not…"

"Hey, you know I don't ask anymore. You're an adult. Not my business. Other than that, everything okay?"

"Yeah. But…" Everywhere. Meaning Katie heard. "She's a new singer they're trying to promote, getting her name out there. It's nothing…"

"Since when do you explain to me about your girls? Like I said, not my business, as long as it doesn't hurt you."

"She's not one of my girls." He rubbed his head. He needed a shower, a long, hot shower that might help him sleep. "Tell Katie I called. Sorry I missed her. I'm not sure when I'll call next. It's insane busy right now. Is she doing all right?"

"It's been a few days." Will stifled a yawn. "She's fine, but try waking hours next time so she can tell you she is."

"Is she talking to you at all?" He fought a yawn in answer.

"A few words here and there. Not for a couple of days. You need to call her. When she's awake."

"Yeah. Tell Tracy I'm sorry and I didn't mean it the way it sounded."

"Good night, Ry. Be careful."

Hanging up, he dropped the phone on the cushion and went in to the shower. Not for a couple of days. She was talking but not for a couple of days? Did he mean at all? Or not as much? Why would she start talking to them and stop? Will hadn't answered whether she heard about Felicia. Would it bother her? Stupid question. He would have to call in the morning, around whatever else was going on. It was nearly impossible to get time without someone hovering, though, and he didn't want someone listening to everything he said.

"Let's *go*, Reynauld."

Ryan opened his eyes to Ginny's voice and rolled over, pulling the sheet half over his head. He felt stiff, and so damn exhausted rolling over took almost more effort than he had.

"You're late already. Have to stop that. You're not nineteen anymore and it wasn't cute then, either. You're going to have to grow up some day and get yourself out of bed on time."

"Not in this business. That's what I pay all of you for. Why are you here instead of Daws or Jim?" Thinking about it, Ryan realized he hadn't seen his tour manager all the day before.

She yanked the blankets off. "Get up. You have ten minutes to be dressed and out the door."

"Damn." He turned enough to try to grab them and cover himself. "I'm in my shorts. You mind?"

"I've seen it before. Get up. I have coffee."

With a groan, Ryan rolled up into sitting mode. It was cold and he shuffled over to turn up the heater.

"Don't bother. You won't be here that long."

"Gotta make a phone call." He found his cell and stood over the heater. Rain pounded the window.

"Not now, you're not." Ginny grabbed it from his hand.

He reached for it. "Two minutes."

"Get dressed."

"Give me the damn phone."

"Get dressed." She walked away.

Stringing together a few words he knew she wouldn't appreciate and yet ignore, Ryan went to turn the shower as hot as he could get it and jumped in. She'd have to wait. He was cold, exhausted ... his muscles ached. His skin stung beneath the steaming water pelting it. Breathing the wet hot air, he reached for the hotel shampoo. Coconut. He hated the smell of coconut and had to put up with it too often. He should've grabbed his own from his bag. It would have to do. He would scrub off the nastiness he could feel trying to overwhelm him and he'd be fine.

Clean enough, he stood with his back turned to let it run down his shoulders. The water stopped.

"Get out and get dressed." Ginny threw a towel in around the shower curtain.

Ryan didn't bother to argue. It wouldn't do any good. The woman was worse than Daws. Where was his guard? Frustrated and spiteful, he stepped out without bothering to cover himself. "Maybe you should send Daws in next time, huh? Or my tour manager. Where in the hell is he?" He scrubbed moisture off his face.

"I have five sons, two exes, and I've been in this business a long time. I'm not bothered or impressed. Let's go." She at least walked away to let him finish. His clothes were on the counter.

With enough pain killers, he managed to get through an interview, a mini photo session, lunch with Felicia's people for some kind of promotion they didn't explain much, and a signing session for that night's show. The stuff with his name on it would sell even higher than the normal merchandise fees. He'd tried to object once. Ginny said his extra effort made it worth it. He couldn't help but wonder how much of the extra she got out of it.

"Where's my phone?" Backstage, he swallowed two more ibuprofen.

"What are you taking?" Ginny reached for the bottle he shoved into his pocket.

"Everything I can get my hands on. Where's my phone?"

"Still not funny, Reynauld. What is it?"

He jerked away when she made a move toward his pocket. "It's fucking aspirin, okay? Where's my damn phone?"

"Aspirin. And that's why you're trying to hide it."

Ryan pulled it out and cradled it in his hand so she couldn't quite see it. "Trade you."

"I've got to stop working with immature children who should be adults. You don't need your phone. You're about to do sound check. We use mics for that."

"Where in the hell is Daws?"

"Taking a day off. Trust me, I'll be as glad as you when he's back."

"He doesn't take time off on the road. It's his fucking job. Where is he?"

The stage manager yelled they were ready for him. He didn't budge.

Ginny sighed. "He's got the flu and he's staying away so you don't get it, but you weren't supposed to know. So you don't. Go to work. You'll have time to make phone calls after sound check." She held out a hand.

He set the bottle in her palm. "Too late to stay away. Hang on to that. You may need it next." A little too satisfied by her sympathetic look, Ryan headed to the microphone. It would have to be a damn short sound check.

Falling into bed, he hoped he'd pulled off a half-decent show. He didn't even want to ask. And he hadn't called Katie since he dropped into a deep stupor as soon as he hit the couch in the dressing room. He knew a couple of his roadies helped him get from there to the hotel and hoped they wouldn't catch it. He should have called her first. It was too late now, and he didn't have energy to open the phone and dial the number.

~~~

"Hey moron, call your brother before he sends out a search party."

Ryan pried his eyes open and threw Daws a suggestion with one hand. He reached for the cough medicine with the other.

"Want me to call?"

"Hell, no. You'll..." He was interrupted by a chest-rattling cough and let Daws take the bottle to open it. He hated those childproof lids. "You'll scare the shit out of him."

"Then you call."

Gulping a couple of swallows of the stuff, hoping it would at least help him sleep, he dropped his head against the hotel arm chair and let his eyes collapse in on themselves.

"How many messages has he left?"

Ryan heard but didn't acknowledge that he heard. It was all he could do to get through shows, forcing back the cough until he got off stage again. He couldn't do conversation.

"I know you're not up to it. Let me call and tell him what's going on."

"I don't want him to know what's going on. Go away, Daws. I gotta sleep." He wanted to lie down, to feel the lush pillow he knew was only a few short feet away, the luxuriousness of the mattress and blankets and his body melted between. The damn cough wouldn't allow it. He'd slept in chairs for four days. He wanted to call. He wanted to hear her voice. But he didn't want her to hear his the way it was. Ryan could cover all right on stage, with music and screaming fans. There was no way he could cover it over the phone.

"How 'bout getting me a beer?" He knew Daws was there, even with his eyes closed.

"On top of the gallon of that stuff you've had so far? No chance in hell."

"Something's gotta kill this. Or at least give me a few hours of straight sleep." The cough took over again. His ribs stabbed him. They were as sick of the cough as he was.

"I'm telling them to cancel tomorrow."

"I'll be better..." Damn cough. "Tomorrow." Grogginess overtook him and he gave into it.

A touch of light filtered through heavy curtains as Ryan pushed himself up enough to find the red numbers of the alarm clock. Five-forty. Four hours or so. A record recently. His body ached like it had a couple of weeks before when he started to catch the damn bug. It was the cough. It made him so damn sore he couldn't think of anything else. Except Katie. He wanted to talk to her.

He wouldn't, sure his voice still sounded like hell, but he checked for new messages. Will, from the night before: "Hey, you want to let us know if you're still alive and kicking out there somewhere? Your guarantee isn't good anymore? I have to guess you are since nothing's been all over the news, but hearing it from you would be good." A pause and then his voice lightened. "Seriously, Ryan, take two seconds and call me back." Nothing more.

Why was there nothing more? Every other message had stated Katie was doing okay. This one didn't mention her. It was a ploy. He hadn't said it on purpose to make Ryan worry enough to call back. It wasn't working.

Yes, it was working. So it was five-forty in the morning. Payback was hell. He hit Will's speed dial number and leaned back against the chair, unable to stifle the cough.

"Ryan?"

Hell, he of course would answer during that. "This is your two seconds. How's Katie?"

"You sound like holy hell."

"Which is why I haven't called. Don't tell her. I don't want her to worry. Is she okay?"

A pause came, although Ryan knew from the muffled voice Will was telling Tracy.

"Will. I'm not in the mood for games. Is she okay?" The cough delayed the response.

"Get a damn doctor if you haven't, you stubborn ass. And yes, she's okay. Although I think hearing from you would be good about now."

"Why?" He doubled over and pushed his hand against his ribs to try to cut the pain.

"Then again, maybe she shouldn't hear that."

"Ya think? Just tell her I called and ... work is excruciating right now. I'll call back."

"Ryan, get a doctor."

"Had one. Hell of a lot of good it did. Gotta get off here. Two seconds are well past." Hanging up, he made his way to the bathroom in the midst of coughing so hard he expected everything inside to come out, and leaned over the toilet. *Hearing from you would be good.* Why? His brother hesitated to say she was all right. Why?

"C'mon." Daws was there, hanging on to him from behind.

Ryan had no idea how long he'd been in the room – hopefully long enough to know he'd called his brother so he would get off his ass about it. He walked him over to the bed.

"I can't lie down."

"Then prop the pillows."

He didn't have the strength to argue.

Ryan vaguely remembered people in his room, something stinging his arm, voices, lights, dark. And Daws was still there, or there again. He heard his voice. Someone else was there. It was still dark, or almost dark. Turning his head to the red numbers, he was thrown off that it had only been three hours ... not even three hours.

He was starving. "Call room service, would you?" Expecting Daws, he started when he saw Kaitlyn.

She sat next to him and set a hand on his forehead. "You're not hot."

"That's a hell of a thing to say to a guy." He studied her face. "Am I still in dreamland somewhere? Why are you here? Not that I'm not glad to see you, but..."

"She insisted." Will walked up behind her. "We heard you cancelled a show. You never cancel shows. Couldn't hide it from her, I'm afraid."

"Cancelled?" He sat up to find Daws. "I told you I'd be fine by tomorrow."

"Yeah, well that was yesterday. You slept through tomorrow."

"What?" He looked at the clock again as though it could tell him the day.

"Yesterday's show was cancelled. Tonight is still on hold."

"Tonight." Ryan rubbed a hand through his hair. He felt less congested and the pain in his ribs was less intense. He looked at Katie. "I'm sorry I didn't call."

She threw her arms around him.

Ryan was a bit embarrassed about her doing so in front of not only Daws and his brother, but Ned, as well. Why was he there? It was too early for him to be up. She felt good, though. After almost two months of the band and roadies and girls drenched in cheap cologne and smoke and alcohol, she was salve for his senses. No cologne. No sweat. No smoke on her clothes. Only her.

"So what do you want from room service?"

He made himself pull back at his guard's voice, catching her eyes first. "Anything. Everything. I'm starving."

"Guess that's a good sign. Think the show's doable or..."

"Definitely. I'm fine and dandy. The show goes on. And apologies to..."

"Taken care of. They're already trying to reschedule."

Katie's eyes were on him, concern too apparent.

He touched her face. "You shouldn't be in here." Ryan looked up at Will and lowered his hand again. "You shouldn't have let her in here. If she catches this ... it's a nasty one. I've been fighting it for the last week." Ryan returned focus to her eyes. "Don't catch this from me. I'll never forgive myself."

"We've mainly kept her away from you, opened windows and such to let the germs out." Will threw him a curious look. "The doctor said after the strong antibiotic he gave you yesterday, you should be safe by this morning."

"Doctor?" Ryan rubbed the top of his arm. "Thought I was dreaming about a wasp sting. Wondered why there was only one." He touched Katie's hand. "I gotta get up." When she moved, he slid off the bed. A wave of dizziness set in and Will grabbed his arm. "I'm all right. Gonna shower quick before the food comes. I feel more nasty than normal."

He stayed under the hot water longer than he knew he should, and yelled through the door to his brother that he was fine and not to be so damn impatient. Turning it off, he scrubbed the towel along his body to get the circulation moving better. He felt stiff and wanted to go back to bed. But he had to get there, to the next venue. He figured it must not be far since they weren't trying to rush him out the door already. He wanted Katie to stay. He wanted her on the bus with him, or plane, or however the hell he was getting wherever he was going.

The smell of food hit him when he opened the door and he nearly forgot everything else.

But not quite. He went to where she stood beside Will. "Up to some traveling? I have no idea where we're heading or how we're getting there, but if you want, and since you're already out here wherever we are now, feel like seeing what this job is like on the road? It's a damn sight more exciting than studio work."

She nodded.

"Yes?"

"Already have it arranged." Daws grabbed the back of his shirt. "Eat. We don't have much time."

The three days Katie and Will were able to stay were marred only by his continuing fatigue and the way his publicist kept throwing girls at him in public around photographers. She also took advantage of the way Katie found refuge at Will's side when in the midst of crowds, catching photos to use as reinforcement of the "she's family" idea. Ryan wasn't sure whether or not he should object. Glad to see how comfortable she was with his brother, he caught his breath the first time he saw her look up at Will with a trusting expression. She answered Will when he spoke to her and he kept anyone she wasn't comfortable with at an arm's length or more.

Although close to Will, she kept distance from Ryan. She watched him and met his gaze and answered when he spoke to her, but otherwise Katie acted like one of the crowd. Her color was even better, which meant she enjoyed the yard, and the sunshine. It was good for her to be there. He expected she might want to stay.

She might want to stay. Instead of returning to New York with him.

He tried not to think of it while he walked with her to the car that would take them to the airport. He nearly asked Kaitlyn to stay with him instead. He couldn't quite do it. She was doing well there, with his brother, as family.

"Call me when you get in." Ryan focused on Will although his senses were tuned into Katie. She smelled of the same light scent he first noticed after taking her to Will's, something from the gift basket his mom set out. It meshed beautifully with her own natural smell, her simplicity and gentleness...

"You plan to keep in better touch this time?" Will threw a sly grin.

"Yes." He touched Katie's eyes. "I will."

She searched his face. "Are you okay?"

She'd asked several times in the past three days, whenever he'd gotten too far into the exhaustion, whenever he was sick of being kept away from her for too long. She always knew when he needed her connection. He nodded. "Still tired, but nothing I'm not used to. Maybe ... one of these days I can do an easier tour, less intense, shorter, and ... you can stay longer. If you want. If this didn't make you never want anything to do with it again. And I wouldn't blame you..."

"It didn't."

"No?" He wanted to kiss her, so he nodded again and backed up. "Good. We'll do that sometime, then." He opened the door and held it, talking over top of the car. "Give Tracy and the kids my love and thank them for letting you be away a few days."

"They'll probably thank you for getting me out of their hair for a few days." He grinned. "Stay healthy this time. Sleep more."

"Yeah."

Katie stood between the car and the open door. Ryan didn't know what else to say, but she put her arms around him.

His lungs expanded and he fought himself to keep the hug casual. "I'm glad you were here." He kissed the side of her face. That was innocent enough. "I'll see you soon. Take care of yourself, Katie."

Her fingers lingered on his waist while she pulled back to get in the car, or at least he chose to believe they did. Maybe she would still want to go back to New York with him.

8

Ryan thought of her fingers against his waist as the plane touched down in Albany. He didn't think he'd ever been so glad to be done with a tour in the six years since he'd started playing the game. Nearly six years. He'd been nineteen, Katie's age. Funny, he'd felt so much older when he was nineteen than he could see her as being. In truth, he had to have been about half as mature, if that. His mom fought against him being signed to a label so young, thrown to the wolves, as she put it. And he probably would've been devoured out there if not for Daws guiding him. Why he did, Ryan still didn't know. He was the one who found him and pulled him away from the man who promised everything under the sun and did nothing. The man was easier to deal with than Ginny, but Ginny, Ryan had to admit, was incredible at her job. She was exactly what he needed.

And Daws stepped in again, accompanying Ryan home. It must've been the "homesick" comment that slipped out. He didn't get homesick. Daws knew he didn't. His guard had watched him closer since, and backed Patricia away from throwing girls and photographers at him. He'd also noticed how careful Ryan was about what he ate, also unusual. Except when he was fighting his stomach.

Deanna said Ryan owed her a day out on the boat and invited herself. Ryan had misgivings about them being there, at his home. Daws had been already a couple of times, for security reasons. But he kept himself scarce and didn't stay longer than necessary. Home time was home time. It was separate, and Ryan wanted to keep it that way. He wasn't sure what to expect with Deanna tagging along.

He fidgeted while waiting for the attendants to allow departure from the craft. It was another thirty minutes to Will's, if traffic was decent. He wanted to get to the car and on the road.

Deanna leaned toward his ear. "Be careful, hon. You'll use the little energy you have before you even get to her." She threw a wink.

"Doesn't take much energy to pilot a boat."

"I didn't mean the boat. I meant what you've really missed. And don't look at me like that. It's not like we don't know."

He glanced up at a passing stewardess, vaguely returning the grin. "Don't know what?"

Deanna set a hand on his arm. "I know you're going to get a lot of flack for it when people find out, but I think you're on the right path, so don't let them tell you otherwise." With his silence, she put an arm around his shoulders. "Take it slow, though, hon. Give her time."

"Anna, we're friends. I don't know what you think you know, but I'm not anywhere near what she needs. She's doing great at Will's…"

"You are so cute when you're in denial. Don't forget how long I've known you." With that, she turned back to Daws.

Denial. He wasn't in denial. She was nineteen, barely. They were only friends. It was all they could be. No matter what he wanted.

On the way out, Ryan gave the stewardess who had chatted with him, only enough to let him know she was a fan, a kiss on the cheek and handed her a signed CD. Then he badgered Daws and Deanna to keep up better so they could get out of there and to the rental station.

Except he was greeted by a swarm of girls who thrust papers and pens at him and snapped cameras in his tired eyes. How did they know? Ryan hadn't even given Will his flight info in order to prevent it getting out somewhere in the communication line.

Ryan acted the part and smiled through wanting to curse. He signed his name a hundred different times and allowed a few photos … and Daws pulled him away with the help of airport security.

"We'll never get through baggage claim now. How in the hell did they find out I'd be here?"

"You're not going to baggage claim. Go on and we'll take care of it."

"Go where, exactly? You're shoving me off by myself in the middle of this? Some bodyguard you are."

Rolling his eyes, Daws grabbed his shoulders, turned him to face the opposite direction, and shoved him toward where Will and a couple of his friends stood, with Kaitlyn. "Get out of here." Daws gave him another shove. "We'll meet up with you later."

Ryan didn't need the extra encouragement. He went to his brother and took his hand, said hello to the friends, and wrapped Katie in his arms. Damn she felt good. More than any of the women who had been in or around his arms over the past several weeks, she felt … amazing. Denial. Maybe he was in denial. The crowd didn't matter anymore. She was there with him, and she felt damn good in his arms.

"Let's go, Ry. There are only four of us and a ton of them as soon as they break through security."

At his brother's voice, he grabbed Katie's hand and brushed the flashing cameras out of his mind.

Relief flooded through his whole being when they finally neared Will's. Katie didn't talk to him through his chatter. But she also didn't pull back at his overly friendly gestures: staying close enough when they walked to brush her arm, addressing her more than the others, touching her back while holding doors for her.

The extra cars parked up and down Will's road made him wonder who would have a get-together on a week night. It was early still, barely dinner time, but he figured it could've waited until the weekend.

Katie caught his eyes when she followed him after he nearly jumped out of the car the second it stopped. He didn't have time to answer her curious expression.

Bella escaped her mom's grasp at the front door and flew out to him. "Uncle Ryan! Look! Come look!"

Will tried to hush her.

With a chuckle, Ryan swept her up in his arms. "My beautiful Bella. Give me a hug and kiss and then I'll come look." She laughed when he pretended to choke from the little arms squeezing his neck. "So what is it? Can I go in and kick off my shoes first? It's been a long tour and I'm tired."

"Nooo, you have to keep your shoes on! It's out*side*!" She wiggled out of his arms and grasped his fingers. "Come!"

He forced her to slow down long enough to introduce Deanna to Tracy and to be sure Katie was fine following with them. Ryan turned the corner to the back of the house, and stopped. The ton of people gathered in the backyard saw him and started yelling, "*Surprise!*"

"What is this?"

Will tapped him on the back. "A late birthday party. Mom's idea. And you forgot it again, I suppose."

Birthday. It was … July 27th. He had forgotten. But he didn't want a party, especially not the first night back. He wanted quiet. He wanted to kick his feet up. When his mom came to give him a hug, he had to fight himself not to say so.

She set her hands alongside his face. "It's so good to have you home again. Will said you were terribly sick. You don't look like you've quite recovered yet."

"I'm all right. But this was unnecessary." He motioned to the yard full of familiar faces – mostly familiar.

"Of course it wasn't. We don't often get you home so close to your birthday. We have to take advantage of it when we do. And Kaitlyn made the cake, decorations and all. She's wonderful in the kitchen. We've had a lovely time."

Ryan turned to find her close to his side. "Did you?"

She held his eyes until the crowd interfered.

Most of the evening, he managed to stay at least somewhat close to her. And she paid constant attention to where he was. If he moved away from whatever group he'd been talking with, she looked over. She didn't seem to need his attention or be bothered that he wasn't at her side. Only … checking on him. Did he look that bad?

When she wasn't at his side, she was with or near Deanna or Will, or she was sitting close to that dog and no one dared get close. The one time a neighbor tried, the dog barked a warning until the woman moved away again. Someone asked Will when he was getting rid of the thing and several others joined in. Katie wasn't comforted by Will's answer that he was still trying to find it a good home.

Ryan grabbed a long swallow of his beer. He didn't believe for a minute anyone would take the dog. Not for anything but security somewhere, at least. And it would bother her when the matter had to come to an end.

"Ryan, happy late birthday."

He pivoted toward the voice and the hand sliding around his waist, and he stepped back. "Why are you here?"

"Your mom invited me." Veronica leaned in. "She still thinks we would be good together. I keep asking her when you'll be home, you know. I missed you last time, away in the Orient with Father. Gorgeous trip, but bad timing. I've missed you loads."

Ryan was aware of eyes on them since they'd been quite the talk around town before he left. For his mom's sake, since *Father* was a long-time friend of hers, he had to be careful. He didn't believe for a second his mom was trying to set them up, though. Veronica more likely gave herself an invitation. But he couldn't make himself speak to her. He walked over to where Katie sat beside the dog away from people. Maybe he would encourage Will to keep the animal.

She stood to meet him. The dog growled until Katie hushed it.

"You spend a lot of time out here with him?"

"Her."

"Sorry, I should remember that. Most of the time I get growled at, it's by women."

Her eyes questioned him.

He shrugged. "Not that I don't ask for it." Ryan lowered to the ground and swallowed the last of his beer. He fiddled with the empty bottle to get it to stand up in the grass.

Katie sat next to him, close enough he'd touch her if he as much as breathed hard. It was a nice respite from people floating around him, chatting and joking and patting his shoulder or asking about the next album and the tour and the girls. About Felicia. He'd repeated several times that she was a singer his label wanted him to help promote, nothing more. Their looks showed disbelief, even with Daws backing him up. Katie had yet to ask about her. Ryan figured she wouldn't, even though she'd heard the questions and had to see no one believed him. It didn't matter if no one else did. He was used to it. But he wanted to make sure she did.

"I want you to know." He hesitated as she put her gaze anywhere but on him. "I'm telling the truth, about Felicia. I know you heard or saw it. Will said it was everywhere. But it was nothing. I was helping her promote for the label, nothing more..."

She touched his eyes.

"And I know no one else believes that, but..."

"I know." She stood, grasped his fingers when he stood up beside her, and went to the gate.

Ryan pulled back when the thing jumped on the fence.

She kept his hand and pulled up the latch. "It's okay."

"Katie..." His voice barely worked. "Don't."

"It's okay. I promise."

Ryan's heart nearly stopped. She was asking for his trust. After all the times he'd asked for hers, he had no choice.

"Don't be afraid of her. She'll know."

"Then I'd say it's too late to make her think I'm not. She probably hears my heart thumping."

With a squeeze of his fingers, Kaitlyn moved inside the pen. The animal was chained, so they could at least back up out of the fence if needed, but the dog stayed still. A light growl emerged from low in her throat when she looked at Ryan but stopped when Katie scolded her.

"Sit." She waited to be obeyed and scratched the thing behind its ears. Ryan felt like a coward remaining a step behind, but he didn't expect the animal to bother her. He wasn't so sure it wouldn't decide he was a threat to Katie, though, and suddenly defend her.

The dog jerked its head to the side. Ryan followed its gaze to Daws, Deanna, and Will.

His brother grinned. "Never thought I'd see this. Thought you didn't like dogs."

"Good. Tell her that." Ryan tensed when it focused attention on him.

"I already told Kaitlyn you don't like dogs. Apparently, she wants to change your mind."

"I meant the dog. I'm within tearing-off-the-arm distance. She doesn't need to know I don't."

Will chuckled. "You might not want to try to pet her. She won't even let me do that."

"Oh, don't worry."

Katie looked at him. "It's okay. You can."

Ryan gave his head a light shake. "No, I'm as close to the edge as I wanna be. Can we get out of here now?"

She ran her hand down the dog's back, gave it a pat, and began toward the gate. The dog whined and followed as far as she could, earning itself another scratch behind the ear.

With the gate latched, Ryan started breathing again.

"Kaitlyn." Will moved closer. "Don't get too attached to her. I can't keep her much longer."

Sadness touch her face before she turned it away. Ryan couldn't stand to see it. She needed the dog. "Why can't you? She's not bothering anyone."

"You kept badgering me to get her out of here and now you want me to keep her?" Will threw him an amused look.

"I've never seen that she can be this docile. Maybe she'll calm down."

"Doesn't matter. The neighborhood is talking about a petition. She scares them. They only haven't out of respect for us."

"Hell, she's tied and in a fence. What are they worried about?"

"You know as well as I do she could get out if she tried hard enough. And I can't keep kids from teasing her, which is making everything worse. I can't risk it." He studied Katie. "I'm sorry. I wish I could."

Kaitlyn returned her gaze, to Will. "Where will she go?"

His chest rose, shoulders falling with the breath. "A shelter. For a last chance. But then...." He stopped. He couldn't tell her.

She walked away. Deanna followed.

"Damn it, Will. One thing she's found that gives her comfort, that she truly cares about, and ... what? They're going to put her down because some damn kids won't behave?"

"I know, but there's nothing I can do. No one will take her and this area has too many little ones roaming around. If I put a big fence all around the yard, it would be different, but I don't want my yard blocked off. We enjoy most of the kids and company and the openness. I can't change all of that for a dog."

Ryan looked at Daws as though he could fix this like he fixed everything else. Except he didn't jump in. And he couldn't. It wasn't like either of them could have the thing in their city apartments. "It's getting late. Isn't it time for everyone to leave? Not that I don't appreciate the trouble. I do. But I've had enough of crowds for a while..."

"Understood." Will set a hand on his shoulder. "I'll start clearing them out. And you know, I wouldn't object to getting another dog, something friendly. A lab maybe, or..."

"Why?"

"Because she likes dogs."

"And she isn't here that often. I won't tour again for ... I don't even know right now."

"Maybe she should stay, even if you're not touring."

Ryan caught his eyes. "Why?"

"This seems to be good for her. She's starting to talk to us. Getting more at ease around company, most of the time. If she gets uneasy, she comes out and sits with the dog and we can get her one the neighbors won't complain about. Mom loves having her and Bella absolutely adores her, like a big sister..."

"Has she said she wants to stay?"

"I haven't asked. I didn't think I should without talking to you first."

Ryan listened to the sounds of the party he didn't want, the laughter and radio in the background, voices. And he looked over at Daws, to get his reaction. Although he wasn't sure he wanted it. He would agree with Will. Ryan knew he would. "Yeah well, it's not up to me anyway. It's her choice. I'll ask her."

"Hey." Will stopped him. "I thought that's what you wanted."

"Yeah. Like I said, I'm wiped out. I don't wanna do decisions or anything tonight." Ryan saw Katie move toward the fire pit. She was probably getting cold.

He headed her direction but was stopped by neighbors who asked if he'd do a couple of songs. "You know, I'm kinda tired of my own voice right now. Maybe another time?" At a grudging acceptance, he continued, until someone gripped on his arm.

"Come on, honey. Play for us." Veronica sidled up next to him.

"Excuse me." He pulled away, dodged someone else who looked like he wanted to talk, and took Kaitlyn's side. "Are you cold?"

She shook her head.

"I'm sorry about the dog. If I could do anything..."

Her eyes went back to the fire.

They stood in silence for some time until he felt a hand on his back and turned. Veronica. She asked again if he would play, with the excuse that his mom wanted to hear the new songs.

"I'll play them for her tomorrow." Ryan brushed her off and put his attention on the lapping flames with orange-red edges, on the contrast of his heated front and night-cooled back. On Veronica pressing against him on one side, and Katie allowing whatever distance he wanted on the other. Except he didn't. He wanted Veronica to go away. He wanted to wrap an arm around Katie's back, to let her know he missed her. He didn't dare.

"Come on, Ryan. Sing for us." She recruited help from neighbors close by.

"I'm not..." His phone interrupted and he checked the number. His life preserver. "Hey, sexy." He answered that way for Veronica's sake. Not that it worked. He could barely hear Dani over Veronica as she kept recruiting. She also threw Katie looks, not that *that* worked, either. Katie paid no attention to her.

"Let me call you back later when I can hear. ... Just as soon as I'm up to being on the phone." He laughed at her answer. "You keep promising that. So come on. ... Uh huh. ... Soon. ... You too. Later."

He tried very hard not to gloat like a cat with its first mouse in its teeth at Veronica's expression.

"Your new girlfriend?" She propped a hand on her hip. "So much for it not being true."

"If you mean Felicia, she doesn't have my number."

"Keeping her on a string, huh? Nice, Ryan. So it was a different new girlfriend?"

He couldn't help himself, regardless of how many were close enough to hear. "Nope. Long-time torrid affair. Excuse me."

Unable to escape alone with Kaitlyn as he intended, somehow he got dragged into playing. He missed part of the conversation that led to an agreement he didn't remember making while he tried to hear his friend's voice over the line.

As the commotion quieted, Ryan sat on the grass and stretched his legs in front of him. Katie was again by the fire, alone, sitting this time, while Will and Tracy and his mom finished ushering people out of the yard and Daws and Deanna chatted with a couple who used to be from New York. Relaxing further, he leaned back, clasped his hands under his head in the grass, and studied the stars. He ignored the last few guests still meandering and hoped she would come join him, admire the night sky with him.

The body that lowered beside his wasn't the one he wanted there. "Veronica, go home. It's late." He closed his eyes, breathing in nature's scent: damp pollen, a touch of smoke that drifted over, the heaviness of late summer air.

"Come with me, Ryan. Your family will understand. They know how I've missed you." She set a hand on his stomach.

He pulled away and sat up. "Don't touch me again."

"You're honestly still mad at me? When are you going to grow up and get over it?"

"I'm not." He stood.

She rose beside him. "You're still pining for that prissy little thing you thought you wanted? Are you kidding? She's moved on. Maybe you should."

Jaw clenched, he stared at her.

"Does that girl remind you of her?" She nodded toward the fire. "That's not what you need. You know it's not."

"She's a friend. Not your business."

"*Riveting* Ryan Reynauld doesn't have girls who are only friends. He has girls who aren't friends but never friends who aren't his girls. Never did have, did you?"

"Go home." He turned from her, using every ounce of control to walk away with his manners mostly intact.

"You need someone who'll take care of you. A strong woman. One who can look the other way from time to time and love you anyway. You know I can do that. I can take care of you. Do you really think she can? She's nearly a kid, Ryan. You would destroy her if you..."

He wheeled back, keeping his voice low. "You have screwed me the only way you ever will. Get that through your head. Never will I ever touch you. Never. Go home. Or find somewhere else to go. If you want, I can give you a suggestion." He escaped into the house, pacing from one room to the next. Destroy her. He would destroy her if.... But he wouldn't. He would never do that to Katie. Any more than he would ever give in to Veronica. She'd chased away the one girl he'd ever really wanted. Accusations. But he hadn't done anything with Veronica and he told her ... and it didn't matter. It was over. He was never able to admit it to his family.

Ryan grabbed a beer out of the fridge, pried off the cap, took a long swallow, and headed back outside. Everyone would be gone. He hoped they would be gone.

As his eyes adjusted to the dark again after the light of the kitchen, he walked toward the glow of the fire. He wanted to sit beside her and let her calm him ... but someone was there. Kaitlyn was standing, moving away ... and the man moved after her. He didn't see Will, or anyone else. Their voices came from the side yard, still ushering people out. And Katie jumped back from the man Ryan barely recognized.

Setting the bottle on a chair he passed, he quickened his pace, saw the man grip her arm and Katie unable to pull away ... and Ryan plowed into him, pushing him away from her, knocking him to the ground. The guy was bigger but no match against Ryan's fury as he punched a fist into his side.

"*Ryan. Stop.*" Will ran up to them and tried to pull him off.

His fist again merged with the man's gut. It felt good, powerful, in control...

Hands on both of his arms pulled at him, pulled him away. He found Katie. Deanna had an arm around her.

"*Who* is this guy? What in the hell is he *doing* here?"

"He works with me." Will helped the guy to his feet and stared at Ryan. "What do you think you're doing attacking my guests?"

"He *grabbed* her. She tried to get away from him and he *grabbed* her. If he touches her again, I'll beat the hell out of him. I don't care if he's the damn president of the company." Daws kept him from moving in again.

"Ry, calm down. I'm sure it wasn't..."

"The *hell* it wasn't. *Look* at her." She was pulled into herself, head dropped and turned toward Deanna. Shrugging away from Daws, he went over to ask if she was all right and she clung to him, her head pressed against his shoulder, fingers clutching his sides. He looked at Will. "Still think it wasn't? Get him out of here." Tracy and his mom were there, also, asking what happened, if she was all right. Daws went with Will and the New York couple to accompany the man out of the yard.

Ryan brushed hair out of her face. "Katie, I'm sorry. I didn't think anyone would bother you here, in the yard..."

She shook her head. "I overreacted. I'm sorry. I didn't mean to cause trouble. I overreacted."

"No. It's not your fault. He had no right..."

"I don't want to cause trouble."

Ryan pulled her in as close as he could, holding her head in his palm. Seething. No way in hell would he leave her. Not with people like that around. Not if ... he couldn't blame Will. He was there, too, or not there when he should have been. It was his fault as much as anyone's, except that man's. He would talk to Will about him later.

Tracy offered to walk Kaitlyn into the house and suggested a hot shower to relax her, trying to coerce her away from Ryan. Katie gripped him tighter.

"I'll walk her in. When she's settled, I'll come help clean up."

"No honey." His mom touched the back of his shoulder. "Stay in with her. We can do this. You've been away for some time. I think it's been a long month for both of you."

She meant they both overreacted. Maybe he did. Will came back and said someone took him home, that the guy didn't mean to scare her.

Ryan looked at Daws. "And the asshole's gonna sue me now, right?"

"Not unless he wants a countersuit and a harassment claim on his record."

He breathed easier. "Don't know what I'd do without you at times."

"Go get some sleep, Reynauld. You're not recovered yet."

With a grin, he convinced Katie to release him enough to walk to the house. They didn't talk until they were upstairs in her room, away from where someone might interfere. He sat beside her on the bed.

"They'll want me to go now."

"Who?" He leaned his head forward to try to see her eyes.

"Your brother. Your family. I didn't mean to ... he kept getting too close. I didn't want to talk. I didn't want him..."

"Katie." He ran a hand through her hair. "No one wants you to go. They may yell at me but they won't be upset with you."

Her eyes met his, widened. "I don't want you hurt because of me."

Ryan chuckled. "Will has never in his life tried to hurt me because he was mad at me. Hell, he's been mad at me plenty. He might yell for a minute, but it's no big deal. And it's not your fault. I'm the one who overreacted. I do that. He's used to it, although ... I want you to know attacking people is not something I do often. I ... I was tired, and tired of people, strangers, and ... I shouldn't have. I'm sorry. It drew too much attention. It wasn't fair to you."

She threw her arms around his shoulders, burying her face in his neck.

"It's all right." He nearly whispered beside her ear, his eyes closed, and held her as close as he could. Her body relaxed. A trace of campfire smoke scented her hair The freshness of nature surrounded her. "I'm so glad to be back here with you. I missed you, Katie."

Drawing back, she questioned him with only a look. And he knew he shouldn't have said it. He had to pull himself from his thoughts, and stood. "I should let you shower. I'll be downstairs..." He stopped when Tracy knocked on the open door and tilted her head as though wondering if it was okay. Ryan hoped she hadn't heard him.

"The kids want to say good night before I send them to bed."

Ryan frowned. "I thought they were in bed. Hell, they didn't see that...?"

"No, they were in here getting ready." She stepped toward Kaitlyn. "I'm so sorry, honey. We never expected he would ever bother you, or anyone. He hasn't before, has he? He's been here several times."

When she didn't answer, Ryan crouched down to look up at her. "Has he bothered you before?"

She shook her head.

"Hey." He touched her face and she pulled back. "You're not okay yet. And he has." At another head shake, he grabbed a deep breath. She wouldn't say anything with Tracy there. And maybe she wouldn't anyway. "Okay. Go shower. Take more than two minutes and unwind while I say good night. I'll come back." He went to the door, paused beside his sister-in-law while he checked to see if Katie was going to stop him, and headed downstairs. She would have told Will. He was fairly sure she would have told Will if the guy had bothered her. She said he didn't. But there was something she wasn't saying.

Ryan gave Matthew and Isabelle hugs and said Kaitlyn was tired and would see them in the morning. Then he went down and out the back door. Will, Daws, and Deanna still sat around the waning fire. He didn't join them. He headed toward the dog. The closer he got, the slower he walked, and he spoke to it when it growled. "Tell you what. I won't bother you if you don't bother me. Deal?" Reassured by the quiet that followed, Ryan sat in the grass and turned his face to the sky. It was hazy, the lightest stars barely visible, but it was still blanketed in glistening speckles of light. As he always had when he was young, he wanted to reach out and swirl his hand through it.

The dog barked. Once.

"Okay Chewy, it's only me." Will's voice was nearly a scold, and he sat facing Ryan. "Is she all right?"

"She's shaken. Tracy's inside with her."

"Ry, I feel worse than I can say. I never expected..."

"It's not your fault. It wasn't fair to bring her here, to ask you to do this." He played with a blade of grass without pulling it out. "I thought I could help her. I thought all she needed was companionship, someone to be there. I was wrong. I should have called a professional right away. Now if I do, it'll look like I'm giving up, and..."

"And you can't."

He abandoned the blade to find his brother's face. "You told me I should, that I should call the authorities."

"Yes, but I think I was wrong. She's been different today since you came back. More ... more animated."

"What do you mean?"

"She hasn't really been here. Of course she was here, physically, but much of the time it was like having a robot or something in the house. There was nothing there when she responded, only as necessary. She's always so extremely guarded we can't even begin to know what she's thinking, how she feels. Today though, and for the three days we traveled with you, I saw so much more going on inside. She's actually *present*, at least more so."

Will shrugged. "It reminds me of when you were little and followed me everywhere. Mom said you pouted and would do nothing but play piano when I went out without you."

"Spoiled ass, even then." Ryan ran his palm over the grass.

"I was flattered, although at times it was annoying. And at times I felt guilty for letting you down because I was in charge of you so often it was hard on you when I suddenly wasn't there."

"You had your own life. I shouldn't have been so demanding. It was absurd."

"It was fear."

Ryan threw him a questioning glance.

"Neither Mom or Dad was around as much as you needed at that age. You needed an anchor somewhere." He paused while Ryan couldn't answer. "It's your turn to be that anchor. But remember, you have your own life, too. There's no shame in falling back on others to help."

"Except I don't know how to be an anchor. I have no idea what I'm doing."

Will laughed. "And I did? Hell Ry, we all learn as we go. Trial and error. Same with parenting. Tracy and I were scared to death about being parents. But you learn. The big thing is that you care enough to learn, and keep learning. It's all you can do." He stood and set a hand on Ryan's shoulder. "She apparently thinks you're doing okay as a big brother. You're still the one she wants to follow around." He nodded to the side.

Ryan turned enough to see her walk toward him, with Tracy. The dog saw her, also, and whined, ducking its head as though calling to her.

She had already returned the favor to another, provided comfort to the dog everyone else had given up on.

Tracy slid a hand around Will's arm and drew him away.

Katie sat next to him, faced the opposite direction close enough he could easily reach her face if he tried. "Do you still want to know what I want most?"

He stared, unable to ask.

"I want there to be one person in my life I care about who I don't hurt."

The emotion was in her voice even if she didn't allow it in her face. Ryan couldn't hide it as well. One person she didn't hurt? He couldn't imagine how she would hurt anyone. His frustration, his backing away when she didn't answer ... she must have taken it wrong. "Katie." His voice was a whisper, a pathetic, failed attempt to hide what he felt. "I'm not afraid of you hurting me." When she pulled her eyes away, his fingers brought them back. "I'm only afraid you won't allow me to keep trying. Don't worry about me. And don't be afraid to be around me. Because I do care about you. I care very deeply about you, and nothing you do will ever change that."

She looked like she was trying to decide whether or not to believe him. Ryan nudged closer and took her in his arms.

Chewy barked. Worried.

Katie pulled back and stood. When Ryan rose next to her, she spoke to Chewy, took his hand, and moved closer to the fence. Then she spoke to the dog again as she pressed her body up against Ryan's, her head on his shoulder.

Chewy quieted.

"Mind getting up early?" He stroked the curve of her back. "I want you to see the sunrise from the boat."

Daws and Deanna invited themselves. He supposed it was good; being alone with Katie after he'd missed her as much as he did was not a great idea. Still, he'd wanted to share it privately. He was quite sure Daws didn't want him to share it with her privately.

At least he had extra hands to hold flashlights while he prepped the pontoon for the pre-dawn sail. It was still chilly and the first thing he did was to get Katie settled with a thick blanket around her. Deanna complained to Daws about not being as thoughtful. So Ryan grabbed another and wrapped it around Deanna, landing a kiss on her cheek.

"You are just too charming for your own good. If I were only a few years younger..."

"Hey, wouldn't matter to me, but you'd have to lose that guy first." Ryan laughed when his friend shoved him away and told him to start the damn boat already.

With the pontoon readied and untied from the dock, Ryan took the captain's seat. A turn of the key and the engine sputtered into a smooth purr. One of his favorite sounds in the world. When he had more time, he'd have a fleet of different types, including one with a lower deck capable of lying down, escaping the sun, or finding privacy.

He pushed the privacy thought out of his head and turned toward open water where there would be no interference, nothing between them and the sun rising from behind the lake and distant shore. Angling so the view was clear from both the front of the boat and the back, Ryan stopped the engine and anchored it, reminded of Will's comment about him being the anchor. Except he didn't feel like an anchor. He felt adrift as though he didn't have one to throw out. *Trial and error.* He hoped it would be more trial than error.

Katie moved from where she'd been sitting next to Deanna at the front of the boat and glided to the back, planting herself, legs crossed, up on the high seat from where she had watched the kids play in the water. Ryan had the definite feeling she had thoughts of privacy, as well. Maybe they were wishful feelings more than definite. He couldn't allow himself to guess what she was thinking. He was likely so off-course his thoughts and hers weren't even on the same map. Still, he joined her, kicking off his shoes and pulling one leg up enough to face her, the other foot propped on the seat below.

The sky started to show a hint of light. He loved the in-between time when it wasn't completely dark and wasn't yet dawn. Katie focused on the stars, or maybe on the moon. He wasn't sure which. It was new – a sliver only, which made the stars brighter. Ryan pointed out the big dipper.

"It looks like we could sit up there."

"In the big dipper?" Ryan wondered if he should admit having considered the idea as a child. Hiding inside the big dipper.

"On the moon."

"Hm, I think I'd rather sit in the big dipper."

"Why?" She dropped her eyes to his.

"It looks sturdier, like we could crawl inside and not have to see over the edge. You know, the heights thing. The moon looks too easy to fall off."

Her focus returned to the sky. "You only fall off if you want to."

This time, he knew where she looked. *Only if you want to.* Ryan knew he was staring at her, but he couldn't stop. The sky began its white glow that turned the black into blue and then into lighter blue, with peach touches. He saw it with his peripheral vision only. His full attention was on her, on the way the light reflected on her, taking away the shadows slowly, steadily. She didn't want to fall any longer. It was transparent on her face, which had become so much less translucent and more opaque, more full and round and soft without looking so dangerous to touch. Her eyes remained on the sky, drifting between the moon sliver and the sunrise. Ryan knew she realized he was staring. He loved that she didn't care.

She met his gaze. "You're missing the sunrise."

"No, I'm not." Regardless of how he wanted to, he wouldn't kiss her. Not there, with Daws and Deanna up front. "Kaitlyn, thank you. I have never seen half as much before I met you as I see now. It's amazing." Her eyes said she was unsure what he meant. "I know I'm not making sense, but it doesn't matter. It's just ... I'm glad you're here."

She studied his face a moment longer, then found his hand. "Thank you." Her fingers tightened. "For pulling me in."

He wished they were alone. He didn't want to have to explain his actions or have them interfered with by his bodyguard ... his friend. Ryan knew he was more his friend than anyone else who wasn't family, except for Katie. His anchor. Will was wrong. Ryan wasn't the anchor. Katie was.

Her body shifted closer, and she leaned forward to find his lips.

He hesitated. Will called him her big brother, or at least hinted at that. Daws was firmly against it. She wasn't as young as he first thought, but she was still young. And yet ... he pulled back enough to see her face, her eyes opening to find his.

"You are afraid of me." It wasn't accusing, or questioning, only simple fact that said she knew.

"No." He touched her hair, smoothing his fingers through it to rest his palm aside her head. "I'm afraid of hurting you. Big difference."

"You don't have to be. I'm not afraid of you." She leaned forward again. "I am afraid of everything except you." Her eyes dared him. Invited him.

He inched back. "I can't." She was too young, too afraid, too vulnerable. And he couldn't do anything stupid with her ... not with her.

She got up and moved to the seat on the side of the boat. He stayed there, grabbed a deep breath, and told himself he did the right thing. His eyes fell to the water to watch fish nibble at the top in search for bugs. Daws would approve. He would tell him he was doing the right thing, being less a moron than usual. But it didn't feel right. And at the same time, it did. He could ask Will, except he didn't want his brother to know he had such feelings for her. He couldn't admit it to him ... which told Ryan he was definitely doing the right thing.

He stared at the sun's reflection in the water, and then went to sit behind her, wrapping his arms around her and kissing the side of her head. A brotherly act. No more. At least she didn't walk away again.

9

This time, Ryan was more than ready to be home. The days at Will's were too confusing. His mind kept going back to selfish thoughts: thoughts of kissing her, of holding her close and losing himself in her scent, of sitting alone in the backyard under the stars. Of him asking if she would rather stay than return to the city and the look in her eyes that was close to real emotion, the shake of the head, the waiting for him to withdraw the question. It was too real there, too vivid. They needed to be at the loft, to settle back in to where they started, and things would be different. She would see what he was instead of acting the romantic position of a boat captain with free time drifting along as he pleased. He had to get back to work: write, get the album done, network, all the stuff that kept him always on the move and out of thoughts of what he should or shouldn't do. He reacted with his work. He didn't think everything to death. That was the problem; he had too much thinking time when he was with her. She pulled him too far out of the shallow-ass shell he'd happily created for himself and he didn't want out of it. It was fairy tale garbage. In real life, she would get annoyed with him always working and always being elsewhere in his head, writing songs or trying to come up with song ideas or drinking with the guys so he could stop thinking of song ideas and ... and of what was missing.

He needed to go back to that – to not thinking.

He glanced at the gossip rag Ginny shoved in front of his face but refused to read it. Another photo and article that showed Katie beside him and questioned who she really was. So what? He'd lost count as to how many there were. None of the photos showed anything except her presence, other than the one where he was holding her hand, only because there was a crowd and he didn't want her separated. There was nothing more for anyone to find.

"Reynauld, you do know we have an album coming out we need to promote? Sales are declining too fast for the last one and there isn't enough interest in this one yet, nothing like for the last two. Want to guess why?"

"They're realizing it's a waste of money." He swerved around his manager to refill his water from the upside down bottle pretending to be a fountain. He much preferred regular fountains, the old metal ones he'd used at the park in between playing ball. The ones that pumped real water from an underground system, not overly filtered tasteless water in plastic bottles.

"Waste of money." Ginny held her spot. "What is wrong with you? You think your music is suddenly a waste of money when it's always been the only thing you gave a rat's ass about?"

"No." He met her gaze. "I think the way it's overproduced is a waste of money. My music ... is rough, raw. That's the way I want it. That's the way I hear it in my head. And then we spend months making it smooth and over-polished and I get this album I don't even recognize. It's not mine. It's theirs. Why do I even bother to write? Hell, just pay for a few songs, stick me behind the mic, and let it go. Would it matter?"

Daws raised his eyebrows, a hint of amusement in his face. Ryan figured he agreed it didn't much matter what he sang, or that he spent so much of his time writing new stuff when he could just as well kick back and relax and let others do the writing.

"You've never said anything about this." Ginny ambled closer. "You don't like how the last album turned out?"

Ryan shrugged. "That doesn't matter much, either. I'm nothing but a voice and a face. Since when did anyone bother to ask what I like?"

Another amused look from Daws grabbed his attention, or maybe it wasn't amusement. Maybe it was ... approval? Did he not like the sound of the CD, either? Ryan had never bothered to ask him.

"Ned put this into your head, didn't he?"

Rolling his eyes, Ryan moved around her and dropped back onto his chair. "So do we have a new schedule or are we sticking with the old one?"

"He complained to Mac about it. He's putting you up to this because he doesn't like all the studio time. I told you, Reynauld, you need to use studio musicians instead of these guys who are great on the road but take more time than necessary in the studio because they're not geared for that..."

"Maybe I'm the one who put it in *his* head. Ever think of that?" His stomach panged and he forced more water.

"No." At his glance she came over and pulled a chair beside him. "I think those guys are pushing you to feel this way. You know the sound is good. You know it has to be different on an album than it is live. You know listeners are used to the polished sound and that's what they expect. This isn't you. It's your band. And nothing against them – they're a great road crew. But for the next one, you need to consider using..."

He shoved out of his chair, paced around the table in Ginny's office, and paused by the big window. What a huge difference between looking out the window at Will's with his yard covered in green and decorated with trees and flowering things. Here, he saw cold gray steel and reflective glass rising from gray sidewalks and cigarette-butt-littered streets. The glass reflection reminded him of sun shining off the surface of a lake, except it was unwavering, still, silent.

Ginny touched his shoulder from behind. "You know I want the best for you. I want your work to shine as much as it should, without being held back."

"I don't want a damn studio band." He kept his eyes outside the window. Around the corner was Katie's building. Ginny had managed to get an office a few floors above the studio to make it easier for her to keep up with Ryan's work and the one other band she managed. They didn't do much touring outside local clubs, so it wasn't a strain on her time...

"Okay." She moved away, her voice circling in front of her and then back to him. "So let's work on this schedule and get back to the original issue. This friend of yours. How about we find her an apartment of her own? At least that way, it looks less..."

"No." Ryan turned. "She doesn't want to live on her own."

"So we find her a roommate. Should be easy enough with..."

"She has a roommate and she's fine where she is."

"Look, Reynauld, I understand she means something to you, but you can as easily see her if she's a couple of blocks away at her own place, and that'll help with some of this." She nodded down toward the paper. "And if we do it fast enough, it won't hurt the new album sales. We can even move her in with Daws until we find her another place..."

"No." Ryan didn't bother to check his friend's reaction. He wasn't moving her out. Unless it was ever her idea. It wasn't going to be his and it sure as hell wasn't going to be his manager's. Or his fans'.

Ginny picked up the paper. "*This* is not helping you. She's *too young*, Reynauld. They can see she is no matter what we say. Do you want to see your sales figures?"

"If sales are down, it's because the music isn't good enough." He started to pace again.

"Don't be naïve. You've been in this business long enough to know better than that. It's all in the promotion. As you said, you could sing all cover songs and it would still hit the top if we promote it well enough, if you're careful about what you're doing in public..."

A sharp pain in his gut stabbed at him and Ryan walked out. He shoved the door closed. All cover songs were just as good. Great. Just what he wanted to hear. Fucking *great*. He could just do cover songs with studio musicians he didn't know and get it done quicker. Why bust his ass to do anything else if it didn't matter?

He didn't answer a greeting thrown at him as he treaded down the gray carpeted hallway toward the elevator. Why did everything have to be so damn gray?

"Hold up, Reynauld."

Not slowing for Daws, he got to the elevator, pounded the button to get the thing to open, walked several steps away, and got caught by a large hand. "Not now. I gotta get out of here."

"And go where?"

"Doesn't matter. Anywhere. Not here."

"She didn't mean it the way it sounded."

"No? I think she did. And what blows is I think she's right. My songs are just like everyone else's. Why bother? Hell, I can sleep instead. Or ... or take a drive. Or throw on some damn disguise and hit a movie. Why in the hell not? It's all the same. A voice and a face. Singing about things that have been sung about a trillion times already." He shrugged and headed to the opening door.

"Ryan." Daws stopped him, waving the elevator on when someone inside held it for them.

"Great, now it's gonna be ten minutes before it comes again. You know how slow this is."

"In a hurry to go where you don't know you're going?"

"Yeah well, what's new?" He took a deep breath, ambled to the opposite wall, and leaned back against it.

Daws pulled out his phone, told Ryan not to move, and walked farther down the hall.

"Calling a shrink?" He muttered to himself. His guard must've heard since he turned and gave him that 'shut the hell up' look before he continued his pace.

Don't move. Hell, he was tired of taking orders and went back to pound on the down key a couple of times. "*Come on* already."

"Let's take the stairs." Daws called from down the hall, motioning with his head for Ryan to follow.

The stairs. Perfect. It would use some of his anger energy. Maybe he'd go all the way down and then back up again.

Daws ended the conversation and closed the phone as he neared.

"You don't like stairs." Ryan eyed him.

"Don't like pouting pop stars, either, but you do what you have to." He opened the stairwell door. "Deanna says Kaitlyn is fine with staying there late tonight. We're going out."

"Out where?"

"Out."

Daws half-pulled him into the apartment until Ryan told him to let go, to let him walk on his own. They'd stayed too late, even after Daws made his point. The barflies were all over him as soon as he walked in, girls and guys, and Daws let it 'slip' that Ryan might stop writing songs.

He never expected the ruckus he got. Much of the rest of the night, he had to listen to girls tell him what some particular song meant to her, how she and her boyfriend made one of them 'their' song, how when they had a bad day, his music pulled them up at night. They asked him over and over not to stop writing.

As though he would have anyway. Even if he didn't ever use them, he had to write them, to get them out of his head so they didn't drive him crazy. But maybe he would keep using them. And maybe he would put his foot down and insist on less 'smoothing' during production.

"Drink the place dry, did you?" Deanna took his other side. "Criminy, you smell. Go shower. And hurry it up so Freddy can get human again, too."

"I gotta go home." Ryan stumbled.

"No you don't." Daws nudged him toward the bathroom. "I'll bring something in to put on. Make it quick and not too warm. Don't want you passing out in there."

"I'm not gonna pass out. But I gotta go home. Katie..."

Deanna turned her face away from his breath. "She's asleep. It's after two. Here, in the guest room. So you have no reason to go anywhere, except to get clean. You know where the mouthwash is. Use it. Don't drink it."

"Hell, I'm not..." He stopped. He wasn't that far out of it. He got sick at the bar because of his damn stomach. But he wouldn't say so. They could think he was that far out of it. In the guest room? Detouring around where they tried to shove him, Ryan went to the guest room door. It was mostly closed but not quite.

"Ryan, she's asleep." Deanna tugged at his arm. "And she's fine. Come on. Leave her alone."

"I just wanna let her know I'm back so she doesn't worry..."

"She's asleep. She's not worried. Come on."

He gave in since he was too wiped out to argue, and ran in and out of the shower, then slipped into the sweats on the counter ... his sweats. Why were they there? ... and went out to find the couch.

She had a pillow at one side already and tossed a blanket at him. "Don't you dare get sick on my floor."

"I'm not gonna get sick." He surrendered onto the pillow and closed his eyes, waiting for them to go away, for the room to get darker, but never too dark. Deanna always had night lights everywhere.

He couldn't sleep. He wanted to make sure she wasn't worried.

Pushing himself up, Ryan made his way to her room and nudged the door until he could see her. The night light glow shimmered over her face, her bare arm atop the blanket. She didn't look worried. She looked peaceful. And he went back to lie down. She hadn't needed him there. She was doing well. He'd been out all day and all night and she was fine.

He shoved an arm against his stomach.

~~~

Ryan hung up with the third radio jockey of the morning, having answered the same questions in various forms each time, threw on his sweat pants and shuffled to the kitchen. It was early. She wasn't up yet. Why they had to do radio interviews at seven a.m., he didn't know. At least the phone interviews were easier to take at that hour than the in-person sessions. He'd refused to do those for the past couple of years or so, as soon as he felt able to refuse. His publicist stopped complaining about it only recently.

Searching through the refrigerator, he pulled out eggs and bacon and a can of biscuits. Kaitlyn had cooked often enough. Since he had time before going out to ... he couldn't even think what it was for at the moment, he would try to make up for his lack of availability with breakfast and chatting. It had been some time since they'd said more than basic daily living stuff. She'd barely even done that, since ... he wasn't sure when. As he'd expected, everything normalized when they got back to the city. Two weeks passed since being at Will's and there was no hint of her even thinking about what he wouldn't let himself think about.

He wondered if she would go with him to wherever he had to be later. A week before when she said she would stay alone at the loft, he hesitated. But she said it was okay. She'd stayed there alone twice since.

Ryan cut open the bacon and started to pull it apart while the oil heated. His mom would yell about him using oil to fry bacon which had enough grease on its own, but it cooked faster that way and he hated standing over the stove turning it twenty times. The bubbles coming up told him it was hot enough, and he dropped the first couple of pieces in.

"*Damn.*" He jumped back when oil splashed his stomach. "Plenty damn hot enough. Shit." Ryan tossed the rest back onto the greasy package, went to the refrigerator, and pulled out the butter.

"Don't put that on it."

He turned to her voice. "Just burned the shit out of myself."

"Use water, not butter." She took the container from his hands, went to the sink and ran a clean towel under the faucet. With a glance at the popping oil, Katie handed him the wet towel and held a dry one in front of herself while she moved the pan to a cool burner.

Ryan watched her, so much more comfortable in his kitchen than he could ever be.

She returned her attention. "Put it on the burn. It won't help in your hand."

"It stings like it's on fire. Butter..."

"Will make it worse." She took it from him and set it against the red spot. He pulled back at the shock of cold but she pressed it softly against him again.

It still stung, but the cold distracted him, almost as much as her hand nearly on his bare stomach, her body close to his, smelling that incredible "fresh from the bed" smell. Ryan claimed the towel and moved back to the stove. "Thought I'd surprise you with breakfast but I didn't mean to do it like this." He should have put a shirt on.

She joined him as he set the pan back on the hot burner. "Bacon doesn't need oil."

"Yeah, that's what Mom says, too, but I always do it this way." He wouldn't look at her.

"You always burn yourself?"

"No. Only about half the time. You were lucky enough to get a show with your meal." He knew he sounded sarcastic, and he didn't exactly mean to, but she was bothering him. In a good way, but not good. "I'm gonna get a shirt so at least it won't hit the same place."

"I can cook."

He looked back from the kitchen exit. "No. I'm cooking." Again, it didn't come out right. But damn, he was annoyed. He had to start dating, or ... something. It had been too long. That's all it was.

In his room, he picked up the phone and waited for Ned to complain about the early call. "Yeah well, I was up. Thought you should be."

"We're not working today, are we?"

"You're not. What are you doing tonight?"

"Me?"

"No, asshole, whoever is beside you making you not use your brain. Who do you think I'm talking to?"

"Since when do you want to know what I'm doing, other than working?"

Ryan scratched his head. "Yeah okay. You can just tell me to get off the phone." He hung up, pulled a shirt over his head, and shoved his hands through his hair, stretching his neck back and forth. He nearly ignored the ring, but decided it would at least give him another couple of minutes to settle himself.

"Did I do something to piss you off you're getting even for?" Ned sounded a touch more awake.

"No. Sorry. Just pissy in general. I need a good distraction tonight. Know anything going on?"

"Ah. A distraction. I might know a couple of girls who could help make something go on tonight. Your place? Mine's kind of, uh..."

"Yeah, as always. I'll be here."

"So, what about Kaitlyn?"

"I would suppose she'll be here, too. Unless she makes plans with Deanna again." He shouldn't have said it. And he wasn't going to explain. "See ya about ... eight or so? And add a few people. I don't want it to look like a double date." Getting agreement, he hung up and suddenly realized he'd left the pan of oil on the hot burner. "Shit." Ryan half-jogged back to the kitchen. It was fine. The temperature was lower. Kaitlyn wasn't there.

Just as well.

How Daws heard about the party was beyond him. The man was impossible to get around. And of course, Deanna came with. Shrugging it off, Ryan went to grab another Seven and Seven. He knew he should make it weaker this time but figured he might as well act the full part of the moron since he was doing a good job of that so far. Katie stayed with Deanna much of the night. Ryan didn't interfere. Space was good. He added even more whiskey. His stomach would just have to tough it out and quit being such a damn aggravation.

"Want to pour me another, too, tiger?"

Ryan forced himself not to roll his eyes at the girl-leech. She'd hung on him since she walked in the door, no matter how often he moved around. He had to wonder why Ned invited that one, the one he'd escaped at one of the last parties. He still couldn't remember her name for anything and she still didn't appear to care. "How heavy you want it?"

She slid up against him. "How about I leave it up to you? I'm a big girl. I can handle it."

"Never had any doubt." He tried not to spill the stuff all over his counter while she pressed her half-naked breasts against his back. Her hands roamed along his front. He also tried hard not to react. It had been too damn long.

"So can you send your little friend home with your guard tonight?" She accepted the drink he'd made weaker than his own. "I'd love to stay. If you'd love to have me."

Ryan considered the offer. He couldn't ask Katie to leave with Daws. She would know. Of course, this girl was making her intentions obvious, anyway, and then maybe Katie would know he didn't plan to ... or think he wanted to ... or could...

"Ryan." Fingers slid down his chest, her voice in his ear. "Yes or no? Tell me if I'm wasting my time."

"How about we take a walk?" He set his glass on the counter.

"A walk? After midnight? What, with your security detail following?"

"No. To the roof. We'll look out over the city." And get away from eyes and from having to ask anyone to leave.

"You? Look over the side of a building?"

"Nah, I'll stay well away from any edges." Her question sank in. "Wait. How in the hell do you know about my heights thing? I didn't..."

"Are you kidding? Everyone knows most everything about you. Height, weight, likes, dislikes. You haven't exactly been reclusive."

For a moment, Ryan had talked himself into believing he was just another guy, that she liked him for him, that ... that anyone he ever met might actually be interested in who he was other than the likes and dislikes, which weren't all exactly true, anyway. He grabbed his glass and took a good swallow.

"Sorry. I won't mention it again." She ran fingers up his arm to his shoulder. Painted bright red long nails caught his eye.

"Doesn't matter." He took another swallow. And set it down. He took hers, set it down, also, and grasped the hand with painted bright red nails. Leading her to the living room, he wondered if there were more people than a few minutes ago or whether they were only starting to bother him. It would be helpful, anyway. They could slip out pretty much unnoticed.

He meandered and visited as they moved to the door, with her stuck to his side. Before he walked out, he glanced over to make sure Deanna or Daws was still close to Kaitlyn ... and caught her eyes. She looked at the girl, at her hand on his stomach and his on the door handle, and looked away. Hell.

"You know what?" Ryan pulled back from whatever her name was. "I can't. Not tonight."

"Ryan..."

"No. Sorry. I ... I can't. Hell, you know I don't even remember your name, although I know you've told me at least three times..."

"Four. And it doesn't matter."

"Why doesn't it?"

She shrugged. "It's not like I want to marry you or anything. We had a really good time together. I thought it might be nice to have another one. Even if you don't remember it. I will." She slid her hands around to his back and pressed close against him, smelling of ... of something smart and sophisticated and high class ... and she didn't care if he knew her name.

Ryan backed up and picked her arms from his sides. "Sorry. Guess that's not good enough anymore. No offense."

"Fine." She yanked out of his grasp. "Your last CD was crap anyway. In a couple of years, no one will even remember your name. Then you'll know how it feels." Trotting off, she grabbed Ned and pressed in from behind.

Crap. It was crap. Like he didn't already know it was.

With a deep breath, he looked over to find Katie, to see if she noticed he didn't go anywhere with the girl. She wasn't there. Moving back toward the center of the room, he still didn't see her.

"She said she was going to bed." Deanna gave him that look.

"She's upset."

"Is that what you were trying to do?"

"Are you crazy? Why would I want her upset?"

"That's what I'm wondering." She walked away.

Ryan couldn't deal with Deanna's attitude until he talked to Katie. He went back to her room, pulling his arm from someone who tried to stop him, and knocked. No answer. "Katie? Hey, can I talk to you a minute?" Still no answer. There was light under the door. He knocked again. Getting nothing, he turned the handle. It was locked.

His stomach churned and he gripped it tighter, tried to force it to turn, called her name, knocked again ... and she opened it, only a couple of inches. "Were you trying to scare the hell out of me?"

She stared, with no emotion. Always, no emotion.

"Can I come in a minute?"

"I'm going to bed."

"I know, but just for a minute. I wanted..."

Daws tapped his shoulder. "Let the girl get some sleep. We'll start filtering people out of here."

"You don't have to." She looked at Daws, not at him.

"I think it's time." He gave Ryan a nudge.

"*Damn*, you're *not* my father. Don't fucking tell me when to go to *bed*."

Katie opened the door wider, still dressed, and swerved around them out to the other room.

Daws grabbed his arm. "You better make up your mind as to what you're trying to do."

"What I'm trying to do? Are you shitting me? I'm not trying to do anything except help her out. I gave her a fucking place to stay when she needed one and then I get yelled at for being too close to her so I back off and now I'm getting yelled at for that. What in the hell am I *supposed* to be doing?"

"Help her out? And you haven't come onto her at all?"

"No." He scratched his head. "Damn. Not ... I kissed her once. It was nothing. Twice. I ... hell." He leaned back against the wall. "I wasn't trying to come onto her, but it wasn't nothing, either."

"I think she should come stay with us for a while."

Ryan raised his eyes. "No."

Daws stepped closer. "Reynauld, if you want to play games with your own life, that's up to you. You cannot do it with hers. You really want her to walk away and go find another ledge?"

The pain in his stomach was almost impossible to hide. He covered by pulling away, following her. Except she nearly ran into him at the corner.

"I'm going to Deanna's tonight."

He couldn't answer. And she walked around him.

As soon as he could manage, he went to the living room and told the rest of whoever was still there to leave. He didn't care how it sounded. He didn't care that the girl who called his CD crap had her hand up the front of his guitar tech's shirt. He wanted them out.

Ryan flopped on the couch as they left. He knew Katie was putting clothes and such into her travel bag. He supposed Deanna was with her.

Daws closed the door behind the last of them and came over to sit in the adjacent chair. "What's going on with you?"

"Me?" Ryan snickered. "Nothing more than usual. I'm an arrogant, conceited bastard, remember? What's so surprising?"

"I never called you that."

"No, guess that was Deanna. Although she didn't use that exact term. It's what she meant. To you I'm just a moron, and I'm sure you're right."

"Get over yourself, Reynauld. If you need something, call. But it better be important." He went to meet the girls when they came out together. "Ready?"

Ryan didn't hear the answer if there was one and didn't bother to get up. He leaned his head back against the couch and closed his eyes. He wouldn't watch her walk out.

A presence beside him opened his eyes again and he barely had time to see it was Kaitlyn before she gave him a hug and got up. He did watch her leave. He didn't react. He couldn't.

Until it closed and he dashed to the bathroom, gripping one side of the sink while he leaned over the toilet to let his stomach release the bile.

She'd walked out.

Ryan washed his mouth and gargled with too much mouthwash. His palms pressed into the sink edges. She'd walked out. And he was too much of an idiot to stop her. He gave up. Like he gave up on the only other girl he cared about. He didn't fight. He backed away and let her leave him. Like he had ... at his father's memorial service. He'd walked out and refused to go back in, sitting instead on the cement steps in the back of the building by himself. Telling everyone who tried to comfort him to go away. He wanted to be left alone.

Except he didn't.

He didn't want to be left alone. He wasn't giving up on her. No more ledges. No more giving up.

After a couple of swallows of Maalox to coat his edgy stomach, he ran back through the loft, not bothering to lock the door on his way out. He could get to where Daws always parked before they left ... except he didn't have to go far. They were still at the elevator. Daws held the door open. Katie stood in front of it, her gaze on the floor.

"Don't go to Deanna's." Ryan slowed his pace and caught her eyes.

"I'm sorry. I was an ass. I don't want you to go, and I won't yell again, and..."

"I don't want to be in your way."

He shook his head. The girl. She meant the girl whose name he didn't even know. "You're not. I'm an idiot. I ... I'm sorry. I don't want you to go. Of course ... I don't mean to try to say you can't. If you'd rather stay there, it's up to you of course, but not because..." Ryan grabbed a deep breath.

She took a few steps closer. "Do you want me here? It's okay if you don't."

"Kaitlyn. Yes. I want you here. Stay. Please, stay."

She turned and walked away. His heart pounded while he thought about how to change her mind. But she took her bag from Daws and walked back to him. Ryan claimed it. And he answered his guard's question before it came. "Don't worry. I promise I'll be good."

"You better be." Deanna touched Kaitlyn's lower arm, the only place Deanna could touch her without making her pull back. "Call me if you need, no matter what time."

"Hell, don't act like she has to be scared of me."

"I never would have thought so, Ryan, but no one knows who you are anymore."

"Katie knows me." He caught her eyes. "Are you worried about staying?"

She shook her head.

"You're sure? Because you can say so. I won't blame you."

"I trust you more than anyone."

Ryan knew it hurt Deanna's feelings for her to say so, but he was so incredibly relieved, he couldn't care.

Away from the stares and back in the loft, he took her bag to her room and turned to find her behind him.

"Why did you let Jameson leave when you didn't want her to leave?"

"Who?" The girl who wanted to stay. "Oh. Jameson. I can't ever remember that name." He probably shouldn't have admitted that. "I let her leave because I wanted her to leave. I wanted everyone to leave, except you." Her look said she knew better. "Okay, for a few minutes I didn't. What can I say? I'm not used to being ... on my own for so long, so to speak. But I didn't ... I can't say this without it sounding as bad as it is. My history with girls ... well, I've...."

She ran a hand up to his shoulder and leaned in to kiss his cheek. Then she moved away to unpack.

"I should let you get to bed." He went to the door and looked back to find her watching him. "I'm glad you stayed."

~~~

"Do you want to pay attention?"

Ryan looked up at his publicist and did his best to ignore the fire in his stomach. "Why? We've been over this already."

"On top of the pictures we've been over already, now we have that groupie of yours telling anyone who'll listen that you're so wrapped around the girl you won't even talk to anyone else. This *has* to be answered. We can't keep ignoring it."

Ryan glanced at the photos spread out in front of him: the first one at the café where they had lunch and various shots taken from the tour, even a couple out by the boat Ryan couldn't figure how anyone got. One of them was nice quality. He'd have to grab a copy of it. "You want me to answer them? Fine. Tell them to fuck off. I don't care what they think."

"Lovely. That'll go over well with parents of the kids listening to your music."

He leaned forward in the guise of being tired and propped his head on his hand, elbow on top of one of the photos. "*Nothing* is going on."

"Which doesn't matter, of course, since it looks like something's going on. You've *got* to get her out of your place. Take her back to your family. Get her out of town. Let this blow over."

"And then what?" He straightened again. "Never see her again? Claim she's related as we started to do?"

"Good first steps."

"Bullshit." He shoved away from the table and bolted from his chair. "Just fucking tell them she's twenty-one. How are they gonna know? So she looks young for her age..."

"Is she twenty-one, Reynauld?"

He dropped his gaze, hands clenching. "It doesn't matter."

"You don't know? Or you won't say?"

Eyes blazing across the room, he didn't care if the whole damn building heard him. "Because it doesn't fucking *matter*. Don't you *get* it? I'm actually being the good boy, doing what I *should* be doing, or rather *not* doing what I shouldn't be doing, and there is *nothing* going on. So it really doesn't fucking *matter* how *old* she is." A sharp pain in his stomach nearly doubled him over.

Daws came to his side and gripped his arm. "It's acting up again."

"Just get me out of here." He looked back at the publicist. "And you'll say nothing about her I don't okay. Understood? 'Cause if you do, you're fired."

Daws walked with him to his rental and kept hold of one arm as though he was going to fly away. "You're not driving." He stopped him from trying to get in his door. "Get in the back."

"Bullshit."

"They're waiting to follow you."

"How in the hell do you know?"

"It's my job to know. Just get in the back and lie down, which looks like a good idea anyway. When they see it's me, they'll back off and I can get you to a doctor without a media circus trailing us."

"I don't need a doctor."

"Reynauld..."

"Take me home." Doctor or not, the last thing he wanted was a media circus. Crawling into the back, he reclined on the leather seat, one arm over his stomach and the other under his head. Ryan couldn't imagine how they could ask him to ship her off to Will's permanently, to not see her again. What in the hell else did he have? They'd already taken his music from him. It was never quite his anymore. And they were already keeping Katie from him enough. Any other guy would be free to be with his nineteen-year-old girlfriend without a bunch of hassle about it. Without having to explain. Maybe they could just tell her age. She was legal. Barely. It still wouldn't look good.

They could say she was twenty-one. If she had no one, who was to argue? Who would know?

Glad Daws listened and took him to his loft, although Ryan heard him call Deanna about a doctor, he straightened as well as he could in order to get into his building without unnecessary attention. The elevator ride was hell, with its lurching starts and stops and people joining them. Deanna was with Katie, in the loft. If Daws told her ... he hoped she wouldn't have said anything, although it wasn't like she wouldn't know, unless he could pull off being tired and say he needed to sleep, getting out of her vision.

As soon as he was through his door, that plan was shot to hell. A sudden urge of nausea sent him to the bathroom. He held his stomach as though he had an actual fire he could quench with pressure. Daws was there, waiting, and held him up while he washed himself as well as he could and gargled a ton of mouthwash to get rid of that taste.

He trudged into the main room and fell onto his couch, his head dropped against the back. Deanna said a doctor was on his way and would be sure not to look like a doctor so there wouldn't be questions from anyone who saw him enter.

Katie lowered next to him and set a hand on his forehead. "You're not hot."

Despite the pain, he couldn't help grinning at her. "Still not a great thing to say to a guy."

Her eyes ... watered. They stayed in control otherwise, but it was so much more emotion than he had ever seen before he thought it was nearly worth the pain to see she still had it somewhere inside. "It's nothing. Don't worry." At another pain, he clenched his eyes and dropped his head back again.

Sliding her arm beneath his head to keep it more upright, she slid the other hand across his chest up to his shoulder, pressing in close. "I'm beside you on the ledge. Remember."

A bleeding ulcer. Close to surgery stage but not quite there yet. Ryan dropped his head back at the words. *Riveting* Ryan Reynauld. Bullshit. He was a pansy putting on a big show. So much for disguising the doctor so no one would find out. The first thing the man did was call an ambulance. It would be everywhere. How his publicist would make this sound less embarrassing, he didn't know. She would change the facts, he supposed, turn it into something more interesting, use it for attention.

And he didn't care. At least the attention would be about something other than Katie.

Weary with the whole thing, he closed his eyes and tried not to dwell on the two mandatory days in the hospital. She would stay with Deanna until he could go home. At least he knew she would be okay there.

Part Two

"You stand there turned away, afraid to let me see
what lies behind the lies you've heard,
   the reasons you won't believe I'm real
   but I see anyway
I see you want to feel, more than you allow
You keep turning, I'll keep moving
   around
  to the other side, 'cause windows have two sides
  and birds are meant to fly..."

(from **Birds and Windows**, ©2000 Ryan Reynauld)

10

"C'mon Reynauld, it's time to get your lazy ass out of bed."

Ryan pulled away. "Leave me alone."

"Sorry, impossible. Your flight leaves shortly and you might want to be dressed."

"Flight?" He shoved at his hair and looked at Daws. "I need time off. You heard the docs. They said I need time off. I'm not doing any damn flight for anything."

"So I should tell Kaitlyn you refuse to take her to England where she still has one relative?"

"What?"

"Told you I was checking into things. Seems she has an uncle in England, musician, believe it or not. An American who floats between the two countries. You're taking her. It'll get you out of here for a while. Of course, you're stuck with us since it seemed a good bargaining chip for Anna to get me to take her over."

Ryan sat up. "Wait. An uncle? She said she had no family."

"My guess is she doesn't know. She also doesn't know why we're going other than to give you time to rest without photographers in your face." An uncle. Musician. Pushing himself out of bed and to the shower, Ryan wondered what kind of musician, and how in the hell Daws found out about him if Katie didn't know.

Rubbed nearly dry, he wrapped the towel around and went back to his room to air dry more before he dressed. He couldn't stand putting clothes over tacky skin, which made no sense, as often as he got tacky, or worse, while playing. Hell, he usually ended up with sweat running down his back into his shorts on stage. Still, he didn't need to start out that way, and hopefully he wouldn't get that way on the flight to England.

Did she have a passport? Why would she have?

He went out to grab Daws and nearly ran into her. When she glanced at his chest, Ryan pulled the shirt he was carrying over his head. "Daws says we're heading out of country. Did he bother to ask if you have a passport?"

"She has one." Deanna's voice interrupted from behind Kaitlyn. "You don't think we know enough to get her a passport for an overseas trip?"

"But it takes..."

"Freddy got it in process when you started talking about dragging her along on tour. He didn't want last minute issues."

"I haven't been overseas since..."

"But you will be. Are you ready to go?"

"Are you insane? I haven't packed."

Daws joined them. "You have five minutes to grab anything I don't already know you'll want. The bag's in your closet. Let's go."

Too frazzled to keep asking questions, Ryan glanced at Kaitlyn and went back to check his bag. After a quick perusal, he closed it and dragged it to the living room. "How in the hell long have you been planning this?"

Daws raised his eyebrows. "Since I had to hold your ass up at the toilet. Not something I want to keep doing. Get your jacket. It'll be colder over there."

In the elevator, no one spoke. Ryan wanted a minute alone with Kaitlyn, to ask her why they knew about the uncle when she'd told him there was no one. Had she lied to him? He never in the world would have expected she would. Maybe it was better they didn't have time alone. He had to sort it through his scattered brain. There was a reason. Or maybe Daws was right and she didn't know.

He tried to get in the back of the car with her but Deanna pushed him up to the front. Why? Did she know what was coming? The question he had to ask? He had the right to ask. The whole thing ... her whole *act* if that's what it was, revolved around her needing his help because she had no one. Was it a set up? Was it all an act to get to him? Another crazy obsessed fan ... it would explain why she'd been trying to get closer, why she'd kissed him when he tried to keep his distance. Why she'd been on the ledge of the building across from where he worked. How long had she been trying, standing by the window waiting to see if he would come up? But how would she know he would?

"You wanna stop for food first? We won't get much on the plane."

Ryan shrugged. "Go ahead if you want. I don't want anything." He switched the radio station away from the whining high-pitched voice.

"You've barely eaten in days." Deanna leaned up and set a hand on his shoulder. "You should try."

"I'm not hungry." His stomach was upset again. Instantly. She'd lied to him. "I hope to hell you packed the Maalox."

"Front pocket, but take it easy with that stuff until you get something else inside you."

"I'm fine." He reached down into his carry-on and took a swallow. He wasn't fine. She'd lied to him. It was an act. Ryan figured he'd seen enough damn acts by this point to know one when he saw it. She could qualify for an Oscar nomination. He switched the station again. Romantic gushy wasn't what he wanted, either.

While his eyes drifted along the city traffic, and while he refused to order anything and kept his head turned so the cashier wouldn't recognize him, Ryan saw her face as it had been when they met. That wasn't an act. The emaciated pale skin wasn't an act. The eyes ... no, it couldn't be. Forcing deep breaths and seeing the images of her expression whenever she looked at him, and the blankness of when she looked at anyone else, the only difference in her eyes, Ryan knew there was an explanation. He hoped to hell there was an explanation.

He refused to eat the chicken sandwich Daws ordered for him and stuck it in his carry-on in case anyone wanted it later. Wasting food was strictly prohibited in his house ... in his mom's house. There were too many times they barely had enough. Waste, even when they did have more than enough, was against the rules.

The hat and fake glasses Deanna threw at him before he got out of the car worked well enough and they managed to get onto the plane without notice. In the commotion of packing stuff into overhead bins, he found himself beside his friend while Deanna guarded Kaitlyn. She seemed nervous. Ryan wondered if she had ever flown anywhere. If she had an uncle in England, he supposed it was possible. Hell, maybe she even had the passport already. When the stewardess asked everyone to take their seats and fasten their seatbelts to prepare for takeoff, Ryan stood and finagled his way around Daws.

"Gonna need to be held up?"

With only a glance to answer, Ryan told Deanna to trade him places. She hesitated, but he didn't back down. Settled again, he found Kaitlyn's eyes. The wariness she had first shown him was back. He hoped to hell it was nerves about flying.

"Have you done this before?" He started with the easy question. She didn't know the actual purpose of the trip. Ryan suspected Deanna was afraid he would let it spill. And he would if he decided to.

She shook her head. Nerves. She was afraid of flying. Of everything except him, so she had said. Still, she also looked wary of him.

"I uh ... haven't been myself recently." He watched her expression although it didn't change. "It's an occasional thing. I've had it for years. I don't want you to worry."

At the engine's slide into a light roar, she looked out the window, her fingers gripping the arm rests.

"And you're more concerned about the flight right now. It's safer than driving, you know."

Turning back, she shook her head again.

"Really. There are statistics. You're more likely to be in a car crash than..."

"I'm not." She continued at his confusion. "More concerned about the flight than about you. I'm not."

A deep breath consumed him. She didn't lie. There was nothing but honesty in her eyes. There never had been. "Katie." He leaned in and pried her hand from the armrest, wrapping it in both of his. "I have to ask you something, and I'm not sure you'll understand why I'm asking. But I need to know." He was glad she didn't pull away. His voice low, the surrounding noise kept it hidden. "When you said you had no one, how did you mean it? Literally? Or no one you want to be around? Or...?" Ryan waited to let her fill in the blank.

"No one I *can* be around, who wants me around." She held a question on her face before deciding to share it. "Am I too hard on you?"

"No."

The aircraft began to back up and the movement startled her, but her attention stayed on him.

He raised her hand, and there, regardless of who was paying attention, Ryan kissed her fingers. "The ulcer is because I needed to get away from work. And I truly look forward to spending time with you without fans following us, and the band and ... and maybe we'll have to rent a boat and go cruise one of the lakes. What do you think?"

She turned to watch out the window, not withdrawing her hand, but not encouraging him, either. Ryan couldn't blame her. The last time she'd encouraged him, he pulled away, told her he couldn't. And he still couldn't. But maybe in time he could. Maybe he could let her know that in time, when everything was more stable, maybe he could.

~~~

Ryan insisted his friends leave them alone for their first night in London. He wanted to take Kaitlyn to his favorite restaurant and then walk along the city sidewalks as though they were residents, sight-seeing without obviously sight-seeing, enjoying the dark and the lights and laughter of Londoners as they bumped from pub to pub in groups and couples.

She barely spoke to him, only enough to be polite. It was all right. He would earn her trust again. Aware it could take longer the second time, he didn't push, didn't grasp her hand as they walked. And he didn't keep her out as long as he would like to have stayed out among the misty summer air. They'd been up for a day and a half and he wasn't sure if she'd slept on the eight hour flight as he did.

Daws had booked a suite, a living area with two rooms and a sofa bed. It wouldn't have been Ryan's choice. It allowed Daws to keep an eye on where he was, if he was anywhere other than the sofa. Not that it mattered; where else would he be? Still, it was grating even if his friend insisted it was for "looks" in case anyone noticed.

Kaitlyn went to bed soon after they returned to the hotel, although Daws and Deanna were still out somewhere and they had the living area alone. With a sigh, Ryan called Will for a few minutes to let him know they were there and all was okay, and kicked back with a droning British voice on the television as company.

The next day was organized sight-seeing, things Deanna wanted to tour while in the city. Much of it, Ryan had already seen: Buckingham Palace and the Queen's gardens, Big Ben, the huge Ferris Wheel that nearly made him sick just by looking up at it, the art museum and shops along the Thames River complete with performers of all sorts, and lunch at a little Greek place with outdoor café. After lunch, a cab to the other end to see the Tower of London and London Bridge and St. Paul's Cathedral. Kaitlyn wouldn't say if there was anything in particular she wanted to see, even though she did go through the guidebook Deanna gave her during the flight. They all exchanged glances when she threw out facts about what they saw, without the book. The longer the day progressed, though, the more withdrawn she became. She said less, looked at sites but didn't pay much attention to them, and refused to meet Ryan's gaze.

She was tired. It took a couple of days to recover from jet lag. And Daws insisted they all go out together that night to a club he'd "read about" or so he said. Ryan knew his friend was chasing leads, looking for the uncle. He couldn't ask, though. It would seem more treasonous to Kaitlyn if they talked about it. He was doing nothing this way except running around London with her. Ryan knew it was possible the uncle wouldn't be found. There was no sense making her think he would be.

Another pub the next night. He didn't mind. It had been some time since he'd been able to jump in and out of bars and sit back and listen to local musicians as one of the crowd. Ryan loved it. He worried about her, though. She refused to sight-see earlier in the day with no reason given, so he hung around and asked if she would go to the hotel pool with him. She refused that, too, but said he should go. He didn't, until Deanna came back for a "rest" while Daws was out on "business."

Hoping Deanna would tell Katie since she and Daws were running the thing, Ryan went for a swim alone, doing laps to the point of near exhaustion in an attempt to work out why she was withdrawing, why she barely spoke to him, and why, if she knew how to swim, she wouldn't. He was more jealous of Deanna the more Kaitlyn looked to her for any kind of communication. He understood the female thing but other than female things, he didn't understand. Was he supposed to take unfair advantage of how vulnerable she was? Let her kiss him and return it as he longed to do when it wasn't what she needed? It was the right thing. He was doing what was right. Why in the hell was it backfiring on him?

More frustrated the longer he was there alone, he pushed out of the water, scrubbed himself dry, and headed back to the suite. He barely started up the stairs before he turned around again and went to the front desk. Finding an available separate room with two beds on the same floor, he booked it and went up to let her know he had, and that she could either stay in the suite or take the second bed in the separate room. It would be her choice. If she wanted distance, she could have it.

He didn't have the chance to ask. The girls were nearly ready to go, with reservations at some restaurant already made, and Daws was about to retrieve him and pull him back. He had only a few minutes to shower and dress and blow his hair half dry.

Ryan almost refused to go, but decided it would be too far.

"How often have you been to London?" Her eyes touched his.

Amazing. One simple question, breaking her silence through the first half of dinner, and all irritation with her vanished. Ryan set his glass of wine down and considered the answer. "Oh, I think ... four or five times. We've done a few shows around here." He wanted to grab her up in his arms.

"Where are the fans?"

He shrugged. "We're not so big in the UK, which is why I like tp play here as I can. We're still at the 'try to win them over' stage and it's nice, more satisfying. Sound crazy?"

She shook her head and Deanna joined in their private conversation. When they went on to the pub, Ryan would attempt to pull her away from the others as he could. There were too many interruptions, from everywhere.

Satisfied that she walked next to him down the sidewalk, close enough their arms touched when they moved for people heading the opposite direction, he risked grasping her fingers, lightly. She could easily pull away if she decided. Instead, she slipped her hand more firmly into his and kept it there as they entered the dark, crowded pub.

It was easy enough to find a table for four since it was still early, and he held her chair and moved his closer to hers than it had been. A young couple recognized him and stopped only long enough to say hello and get his autograph.

Katie tried his wine when he offered although she didn't like the other he'd had at the restaurant. Ryan figured he would keep switching until he found what she did like since she didn't know. She drank water. He could rarely get her to drink anything else.

Applause spattered through the room, close to the stage, and Ryan looked over to see the band wander up to take their places and ready their equipment. He found himself longing for the days he could wander up to a small stage without security, with some applause from a few loyal fans and a few who were only being polite. Although, he had to admit it wouldn't be long before he'd want to return to huge auditoriums and so many offers he couldn't take them all.

One of them looked familiar and Ryan sipped his wine while he tried to decide who the musician reminded him of ... and Katie got up and walked away.

He exchanged looks with Daws and went to follow. As fast as she was moving, she was out on the sidewalk before Ryan caught up with her. She didn't stop at her name. He had to grab her arm.

She swung around. "Why didn't you tell me?"

"Tell you what?"

"That's why we're here? Why? How could you not tell me ... *ask* me? I've been waiting. You didn't say anything. *Why?*"

"Your uncle."

"You knew." She pulled away and nearly jogged down the sidewalk, in the opposite direction from which they'd come.

He caught up. "Katie, stop a minute." Ryan expected it might not be a good idea to take her arm again, so kept walking. "This *wasn't* my idea."

She paused. "You knew."

"Yes."

Her pace quickened.

"But I didn't think we'd actually find him. I figured ... you said there was no one. I didn't expect to find anyone..." His voice trailed off and he stopped, calling her name to let her know.

She kept going.

He wondered how far she would walk down a mostly dark London sidewalk by herself. "Katie..." He was too tired to chase her, worn out from the pool, weary from the wine at dinner and at the pub, his stomach telling him wine was the last thing he should have put in it. Still, she didn't stop. So he pushed himself to start after her again. "Hey come on. I'm too *tired* for this." Still, she kept going.

Coming to a stop, Ryan vacillated between worry and anger. Did she expect him to let her walk away by herself? She had money for a cab if she needed one. Ryan had insisted she carry a few British pounds, in case. Still, it was the middle of a city in a foreign country, dark, and a Saturday night when too many single men were out drinking and looking for company.

He started to follow again when she turned a corner, and picked up his speed despite the fire in his stomach. He didn't see her when he turned the same direction. His heart nearly stopped, then started beating loud enough he could hear it. "*Katie?*" His yell turned a few heads but not the right one. His fast walk became a jog; his head turned everywhere he saw movement. There were several open restaurants and pubs and he glanced in each as he passed. She had to have gone into one of them. Getting farther down than he figured she would have gone, Ryan turned back, crossed the road, and looked into businesses open on that side.

Then he grabbed his cell and dialed Daws.

"Hey, where are you? Think we found the right one."

"Well that's *fuckin' dandy* but I don't know *where* in the hell she is."

"What do you mean?"

"What in the hell do *you think* I mean? She walked *away* from me. She is truly pissed off and wants nothing to do with me now. Thank you for this. Some *stupid* fucking idea this was. *Why* do I listen to you?"

"Reynauld, calm down. Where are you?"

"I'm in the middle of fucking London with *no* idea where she is. Did you *not hear* me?" He ignored the looks he got for screaming into the phone while he rushed up and down the sidewalk and looked through windows.

"All right. We're on the way. What direction? What street are you on?"

"Left."

"Left from where?"

"From the fucking pub where you apparently found an uncle she *doesn't want* to see. Where in the hell do you *think* I mean left from?"

"You're going to have to calm down. They'll arrest you for public disturbance."

"Tell me to calm down again and I'll *break* your fucking jaw when you get here." Seeing a road name stuck to the side of a building, he gave it to Daws and hung up. He would have to go into any place that was open. But then she could leave another and he wouldn't see her. At least out on the sidewalk, he had a good chance of spotting her from wherever she came out of ... if she was still on this street somewhere and not down farther or around a different corner.

"Are y' alright, mate?"

He swung around to the hand on his shoulder and apologized when the man jumped. "No, my girl is here somewhere. She's pissed and I have to find her."

"Canno' hold her drink?"

"What?" Still looking around at every movement, Ryan realized the phrase difference. "No, not pissed drunk, pissed angry ... American-style pissed."

"Ahhh. Y' want help lookin' around?"

Ryan wondered at the stranger offering help, but he couldn't refuse it. He gave him a brief description and his phone number, thanked him, and crossed the road again, still trying to decide if he should go in and search or stay where he was or try another street.

A couple more times down the sidewalk, going farther than before to peer down both directions at the intersection, and returning, Ryan stopped. He leaned back against a brick building, dropped his head against it, and forced breaths. Why had he let her get so far ahead? She felt betrayed. She'd asked if she was too hard on him. And she thought he was trying to find someone else to dump her on, he supposed. He should have told her. He should have said he didn't want to dump her, to let her go with anyone else. He should have just said he was falling for her and trying hard not to, that he was afraid it would hurt her. He should have let her kiss him if it was what she wanted.

The pain in his stomach worsened and he knew he deserved it. Where was she? She couldn't be out there alone ... alone. He promised she would never be alone, but she was. And it was his fault. Even if she was the one to walk away, it was his fault. He betrayed her, as he stupidly thought she had done before. *No one she could be with.* So she knew where to find the uncle, but she couldn't be with him. Why? Why hadn't Ryan asked why there was someone she couldn't be with?

The one that looked familiar. Ryan hadn't thought about it at the time, but his accent sounded American with some British absorbed into it. Why did he look familiar? Trying to picture his face again, Ryan felt a soft hand on his arm.

Deanna.

"She walked away. My stomach was burning like hell and I stopped, only for a few seconds, but she was moving fast, around the corner and..."

Deanna put her arms around him. "Don't worry. We'll find her."

"How?" He pulled back and glanced at Daws but didn't dare say what he was thinking. "I've been up and down here, trying to look inside but I don't know ... she could be half way to anywhere by now. If ... if something hasn't happened." He pressed a hand against his stomach.

Her touch to his face did nothing to calm him. "She's smart, honey. She's probably inside somewhere trying to be alone for a few minutes."

"She *can't* be alone. Don't you *get* it?"

"Ryan." Daws pushed in. "Go back to the hotel and see if she shows up there. We'll keep looking around here and call..."

"No way in hell. I'm not leaving here until I find her."

"She knows where the hotel is. When she's ready, she'll go back."

"She doesn't have a fucking key because she wouldn't take it. How would she get in?"

"The front desk..."

"She *doesn't talk to anyone. Damn*! Don't you *understand* how *serious* this is? She doesn't..." He shoved away from them and paced the sidewalk again. Yes, maybe most people would go back to the hotel, but he couldn't imagine she would. Where would she go? With a horrid thought hitting his brain, he moved to the edge of the sidewalk and peering up at each building. She wouldn't. Ryan knew she wouldn't, but he wasn't completely sure she wouldn't.

He heard Daws say he would go back the other direction and look inside pubs, leaving Deanna with Ryan. He argued he didn't need a babysitter. She said she would take the opposite side of the street.

With a glance at his phone, Ryan cringed finding an hour and a half had passed. Something had happened. She knew his cell number. If she'd gone back to the hotel ... if she'd found the courage to ask to be let into the room, she would have called by now. Where was she?

Exhausted and burning with pain, he leaned back against a building and crouched down, dropping his head into his hands. He was a moron. Daws was right. He handled everything wrong. He should have found her real help right away. She still could have stayed with him, but maybe someone could have helped them both figure out where to go from there.

He jumped when Deanna touched his head.

"Freddy found her."

Forcing himself to his feet, he almost didn't want to ask.

"She's fine. She went back to the hotel. She's been waiting there, in the lobby. She won't go up to the room with him so he's sitting with her. I've called a cab. It'll be here in a few minutes."

Ryan bolted to the edge of the sidewalk to watch for it. He couldn't just stand and so walked in the direction of the hotel. Deanna was right beside him but he couldn't talk to her. He couldn't talk. He had to see Kaitlyn. Daws saying she was fine meant next to nothing to him. He had to see her.

The cab ride was too long, though the distance wasn't far, and he jumped out and let Deanna pay the fare. He'd pay her back later. He had to see Katie.

She was curled on the edge of a big couch in the corner of the huge lobby, one leg pulled up with her arms wrapped around, her attention on anyone who came anywhere close. She unwrapped herself when she saw him, standing, staying beside the couch. Her eyes were wary.

He stopped several feet away. There were people around, not close, but around. "Are you all right?"

She stared, silent.

"Kaitlyn, I'm sorry. I didn't ... I didn't think we'd find him and ... I didn't know..."

"Your stomach is bad again." She studied his movements.

"I was scared to death. I was afraid..."

"You want to leave me here."

"No. Katie, I don't want to leave you anywhere. I didn't ... I was hoping we wouldn't find him. Is that horrible? I was afraid ... if you found family, you wouldn't need me, and I want you to need me."

Emotions broke through her always-the-same expression. She fought watering eyes. "It wouldn't matter who I found."

A deep breath consumed him, gave him time to consider her words. *It wouldn't matter.* Starting toward her slowly, he nearly jogged the next few steps and closed her in his arms, clasping her head against his shoulder. "Don't run from me again. Katie, don't run from me."

Daws suggested they move upstairs to the suite. Yes, he wanted privacy. And he hoped Katie would agree to move to the other room with him. He wanted to be able to wake up and see her in the next bed.

Explaining the second room, he used the excuse of needing time to talk to her alone, but only if she was comfortable moving. She nodded and went to get her things. Deanna suggested she and Daws would move instead so Ryan and Katie would have private rooms. He brushed it off as she returned to him. He didn't want that much separation.

As they settled into the smaller space, Ryan fidgeted with the air and the curtains and moved stuff around that didn't need to be moved. He wanted to be on his feet, to keep things flowing, to prevent the awkwardness he felt in not knowing what to say to her next. He wanted to ask about him, about the uncle and why she didn't want to see him, but he figured it wasn't the best place to start. There were so many things he wanted to ask. And he didn't know if he could. If she would want him to ask. If she would answer or ignore the questions.

He paused at the curtains and peered out into the semi-dark of London. A light fog covered the ground enough to make the street hazy. Still, it was a nice view. The hotel was in the heart of the city and he could see people drift along the dark sidewalks luminated by street lamps and by businesses with well-lit windows and doorways. Where were they going? Were they local or travelers? What had they done with their days? What would they do with their tomorrows?

Ryan turned when she touched his back. She didn't speak, except to throw what looked like an invitation with her eyes, waiting for him to react. The room was warm and she had removed the light sweater she had over a fitted tee while they were out, hiding herself more than she was now. She had a nice figure since she gained enough weight to look healthy, still small but more feminine, round enough....

He touched her hair, pushed one side behind her ear to find more of her face. "Why don't you want to see him?" He hadn't meant to ask, but it came out.

Her chest rose and fell. "I tried. After ... when his band was playing close by, in another town but one I could get to, I went ... I wasn't supposed to go. It was against the rules and I knew ... but if I got to him, I wouldn't have had to go back." Emotion had started to grow in her voice and she stopped until it was under control again. "I thought ... when I was little we ... I thought he would..." She stopped again.

"You expected he would take you in. This was after you lost your parents?"

She nodded, barely.

"And he wouldn't?"

She bit her bottom lip, only for a second. "They wouldn't let me see him. I told them I was his niece and they wouldn't believe me. I ... I left a note ... to tell him where I was."

"They?"

"Security. It wasn't like tonight. It was ... a big place, lots of security. Like at yours."

"What was his band's name?"

Her eyes touched his. She didn't want to answer. And it wasn't what mattered.

"He didn't come find you."

She shook her head. "I wrote letters, a lot. I asked him to come."

Letters ... and security. "There's a good chance he never got them."

"They said they would tell him."

"Yeah. Well, I rather doubt they did. They get stories like that all the time, some girl who claims to be related or a friend or ... anything to get backstage. They can't pass along all of those notes or letters. There isn't enough time to read them all with everything else. I barely read any of mine." He slid his hand down her shoulder to grasp her fingers. "You were close to him when you were young?" A nod answered. "Why didn't they contact him? The authorities should have..."

She walked away and sat on the edge of one of the beds, a leg pulled up underneath.

He was pushing. Ryan knew he was pushing. But something told him he couldn't let up, not now while she was saying so much. He went to her side and wrapped his arms around her.

"I wasn't there." Her head dropped onto his shoulder. "I ran." Her fingers tightened. "There was ... a stranger. Dad was away. My stepmom told me to hide."

Ryan felt her shake and held her closer. A stranger. In the house, he assumed. He wouldn't interrupt to ask.

"But she screamed and she kept screaming and ... I wanted to help. I ... went back to find the phone and called his work to tell him to come and ...." She stopped; the shaking grew worse.

Ryan stroked her hair. "You're all right now, Katie. Breathe a minute. It's all right now. You're safe."

She shook her head. "He saw me ... and I ran. Outside. It was cold and ... I kept running because I heard him. He yelled at me to stop. He said ... he said he would kill them both if I didn't stop, and I did, but he got closer and he was big and ... I kept running."

Eyes clenched, Ryan couldn't say anything. He held her, stroked her hair, and kissed the side of her head. After quite some time, he felt her start to relax, her breathing slow. He kissed her head again. "How old were you?"

"Eight … seven." Her head shook. "I forget."

"I don't understand. Did you go to a neighbor's? Wouldn't they have taken you to where the authorities could find your uncle?"

"There were no neighbors. We were … out … just moved, to … it was like a forest. I don't remember where. I didn't know anyone."

"If you told them your parents' names…"

"I couldn't." She tensed again. Pulling from his grasp, she returned to the window.

He followed but didn't impose on her space. He waited close by.

"I can't. It's too much. I can't…"

"Okay." He moved up and touched her back and she jumped. "I'm sorry. Should I…?"

Kaitlyn fell against him and held him the way she did when he pulled her from the ledge. She blamed herself for her parents' … murder? Were they? Or did she only think they were and get too scared to go back to check? Had she been hiding from the truth the whole time? They would have found her, though, if they weren't.

Either way, she'd had enough for the night. They would talk more about it another time when it wasn't so late and she wasn't so worn out. When he wasn't. He had her back. She was talking to him, more than ever. Maybe he hadn't screwed up as much as he thought.

"Do you want to shower before bed? It might help you unwind."

She shook her head against him.

"Katie…" Ryan stopped, with no idea what he planned to say.

After a few minutes of quiet while she stood and held him, she met his eyes. "I'm sorry I scared you. I … seeing him … I've tried to forget…"

"That's understandable. And I should have told you what we were doing. But I didn't want your hopes up if…"

"You didn't want to find him."

Choking on his guilt, Ryan wished to hell he had never admitted that. "I uh … I only meant … I know, I'm a selfish ass. I always have been. But I can't…." With a deep breath, he figured he might as well say it all and quit trying to pretend he was more than he was. "I don't want him to take you away from me. I don't want anyone to take you away from me. I … I have never felt as alive as I have since I met you and … I feel more for you than I wanted, than I should, and I'm trying very hard not to. I know I'm not … you need something better than this. I can't…."

Her hands slid around from his lower back to his stomach, up, nearly to his chest. Her eyes were on his. "It's okay."

Okay. Ryan wanted to ask her exactly what was okay. That he felt the way he did or that he could kiss her the way he wanted to kiss her?

Which did she mean? Why was so much of what she said in code?

When he didn't answer or react, Katie pulled away.

He caught her hand. She didn't look at him when he moved back in front of her, when he raised the other hand to her hair, again brushed it out of his way. And she didn't stop him when he found her lips.

It was a soft kiss, wary, questioning, all on his part. Until she returned her hands to his waist, slid them around to his back, pulled herself in closer. And he let go of shoulds, of Daws's voice in his mind telling him to be careful, she was too young, it was too dangerous for his career; of Will referring to him as a big brother; of his mom accepting her as family, as a daughter; of his own misgivings. He wrapped a hand around the back of her head, held her into him, kissed her more deeply, watching for signs she wanted him to stop. There weren't any. No hesitation, no drawing back, no pushing away. She allowed him as close as he wanted to get.

As he realized he was starting to want way too much, he broke off the kiss and moved his lips to the side of her head, to just above her ear, to her ear lobe she'd kept hidden from him for so long. Her head tilted back, fingers dug deeper into his skin, her breath became more rapid, raising her chest against his at regular, quick intervals. Her eyes were closed, trusting him. Wanting him.

Ryan studied her face while he moved his fingers against it, caressed her closed eyelids, her cheek, her lips. And he realized how blind he'd been. She wanted him. Possibly more than any girl he'd ever known, Katie wanted him honestly.

He kissed her again and paid more attention to her movements than to his own, to how she reacted to everything he did, every move of his fingers, his lips, his body pressing in.

They were close to the bed. He moved them closer, slowly, not breaking contact. She tensed. Too far. He was pushing too far. It was why he'd kept so much distance. He knew he would push too far.

"I'm sorry. I didn't mean to suggest..."

"It's okay."

Ryan found her eyes. "What's okay, Kaitlyn? What exactly is okay? Tell me."

She ran fingers down his chest. "What you want."

What *he* wanted. She was giving in because *he* wanted it? He shook his head. "I can't..."

"I belong to you."

The phrase pushed him back, away from her. It was gratitude. She was offering herself ... as gratitude? Because he wanted it? No. Not with her. He had to admit it wasn't something he would usually turn down, but she wasn't like the others. He had never in his life been with a girl who wasn't fairly experienced. Being with him wouldn't have changed their lives one way or another. It didn't matter. "No." He stepped back farther. "Not because I want it. Not because you think you owe me something. You don't owe me anything. I won't do that to you, even if you think it's okay now. Because you won't. It won't be okay. I'll lose you."

"No."

With another couple of steps backward, Ryan felt the urge to go find a pub, a crowded pub, and get lost within it, within some stranger's arms who didn't matter to him and who he wouldn't matter to. It was easier.

"You're the only thing I still have that I would care about losing." With that, she returned to the window.

Ryan saw an image of a small bird with her wings clipped as he gazed at her. He was the only thing she cared about losing? What about Deanna? They'd become close. At least he thought they had. She was opening to his family. She was doing so much better. Why was he still the only...?

His lungs ballooned so full it almost hurt. Moisture tinged his eyes. It didn't matter if he was good enough. As he told Daws, it only mattered that he gave a shit. As Will said, it mattered that he kept trying.

Her hair fell soft over her shoulders, the wispy ends showing it hadn't been cut in some time. The straightness of her back – she always carried herself well – rounded into the arch of her waist beneath the shirt that showed every curve. The Dockers she wore instead of jeans – she wouldn't wear jeans – highlighted the roundness of her thighs. And he was the only thing she cared about losing. He saw her face again after he'd kissed her, while he explored it with his fingers, after he kissed the scar on her ear she no longer hid from him. She'd told him of what had to be her greatest guilt. She said he wouldn't lose her. It didn't matter who she found. Maybe part of her didn't want to find her uncle for the reason Ryan didn't want to find him. They were afraid he would try to pull her away. She didn't want it any more than he did.

Ryan went to her. He slid his arms around her waist from behind, his body nearly against hers. She set her arms over top his and leaned back into him. Her stomach swayed with a quick breath.

The sensuality of the movement along with the light turn of her head to be even closer was more than he could ignore. He wanted her. It was an intense struggle not to allow himself to let her feel just how much he did as she stood melded to his body. As he kissed the side of her face. As she squeezed his arms.

"Katie." He was losing all control. He couldn't quite yet. "There's something I have to know." He continued at her silence. "Are you ... would I be...?" He noted the slight shake of her head and turned her around to face him. Her eyes were cast down, away. "I'm not ... this isn't some kind of judgment. I don't want you to think ... it's only, you're so young and if ... you should wait ... if it would be..."

Her eyes raised and a tear escaped. Her head shook again.

"No, don't." Ryan wiped the moisture from her face. "I didn't mean to upset you and I'm not ... hell, everyone knows I'm ... well, I only ... I didn't mean to pry, or to suggest..."

"I wish it could have been you." Her voice was weak, shaky, and her eyes were avoidant.

"No, Katie, I'm ... I don't think I could ... I mean if ... it doesn't matter. Don't think it matters to me." Ryan leaned in to kiss her. He didn't want her upset. He didn't want her to think he was judging, as though he had any right. She calmed with his touch, his attention, his wanting her that had to show through every part of him. Almost every part. So far, he was still able to maintain partial control. "Promise me something." He whispered beside her ear, only barely in partial control. "Stop me if you want me to stop. Don't ever agree to anything I want if you don't want it, too. Promise me, Katie." He kissed her ear. "Promise me."

She nodded.

Ryan hoped to hell she meant it. His control evaporated.

Lifting her into his arms, he turned toward the nearest bed, and then set her back down. "Hold on. Don't move." As quick as he could manage, he went to pull the bedspread down out of the way. He'd seen and heard enough to know he wasn't about to put his naked body on top of the thing, or hers. The sheets were at least bleached.

She'd listened and held her position where he set her down. By this time, there was no mistaking his intentions and he was relieved she didn't flinch at his return. Instead, she wrapped her arms around his neck and dropped her head against his shoulder when he picked her up.

"Sorry, that wasn't very romantic. Should we try this again?"

Kaitlyn raised her head, moved a hand to the back of his, and brought his lips close enough to reach them. He continued the kiss as he lowered her to the bed and leaned in against her. She was nervous, slightly stiff although her fingers gripped his shirt and pulled him closer, and he reminded himself to take it slow, to pay attention to her reactions, to any sign he should back away. He ran a hand down her arm and up again, around the top edge of her tee, up along her neck to her face, and kissed her more deeply. She didn't withdraw in any way.

He wouldn't be her first. He wasn't taking anything from her. And she wanted him.

Sitting up, he unbuttoned his shirt. Kaitlyn watched, waited. He dropped it on the floor and leaned back in; her hand brushed up against his bare skin and onto his back. He kissed her neck and her head rose to allow him access. Encouraged by the way she went along with his every movement, and the way her chest rose and fell heavily, the way her eyes closed at certain moments and then found his again, Ryan went farther. His lips traced from her lips to the edge of her shoulder while his fingers pulled the fabric away enough to find more bare skin, down her soft pale chest to above her breasts. She still didn't show hesitation.

He slid his hand under her shirt, to her stomach. It moved under his touch, reacting to him. He took his time exploring the curves, around to her waist, up to her rib cage. Her skin was incredibly soft. He could revel in laying there all night caressing her, dwelling in her reactions, in her fingers pulling at him. He loved the way she pulled at him, gently, possessively. Her breath caught when he moved his fingers higher, when they slid up and around to cradle her breast. He paused, making sure she was still okay with it, and she pulled at him again, closer.

Ryan had to kiss her, to connect as much as he could, to be sure this wouldn't feel like a fling, to be sure she couldn't think it wouldn't take over and consume them both, lock them into a joined path. It would. It never had before, not for him, but with her, it would. She had to know it would.

Her fingers slipped barely beneath his jeans at the small of his back. Encouragement. Saying yes. She knew it would. Her eyes said she knew it would. They were more intense than he'd ever seen.

He wanted her shirt out of the way. And her bra blocking his fingers from her bare skin.

The ab muscles he worked on so often when no one was around contracted as he pulled them both up to sitting. Ryan gripped the hem of her shirt and slid it up ... but she stiffened instead of raising her arms to allow him to pull it off.

"Katie?"

Her chest rose and fell. She refused her eyes.

He sighed and released her shirt. "Okay." Damn. He knew she wasn't ready. He'd have to go stand in the cold shower forever.

She grabbed him when he started to get up. "No."

"No, what?"

"I want..." She pulled her eyes away.

"What do you want?" He ran fingers through her hair, his focus on her face. "Tell me what you want."

"I want this."

"Do you? You don't seem sure. And it's all right..."

"Can we turn the lights out?"

Ryan frowned. Okay, she was shy. He knew that. But did it make that much difference if the lights were on or off? It was still all the same thing. "How about we turn them down instead of off?"

She touched his eyes.

He got up and went to turn on the bathroom light, pulling the door most of the way shut, and then switched off the room lights. Too dark.

He nudged the door open a bit more. And he returned to her. "I know, I can still see you. But I want to see you, Katie. I won't make love to you with it so dark I can't see your face. If you want to wait..."

"I have scars."

Scars. Ryan tilted his head, letting it grasp his mind. She had a hell of a lot of scars, apparently not all mental and more than her ears. "You're afraid that's going to bother me? Turn me off? I can't imagine..."

"On my back. They're ugly."

Ugly. Not a word he could connect with her in any way. He let that go. "How? How did you get scars on your back?"

She shook her head.

"Okay, you know what? Tell me later. If that's the only thing stopping you, I'm not going to let it stop you. I'm not going to let it stop us." He brushed fingers along her face. "You want this."

"Yes."

"Yes." He gave her a light kiss. "So do I. More than I ever have before. I want this. And not just tonight. I want *us*."

Her eyes glistened.

Ryan kissed her, long and deep, and slid his hand up under the back of her shirt. He felt her tense and pressed closer until she wasn't. Until she melded back into his body, as close as she could get, pulling him with her soft grasp.

This time, she raised her arms to let him remove the shirt. And he got up to move around behind her. Ryan cringed at what he saw. He'd expected ... he wasn't sure what he expected, but not this, not long welted scars running from the back of her shoulders down across the width of her back. Several of them. He had to give himself a few seconds before he tried to talk. But he couldn't talk. She would hear it in his voice. She would hear his anger, his need to find out who did it and beat the living shit out of him. Later. Not tonight. Tonight, he wanted to be with her, erase as many of her scars as he could.

He brushed fingers through her hair and leaned in to kiss the side of her head. Then he let his hand slide down over the scars. She scrunched her shoulder blades together and he moved his hand. "Are they still sore? They look healed."

"They're ugly. Don't..."

"Katie." He kissed her shoulder. "Relax." He ran his fingers down the arm she had tucked around her bare stomach and grasped her hand. His chest pressed in against her back. She tried to turn.

"No. Hold still. It's fine." He pulled her hand up to kiss her fingers and released it. Her skin was warm against his lips as he moved them from her shoulder down to the top of one of the scars. Her muscles tightened again but he continued, planting kisses all along each one, trying somehow to help the memory of it heal. To let her know she was still beautiful, sensual, that he still wanted her passionately. Her body loosened, gave in to him. She reached behind and gripped his leg.

"Still yes?" He asked in between kisses rising back to her shoulder.

"Yes."

Ryan unhooked her bra. She took it off. And turned to him, her eyes moist.

His heart pounded the way it had on the ledge, except he didn't feel sick this time. She was his. He saw it in her eyes. Felt it in her touch. Yes. She belonged to him, not the way he'd understood it when she told him she did, but ... the way she meant it. Because she wanted to belong to him. They were bound. Forever, he would be bound to her.

Her exploration of him began shyly, fingers barely touching his chest. He let her lead as much as she would and took over when he could see she wanted him to take over. She didn't act at all experienced. He'd never been anyone's first time but it felt that way. Maybe it had been a one time thing, quick and ... meaningless. Ryan couldn't help but hope it wasn't, for her sake, but this ... he knew without doubt it had never been like this for her. It had never even been like this for him. The deep emotional attachment he'd heard of had always been lost on him. He wasn't sure he was even capable of it.

Then again, he could have been wrong.

The way she touched him, and the way she released control enough to show more on her face than she ever had, the way she moved with him, leaned up into him, claimed him, told him he was very, very likely wrong.

Lying uncovered on his back, Ryan stroked Kaitlyn's skin as she curled against his side and snuggled into his shoulder. He had definitely been wrong. He had it in him to feel the deep emotion, maybe too much. He hurt for her. He wanted to know everything, and yet he didn't. He wanted to keep her wrapped within his arms every minute to be sure no one else could ever hurt her again. And he wasn't about to let any relative she found take her away, not without a fight. Unless she wanted it. If she did, if she chose to go with any relative away from him.... She wouldn't. She belonged to him, as she said.

Moisture on his skin where her head rested distracted his thoughts. She wiped at her face.

No. His stomach hurt suddenly. And he rolled her onto her back to be able to see her. "Katie..."

"It's okay." She tried to duck back into him.

"Okay? You're crying? How is that okay? You should have told me to stop. I..."

"No." She touched his face, shook her head. "I ... I didn't think I could ever want this. I didn't think ... I could ever feel like this. I'm not upset.

I'm not."

Not upset? With tears running down her face? "I don't understand." He wiped at them. "You've ... you've done this. You said..."

"Not like this. Not...."

"Come on, Katie. You have to tell me what you're thinking because I'm kind of confused right now. If I've hurt you..."

"No. Ryan, no. You didn't."

She said his name. It was the first time she'd ever said his name. It was beautiful.

"It ... it was the first time I wanted to. The first time it was..."

"Wait." He straightened. "You've agreed before when you didn't want to?"

"No. I didn't agree." She turned her eyes away. "I didn't want it. I didn't think I could, ever." More tears fell.

His skin prickled. "You were forced."

Katie rolled in against him, clinging to his bare skin, her head buried into his chest.

"Why didn't you tell me? This ... it had to be hard for you..."

Her head shook. And she pulled back to see his eyes. "I ... didn't want you to ... to think about that. I didn't.... It wasn't. I wanted to know ... how...."

"How it's supposed to be?"

She nodded.

"You've been too hurt too often. Why? How much more is there I don't know yet?"

She ducked back into him.

"Stupid question. I'm sorry." Ryan kissed her head.

"Don't think of that." Her voice was muffled by his skin. He could feel her breath as she spoke. "Next time. Don't..."

He rolled her onto her back and sat halfway up, leaning over her, his hands on both sides of her face. Words wouldn't come. So he kissed her. A kiss deep enough she couldn't possibly think he had anything on his mind except her, except being with her. And he wanted to be.

She pulled him in.

11

Sunday, he ordered breakfast in and called Daws to tell him she was overly tired and needed the day to rest. He wanted her to himself. They went to the hotel restaurant for lunch, tucked away in a corner talking much longer than their server appreciated. Ryan tipped her well to ease her annoyance. After lunch, Katie agreed to a leisurely walk in a less touristy part of the city and they grabbed gelato from a vendor and found a grassy spot to rest. They returned to their room for the remainder of the afternoon and evening, made love in the light of growing dusk, ordered room service, and found a movie while giving in to the night and each other.

On Monday, Ryan insisted Daws say whatever he had to say about the uncle in front of Katie. Anything he knew, she would know. Daws hadn't spoken to the musician or his band but made casual inquiries while he chatted with others in the pub. He was American, with a work visa that allowed him to stay in England much of the time with his girlfriend. He also had a home in Montana, out away from the crowd, so they said. Daws told her he would be playing at another pub in the city on Wednesday night. She didn't comment.

She treated Ryan the same as she always had when they were around Daws and Deanna. He followed her lead and kept their advanced relationship private, although he had to try harder than she apparently did and he caught Daws studying him occasionally. The moment they found time alone, however, Katie stood closer and often touched him, and she didn't hesitate to let him know when she wanted him to kiss her, or when she wanted more. It was subtle, always a hint, but he was learning to read her well and she showed her appreciation by opening to him. The second anyone else was around, she closed.

On Wednesday, she began to withdraw, even around him alone. It was because of their plans to go to the pub to see her uncle. She wouldn't say anything about him, or promise to even let him know she was there, but the later in the day it got, the more she closed inside herself.

And it was time to go. Still in their room, he walked up behind her and wrapped his arms around her stomach. "I want you to know that whatever happens, I'm still here. And I'll be hoping...."

She turned in his arms. "I'll stay with you as long as you want."

"Are you sure? 'Cause you know, if you would ever be happier ... I uh..."

"I couldn't be."

He touched her face, sliding his fingers down her cheek to her neck. "No? I have yet to see you smile. Not even half a smile. I want that. To see you able to smile again, whatever it takes, even if it's not with me."

She fell against him, holding tight. "What if I can't? Ever?"

"Then I'll have to keep trying. Forever, if need be."

"I don't know if I want to see him, if I can talk to him."

Ryan pulled back to find her eyes. "Don't talk to him if you don't want to. I will. And don't worry, I won't say much. Give me a sign if I say more than I should. Tell me if you want to go and I'll take you out of there, anywhere you want to go." He thought he saw her begin to relax. "It'll be all right. I won't leave your side."

Daws and Deanna kept an eye on her at the pub from across the table. They were far enough back the band wouldn't see them, but close enough Katie could watch her uncle. Daws asked privately if Ryan recognized him. He had to admit he only did somewhat and dropped his jaw hearing the name. Everyone in music knew that name. Her uncle was the guitarist from Foresight? The band Raucous helped propel to the top. And Katie had never mentioned him.

She remained tense, forcing whatever she felt not to show while she kept her gaze on her uncle, except at certain times when emotion started to slip through the tiniest bit. Ryan was envious of her control. He was also glad she didn't stay so controlled when they were in bed together. It was the only time he saw any real expression in more than her eyes.

Her glance made him wonder if she knew where his mind had wandered. It was wrong. He shouldn't have gone there while she sat in the foreign pub trying to decide whether to face her uncle or stay hidden. "So you grew up knowing about the life of a musician?" He had to ask.

She shook her head.

"No? You said you were close."

"He wasn't allowed to talk about it to me."

"Wasn't allowed?" Ryan couldn't resist a chuckle. Who would've told him he wasn't allowed to talk about his career?

"My father didn't approve. He said it was dangerous, a bad role model."

Bad role model. Her father didn't approve of musicians, at least not rock musicians. Ryan was nearly selfish enough to be relieved he wouldn't have to fight for the man's approval. Luckily, she turned back and didn't see him fight himself not to be so selfish.

He could see the resemblance. When the uncle turned to the right angle, Ryan could see similarities between him and Katie. He looked like a kind man, with crinkled eyes and a nice smile given freely. Ryan wondered how like him she would be if she hadn't dealt with as much as she had. Would her smile also be so free and easy-going? Would her face glow with the same kindness? Probably it would. Shifting his position, he grasped her fingers. It would only look like he was helping her not be nervous, as he had done so often, although the look Daws gave him said it didn't. Deanna nudged her boyfriend to stop the gaze and gave Ryan a soft grin. Katie squeezed his fingers.

When the band announced a break, Ryan stood. "Come on." Without giving her time to change her mind, he pulled out her chair and didn't object when their friends got up to go with. More moral support couldn't hurt anything, he figured.

Katie moved behind him when they got close although she kept his hand.

Her uncle was fixing a string on his guitar, his band members on both sides. Ryan walked up in front of him. "Excuse me."

"He is busy, mate. Can I help ya?" The younger guy who played bass stepped half between him and the uncle.

"I only want a couple of minutes." Ryan tightened his grip on Katie's hand when she tried to pull farther away.

"If the girl wants an autograph, make her ask herself, if she can stop hidin' behind you." He studied Katie curiously, and with too much interest. "Anyone lookin' like that will not have trouble getting one. You, on the other hand, migh' have a harder time." The bassist grinned. Daws moved closer to Katie.

"Let him alone, Conner. He is American, by the accent. My only fan still left there, in all possibility." The guitarist laughed at his own joke without giving Ryan more than a glance. "What is it that you want, lad?" Still, he gave his attention to the guitar, restringing the thing in a quick, expert manner.

"I wondered if the name Kaitlyn Murray meant anything to you."

The instrument nearly dropped to the floor. "What did you say?" He stood.

"An American, also. I think she knows you."

He let the bassist take the guitar. "How ... you know Kaitlyn? What do you know?" His eyes were a lot like hers, also, especially now that they were serious, tense.

Ryan felt her body press closer. "She's a friend of mine. Lost some people a long time ago. When she was seven or eight."

He looked close to collapsing, enough that a couple of his band mates stepped in and asked if he was all right. "She's alive." He waited for Ryan's nod. "Where is she?"

Ryan turned and encouraged her to move up beside him. She raised her head slowly to her uncle's face.

The man forced his breath while he studied her. Tears came to his eyes. "Katie, my love, is it really you?"

She remained still.

Her uncle stepped up and threw his arms around her, enveloping her in a large, protective hug. A woman came to his side and asked what was going on, and he still he held her. Ryan watched Kaitlyn for signs he should interfere. She didn't exactly return the hug; her hand was still in Ryan's. But she didn't seem to need interference.

Finally, the guitarist stepped back to again look at her face and the woman insisted on an answer. "It's Katie." He was nearly breathless, his eyes locked from his niece.

"Katie? You don't mean ... *Robert's* Kaitlyn?"

She glanced at the woman.

"Yes." Her uncle only looked at her, still studying her as though trying to convince himself she was real. "Yes. It has to be. You look so like your mother." He touched her face and she flinched.

Ryan moved an arm around her back. "It's all right."

The man gave her a curious look. "You remember me. You were young, I know, but you must remember me. Every spare moment I had I came to spend with you, to the annoyance of your father. You do remember?"

She nodded.

"W*here* have you been? We have been looking everywhere, for so many years. *Where* have you been?"

She backed up when her uncle tried to get closer.

"Your father ... you have contacted him, I hope? If he found you and didn't call me, I ... does he know?"

Her father. Katie stared. Ryan asked for her. "Her father's alive?"

"Of course. We are not as old as you lads seem to..." The expression changed from annoyance to curiosity. "You're that singer. The one magazines trash as too rebellious for your type of music."

It wasn't the time to talk music, as much as Ryan was honored Nick Hollister knew who he was, but he supposed he should introduce himself. "Ryan Reynauld. Where is her father?"

Katie pressed closer.

Her uncle looked back and forth between them, with an occasional glance at Daws and Deanna. "He doesn't know. Robert doesn't know yet..."

Hoping Katie would tell him if he said too much, Ryan took a chance. "She didn't realize he ... she thought..."

"My love, are you all right? You look more in shock than I am even. Will you speak to me, tell me ... you are still my Katie dove."

She walked away.

This time Ryan followed immediately, not about to lose her in the city again. She stopped outside the door, checked to see who was there, and fell against him.

"Okay, it's okay." He held her in and stroked her hair, resting his palm alongside her head. After a minute, he asked her to walk. When Daws called, Ryan told him to stay put until he let him know if they were returning or if she needed more time.

He followed wherever she wanted to go and she walked a fair distance. When he started to get tired, Ryan knew she had to be also, and pulled her into a little pub. Settled at an out-of-the-way table, he ordered a bottle of wine to share.

Leaned back in his chair, he scanned the place, giving her time to decide whether she wanted to talk and himself time to decide how to consider the extra complication of Nick Hollister being her uncle, an uncle she maybe wouldn't want to see again. An uncle somewhat attached to his best friend's past. Ryan would have to be careful about conversation, both for Kaitlyn and for Dani. It was no secret he and Dani were close. Everyone who followed the current music scene knew. He wondered if Nick Hollister still did.

After all the silence between them he could deal with, he grabbed a swallow of wine and crossed his arms atop the table. "Is he your mom's brother or your dad's?"

She raised her eyes. "Mom's. I didn't know her. Not much. He talked about her a lot so I wouldn't forget all the way." Her hand shook when she raised her glass. "How much do you know about him? From his music?"

"Not much, only his name, the band's name. Damn good on that guitar when he tries. He seems decent." Ryan leaned in. "And awfully glad to see you."

She set the glass down after a small sip, and sighed. "I didn't know." She spoke to the table.

"About your father." When she didn't answer, Ryan moved his chair closer. "Why did you walk away? I know you wanted to see him. I know he wants to see you, to talk to you..."

"I can't."

He rubbed her fingers. "Why?"

"I don't want him to know."

Ryan guessed what she meant. "I won't tell him how we met. He doesn't have to know that. Daws won't say anything, either."

She shook her head.

"That's not what you don't want him to know?"

With still-trembling fingers, she took another sip of wine. "I'm not ... what he thinks ... the same. I don't want him to know anything ...

between then and now. I don't want him to know."

"He's your uncle and he loves you. I can see it in his face. It'll be all right."

"I mean my dad. He's ... I didn't know he was ... he can't know."

Her dad. Of course. She'd tried to contact her uncle but only when she thought her dad was gone. "Katie, you can't refuse to see him. Choose what you want to tell him, but..."

"You don't understand. I'm not ... I'm not, anymore."

Ryan took her in his arms. Not what? What she used to be? Or just ... not? Did she feel non-existent? She couldn't. Ryan felt her full existence when they were together. It was there. She had to know it was still there, whoever she used to be, whoever she still was. She could hide it as much as she wanted, but it was still there.

"Your dad needs to know where you are, that you're still here, and you're okay." Okay wasn't the right word and he knew it wasn't, but he couldn't think how else to say it.

"Would you want to know?" She captured his eyes with a rare intensity. "If it was your daughter and ... with what you already know ... would you want to know?"

He hesitated, trying to decide if it could hurt him more as a parent than it did as her friend, her lover. He wasn't a parent. How could he answer? When she looked away, he set his hand along her face and pulled her back. "Katie, I can't answer that for him but I can't imagine it would be as hard as not knowing anything, as it would be to wonder for the rest of my life what happened." He brushed fingers through her hair. "Besides, I'm more concerned about you, and I think you really need to find him again. Maybe it'll help you start finding yourself again."

Her eyes watered and she turned them away.

"I'm going to call Daws and ask him to bring your uncle here when he's done playing. You don't have to talk to him but I think you should at least be around him a while. The rest of us will do the talking. But I want to watch him react to you. I need to see if he's worthy of being an uncle to you. Because maybe he doesn't know you anymore, but I do. And I really think he'll want to know you for who you are now."

He could tell she didn't believe it, but she didn't argue or stop him from calling.

A bottle of wine wasn't the best idea Ryan had. On top of her stress and travel fatigue, Katie showed the effect of two small glasses she'd sipped by the time the others joined them. He wanted her to relax. He didn't want her to look like he might have to hold her up when they left. Ryan had less than she did since his stomach complained after the first one.

The woman who took Nick's side at his show was with him, as was Connor the bass player. Nick introduced her as Rebecca and the bassist was her son, apparently not his.

Deanna claimed the chair next to Kaitlyn before Nick could. "Is the wine to share?"

He saw the question on her face after her quick study of Katie. "Go ahead. We're done with it."

"Oh lovely, Ryan. You could have at least pretended you planned to share instead of acting like it's leftovers." She grinned at him.

"You know me too well for that." When she tried to offer him more, he covered his glass.

"So." He pulled Nick's eyes from Kaitlyn. "I have to say I'm pretty honored you recognize me, never mind the rebellious thing, which of course is all hype." He looked over at Daws choking on his wine. "Ignore him. It's hype."

"And why would you be honored that an aging musician playing unknown clubs knows your face?"

"Are you kidding? I do know who you are. Took me a little time but my mind was elsewhere. Everyone into music at all knows your name."

Nick grabbed a big swallow of the wine. The face he made said it wasn't one he liked. "You don't have to flatter me. You brought my Katie back and that's more than enough points in your favor, the way I see it." He raised the glass in a salute, watching Ryan over the top as he took another sip.

"Points?"

"Should I not presume you're close to her?" He glanced toward their arms coming from under the table entwined. "Though if you would let her speak now and then, it would be good. I haven't heard her voice in a lot of years. And she has such a beautiful voice. You've heard it? Is that how you met?"

Ryan found avoidance in her gaze. Her voice? "You mean as in..."

"Do not tell me you don't sing anymore, my love." Nick's eyes were searching. "You used to sing to everything anyone would play, even the television."

Ryan didn't dare ask. He was supposed to keep conversation away. "I've kept her busy and it can be hard to get a word in around me at times." He squeezed her fingers.

"And how long have you known each other?"

It wasn't going to work. "About four months."

The woman, Rebecca, thanked a server for the beer she'd ordered for her and Nick. "So this is new then. And Nick is assuming more than he should, as normal." She grinned at Katie. "It is wonderful to finally meet you, although I feel like I have with as much as he's talked about you. He's been so worried, as is Robert." She tapped Nick on the arm. "We'll have to go. When she goes to find her dad, we should go, also."

"Any excuse to get over to the States, yes?" He teased with a grin and looked back at Katie. "I haven't called him yet, although I should. Or maybe you want to call? It's about eight in the evening there. He should be home." He pulled out a cell, played with it, and held it out to her. "Just hit send."

She didn't move to take the phone.

"Wait on that."

"Wait?" Nick eyed Ryan. "You have any idea how much he's been hurting since he lost her? I feel like an ass waiting as long as I have."

"She's not going to call. This is a lot at once. Give her some time."

Nick straightened, brushed Ryan off, and focused on her. "Have you not wanted to find us? Is there a reason you made us wait so long to let us know you're still alive? Why here? Why did you come to me first? Your father ... we've had our differences, but he was a good father and he deserves to know." He leaned toward her. "Kaitlyn, where have you been?"

She edged closer to Ryan.

"Foster homes." He answered for her, only enough.

"Does she not talk?" Her uncle's voice hinted at anger.

"Not much, no." And he wanted to get her out of there. She was withdrawing too far. "Putting her on the phone with someone she hasn't seen since she was eight is not a good idea. How is he going to react if she won't talk to him and he can't see her?"

"She was seven and he's her father. Why..." Nick redirected his gaze. "You *would* talk to him."

Her fingers tightened. She stayed quiet. When Deanna explained how they'd learned about Nick and immediately made arrangements to find him, and that Katie didn't know, Nick got up, flustered. Ryan felt for him but he had to put her first. He leaned in to tell her it would be fine.

She jumped. Her head shot into his nose.

He covered it with a hand, trying not to grimace at the stabbing pain that surged all the way through his head while Deanna asked if he was all right. "Yeah." He felt moisture and pulled his hand back enough to find blood covering it.

"I'm *sorry*." Kaitlyn pushed a napkin into his hand. "I'm so sorry. I didn't..."

"No big deal." Accepting another one from someone else, Ryan refused when Daws tried to pull him away to the restroom. He couldn't leave her with her uncle at her side explaining he'd only touched her shoulder and studying her so closely. Deanna told him to pinch his nose. The pain stopped that idea. Servers asked if he needed medical attention. He had to get out of the main room, away from the stares.

Kaitlyn stood when he did. She pushed hair from his face, her own too upset. "I'm sorry..."

"It's nothing. Don't worry. Are you going to be okay here with

Deanna while I clean up?" She agreed and he told Daws he didn't need to be accompanied. He wanted his friend to stay with her, also. Ryan didn't argue with Nick when he said he would walk with him since it sounded less an offer than an insistence.

Regardless of how idiotic he felt walking through the pub holding bloody napkins to his nose, Ryan figured getting Nick alone for a short time could be good. He would tell him ... what? How much could he say? Katie didn't want him to know anything.

At least the can was empty. Cleaning his nose was pointless. It hadn't stopped.

Nick pressed fresh paper towel into his face. "Hit you good and hard it looks like."

"And she's going to feel guilty no matter what I say. Damn." He pressed against it as hard as the pain would allow.

"So can you talk while letting it clot?" Nick leaned against a sink.

"Sure." Ryan grabbed more paper towel and ran them under cold water. Cold restricted blood vessels. He didn't want to talk long.

"Why are you here? How do you know about me if you didn't know about her father?"

"I don't know. Daws handled it. But she didn't think he was alive. She said there was a robbery of some kind, and she thought both he and her stepmom..."

"She remembers it?"

"Yeah."

"They've been trying to figure out what happened ever since. Andrea, Robert's wife, was taken to the hospital. She barely remembers anything, except he attacked her and stopped suddenly, and took off. She's pretty sure he didn't plan to leave her alive. We haven't seen Kaitlyn since. We don't know ... what did she say? What happened?"

Ryan pulled the wet towels away and checked the mirror to see if the bleeding had stopped. Nearly. "She ran. She saw him and she ran. He followed, yelling a threat about killing her parents if she didn't stop, but she didn't. And I think she's been carrying around the guilt that she's the reason he... but if they're alive..."

Nick pressed a hand to his forehead, rubbing it back through his lightly graying red-brown hair. "That's why she didn't come back." He dropped the hand with a deep sigh. "Stop yet?"

Ryan checked. "Maybe." Dropping the wet, red towels into the trash, he grabbed a clean one and dabbed it under his nose, glad for the distraction. Had he said too much? He hadn't really said anything. Still...

"Where did she go?" Nick stepped closer. "When she ran?"

"I don't know. She didn't say. Really, she hasn't said too much about anything. She's ... she barely talks to people. I've only heard her talk to Deanna, my mom once, and my brother a couple of times. But otherwise, she doesn't."

"She talks to you."

"Yes. Sometimes. Not always."

"Then you're not as close as it looks."

Ryan hesitated, unsure how to explain without saying too much. No way could he say just how close they were. Her uncle would never understand at this point, until he got to know her better, until he could realize...

"Riveting Ryan Reynauld." Nick crossed his arms in front of his chest. "I know of you. Your reputation with female fans is as known as your name, and I know enough not to believe everything I hear, but I also know what it's like in that world. I'm not so old I've forgotten. Not that I'm criticizing. I had my share of exploits. You'll understand why I'm asking then. Why I have to be concerned about my niece."

"Of course." Ryan knew straight-forward answers were his only choice, no matter how much Daws would warn him to stay quiet. This man would see straight through anything else. "Met her on my way to work. She needed a place to go. Said she had no one. I was there at the right time, so I gave her my guest room. I uh ... I was concerned enough I took her to work with me, to make sure everything was okay."

"Looking out for her? And that's it?"

"No." He wasn't going to lie. He couldn't. He could, however, avoid the full truth. "I care about her. She's taught me a hell of a lot in a short time. I enjoy being around her, talking or not. It doesn't matter."

"And you do know she's seventeen? A child still, even if England says that's not a child. As her uncle..."

"No." Ryan gave up using his nose as a distraction and met Nick's gaze. "No, she's nineteen."

He raised his eyebrows. "You don't think I know my niece's age? She was more than a niece to me. She was like a daughter. I helped take care of her after her mom, my sister, passed. I was there for her, before that, and after. I nearly died inside when we lost her, as her dad did. I *know* how old she is."

Ryan looked away. She said nineteen. He'd made sure. At times he found it hard to believe ... but she said she was.

"Why did you think she was nineteen?" Nick moved closer yet.

He didn't want to say. Why would she tell him that? Why...

"Why?"

The voice echoing his thoughts threw him into a whirlwind of emotion. Why? He couldn't doubt her again. He had once and she made him feel like an idiot when the truth came out. He wouldn't do it again. At the door opening, he was relieved as hell to see his friend.

"Still alive in here?"

They'd been too long. Katie was probably worried she'd really hurt him. "Yeah. I guess it's not going to start up again."

"Good thing. They're kicking us out. We've already held them open too long." Daws glanced between the two of them. "They did offer to call a lorry if you need one."

"Nice of them." He started toward the door.

Nick grabbed his arm. "Did she tell you she was?"

With a pause, Ryan knew he couldn't say she did, true or not. "I don't know. I may have misunderstood, or maybe I didn't hear her right. Her voice is usually quiet when she does talk and I always have so many people floating around…" His fib and shrug didn't quite settle with her uncle, according to his expression, but Ryan slipped out around Daws and went back to find her. He tried to keep distance when she threw her arms around him and asked if he was all right. She couldn't be seventeen.

"Hey, do something for me." Drawing Daws away from everyone else while they waited for taxis, Ryan glanced back to be sure he wasn't overheard. "I need you to trade us rooms. I want the suite…"

"Already done. Had them switched while we were out." Daws eyed him. "What did the uncle say? A warning?"

"Not quite. But … I don't know. Something doesn't add up."

"No shit, moron. Haven't I been telling you that?"

"All right, save the 'I told you so'…"

"Reynauld, you've gotta back off. This is going to cause trouble for you even if you are trying to play hero. The hero is always the one who gets burned. I don't want to see that happen."

Ryan threw a grin. "If I didn't know better, I might think it was me you were worried about and not your job security."

"That's what you get for thinking." Daws walked away, back to his girlfriend.

With a chuckle, Ryan followed. He took Katie's side but not too close. Nick wanted to know where they were staying and if they could drop by in the morning.

"Sure. Brunch at the hotel maybe?" Ryan gave him the hotel name and turned to his guard. "What in the hell room are we in? I know by walking to it but…" Leaving them to discuss details, Ryan was glad her uncle didn't plan to follow tonight. He was trying to decide what to say to Katie, whether to ask about her age again. It wouldn't be a good time, though. She was already shaken enough and as late as it was, they needed sleep. Talk would wait.

But she came to him. Ryan settled into his own room in the suite and was staring at the ceiling considering Nick's words when she knocked. She didn't speak as she walked toward him, as she hadn't since asking if he was all right.

He remained still, not persuading or discouraging her approach, until she tucked herself under the blankets, at a distance. "I figured you'd be asleep already. It's nearly two." He reached over to brush a strand of hair from her face.

She moved in, accepting his arm around her shoulder, laying her head on his chest. Her breath warmed his skin; her fingers slid across his bare stomach beneath the covers. She was looking for comfort. He could feel it, how much she needed that, and he fought himself. Now that he knew, he couldn't. He wanted to, with every part of his being he wanted to, but he couldn't. He didn't lie worth a damn. He would never be able to convince anyone he hadn't been with her after he'd been told she was seventeen if he had. Before he knew was different. It wasn't, but it was. And he couldn't.

Her kiss nearly changed his mind, but Ryan forced control he didn't have, pretending he did, yelling inside his own head that he did, that he had to have. And soon she was asleep against him. He hated knowing he let her down.

At brunch, Nick said he and Rebecca would return to the States with them. Daws had given them flight information and they'd managed to get on the same plane, all in coach except he and Katie with first class seats, which made Ryan uncomfortable. Nick shrugged it off. He'd done first class plenty and now enjoyed blending in with everyone else. Deanna offered them a room at their place. The plan was for Nick to let Robert know he was in the country and would stop by with friends. It was yanked out of Ryan's hands, with no input from Kaitlyn, either. She still didn't speak to her uncle.

Ryan worried that she hadn't even said a word to him since the pub. He had to get her alone, away from Nick and Daws and all of it. He watched her barely eat, seemingly oblivious to the fact anyone else was around. He knew she wasn't, that she was maybe painfully aware of just who was around and how her uncle was trying to get her to talk. She had to talk to him. For her own sake, if nothing else.

"So, we're heading out of here tomorrow." He glanced at her between swallowing syrup-soaked pancake. "Anything else you want to do first?"

She allowed him her eyes.

Nick was watching. Ryan had to get her to answer, to show her uncle she would. "A boat. We haven't done that yet." He at least got a reaction, a slight uplift of her face. "You should've thumped me upside the head. I forget everything. You know that by now, right?"

Deanna leaned in from Kaitlyn's other side. "Like your room number? I swear without Jim or Freddy you'd always be roaming the hallways trying to find your way."

"Yeah well, Katie would've been able to tell me last night. She's good with numbers."

"Is she?" Nick looked at her over his coffee cup.

"Oh yeah. It's been a big help. I had someone throw me a phone number I had to have, with nothing to write it on and of course I forgot it, but she didn't."

"Her dad is good with numbers." Nick held the cup with both hands, elbows on the table, all attention on his niece. "Remember how Andrea would do the budget and not bother with a calculator? She'd give the numbers to your dad while he was doing other things and he'd throw back the total without thinking much about it. Coulda been a circus act."

Katie pushed at her eggs, moving the soft yolk centers she'd eaten around to the side of her plate.

"She likes her eggs scrambled. Won't eat raw yolks. Figured she'd changed her mind when you ordered them that way for her."

Under Nick's scrutiny, Ryan wasn't sure how to answer. Why hadn't he figured that out by now? She always scrambled them when she cooked, or turned them into omelets. He always made them sunny side up as he liked. He was sure she ate them before, though. He had to ask why she hadn't told him, getting only a touch of her eyes in response.

Letting it go, since her silence was frustrating him, he went back to his pancakes and conversation. "What does her father do? Accountant?"

Nick swallowed coffee while he moved his gaze between the two of them. Studying the relationship. "Engineer. One of the big wigs at the company. Gets kind of full of himself but guess he's earned it since he worked up from the bottom, unlike most."

Katie's eyes rose to her uncle.

"He was still on the ground floor of the place last time you saw him." Nick's voice was more gentle aimed at her. "Work became his escape after...." He shook his head. "Damn, he's going to be glad to see you. Wish we could get a flight out of here today. One less day for him to wonder."

Ryan looked at Daws.

"How soon?"

"I'm taking her out on a boat first. Not sure how yet, but I promised. So not early. If you can do it."

Daws nodded and got up.

Rebecca stared after him. "He'll never get one for today, for six people. This is busy season and there are only a few flights going to the States each day."

"If it can be done, he'll do it." Ryan turned to Katie. "If you're okay with leaving tonight instead. If you aren't, tell me and I'll go stop him."

She shook her head. No. When he started to get up, she grasped his arm. "It's okay." Her look belied her words.

"Katie, tell me. Honestly. If you want to wait until tomorrow…"

"I want to see him." Her eyes fought moisture.

"Yeah?"

She nodded.

"Good. I would guess he'll get it done. There's not much he tries to do that he can't. Don't know how, and I'm not sure I want to know, but he does." He took her hand. "You're all right, then?"

"You'll be there." It wasn't a question, except in her eyes.

"Of course." He knew Nick was paying attention, likely to everything … the hand holding, the eye contact, the fact that she spoke only to him, and the way she relaxed at his touch. He would have to be careful. The conversation the night before wasn't a warning in particular, but it was close enough. And he couldn't blame him. She was young, too young for such an intimate relationship. But then, Nick didn't understand. He didn't know what she'd been through or why … why it wasn't exactly as wrong for her as he would think not knowing. Or maybe it was and Ryan was trying to convince himself it wasn't.

He didn't want to let it go.

Daws returned with a seven thirty-five flight time and a reservation for a boat tour, for only Ryan and Katie. Deanna wanted to ride the giant Ferris wheel before they left and Nick and Rebecca had last minute arrangements to make. Even so, Ryan wasn't sure why Daws was purposely allowing him privacy with Kaitlyn when he'd been so intent on not allowing it. He wouldn't dare press the issue.

12

Nick's self-invite to stay at Ryan's place instead of with Daws or a hotel made Ryan more uncomfortable than he wanted to admit. His guard wasn't going the next morning to Montana where Katie's dad still lived. Daws didn't think it was their place to interfere and didn't expect Ryan to need guarding "up there in the mountains" with Kaitlyn's family.

As they sat and chatted about music, Nick unwound, joking with the grin he gave fans while on stage. Ryan had seen it often on Foresight's videos. The more they talked, the more he enjoyed the man's company – Nick Hollister, the guitarist who had remained rather mysterious and kept himself hidden other than on stage. Ryan knew his work. His lyrics were impressive: poetic and deep, with meanings as hidden as the writer. The music was more complicated than critics gave him credit for. Ryan knew it was since he'd played some of it while learning his instrument. Nick's voice was his weak point and it was only weak on certain songs. On others it was fully intense and made an otherwise un-notable song a must-listen.

Nick, in turn, complimented Ryan on his music. Said it was among his favorites of the new generation.

"This gets tiring, doesn't it?" Rebecca leaned toward Kaitlyn. "They could go on like this all night. Don't let them keep you up, honey."

"Ah, she's right." Nick scratched his stubbled chin. "We should call it a night. Tomorrow..." He looked at Katie. "Is there anything you want to know before tomorrow? So much has changed. If you want, I can fill you in. Or if you'd rather wait and let your dad tell you everything, that's good, too."

Katie watched as he scratched the other side of the dark shadow on his face. "You need to shave."

A smile curled Nick's mouth. "As always." He looked tempted to go wrap his arms around her. "You never liked the scraggle."

"It poked my face."

He chuckled. And grew serious again. "I've missed you, my Katie dove. Guess you're still in there, huh?"

"I tried to find you." She let Ryan repeat what she'd told him about not being able to get through security, about the letters.

Nick rolled his eyes with an exasperated sigh. "I never got them. They never told me. I would have cancelled any show in the world to go to you, Katie. I'm so sorry I didn't know. I would've come for you."

She dropped her gaze and Rebecca again suggested they get some sleep. Agreeing, Ryan went back to to grab sweats before he turned his room over to his guests. Katie stood when he returned, gave him a soft hug, and told him good night. As she started away, Nick told her not to let the bed bugs bite. She caught his eyes, went back to him, and gave him a hug ... a long, tight hug.

Nick called his brother-in-law in the morning before they left. From the side of the conversation Ryan heard, it sounded like Katie's dad wasn't keen on the idea of him bringing "company" over.

Just before the last leg of the cross-country flight, Nick called back and again got some kind of argument. "Robert, listen to me one minute. You need to be home tonight. I don't care how busy you are at work." He paused with a look at his niece. "Sit down because this is going to be a shock. ... Kaitlyn is here with me. ... Are you there? Don't have a damn heart attack. You've been waiting a hell of a long ... of course I mean your Kaitlyn. Do you think I would do that to you? ... Yes, she's right here and no, I'm not putting her on the phone. She doesn't like phones ... Robert, we'll be there ... no, don't meet us at the airport, that's no place for this." He gave her a half-grin. "She looks like her mother, even more than she used to, except a fair bit smaller ... I know what you asked. It's hard to answer, but we'll see you soon. ... Robert? ... Hey Andrea, is he okay? Still breathing? ... Yes, she's right here ... yes ... yeah, me too ... we'll see you soon. You might want to stay with him until ... okay."

He hung up and took a deep breath. "Well, better get going. If we miss the flight, he *will* have a damn heart attack."

Katie moved toward him. "His heart isn't good?"

"No love, it's fine. He's fine, healthy as a mule and still as stubborn as one. It was only an expression." He touched her arm, carefully. "I didn't mean to scare you. He'll be pacing until we get there and trying to decide whether to go to the airport, which is why I didn't give him the flight information. I don't want you to have to do that in public."

She nodded, not quite sure about his reassurance.

On the way, Ryan considered Nick's description of her to her dad. She looked like her mom except a lot smaller. He wondered about her dad's size. Was he a small man? Ryan couldn't help but hope he was. He'd heard girls tended to go for guys built much like their fathers. Her uncle wasn't small. Ryan figured her mom must not have been, either.

~~~

Nick pulled the rental up to a large, modern two-story house with beige siding and brick accents. Set slightly away from the road, as the others in the neighborhood were, it boasted a huge front lawn bordered by trees of all kinds along each side, with perfectly groomed grass. A two-car garage connected to the house with a passageway. The security company sign beside the mailbox at the start of the cement drive was repeated close to the front door.

Ryan noted a large pole in the midst of a shrub garden holding a big light. A security light. He imagined at night it illuminated the whole yard. Lights over the garage door flashed on when Nick got close. Motion sensors. Ryan half expected to find a camera somewhere on the property.

"This is it." Nick looked back at Katie. "They moved, just after.... Andrea couldn't stay in the house. This is the third one since. I think they're settled now."

Ryan saw the front door open and a man step out on the porch, grasping the door frame for support. He wasn't a small man, but he had to be Katie's father; the resemblance was remarkable.

She stared from inside the car while Nick and Rebecca got out and went to talk with him. Ryan took her hand and opened his door. She slid out behind him and positioned herself so he half hid her from view of the others. A brief thought of being like the earth positioned between the sun and moon flashed his mind. A woman came out from the house. Andrea, he supposed, Katie's stepmom.

The man walked forward, unsteadily, his brother-in-law at his side.

Katie pressed in against Ryan's back and held his arm.

Nick introduced him to the couple but Ryan knew they weren't listening. They didn't care about him, or even who he was, at the moment. Andrea's tears fell. Katie's father forced their control.

Ryan moved to the side and drew her forward. She gave him her eyes, a frightened look mixed with a strange emotion he couldn't place. And she stepped back when her dad tried to grab onto her.

Nick interfered. "Give her a few minutes, Robert. It's been a long time."

"She's my *daughter*. Kaitlyn. *My Kaitlyn*." Deep quick breaths gave him a shaky appearance. "Are you all right? Just tell me you're all right. You're ... you're not much bigger than when I last saw you. Do you eat? Have you been taken care of?" He stepped closer.

She moved back.

"We should go inside." Nick nodded toward a neighbor's stare.

"Yes." Robert was still intent on his daughter. "It's a new house. You don't know it, but we have your things. You have a room. We always ... when we move, we always have your room ready for..." He stopped, emotion choking his words.

"It's been a long couple of days and she's exhausted. Let's go in."

With a reluctant nod toward Nick, her father led them to the door. He left his wife to speak to Ryan, to welcome him, although the way she stared made it feel more like an inquisition. Nick and Rebecca took the rear and Nick called a hello to the nosy neighbor. The man turned away.

"You're a friend of Kaitlyn's?" Andrea studied Ryan as they entered the living room: a large, sparse, brown and beige room with tiled floors and a lightly patterned area rug with only a trace of color. Burgundy. He hated burgundy. It looked like dried blood, warning him to be careful.

"Yes, I'm a friend."

"Long time?"

"No, only a few months."

Nick set a hand on his shoulder. "He helped her find us."

"Oh, I can't take credit for that. It was Daws ... my ... a friend of mine. The man can do anything." Ryan was more uncomfortable than he ever remembered feeling, in the house that belonged to Katie's parents, trying to explain the relationship he couldn't say much about. He hoped to hell they wouldn't ask him much. With Nick's amusement and the glance between him and Andrea, Ryan felt like walking out. Of course he wouldn't. His discomfort had to pale in comparison with Kaitlyn's. He had to stay with her.

When Robert raised a hand to her face, she jumped and grabbed Ryan's arm. He threw a silent accusation at Ryan but addressed Nick. "What is this? Why is she afraid of me?"

"It's been a long time. She needs time to get to know us again."

"How long have you known? When did you find her? How *long* did you wait to tell me?"

"Calm down."

"Don't tell me to calm down. You tell me *yesterday* you're bringing friends to visit with no explanation and today I find it's my *daughter*? How *long* have you known where she was?"

Katie backed away, farther behind Ryan.

"Robert, you're making her nervous. You've got to calm down."

"Nervous?" He looked around him at her. "Of me? Why?"

Her grip on his arm tightened and Ryan set his other hand over hers. "Of people in general, not only of you."

The man stared a moment, then pivoted and stalked out of the room.

Andrea threw a sympathetic glance. "He's been ... this isn't him, not the father she used to know. He's been so lost since.... I'm sorry. But he'll calm down soon." She focused on Kaitlyn. "He's still a good man. He's just shut himself off so much..." She stopped when his footsteps signalled his return.

Holding a picture frame, he faced it toward his daughter. It was them, together. She looked about six or so and was giving him a huge smile, her hands on both sides of his face. "Do you remember any of this, anything from when you were here?" He tried to hand it to her.

She wouldn't take it. Her eyes turned away.

"What's wrong with her?"

Ryan caught Katie's glance at her dad's question. "Nothing. There's nothing wrong with her. She doesn't like to talk, but..."

"My Kaitlyn is a chatterbox. She loves to hug. She isn't afraid of her father. *Don't* tell me there's nothing wrong with her." He moved in. "What's happened to you? What have they done to you?"

Katie pulled away and headed out the door. Nick stopped Robert from following and told Ryan to go ahead and give him a call if he needed.

He caught up and grabbed her hand. "Hey. Stop a minute."

She did, but she wouldn't look at him.

Ryan brushed hair from her face. "He's only in shock. He's upset. He didn't mean to hurt you."

"I don't know him."

He rubbed a hand down her arm. "You've both changed. It'll be hard. You can take your time, get to know each other again..."

She shook her head. "Take me home. I don't want to be here."

Ryan wanted to take her home. He wanted to take her out in a boat and away from everything. But he couldn't take her from the father who desperately needed her. And he couldn't let her leave things that way. "Let's walk a while and we'll go from there. Okay?"

They walked around the quiet little town until they came to a big park and he led her over to a metal swing set with droopy cloth seats. Ryan held one while she reluctantly sat down and lowered onto the one beside it. She rocked herself with her toes on the ground, staring at the sand.

"Is this anything like your other town? Or anywhere close to it?"

She shook her head.

"I guess that's good, right? Or not?"

"Don't leave me here."

His breath stopped until his body forced it to start again. Getting up, he went over and crouched in front of her, set his hands on top of hers where they held onto the metal chains and peered up into her eyes. "I won't leave you, Katie. Whatever happens, even if ... if there's any reason we have to be separated for a short time, I won't leave you. Like we did for the tour. I'll come back. I promise."

"He'll make you leave. If we stay, he'll make you leave."

Frowning, Ryan pondered the thought. "Well, it's a free country. I can stay wherever I decide to stay, if it comes to that. So can you."

She stared, waiting. For what, he didn't know. Except ... she couldn't. She was seventeen. Ryan had nearly forgotten. Would he? Would he insist Ryan stay away? Not without reason. There would be no reason. They wouldn't tell him ... anyway, he couldn't imagine Katie would tell him, and no one else knew. Daws suspected, but he didn't know. And anyway, they hadn't since he found out. And she wouldn't talk to anyone else. They needed him to stay.

His phone rang. Nick. They didn't need him to stay. She talked to Nick. Not a lot, but enough. "Yeah?"

"Are you lost yet? Need directions or a ride?"

"No, I don't think so. We're at a park not too far away."

"A park." He mumbled something Ryan couldn't hear, then came back. "That's probably as good a place as any. The kids just got home from a birthday party. We'll meet you down there."

"What kids?"

"Oh, Robert's and Andrea's. They have three boys. The park will be a good place to let them meet their sister."

With sudden silence on the other end, Ryan didn't have time for more questions, or to protest. "Um, apparently you have brothers."

She kept her eyes somewhere in the distance.

"They're coming here. Nick thought it would be a good place to get introduced. I didn't ... there wasn't time to ask you before he hung up but I can call back."

"How many?"

"Three. Don't know how old. He didn't say." Ryan stood and offered his hand.

They wandered the park amidst the first threat of dusk's approach. The air was reminiscent of Vermont although dryer – August warm but fresh, pollen-scented, ocassional traces of something floral wafting over from a colorful bush. They passed a little baseball field and he couldn't help grinning at the metal water fountain at its side. Days of running bases and then stopping to let the water splash the outside of his mouth before it got inside surged to his brain. His parents and brother sitting on the gray-wood warped bleachers cheering him and his team no matter how badly they did. His coach trying to remember his name since he was new. Always the new kid. In some places, most of them were always new kids and it didn't matter so much. In the place that became his favorite, nearly none were new, except him. Until he wasn't. Until they moved again.

He enjoyed the walk after the day of flying. Katie slowed, though. Tired, he supposed.

Spotting a big metal merry-go-round with fraying orange paint, Ryan took her that direction, then sat at its edge and invited her to climb on. She sat on the inside closer to the middle with her leg against his. Her hand gripped the back of his shirt when he used one leg to push the thing in slow circles. Backward. And she turned to face the other direction so she wouldn't be going backward, getting even closer.

Once it was going fast enough, Ryan propped his foot on the edge of the metal, touched her hair, and leaned in to kiss her. "It's going to be all right, Katie. Remember, no matter what, I'll never leave you and I won't ever let you be alone. I promised. And I still promise."

She held tight. When they heard voices in the distance, she backed up – not far, but far enough.

The boys were young, a fair amount younger than Kaitlyn. They bounced along loudly chatting while the smallest grasped Nick's hand and another hung alongside Rebecca. Obviously, they knew them well and were glad to see them. They looked different mixes of their parents, all with touches of red glowing through their shades of dark blonde to light brown hair.

Ryan climbed off to meet Robert's children, his other children. Katie stayed where she was, arms clasped around her knees. Nick spoke to her first, saying the last time he'd seen her on a playground, she was the size of the youngest child, rubbing the head of a boy he introduced as Curtis, barely six. The middle boy, Stephen, was seven. Katie didn't respond to their greetings, but she stared when they introduced Paul.

"You remember Paul, don't you?" Andrea set an arm over the oldest boy's shoulders. "He was still a baby when you ... when we lost you. We thought we'd lost him, too, but..."

Kaitlyn scrambled off the merry-go-round and walked away. Her dad called to her. She didn't stop.

"She's overwhelmed." Ryan half-grinned at the boys exchanging glances and went to catch up.

She kept walking.

"What is it about Paul that spooked you?"

She stopped and caught his eyes. "I left him in the woods. He was crying. He was ... he said ... he's not supposed to be here. He said..."

Ryan raised a hand to her face. "Slow down. Paul was crying. During the robbery?" He watched her nod, fighting for control. "You took him outside to hide him?" She nodded again. "Then, you maybe saved his life that way. Right?"

With a glance back over at the boy, Kaitlyn started walking again.

He took her hand to make her stop. "You can't walk away from them. This is your family. Whatever happened..."

"No. I let them get... I ran. I ran instead of staying like he said because I was afraid. And he said he ... he said he killed them because I was running, because I didn't go back. I can't..."

He took her face again, raising it to his. "You were only a child. There was nothing wrong with running..."

"He said he would ... and I didn't go back. I didn't want him to..." Her breathing grew heavier, faster. "He ... tried to ... to touch me, to... like he was to...." She pulled her face away. "I was afraid."

"Come here." Ryan grabbed her hand again and nodded toward a little bench surrounded by shrubs. She sat close. He could hear the boys playing and calling to each other. The peacefulness of the park with its bright green grass and dark green leaves, a gentle breeze pushing soft clouds along, and flowers of varying types, combined with the laughter of the boys' voices was such a huge contrast to Katie's demeanor, the thoughts that rushed back into her head. Or maybe they never left. Or never left her alone.

He touched her hair and she jumped. He didn't back away. Instead, he slid his fingers alongside her head and cradled it in his palm. "You have to forgive yourself. You did nothing wrong."

She focused on the ground and he followed her gaze to where ants were carrying bits of crumbs to their hill within a crack in the cement. Once small crumb at a time. It was all they needed.

"Katie, you were a child. You were scared. There was nothing wrong with running, protecting yourself. And look at them. They're fine. Paul looks perfectly healthy and happy. Your stepmom seems to be okay. All this time you've worried about what happened to them, and they're okay."

She fell against him, trembling.

"Now we have to get you okay." Ryan kissed the side of her head. He would get her to okay. Whatever he had to do, however long it took, he would get her to being okay. He hoped seeing them, knowing they were all fine, that her running hadn't destroyed them as she thought, would help move her along the path to recovery. "Come on." He pulled back and stood. "Let's go get to know your brothers. I'll do the talking. I'm good at that." With a grin, he waited until she accepted.

Paul recognized Ryan and timidly asked about his work. He figured it was safe territory, although he hadn't wanted the focus on himself. It helped Katie relax, though, especially when Nick joined in. Her father didn't appreciate it. There was apparently strain between the two men and at least part of it seemed to have something to do with Nick's career. Katie had said her father didn't approve.

"Does she know how to talk?" Curtis inched closer on his knees.

"Of course." Ryan smiled at him. "But you see, I talk so much she stays quiet to balance me out."

"Daddy talks so much, too. And Stephen talks all day and all day. But Mommy still talks to us."

"Curtis, be polite." Andrea pulled him back. "She's trying to get to know us again. And remember what I told you about listening?"

The middle boy, Stephen, rolled his eyes. "You learn more when you listen than when you talk."

Curtis tilted his head at Kaitlyn. "You must know *lots* by now."

"It's time for your bath. Stephen, run up and get it ready for him." At their father's request, the two younger boys jogged up the stairs.

"You are staying with us tonight, I hope?" Andrea turned her focus from Kaitlyn to Ryan. "The boys can camp in the basement. We always have Kaitlyn's room ready for her..."

"I have a hotel booked." Ryan grasped Katie's fingers.

"Kaitlyn will stay here with us. If you're more comfortable at a hotel, that's fine..."

"Robert." Nick threw him a warning. "I think it's been enough for her today. Getting away from it overnight will be better."

"Getting away? She's been away. This is her home."

"Not anymore. You can't expect her to settle right back in."

"The hell I can't. This is her home."

Andrea interrupted. "Robert, we should ask her. She's no longer a child. Ask what she would rather do."

"She won't say a word to me. How do you expect to get an answer?"

Katie unwrapped herself and stood, her fingers still locked in his. He rose to her side. "You're ready to go?"

She nodded.

Nick gestured a shrug with his hands. "There you go. You have your answer."

"Kaitlyn." Her father stood. "I think it would be better to stay with us than to go to a hotel with *him*. You have no business, at your age..."

"Hell, Robert, she's been living with him for months. There's no point in worrying about it now."

Ryan jumped in at Robert's glare. "She has her own room. She's been staying at my place, but she has her own room."

"Be that as it may, she is home now. This is where she belongs." He faced Ryan as though inviting him to leave.

Ryan met his gaze, wishing to hell Daws was there. "Mr. Murray, this has been a lot for her to handle. She thought ... she didn't even realize you were still alive until a few days ago and she needs time..."

"Why wouldn't I be?" He looked over at Katie as she again moved half behind Ryan and gripped the back of his shirt.

"She's been through a lot. I think talking more tomorrow would be better." Ryan knew he was pushing it. The guy obviously didn't like him, or didn't like his career. Ryan always had trouble discerning which was which when he ran across the attitude. He supposed it was really all the same.

"What is your interest with my daughter?"

He hadn't expected that question, although he supposed he should have. "She's a friend and I care about her. I've been trying to help..."

"Help what, exactly? It doesn't look like you're helping much of anything. She's so jumpy she's..."

"That's not his fault." Nick moved next to Ryan. "She trusts him. That should tell you enough for now."

"Should it? How long have you known him? Is this some set-up of yours?"

"I knew nothing until a few days ago. I met him when he brought her to find me."

"A few days ago. And you're defending him because he's a musician, I suppose, like you're all that damn trustworthy, right? Is that what you're trying to tell me?"

"Look." Nick cast his eyes to the floor and raised them again. "Leave your feelings about me out of this. It has nothing to do with his job, or mine. I can see Katie trusts him. I can also see she doesn't trust anyone else. If it was Ryan making things hard for her, why would that be, Robert? Think about it."

"Yet, he took her all the way to England to find you instead of coming here. Why would that be, Nick?"

Ryan shook his head. "We didn't know where you were. We didn't even know you were alive. If I had known..."

"And you still haven't told me why you think I wouldn't be."

He felt a huge foot in his mouth. "I can't say."

"You *can't say* and she won't speak to me, and you expect me to let you walk out the door with her?"

"It's her choice where she goes."

"She's seventeen. She's not old enough to make that choice."

Ryan grimaced. He should have admitted to her what Nick told him.

"No." She moved back up to his side. "I'm nineteen, like I said. I just turned..."

"Kaitlyn." Robert moved toward her, stopping when she pulled back. "You told him you were nineteen? Why?"

She found Ryan's face again. "I am. I ... I got out of school almost two years ago. I graduated early, a half year..."

"You're seventeen. You won't be eighteen for two months yet, in October. The twentieth." Her dad's dark eyes pierced the air between them. "I have your birth certificate, and I was there, Kaitlyn. I do know when you were born."

She shook her head.

Ryan touched her arm. "Did you give them the wrong date? The foster agency. You were so young. Maybe..."

"No."

"Foster agency?" Her dad hedged toward Ryan, apparently trying not to spook Katie. "What foster agency? Why in the hell didn't they return her to us?"

"I don't know." Ryan glanced at Kaitlyn. She didn't seem bothered by what he was telling her father. "I only know she was in foster homes."

"Why didn't you tell them where to find us?"

She stared at him. And she backed away. "I want to go."

"Okay." He expected a fight from her dad, but Ryan told him he was taking her to the hotel so she could relax and they would return the next day. Except Robert didn't argue with more than a warning to have separate rooms, and to use them, with a reminder of her age. Ryan assured him they had two rooms booked. Nick gave him the keys to the car. He and Rebecca were staying at Robert's.

They did have two rooms. Adjoining. Ryan doubted they would use them both, as upset and quiet as she'd become. But he set her bag in one, opened the door that led to his room, then went to unlock his door. She followed. She wouldn't even stay there alone long enough for him to open his part of the double door.

"Would you rather stay over here?"

She didn't answer, unmoving, watching him.

"I'm taking that as a yes. Let me get your bag, then." He grabbed it and returned, setting it on the luggage stand. "We'll have to at least unmake the bed so it looks slept in, use both rooms just enough. In case anyone pays attention." At her continued silence, he went to her. "What can I do to help you deal with this?"

"I don't belong with them. I don't know them."

"Katie, I'm not trying to leave you here. Okay? Don't think that's what this is about. It's for you, to help you...." He stopped, not sure what he thought it might help. Maybe it would have been better to leave things as they were, to keep her separate from a past she didn't recognize any longer. Her father expected her to be the girl he remembered. Ryan couldn't see that she was even still there – the smiling, carefree girl in the photo. He didn't even get glimpses of her.

Steering toward less complicated shores, he moved them to the edge of the bed, lowered beside her and took her fingers in his. Such small fingers. Her dad mentioned being surprised at her size. "You graduated early?"

"Half a year." She watched as he played with her hand, his arm entwined with hers. "It was December. I had the credits."

"According to what your father said, it was a year and a half early. Did you do okay?"

"Yes. He's wrong. I was ... seventeen. I was seventeen *then*. I ... I just turned nineteen. In May. I didn't lie to you. I wouldn't lie to you." She went to the window and pushed the curtain back to stare into the dark.

Ryan moved behind her. "I know you wouldn't. I'm not upset with you. But Katie, your dad would know. He wouldn't forget. They had to have changed your birthday. Why?"

In the silence, he ran his fingers up her back, over the scars hidden from everyone but him, to her shoulder. He snuggled in close, the side of his face pressed against her hair. Their reflection glimmered back at them from the window. As small as he was, standing next to her made him look larger than he had ever in his life seen himself as being. The longer he studied it, the more the image tore at his soul. They looked like two lost spirits waiting to be let inside, out of the dark, away from the moon beckoning them to surrender to it. The moon had no light of its own, and no warmth. Like the window, it could only throw back an imitation of what it saw. It made people believe there was a man within, that it had illuminating powers, when there were nothing but craters. Scars from being knocked around. Disguised by false light.

Ryan yanked his thoughts away. "Let's go find something to eat. I'm starving."

Katie turned and met his eyes, holding them. In the half-dark of the hotel room in her father's town. In the half-knowledge that had more potential to interfere than either of them appreciated but neither would vocalize. She touched his chest, over his heart. "I'm not stupid. Or crazy."

"Of course you aren't." He stroked her face with the backs of his fingers. "Hell, anyone who can graduate a year and a half early and do okay has to be pretty damn smart in my book." He grinned although it felt sorely out of place.

"They said they pushed me through, made it easy so they didn't have to keep me there."

"Who said that? The teachers?"

"Other kids. They wouldn't talk to me. They said I was crazy. Everything I said, they laughed at, until I wouldn't say anything. Every school it was the same. They didn't understand the way I talked. I read a lot. I..."

"They were jealous." He tugged her chin up to find her eyes. "It was too easy for you. It made them feel bad, so they tried to hurt you. It wasn't true. I know it wasn't true."

She pulled away.

With a sigh, Ryan moved up again, wrapping arms around her from behind. "It's like finding you're a whole different person than what you thought, isn't it?" Through silence, he waited, giving her time. "You know, I'm the same. That's why I don't go home much. Because I'm not the person on stage and in the studio I was while growing up, either. That guy was going nowhere, afraid of everything. He couldn't do what I'm doing now. So I stopped being him and started being what I needed to be for what I wanted. But going home reminds me of him since that's what they still see, and it's hard sometimes to know which I should be..."

"How did you stop being afraid of everything?"

He kissed the side of her head. "I didn't. I just tell myself I did. Like the heights thing and the ledge. It was an act. I told myself it didn't bother me, that it was a stunt..."

Katie turned and caught his eyes, questioning.

"Only the fear. Not the rest of it. Not anything I said to you. Only the acting part that took over and made it about promo."

"How do you know which is the act?"

Caught as off-balance as if he were back on the ledge, Ryan had no idea how to answer. How did he know? Maybe he didn't anymore.

"You're hungry." Walking to the door, she waited for him to join her.

The back corner of the hotel restaurant maintained their privacy, but the meal was quiet. She was lost in her thoughts without wanting to share. Ryan was glad Nick and Rebecca stayed at the house, but he had to wonder how much Nick was saying. Of course, he didn't know much, so there wasn't much he could say.

He was glad to get back to their room. Since people were in the hallway, he opened her door and waited until she closed it again before going to his own. The last thing he wanted was for someone who might know Robert to make suggestions if they found out who she was. Katie had one adjoining door open by the time he opened the other.

"Come on." He took her back into her own room. "We'll use this one for a while. Do you want to shower? I'll be right here." Getting a nod, he switched on the television for company and pulled the sheets out of the bed corners on one side to lie back against the pillow. At least it would look used.

Kaitlyn returned quickly, as always, and before he bothered to get up, walked around to the other side of the bed and cuddled against him. She smelled of scented soap and fresh shower, her skin warm and damp.

An urge he didn't want rushed in and he fought it back. Seventeen. Nearly twenty was one thing, still too young, but seventeen? No, that wasn't good. It meant he'd ... he could be brought up on charges if anyone found out. The urge turned to a churning. He went to his room to find something to soothe it.

He considered a quick call to Daws while he took a couple of swallows of the stuff, but Kaitlyn walked in. With a glance at the bottle in his hand, she went back to her room.

Damn. She would think it was upset because of her. He couldn't argue. He also couldn't let her think it was. He sure as hell didn't want to say why. Stepping into her room, he told her he was taking a shower and would be back in a few minutes. He expected it might be longer. He needed time to think, to unwind. Seventeen. It was wrong. He'd known it was. And he'd been so arrogant about doing the right thing. What an idiot. He'd known she was too young. He had known.

Free of his restrictive clothes, he checked the warmth of the water and stepped in. Maybe he had known. But he cared about her more than he had any other girl in the world. He didn't push. He tried to avoid it. She ... was so relaxed in his arms, after she got over her initial fear caused by the experience ... how long ago? She hadn't said. She said she was forced, but not when. How young was she?

His stomach shot an intense pain and he dropped his head back to let the water pour over his face. She'd relaxed in his arms afterward. It seemed to soothe a lot of her fear, not only at the time, but ever since. Ever since, she'd talked to him more, told him more about herself. Was it wrong if it helped her feel better about herself, less scared?

Of course it was. He was trying to rationalize it. Any way he tried to make it not wrong, it was.

Shoving the faucet back to the wall to stop the water, he scrubbed his body with the rough hotel towel and wrapped it around his waist to go find something comfortable to put on.

She was there. In his room. On his bed, reading the hotel booklet about the area, she met his eyes. She didn't look like she thought it was wrong. She looked like...

Ryan fought his immediate reaction and made small talk while he gathered his briefs and a pair of sweatpants and returned to the bathroom to dress. With a couple of deep breaths, he went back out to her, to the other side of the bed, and pulled out the sheets before propping a pillow against the headboard and grabbing the television remote. She moved next to him. He offered an arm, and clenched his eyes when she cuddled in against his bare chest.

Assured she was asleep, still with a hand wrapped over his arm, Ryan crept out of bed and grabbed his phone. Taking it to the other room, he dialed Dani. She was in a chatty mood – he'd caught her at a good time and was grateful to be able to listen to her recent events instead of having to talk about his own.

"So what's up with you? You've hardly said anything."

So much for avoidance. "Too much to talk about over the phone."

"Ry. Hold on." Background noise of a TV mumbling and voices debating dissipated. "Okay, what is it?"

"Told you, I can't do this over the phone. What's your schedule like next week?"

"Um, don't know. I'll have to check. You know I'm a one-day-at-a-time gal. Let me ... hey, are you okay? Something I can do?"

"Probably not, and if I'm stupid enough to tell you about it, you'll probably not want to help."

"You know better than that. I'm always willing to help you through the stupid things you do." A teasing note in her voice only made him feel worse. "Ry? What have you eaten today?"

"What brought that up?"

"You know why I'm asking. How's the stomach?"

He gulped a breath of air. "Well, it put me in the hospital for a couple of days a couple of weeks ago..."

"Ryan! I thought that was a stunt! It sounded like it..."

"It was supposed to. Glad it worked."

"You're better now?"

"More or less, but damn I could use your company."

"Are you at home?"

"Nah, I'm ... hell, you'd never believe it. Find out how next week works. Phone's always on. But I gotta go. Tell Brian he better be taking care of you."

"Yeah, tell Daws I said the same and I'll be taking his head off for letting you get so bad without even calling me."

"He'll be terrified."

"Ryan ... you know how you matter to me. You better take care of yourself. Understand?"

"Me too, Dan. Night." Hanging up, he shoved a hand through his hair. He shouldn't have called her. She would worry now until they got together, if they did. Rarely did it ever work. He hoped it would. Although he knew this time she would definitely have *his* head, never mind Daws.

13

He could barely read Daws's number in the dusky morning light, and Ryan considered ignoring it. Too damn early for a phone call. When Katie stirred beside him, he figured he better answer while it was still possible it didn't wake her. "What?"

"What's going on, Reynauld?"

"I'm asleep. Know what time it is? Hold on." He pulled it from his ear and eased out of bed. Her eyes opened and he sat down again to give her a quick kiss and told her to go back to sleep, then took the phone to the other room. "Yeah okay, are you calling this early for a reason?"

"You called Dani last night. Scared her half to death. What's going on?"

"She didn't actually call you?" He rubbed his head.

"Got a message late last night. Pretty pissed off. You didn't bother to tell her about the hospital before last night and then wouldn't say anything about it? Is there something wrong with you?"

"Hold on." Ryan looked in at Katie to be sure she was still in bed and walked to the back corner of the other room. "Daws, she's not nineteen. She's seventeen. They lied to her about her age. Changed it." Listening to silence, Ryan could just see his friend's face. "She didn't know. She wouldn't have lied to me…"

"Stop right there." A pause. "Okay, don't tell me what no one needs to know. Got it? She's there with you now?"

"The other room. Adjoining."

"I know, moron. I booked them that way. Tell me you're using both."

"Yes." It was true. He was using one for phone calls.

"Yeah, okay. What about the father? How's that going?"

"Not so good. Doesn't like musicians, apparently, and Katie … she's afraid of him or something. Wants to leave. He wants her to stay."

"Hell. I kept telling you…"

"Not the time. We gotta go back this morning. Nick's trying to help but he and her dad don't get along well."

"Reynauld, listen to me. Get her comfortable with her family and encourage her to stay."

"She doesn't want to stay…"

"I don't want your ass in jail, either. I don't want your albums burned in protest by fans who think … just get her to stay. Come back to work. Visit. Call. She's not alone anymore. She has family. Step back out of it."

He shoved a hand through his hair, grasped a handful, and looked toward the ceiling.

"Way I see it, if her father wants her to stay and she's seventeen, you've got no choice. It'll be better for her…"

"She's afraid of him, Daws. She barely remembers him and she's not who she was, which is what he wants…"

"They'll have to work it out."

"*Damn*. Do you really not give a shit about her yet? I know you can be a heartless bastard, but still…"

"Ryan. How do you think she's going to take it if her father has you locked up? Wanna stop and think about that?"

"He can't. He doesn't know we've done anything and she would never tell him…"

"Holy hell. You just can't keep your mouth shut."

Realizing he'd practically admitted what he shouldn't have, Ryan lowered onto the bed and leaned forward to rest an elbow on his knee.

"You haven't said anything to Nick?"

"No."

"Thank the Lord for that. Try to keep it that way."

"I'm not *that* much of a moron. I tell you everything. Doesn't mean I'd…"

"Okay. Just do me a favor and try to avoid saying much to anyone. Get her comfortable there and get your ass back to work. Let me know when you're ready and I'll get the flight."

Ryan was too tired to argue. He knew Daws was right. He knew he had no choice. Still, he'd promised. Leaving her with a family she didn't know would be too much like leaving her alone. And he promised.

~~~

"She needs to stay." Robert peered at him through wire-framed lenses. "I think you know that as well as I do. She needs her family."

Ryan tapped his foot against the stone floor. Maybe. They'd been there three days and Nick was doing a decent job helping Kaitlyn relax around her parents and brothers. Paul seemed to pull her out some, also. He was a quiet child with an easy manner, unlike his more hyper siblings. And he never asked her anything about herself. Ryan could see she appreciated it, especially when her dad constantly asked.

"Ryan." He demanded some kind of answer, or at least attention.

"I don't know. I think she won't want to…"

"Not if you don't suggest it. You influence her."

"No." He stiffened.

"Even if you don't mean to, yes, you do. You know I'll insist either way. I have that right and I will, but it would be easier on her if you support that decision."

"And she'll think I'm trying to ditch her. I told her I wouldn't."

Robert stood with a sigh and paced around the breakfast nook. Ryan sipped at his weak coffee and focused out the big windows on tree branches dancing in an unfelt breeze. It was nearly three-four time, a triangular movement, and words came to him, bits of lyrics to match the tree timing.

"I lost her too early." Robert had stopped and was staring out the same window. "I should have had these past seventeen years with her, to help her grow up as she should have. Ten of them were stolen from me. From her. You can't understand, until you have children, what a loss I've been dealing with, how ... how it changed me. I didn't used to be like this, stiff and ... obnoxious. Yes, I know I am, but I had to get by, to learn how to live with it, the not knowing. You can't understand..."

"No, I can't. But it's Katie I'm concerned about most. She's been let down too often, hurt too often, and I can't do it to her. I can't let her think..."

He turned. "So tell her that. Tell her you're not *ditching* her, that you're doing it *for* her, that it's best for her..."

"Is it?"

"Being with her family, as she should have been, instead of...." He dropped his stare, silent before returning it. "What is it that you want or expect from her? Why are you doing this?"

"Expect?" Ryan shook his head. "I don't expect anything. I'm trying to help..."

"Why?"

He was stunned enough by the question he couldn't answer.

"No one does anything for a stranger without wanting something, especially from a beautiful young girl..."

"Maybe some people do." Ryan stood, held himself straight and acted like he had more dignity than he did. "I reached out to her because she needed *someone* to reach out to her. Nothing more. She needed help. If it had been anyone else who needed the same kind of help, I would have done the same. It has nothing to do with how she looks or her age. She needed ... someone. I don't expect anything. This isn't about me. And it's not about you. It's about her, about ... making her realize she has reason ... like any of us, to ... to be, to grow and ... to find something better."

"Better than what?"

He couldn't say. He wouldn't betray her trust. "Than whatever came before that's made her so afraid."

"You know more than you're saying."

"Yes."

"You want to fill me in? Maybe it would help if I knew..."

"No. She'll have to tell you, if she decides. I won't. It's not fair to her."

Robert turned again, watching the dancing branches in three-four time. "And when do you plan to leave here and return to your job?"

He overlooked the insulting way Robert said *job*. At least he could answer that one. "I have to be back by Tuesday at the latest, and that's pushing it. They're already yelling, but I do want her to have time to get more comfortable..."

"Why does it matter to you?" Her father twisted back, the stare fully intact. "If you're trying to take her away again, why does it matter how comfortable she gets here?"

"This isn't about you. No offense, but it's not. You have family around who's here for you. You seem to be doing fine, working and living like everyone else. This isn't for or about you. And I know I sound obnoxious now, but my concern is for Katie. We helped her find her family for *her* sake, not for yours. We thought it would help. I'm not so sure it did. But I still hope..."

"If you ever in your lifetime have children, you'll realize just how obnoxious you're being. I hope you don't ever have to deal with such a loss."

Ryan nodded. "Agreed. But it's not about me, either. We all have our issues to deal with, but I don't think either of ours even comes close to touching hers. There's plenty *you* don't understand."

"Well, since you refuse to let me in on my daughter's life..."

"I had no one to tell me. She did, after I earned her trust. I won't destroy it now. She has to have someone she trusts and she has to know she always can." It was the wrong thing to say to her father. Ryan knew it was, but he was being cornered. Or he felt defensive enough to seem cornered.

"As though she should trust some singer she barely knows more than she trusts her own father. Is that fair to her, Ryan? Is it fair to her to encourage that?

"I'm not..."

"Yes, you are. You're letting her lean on you so thoroughly she thinks she doesn't need anyone else. But it's not true, and you know it's not true. No one should have only one person they lean on, because that doesn't always work out, especially not with a stranger who's helping only from a desire to be a good Samaritan for once in his life to make up for everything else he's never done for anyone."

Ryan dropped his eyes.

"Hit a sore spot? Does it sound familiar at all?" Robert walked closer. "Don't think I don't know. I can see through you, as I saw through Nick. You're the same. Big names and adored by thousands of people who don't know you, all the while knowing you're nothing to adore, that you're nothing but an entertainer who escapes from himself behind a curtain instead of living out here in the real world with us working stiffs who have nowhere to hide."

"You have no idea who I am." With false bravado, Ryan met his stare.

"No? Do you have any idea who you are?"

"This isn't about me."

"Isn't it, Ryan? Isn't it about *your* need more than about hers? Because I think you're propagating her need of you purposely in disguise because it's actually you who needs her." He paused. "No one does anything for someone without personal reasons. No one. I admit my personal need to get to know my daughter again to help heal my own loss. Find the man inside you and at least admit your own need. You know it's there."

His own need. His own need ... was to keep her beside him, not only for her, but for himself. Yes, he needed her.

Unable to admit it to her father, Ryan walked away.

~~~

He paced around the hotel lobby. Surprised she agreed to stay at her father's overnight when Ryan suggested she should, he cringed to find he wished she hadn't. He was right. Robert was right about everything he said. He wasn't doing it for Katie. He was doing it for himself. He needed her. He wanted her to want him more than anyone else. He wanted to be her good Samaritan, a white knight who gleamed in her eyes. Adored by thousands ... yes, by thousands who didn't know him. Fan adoration meant nothing but a paycheck, and that he could *live* his music instead of getting to do it as he could around a "real" job as a working stiff. He'd been that. He'd worked fast food, retail stock room, he bailed hay ... he knew what a real job was. And whatever her father thought of him, Ryan knew what loss was. He still missed his own father every day of his life.

Grabbing his phone from his jeans pocket, he dialed his brother.

"What's wrong?"

Will's voice comforted and disturbed him. He didn't know what to say, and a couple of people were staring. Moving out the doors, he headed ... somewhere, away from people.

"Ry?"

"Sorry, had to move elsewhere."

"What's going on with Kaitlyn?"

With a sigh, he told his brother the basics of how her father wanted her to stay, how he wasn't sure he should suggest it, and how he wasn't sure how she would take it or if she would misunderstand.

"What does she say about it?"

"Nothing."

"At all? Not even to you?"

"I haven't asked. Her father did, but she wouldn't answer. She won't talk to him, and I can't see…"

"They don't get along?"

Ryan frowned. "Well, things have changed a lot. He expects her to be as she was. You should see the pictures of her. She was … anyway, I think she's afraid of being pushed to talk about the past ten years when she doesn't want him to know."

"But you know?" His voice sounded cautious.

"Pieces. A few things she's said, not much. Enough to know why she doesn't." He walked out into the parking lot when the people who'd stared inside began to approach. "Will, he accused me of wanting her *not* to trust him, or talk to him, so she would stay dependent on me. I didn't know how to answer."

"Is it true?"

He continued his walk around the mostly empty parking area, keeping track of where the people were. "I don't know. Maybe."

Will was silent until Ryan heard a deep breath through the receiver. "You remember when I started to get serious about Tracy? How Mom reacted?"

"Yeah, she freaked like she would never see you again."

A chuckle came over the line. "It's natural when you've had so much responsibility for someone you care so much about to protest when you start to lose it. It was nothing against Tracy. You know Mom adores her now. And do you think it was easy for us to watch you walk away when we knew we'd hardly see you for who knows how many years? Think it was easy for me after I half raised you? Should I have tried to talk you out of it?" Will waited for a response he didn't get. "Ryan, letting go is a bitch, and I'm sure Tracy and I will feel the same about the kids when they grow up and move on, but it's part of life."

Letting go. Will was telling him to let go; he'd done his job, or much of it. "Yeah." The staring couple had been joined by others and were all looking over at him. He headed to the building and wondered if he would also have to call Daws.

"Hey." His brother's voice pulled him back. "Ask her. Don't suggest either way. Just ask her what she wants. She'll let you know."

"Yeah."

"And Ry? We're always here."

"Thanks. I have to go. Tell Tracy and the kids hi for me." Ryan ended the call but kept the phone in his hand, walking faster to push inside the hotel. He didn't wait on the elevator; instead, he jogged up the stairwell and locked himself inside his room. Trying to decide what to do with his night, he knew he would have to wait until the snoopy people went elsewhere. And he hoped they wouldn't spread it all over town.

Around seven, he couldn't stand to be cooped up alone any longer, even with Dani calling and keeping him on the line forever, as she had at least once every day since he worried her. Alone. He couldn't take it for more than two hours. He couldn't imagine ... but she wasn't now. She was with her family. It would be better for her. Maybe.

Ryan pushed his shoes back on and grabbed his keys and phone. He'd take a drive and find somewhere to be around others, somewhere dark and crowded where he could get lost. Barely into the hallway, though, he saw them: a large group of girls who closed in and shoved paper and markers at him, clinging, flashing cameras ... and he couldn't go back in the room. The longer he stayed, the more there would be until he was good and stuck.

As politely as he could manage, he chatted and signed and smiled and nudged through to the elevator. He wouldn't let himself get trapped in the stairwell with them. They followed him all the way, as many as could fit in the small elevator, through the lobby where more joined the throng. Hotel clerks tried to help as they could but it still took forever to get out to the parking lot where he jogged to his rental, to Nick's rental.

Locked inside the car, Ryan pulled out while he could and headed down the road. He started to call Daws. No, he wouldn't bring his friend back to work during his rare time off. He would simply find another hotel and ... and all of his things were in the room. He couldn't go back, not alone.

With Huey Lewis and the News happily singing how "alright" it was, he headed away from town in search of something somewhat jaded and not too populated. It could take as long as it needed to take. The drive in the dark would do him good. If not for Katie, he'd simply keep driving out into nowhere and worry about finding himself later. As it was, he could go until he was too tired and pull into whatever hole-in-the-wall he came across. In the morning, he'd drive back again to find her.

Although Huey was alright, Paula wasn't working for him and he buzzed through stations to find something heavier. He stopped at the Crüe and had to laugh at the irony of wanting a heart kick-started. His sure as hell had been. Maybe for no reason, as things were going.

A barely-lit sign broadcasted The Hillside Tavern and Grill and he couldn't help think they could be slightly more original. Yeah, they were located on a hillside. Big surprise in Montana in the midst of mountains. Did they have to announce they were as though people wouldn't know otherwise? Okay, he was being snippy. But he also couldn't help think that by the look of the place, he might be willing to drink there but he wasn't so sure he'd want food. Alcohol was bottled and safe enough. Possible food poisoning was not on his to-do list.

It would have to be good enough. He didn't want to get too far from her. In case she'd call. Would she remember his cell number? Stupid question. She remembered numbers. But would she use it?

Gravel crunched beneath the tires when he turned in. He grimaced at an unseen pothole.

Throwing the thing into park and turning off the engine, he called Nick. Her uncle could at least tell him she was doing all right. Except he sounded hesitant to say she was and asked if he wanted to talk to her.

"No, I don't want to interrupt unless she needs to talk. I just … I wanted to be sure you'd call my cell instead of the room if you need to reach me since I'm not there." Explaining, he wasn't sure he appreciated the laughter at the other end.

"Where are you now?"

Ryan repeated the name on the sign, and thought he managed to do it without a condescending tone.

"I know the place. Are you going to be inside?"

"Yeah, it's a nothing bar. Can't be too many people in there and probably a bunch of men who won't give a shit who I am. Not a place I'd take a girl from the way it looks."

"Should be fine. I'll be there soon."

"Nah, no need. I'll just head down the road and find somewhere else to sleep…"

"Not much that direction for a hell of a long ways. Stay put. I'll be there."

"Thanks and I'm sorry about the interference…"

"Hell, you're apologizing to the wrong guy. Glad to help." The phone clicked.

Only Nick came. Ryan flagged him from a corner of the bar where he'd stayed to himself despite the attempts at socializing by a few friendly drinkers. It wasn't as bad inside as he expected. It was as clean as his apartment before Katie moved in, and there were a few women who laughed with the men flirting, but no one was overly intoxicated or overly interested in talking to him.

"You look safe enough." Nick grinned and greeted the bartender by name when offered his usual. With a side nod, he set a hand on Ryan's shoulder. "This is a friend of mine. Hope you're treating him right."

The bartender raised his eyebrows. "Yeah? Unfriendly sort for being a friend of yours."

"He's had a rough day. How about a refill of whatever he's drinking?"

Ryan glanced around the bar when a couple of others yelled a hello to Nick. "Shouldn't we make ourselves scarce?"

"You're all right here. Sit."

"They know my car."

"Do they?" Nick shrugged. "We'll worry about that tomorrow.

Anything personal in your room Becca can't grab?"

"No. My stuff's in the suitcase. I don't bother to take it out."

"Yeah, not much point in that when you're always putting it right back in again."

"Is Katie all right there? She didn't mind you leaving?"

"I think she's more worried about you. She'll be fine."

Left alone with Nick other than casual chit chat from a few who knew the guitarist, Ryan started to unwind. Still, there was the issue of where he would stay. As he drained his second beer, he waited for privacy to ask where he could go.

"Back to Robert's. Probably not a good idea to leave you alone anywhere around here now."

"Her father's house? He doesn't want me there."

Nick studied him. "Any reason we shouldn't let you be?"

"What?" Ryan refused when the bartender asked about another beer. "Other than the fan club finding out?"

"They won't bother him. They know better." Nick took another swallow. "He has friends in all the high places around here. Everyone knows it. Cops would be all over the place if they even tried to gather around his house."

All the high places. The thought made Ryan shudder.

"So what are you going to do about Katie?"

"What am I going to do?"

"Are you going to follow orders and suggest she stay?"

Lowering his gaze, Ryan scratched his head. "Not like I have any choice in the matter."

"You can encourage it or fight it. Just wondered which you plan. So is she."

"What did she say?"

Nick shook his head and emptied the bottle. "She's not saying anything, to anyone."

"She was talking to you. She has been."

"Only if you're around. Not otherwise."

Ryan's stomach spasmed. He shouldn't have had the second beer. "How can I suggest she stay when she won't speak to anyone? How can he ask me to tell her I think it's a good idea when it's not? It's not for me. If I thought it would be better for her, it wouldn't matter that I don't want to leave her here. But I don't think it would be. I think she would feel..."

"Abandoned?"

An unintentional gasp filled his lungs. Abandoned. Nick knew it. He understood her. If only her father did. "I can't." He bounced his foot on the metal rod of the bar stool. "I can't tell her I think she should stay."

"Robert will be furious."

"Yeah."

Silence penetrated as they pretended to watch the game on a small television across the bar. Furious. He knew all the highest people. Wonderful. But as long as he didn't find out how close they were, how close they had been, he could do nothing. Maybe.

"Ready to go? Katie'll get mad if I keep you too long. She tried to come with but Robert suggested it wasn't a good idea." Nick shrugged. "I figured it wasn't worth a fight to win the little battle."

"Why don't you get along with him?"

Nick's face reflected both amusement and irritation. "He married my sister."

"So?"

"So I didn't approve."

"Oh." He wouldn't ask more. Ryan imagined it was enough. "What happened to her? Katie hasn't said."

His jaw clenched for only a second. "She got caught between two worlds." He stood and paid the bartender, insisting on both tabs. "Let's go. She'll worry."

Caught between two worlds. Like Katie was? Did her mom have to choose somehow between her husband and her family?

He didn't argue when Nick said to leave the rental. Sliding into the green Plymouth, Ryan watched the lights from the bar in the rear view mirror until they faded away.

Katie threw her arms around him when he stepped in the door. "Are you okay?"

"It was nothing, only an annoyance." He pulled back to find her face. "Are you?"

She didn't answer. Her eyes said she wasn't.

"We were talking about how she should stay here with us. Tonight shows even more why she should." Her father moved in, glancing between them.

"For hell's sakes, Robert. You had to do that while I was going after him? You couldn't wait?" Nick shook his head. "That's the kind of shit you did to..."

"Don't give me that attitude. I don't want my daughter around it for the same reason I didn't want my wife around it. It's no place for a lady."

"Excuse me?" Rebecca threw her shoulders back.

"I mean nothing against you. But you're not seventeen years old."

"No, but I was, and I don't see that it hurt me."

"Didn't it?"

"*Robert.*" Nick threw a glare. "Enough. This is not about us and it's not about Marlisse. Don't take it out on Katie."

"I'm taking nothing out on her. I'm trying to protect her..."

"Like you didn't before?"

Robert's face clouded. "Get out of my house."

Kaitlyn released Ryan's arm and went to her uncle. "Don't."

His face softened. "I'm sorry. I shouldn't have said that. I don't want you caught in between, also. This is not fair to you. I stayed out of it more than I should have with your mother and I won't make that mistake again."

"Don't talk like it was my fault, like I was the one..."

Nick set an arm around Kaitlyn's shoulders. "Look at her, will you? Are you paying attention to the fact that she didn't say a word to anyone when he wasn't here and now she is? You want to take away her security zone? You think that's a good idea?"

Kaitlyn's eyes were on the floor. It was too much. She was too stuck in the middle. It had to be her decision. But she didn't want to choose, between her uncle and her father ... or between him and her family. It wasn't fair to ask.

"I um...." He moved in beside her. "I have to go back in two days. The pre-tour is coming up in a couple of weeks and I should be there already. It's a short one, remember? Just several dates in smaller places we don't usually get to, kind of half shows, simple.... Maybe, instead of staying with my family this time, you might want to stay here? Not that you can't come with me. You can, of course..."

"Even *he* is suggesting it's not good to have a young lady around it. Are you getting this, Nick?"

Ryan met Robert's gaze. "No, that's not what I'm saying. She would be perfectly safe. I have the world's best security. But it's always crowded and tiring..."

"Security for yourself..."

"For whoever needs it. Daws, my main in-charge, knows I would expect her safety to come before mine. It would be safe..."

"Like tonight?"

"I was on my own tonight. That doesn't happen much."

Katie set a hand on his chest. "You're staying here. Not on your own." It wasn't a question.

"If I'm allowed."

"If you leave, I'll go with you."

"Well." Robert cleared his throat. "That's fine, since Nick already invited you, but the rooms are full. You'll have to take the couch. It's the best we can do without a rock star mansion."

Andrea again said the boys could camp downstairs. Robert argued.

Ryan shrugged. "The couch is fine. I sleep on my own often enough when I have company since my place isn't that big. I'm actually really far from a rock star. More like a pop jester." Robert stared, not getting it. "You know, like Elvis was the king of rock? I'm the underling of pop who amuses everyone with a claim of talent. The court jester of music."

Her father wasn't impressed with the joke, but Nick grinned and tapped his arm. "Usually the most worth listening to. Come on. I think coffee would be good about now." He glanced toward Andrea. "By the way, I think she would argue since she's a fan of yours."

Raising his eyebrows at Nick, he looked over to see Andrea blush ... and Robert clench his jaw.

~~~

As he watched Katie's parents interact, Ryan felt even more out of place.

His parents, while he still had both, had run the house together. There was no "in charge" – the rules were set and they all did whatever needed to be done. He and Will helped cook, clean, and did their own laundry as soon as they were old enough, as well as mowing the grass and taking out the garbage. Decisions were made by mutual agreement other than certain things one of his parents allowed the other full say about. If there was an "in charge" parent, it was his mom. Will's wife, also, was mainly in charge of her house and the kids other than when she sent them to their father for a second opinion, as though it was needed. Every girl Ryan dated, which didn't include his tour flings, was the same: strong, bold, independent. As was his manager. And his publicist. And pretty much every woman he spent any amount of time around. Andrea seemed to be none of those. He figured Katie had seen way too much of her simply taking orders and keeping opinions to herself. She needed to spend more time with Will and Tracy, and his mom. If he could get her out of her father's clutches. He was starting to have doubts about that.

Ryan sipped at a glass of cranberry juice Katie pushed at him, insanely glad he'd be back at his own place the next day. Daws had arranged flights for both of them, although it hadn't been quite settled that Robert would allow it. Ryan wouldn't leave without her. It was too soon. She needed time.

He figured he should to get it over with and find out what kind of resistance he would have. While they sat around the dining table finishing their custard, he mentioned that Deanna hoped Katie would attend yoga with her in a couple of days.

Her eyes barely touched his before Robert cleared his throat to interrupt. "Yoga? Is that something you're interested in?"

She held her spoon mid-air, waiting....

"I'm sure they have it somewhere around here. Andrea can check."

Ryan was about to have a fight on his hands.

"Don't start that shit." Nick banged his beer on the table, with a stare at his brother-in-law. "You know she needs to go back where she's comfortable."

"Don't speak that way in front of my children."

"They hear worse at school."

"They aren't at school. They are at my table."

"Fine, but you know she's not ready to stay here. You've found her, Robert. Ease back into it."

"You have no say in this."

Nick leaned back in his chair, his chin raised. "And neither does she, right? Like no one else has a say in anything around here? Only you."

"Stop or get out."

A sarcastic laugh escaped while Nick shook his head. "Your answer to everything. Worked well, has it?"

Bolting from his chair, Robert dismissed the kids and told his wife she could clean up. They were done.

Katie started to grab things from the table. Her father told her to leave it, there would be plenty of time to help on days she didn't have company. She obeyed only for a couple of seconds and continued around the side of the table where Nick stood, away from her father and into the kitchen. Rebecca remained with Nick. Ryan decided he'd rather help clean up, but he couldn't. She needed him to stand up to her father.

"Mr. Murray." He pretended to clear his own throat while he tried to make it work. "If you'll allow her to return with me, to let her settle in and get her bearings, I'll ask again if she wants to stay here while I'm out running around..."

"This isn't up to you, either. I'm her father and for another two months, it's my decision. Maybe more than that, considering the circumstances."

Circumstances. He planned to use her silence against her. "You don't want to do that."

"Excuse me?"

"It would make everything worse."

"And you think you know what's best for her?"

"No." Ryan imitated the way he'd seen Daws show his determination to get what he wanted. "I think it would be best to let her make her own decisions."

"You say that because you know what she'll decide."

"I say that because I care about her."

"And I don't?" He glowered.

"Then ask her what she wants. She's not seven anymore. Give her the respect to *ask* her." He grabbed a breath. "If I thought she would rather be here, I would want her to stay."

Katie and Andrea returned to gather more dishes from the table.

They were stalled by the staring match. Ryan stepped back, conceding only enough, and began to help clear the table.

"You should finish this." Katie held his glass of half-empty juice, her eyes searching his.

He couldn't argue with her. She wanted it, said it was good for his stomach, and he couldn't argue. He would let her know he could allow her to take charge and take care of him as she felt she needed.

14

Daws yanked Ryan's shirt to pull him back a ways, leaving Katie and Deanna to continue toward his loft. "How'd you get her out of there?"

Ryan shrugged. "Told him he should ask her what she wanted. And … she agreed to go back and stay with them at the end of the month when I'm on tour. She doesn't want to, but it helped him give in this time."

"Or he gave in so he'll have time to gather evidence to keep her away from you."

"Evidence of what?"

"Is there any? Other than your history. Anyone but me know anything?"

"No."

"Not even your family?"

"Hell, they think I'm trying to be a big brother to her."

"Would've been a better idea." Daws started walking again. "You've got a hell of a support system there. Likely a damn good thing."

"You expect trouble."

He stopped and met Ryan's eyes. "I expect a whole hell of a lot of trouble once this gets out, and it will if you go against her father. Should've left her there." Daws moved ahead to go unlock the door for the girls.

Ryan plopped on the couch and kicked his socked heels up on the coffee table. Deanna insisted on staying for dinner and helped Kaitlyn cook, and now showed no sign of being willing to leave. A look from Daws told Ryan there was no point in trying to convince her.

"Tell me more about your brothers, honey." Deanna took the space on the couch beside Ryan while Katie claimed her chair. "He said they were a lot younger than you, right?"

She nodded. Her tea was cradled in her hands.

"Did you get along okay? I have a younger brother and an older and they were always on my nerves. Still are most of the time." She waited but Katie glanced at Ryan to let him take over.

"They're great kids. The youngest is something else. Always on the move. He's six." Ryan knew Deanna's look meant she didn't want him to answer for Kaitlyn but Katie wanted him to, so he ignored it. "Stephen, the middle one is super talkative. Paul, he's eleven, is the serious one.

And very smart. We talked about music some when his dad wasn't around to stop it."

Deanna frowned. "Stopped talk about music? Why?"

Ryan explained the basics of the conflict between Nick and Robert.

"So the last place he wanted her to be..."

"Anywhere around a musician."

With a swallow of her wine, Deanna turned back to Kaitlyn. "Maybe you should come stay with us. Your father might have less trouble with that, even if Freddy is involved with it, it's not the same, and ... it would look better..."

"Hell, don't you start that shit, too." Ryan jumped up from the couch. "*Look* better. Is that all that matters? How it *looks*?"

"Reynauld."

He shrugged at Daws. "What's it going to matter now? She's been staying here for months. What difference is it gonna make?"

"You know that without asking."

"Because we thought she had no family. Because we thought ... she thought she was nineteen and she's not? Yeah well, so what? It changes nothing. What's happened has still happened. It doesn't erase because we didn't know. It's still all the same."

"No, it's not." Deanna stood beside him. "You didn't know. That matters."

"Maybe it doesn't."

"If this gets to the press, it does. It can destroy your career, Ryan. You know if her father makes it an issue, if he decides to say you took advantage, they'll jump all over it whether it's true or not. You won't get booked anywhere. You might as well walk away now..."

"No." Kaitlyn moved between them and set a hand on his chest. "I won't let it hurt you. I won't let him."

With a light grin, he brushed fingers down along her face. "I don't want you to worry about me. I want to know what you want. Honestly. Whatever it is."

Her gaze held almost steady. "I want to not hurt you." She wrapped around him, her fists clenched in his shirt and pressed against his back.

Ryan lowered his head against hers and closed his eyes. He heard Daws – from a few days before – ask how she would feel if he ended up behind bars. If Robert did use her silence against her, if he claimed "circumstances" made her a target, it could happen. And it would be too much for her to take, harder on her than on him. With his status, he would be all right. They'd take care of him. But he wasn't sure what she would do.

"Promise me something, Katie." He kissed the side of her face. "Promise me you'll be okay. No matter what. You take care of yourself. Do whatever you have to do to be okay. Tell them anything you need to tell them if it will help you. Never mind me. Take care of yourself first."

She didn't move.

"Kaitlyn." He forced enough space to find her eyes. "Promise me."

Her head shook, lightly, but enough he knew she wouldn't agree.

"Don't do this. We've come so far." He raised her chin with his fingers. "Please. I have to know you'll be all right. The rest of it doesn't matter unless you are."

"You should have left me there." Her voice was nearly a whisper but it dropped a weight on his heart. Left her there. He didn't at all believe she meant at her father's.

"I told you to go back inside. You should have."

His whole body tensed and he grabbed her hand when she started to move away from him. "No." Capturing her within his arms, he felt her distance, withdrawal. "No. I may have done everything else wrong, but not that. *Not* that." He kept her locked in against him, moved his hand over the back of her head, and pulled her as close as possible. Should have left her there. No. He wasn't going to lose her.

"Daws."

"Yeah."

"She's staying here tonight. I don't give a damn how it looks. She's staying here."

"Yeah. Want us to stay?"

"No. I want you to go."

Ryan heard some shuffling about and Deanna's protest and Daws telling him to call if he needed anything ... and the door closed. He felt himself breathe more deeply with the sudden quiet and privacy of being home with Kaitlyn. Only Kaitlyn. It wouldn't feel like home without her anymore. It never quite did before her.

He didn't bother to say anything more. She didn't want more words. He couldn't think of any that would change her mind. Instead, he kissed the side of her face, her ear, shifted to reach her neck. She raised her head to allow better access and released his shirt to stroke his skin underneath. Ryan didn't care how damn old she was. He didn't care what anyone would say. He wanted her to not be sorry she came in off the ledge with him. He wanted to bring more pleasure into her world. He would take her boating ... when, he wasn't sure. His schedule would be packed getting ready for the tour. But he would make time.

Moving to her lips, he felt tears on her cheeks and found her eyes.

Her hands moved up to his chest, head ducked toward him.

"What is it, Kaitlyn? What are you thinking?"

She dropped her forehead to his shoulder. "I want there to be one person I care about who I don't hurt." Her fingers slid to his side, again clenched his shirt. "I wanted it to be you."

"You haven't." He caressed her lower back. "And if someone else does, it's not your fault. Remember that. It's not your fault if they don't understand. I won't regret it. And I'll bounce back, as long as I have you to bounce back to." He insisted on her attention. "I'm glad I found you. Glad we found each other. Nothing will change that. I can't tell you how much I'm glad you're here with me."

She kissed him, pressed in, made it deeper. Her frustration changed, turning into ... into passion, more than he'd yet seen from her.

His body reacted quickly, too quickly, and she whispered next to his ear. "I need to shower."

"Mmm." He pressed his lips against her neck and enjoyed her fresh, soft scent. "Yeah. Me too." Casting a quick question at her eyes, he grasped her fingers and walked backward, wondering if she would object. He didn't want to leave her side long enough for two showers, even two quick showers. She went with him, far enough to turn him back around, and took the lead. He started the water and let it warm while he pulled his shirt off. Her gaze fell against his bare skin. This time, she didn't insist on lowering the lights, not like it was possible in the bathroom, but she either didn't think about it or decided to let it go, to stop hiding.

~~~

"Hey, Kaitlyn and I are going out since you're ignoring us anyway."

Ryan and Daws looked over at Deanna in tandem from the sound board. Kaitlyn was waiting for his reply, her eyes on him.

"Where're you going?"

Deanna shrugged. "Girl's day out. Manicures, shopping, maybe a hair trim. I need one badly enough it's making me grouchy."

"Yeah, it's horrible." Ryan couldn't help tease. Deanna's hair was always perfect – casually perfect, but always 'done' as she called it. He wondered if Katie would let a stranger mess with her hair, or her nails. "Wanna meet for an early dinner? I'm starving already. I'll have to come back after, but they gotta let me take time to eat."

"Where?"

"Anywhere close."

A sparkle lit her face. "The View?"

"Great." He turned back long enough to nod at his tech's question.

"I was kidding."

He knew she was. Ryan never agreed to go to the forty-seventh floor restaurant at the Marriott Marquis or to the forty-eighth floor buffet lounge above it. Deanna loved the place and she pulled Daws there now and then but Ryan refused. The thought of the wrap-around windows that high up usually made him nauseous. But it didn't this time. Katie would love it. "It's fine if you can get us in and if it doesn't take forever. Say ... two hours or three? Call Daws and tell him."

"Ryan, you don't want to…"

"Yeah. You know, I can't stay terrified of the thought forever. It's closed in, after all. Not like I'm gonna fall out." He got up and went over to Kaitlyn. "It's supposed to have a fantastic view of the city, not that I can verify personally. What do you think?"

She looked amazingly close to a smile, or at least a grin. "Okay."

He touched her arm, wary of watchful eyes. "Have fun. Deanna has my card. If you find something you like, get it. Are you coloring your nails, too?"

She shook her head but Deanna jumped in. "Well, of course. Heck, if we're living it up at The View tonight, might as well go all the way. You'll see what color after she decides." Grabbing Kaitlyn away from him, Deanna threw a wink at Daws and pulled the girl out by the hand. Ryan hoped it was all right to let her.

The past four days, even as stuffed with work as they were, found Katie relaxing, returning to where they'd been before the England trip. She was talking more, not only to him but to Daws and Deanna and an occasional word to Ned who kept bringing her trinkets or books or a handful of wildflowers he said he picked up at his sister's place out in the suburbs. Ryan couldn't figure what the drummer was trying to do, but since he showed up at the loft with a clingy girl the night before, Ryan figured he wasn't trying to hit on her.

Nick called once a day, usually from Robert's, to check in and she spoke to him briefly over the phone. He had the idea Robert didn't bother to try. The plan was for Nick to come to New York and stay a couple of days before Ryan left on tour, then escort Kaitlyn back to her father's house. Rebecca had returned to England, to her job that was flexible but only to a point. Ryan didn't have a confirmed answer as to whether Nick would stay at Robert's the whole time Katie would be there. He hoped to hell he would. Either way, she would be able to reach Ryan whenever she needed as soon as he bought her a cell phone. It was next on his to-do list. He wanted no barriers. She had to know she could reach him, always.

"Here." Daws shoved a shirt and tie at him still on a hanger. "There's a dress code."

"Why do you have my clothes in your car?"

"Because you can't wear that old nasty T-shirt, even if we're doing the lounge instead of the restaurant. Change. We're already late." While he threw orders, he pulled his own button-down shirt over his white T-shirt.

"Not my fault."

"No? You had to argue every point, did you?"

Ryan shrugged and pulled his neon green T-shirt over his head. "It's my show, isn't it? It's my name pulling them in."

"Since when do you take an interest in background effects?" Daws eyed him across the car roof.

"Always did. Just never insisted on anything before. And this shirt isn't nasty. What's wrong with it?" Holding his tee in both hands, he checked for stains or holes. Someone else in the garage commented about his public nudity. He was only half nude and they were in an enclosed parking garage, not public, so he pretended not to hear.

"Reynauld, get dressed. Deanna will have our heads."

Ryan laughed. "Must be interesting to be so in charge of everything everywhere except with your very in-charge girlfriend."

"Nice not to be on occasion. And talk to me about it again when you decide to be in charge of yourself much less anything else." With a glance, he slid onto the driver's seat and started the engine.

When he decided to be in charge of himself. A flash of anger fizzled into the annoying thought that he couldn't argue. What did Ryan know about being in charge? He'd never had a chance to be. Pulling the shirt on, he tossed the hanger on the floor of the back seat and got in the front, buttoning it underneath the seatbelt while Daws began the short trek to meet the girls.

Ryan attempted to put on a comfortable act within the walls of the Marriott Marquis. He also tried not to laugh at the sight of his old tennis shoes atop the black and white polished marble floor. Daws had donned a jacket to help complete his look. Ryan was pushing it far enough with the collar shirt hanging over his black jeans and a skinny black tie streaming down his chest. And his tennis shoes. He had to go back to work. He wasn't getting too uncomfortable in the meantime.

"Look at you." Deanna grabbed the top of his arms and stretched back to eye him. "Nice to see you look like the gentleman you aren't." She winked and released him to admire her boyfriend with a hand soft against his stomach. "How hard was it to force his transformation?"

"Told him to put it on." Daws nodded at someone who greeted him and complimented her on the new haircut and dressy, feminine version of a business suit that allowed only enough cleavage to see she had it.

Ryan turned from the ease between them he was often jealous of and circled his eyes around the lobby. He noted a few small groups of people here and there but no one did more than throw him a glance. He supposed his unfriendly reputation had done its job fairly well, at least with this crowd. Some people were more sensitive about being ignored than others. "Where's Kaitlyn?"

"Ladies' room. We had a blast today."

"Yeah? You both did or you did?" He continued the search.

"She's fine. Relax. And we both did. We decided before she went back to visit her family, she should spruce up enough to show them how well she's doing here."

Spruce up? "What do you mean? What'd you do?"

Deanna nodded to his left and he followed her gaze. It took a second to realize it was Kaitlyn and he couldn't help staring, even if it was rude.

"Looks nice, doesn't she?" Deanna nudged his back when Katie stopped in front of him. "A gentleman would say so."

Ryan studied her head to toe, starting with the hair cut. The wispy uneven ends were gone, leaving a fuller, straight cut barely touching her shoulders and rounded up along the front. The bangs were still long but trimmed to frame her face, ears still covered but not obviously. He thought she might have a touch of color on her cheeks and eyes but it was subtle enough it could have been a bit of natural pink from being in the crisp early fall air. Her blouse was soft and feminine, fitted nicely, and dark, dusty pink with a sheen suggesting elegance. It was tucked into a straight skirt falling to her calves. She didn't look like the same person. Definitely not the girl he'd found on the ledge wearing too-large men's clothing.

"You look too good to be seen with this scrounge and he knows it." Daws made up for Ryan's lack of words. "Hungry?"

"Yes." Katie answered his friend, flashing her eyes back to wait for Ryan to regain his senses. "This is a good color for you. It's nice." She touched the cuff of his sleeve. Blue. Royal blue. His least favorite of the button shirts he didn't like.

"You're beautiful, Katie. Well, you always were. I don't mean only because ... I mean, you look great, like always except...."

"Such a sweet talker." Deanna took Kaitlyn's arm. "Come with me. They'll catch up when he takes that huge foot out of his mouth."

But she didn't go. She moved closer to Ryan, close enough he could feel her warmth, smell ... a new scent, like cookies but less sweet. Her eyes were on his. "Thank you. Does it look like I'm doing well here?"

He grinned. "Oh yes. It looks like you're doing very well here." Ryan offered his arm and didn't bother to gloat when she took it instead of staying beside Deanna. Daws was right. She looked too good to be by his side, and he was so hyped by the thought he could barely restrain himself from yelling at everyone to look at her, to look at how far she'd come, how he hadn't completely messed up. How she made him look better.

As though the glass elevator to the thirty-eighth floor wasn't bad enough, Deanna requested a table beside the window. Ryan forced a gallantry and didn't object. He steered Kaitlyn in front of him and focused on her as he held her chair instead of looking out. He didn't suppose he would eat much. It was worth it, though. Her gaze was turned to the city, in awe of the scenery after being in awe of the lounge with its glamour and glitz and revolving floor. Ryan couldn't have even written how glad he was to see her enjoy the view: not his view, but theirs. Something altogether different than either would have seen alone.

~~~

At the gate, Ryan took Kaitlyn's hand and kept her from boarding for as long as possible. Nick noticed, as he had every time Ryan touched Katie in any way over the past two days, but he didn't comment. Her uncle fit right in with the chaos of tour planning, of long hours and bullshitting with the crew, gratefully thanking anyone who recognized him, refusing to give his opinion when asked saying it was Ryan's show, not his. And Katie adored him. It grew more obvious the more they were together. She didn't flinch anymore when he set a hand on her shoulder or back. She didn't pull away. She was especially attracted to his laughter. Nick laughed easily and heartily. It appeared to be a balm to her soul every time he did.

Yes, she would be fine at her father's as long as her uncle was around.

"We have to go." Nick touched the back of her shoulder.

She nodded and gave Ryan a hug, a long close hug.

"I'll call you." He spoke beside her ear and caught her eyes when she moved back. "And you have your phone. Call me any time. If I'm on stage, I'll call back. It might be late, so I'll leave a message if you're asleep. But I'm here. You know I'm here..."

"I know." She leaned in to kiss his cheek. "Be careful of your stomach. Eat some green stuff."

He chuckled. "Yeah, I'll try to force it down."

"And cranberry juice."

"I think that's growing on me." He wanted to kiss her, fully on the lips, not on the cheek, but not in front of Nick and the others in the boarding area. Some were staring already through his guards standing close by. "You take care of yourself. Enjoy your brothers. I hope ... it'll be easier with your dad if I'm not there. It'll be fine."

"Come on Reynauld. People are gathering." Daws pushed at his back. "Have a good flight." He nodded to Kaitlyn and took Nick's hand.

Ryan didn't want to let her go. Something inside said to refuse.

"Katie, they're holding the gate." Nick's voice was soft, sympathetic. "It'll be all right, like he said, but we have to go." He gave Ryan a handshake and wished him well on tour, and guided his niece away, down the little hallway that led to the plane.

Without him.

But she was doing well. She would be fine. And it was only three weeks. A long three weeks. He'd gotten used to her being there, at his side during the day and every night. She'd come to his room every night until Nick arrived.

He wandered over to the ceiling-to-floor windows where he could see the jet. He hadn't even been able to kiss her before she left. Reluctantly allowing the small crowd to pull him back to where he was, who he was, he forced smiles and signed his name and posed with a couple of girls ... and saw Kaitlyn's plane edge away, back up slowly, then move forward.

Without him.

15

"*Not in. Go away.*" Slumped on the hotel couch, Ryan didn't bother to open his eyes. Whoever was knocking should know better. He was tired. They needed to leave him the hell alone so he could rest before the night's show. Another knock told him it must be one of the new crew guys who hadn't yet learned his routine. Whatever. He wasn't getting up.

The door opened and he pried his eyes apart. "Whoever in the hell is bothering me is *fired.*"

"You can't fire me. Just tell me you're at least part dressed so I don't embarrass you."

"Dani." He couldn't see more than the hand holding the door.

"Got the key from Daws since he said you wouldn't answer. Are you covered enough?"

"Too much." He pushed up from the couch to meet her. "Damn it's good to see you."

With a grin, she gave him a hug, holding tight for the longest time – her usual greeting when it had been a while. "I won't stay if you're too tired. Had to let you know I was here." She slid her hands down his arms to grip his fingers. "You are wiped out. Rest and I'll catch up with you when you're not a zombie. I can hang out with Daws."

"No way in hell." He backed up to lead her to the couch. "You didn't tell me you were coming."

She sat close, one leg pulled up and turned to face him. "Last minute. Had a bitch of a time finding where you were. In hiding or something?"

He laughed. "Yeah, from an angry father."

"What?"

"Kidding. Mostly. Nah, I'm not even sure where I am. Whirlwind thing." He studied her face. "What's wrong, Dan?"

Her chest rose slowly. When it fell again, her whole body seemed to fall with it. "Needed to be away from everything. You know how it is."

"Yeah. But there's more. What is it?"

She tilted her head in a shrug. "I came from home. Had to get out of there. Who needs the reminder that you can't live up to expectations when you're in the middle of doing something they all know is incredibly stupid? Didn't feel like trying to explain."

Ryan frowned. He doubted they felt as negative about it as she made it sound. She was always too damn hard on herself.

"Anyway, what's this about an angry father? Mess with the wrong girl this time?"

"Maybe."

"Wait." She shifted, moving closer yet. "This have anything to do with that kid you took in? Young girl, right? What's her name?"

Ryan told her. Everything. He could never keep anything from Dani. He never wanted to keep anything from her.

Her nod told him she had no idea what to say. Unusual for Dani. He always treasured her advice. She was the only one who understood him as well as he understood himself.

He had to push her to say something. "So I bet whatever you've done you think is incredibly stupid can't top this one."

"Hm. Maybe it does. But how about one thing at a time? What do you plan to do about it?"

With a deep breath, he slumped back against the couch. "I don't know. No suggestions?"

"Well." Leaning in against him, she accepted his arm and rested her head on his shoulder. "Not that I'm the one to ask for relationship advice, but ... I'd say she's awfully lucky to have you. If you need back up on that, I'm here to give it. Although with my history, I'd do you a bigger favor by staying away."

"You better not." He grasped her free hand and pulled it to his chest. "You know I need you." He felt her sink into him. "Your turn. What's wrong?"

~~~

"Reynauld, what's with you tonight?" Ginny pushed at him during the three minute break where he let the music take over and walked off stage to grab water.

"Why?" He grabbed his phone and checked messages. Nothing.

"You look like you don't want to be out there. Want to wake up and get back to work?"

"Do I?" He didn't really have to ask and his manager didn't bother to answer. "So refund them and I'll quit now."

Yanking the phone from his hand, she stared him down. "These people, your *fans*, paid a hell of a lot of money and gave up their nights to see this show. If you're going to get so full of yourself you don't care about that, tell me now. I'll refund them. And that's the last thing I'll do as your manager. But let me tell you, no one else will pick you up if I dump you."

"Someone get me a beer instead of *this*." He nearly sloshed water out of the glass while plopping it down.

"Ignore that." Daws stopped someone who started for it. "Stick with the water, Reynauld. I have no interest in taking your ass back to the hospital."

"Then don't." He yelled again for a beer, confusing the roadies trying to decide who to obey. Ryan didn't believe it would be him.

Daws backed Ginny off from her tirade and pulled him over to a quieter spot. "Wanna tell me what's going on?"

"No." He tried to maneuver around the guard. Pointless.

"Try again. You've been edgy as hell since Dani left. If there's something you've gotta work out with her, call her after the show, but leave it until after the show. Get out there and do your job first."

"It's not Dani." He swallowed a gulp of water. "Not all Dani. And nothing to need to work out with her." Nothing he could admit.

"Kaitlyn. Still haven't reached her?"

"He won't let me talk to her. Since Nick left, she hasn't answered her cell and her father won't put her on the phone when I call the house, and I don't know if he even tells her I call."

"Nick wouldn't have left if she wasn't okay. And whatever her father does, she knows you're there and you'll be back. Hell, we all know you will. It's only another week. Do this and then we'll go tell her in person."

"We?"

"Think I'm letting you go by yourself after the rescue needed last time? If they know you're mixed up with her, they'll be watching for you. Now go. Put your head in the show and we'll take care of this later."

~~~

Four more days.

Ryan had four more days of tour before he could return to Montana and see for himself how she was doing. At least Nick answered his phone. He said she was fine. He called to check in daily. She hadn't talked to him the past few days while fighting an illness most of the family had, but he was kept informed and she was pulling out of it. Something didn't add up, though. Why would she talk to Nick and not to Ryan?

She was angry with him? For leaving her there? But it wasn't his decision. It was hers. Her father was blocking calls. He had to be. She would never refuse to talk to him.

Jumping up from the bed where he'd been lying on top of the comforter unable to make himself undress, he decided to try again. He would call every day even if it didn't go through. At least he was trying. What time was it in Montana? Hell. He had no idea what time it was in Montana from wherever he was.

He dialed his guard and paced until the gruff voice came on the line, asked about the time difference, ignored the why, asked again, and got a slight pause before the answer. Ten-thirty. Not an outrageous time to call.

When Katie's phone again went to voicemail, Ryan grabbed an annoyed breath and leaned back against the hotel headboard, shoving the pillow up higher. He'd have to call the house. Maybe someone besides Robert or Andrea would pick up for a change. Three rings ... four ...

"Hello?"

It wasn't Robert or Andrea. "Paul?"

"Yes?"

"Hey, it's Ryan. Is Katie around?"

"Ryan?" His voice lowered. "I can't put her on but I'll give her a message if...." He stopped. Silence.

"Paul? Still there?"

"Why are you calling my house so late at night?"

Robert. Great. "Where's Katie?"

"Look. I've been trying to be nice about this and make it easy on you both, but I want you to stop calling." He quieted Paul's protest in the background. "She doesn't need your interference."

Interference? "Why don't you tell her I've been calling and let her decide whether it's interference or not?"

"She doesn't need you. She needs professional help. I have a therapist working with her..."

"No. You can't. She doesn't like doctors..."

"She's afraid of them, like she's afraid of everything else. That has to stop. She can't keep living that way, so dependent on one person she won't make a move without him."

"She's not."

"Oh? Is that why she hasn't spoken a word since she's been here?" He waited through silence. "I don't want you to return next week. I want you to leave her alone. Let this have a chance to work..."

"Does she talk to him?" He didn't get an answer. "The therapist? Does she talk to him?"

A pause. "Not yet."

"Then what good is it doing her?"

"He said it would take time..."

"She *won't* talk to him. And tell me she is not *ever* alone with him. One of you is always there..."

"He's a professional, good reputation. I've known him for many years..."

"I don't care if he's the best known shrink in the country. You *can't* leave her alone with him. And you're making things worse. Let me talk to her..."

"Stop calling here. And if you come by, I will not allow you in. Save yourself publicity you don't want." The phone clicked.

Publicity he didn't want. A threat. As Daws said, the man would make an issue of her age if Ryan pressed him. He would question their relationship.

But Ryan couldn't stay away. He couldn't allow Robert to keep her locked away like a prisoner ... with a shrink. *I won't go back there.* Her words echoed through her brain. *I'm not crazy.* She was terrified of shrinks. She hadn't talked to anyone since he left. He had to get her out of that house, away from it.

His stomach twisted into a gazillion knots, he went out to the suite and to his friend's room. Ryan pounded until it opened.

"Damn, the phone call wasn't bad enough? Go to sleep and let me do the same."

Ryan shoved a foot in front of the door to keep it from closing. "She doesn't know I've been calling and he has a shrink talking to her, leaving her alone with him. He told me not to come, to stay away, but she hasn't said anything to anyone, not since Nick left or since she's been there; I'm not sure which since the stories are different. Paul protested when Robert told me not to call again." He ran fingers through his hair, distracting himself from the pain in his stomach. "Daws, they're going to undo everything, make everything worse again until..."

"Until she finds another ledge?"

Suddenly nauseous, Ryan rushed to the bathroom and gripped the sink edge for support.

"We'll cancel tomorrow, say you're sick. Get your stuff together while I make calls. Let's go get her."

"I thought you were against this." He turned the faucet on, focusing on the cold water as he rinsed his mouth.

"Tried that. Didn't help anything. Are you going to stand there and argue?"

Ryan made his way back to his room and was barely able to throw the few things he'd pulled out back in the suitcase.

The car ride was hell on his stomach, but they didn't dare fly until they reached a less populated airport where he wasn't supposed to be. He dozed off and on, and as soon as it was a decent hour and before they reached the little local airport that would get them most of the way there, he called Will. If all worked out, he would take Kaitlyn there for the last two days of tour and then go back to get her. She liked being at Will's. Two days would be fine, even if she was shaken.

"Ry, be careful with this." His brother threw a warning tone.

"I was trying to be. I can't anymore."

"If he thinks you'll interfere with his daughter's well-being, there could be more trouble than you expect. I know if it were my daughter..."

"But he doesn't know her anymore. She doesn't *want* to be there..."

"A lot of teens don't want to be with their parents. It's not necessarily as bad as they think it is or act like it is. And you can't understand until you've been a parent..."

"Hell. And no one else understands things about her that I do, parent or not."

"Okay, I'm not debating that, just be careful. A friend doesn't have the same rights as a parent. You said Daws is with you?"

"Yeah."

"Good. Do you want me to come?"

Ryan pondered. He wouldn't mind having his brother there, but he also didn't want to look like they were ganging up on the man. "No. Not yet. I'll give you a call. It may be nothing and we'll be headed your way as soon as we get a couple hours of sleep." Ending the call, he leaned his head against the head rest, his eyes focused somewhere out the window. *Until you've been a parent.* Maybe he couldn't understand a parent's view since he wasn't one, but there was so much he understood beyond what they did. Things she would allow him to know she would be embarrassed to let her family know. Will should understand that much. He was married, after all. He and Tracy had to be closer in so many ways than a parent and child were. In different ways. More intensely personal ways. Of course, Will had no idea Ryan and Kaitlyn were so intensely personal.

With his stomach pressing at him again, he returned to song lyrics running through his head to distract his thoughts...

"Hey."

A nudge opened his eyes.

"This it?" Daws nodded toward a housing development gate.

"Yeah." Ryan straightened and pointed out directions, stared at the playground where he and Katie escaped that first day, and prepared to jump out of the car as soon as it stopped.

"Ryan." Daws slowed the vehicle. "Take it easy and don't antagonize him. Let me do the talking if you can't hold your tongue well enough."

"I'm not going to leave without seeing her."

"Understood. Just take it easy. Try to keep it sociable, for her sake."

"There." He pointed at the house and forced deep breaths. It was after noon. Maybe Robert would be at work. "What day is this?"

"The twentieth."

"No, what day? Thursday?"

"Saturday."

"Hell." He took another deep breath as the car's movement stopped and barely heard Daws tell him to wait as he near-sprinted to the door and rang the bell.

Watching for signs of life, he thought he saw a shadowed movement beyond the window and rang again. Nothing. He walked over to the garage and looked in the window. Both cars were there. They were home. He went back to the door and rang again.

Too frustrated for the deep breaths to help, he shouted at the house. "*I'm staying right here. You're going to have to open the door.*"

"Reynauld." Daws nodded toward a police cruiser approaching.

"So what? I'm doing nothing wrong. He can't keep her prisoner."

"Let's do this through legal channels. You don't want it in the press."

"I don't *give* a damn about the press. I can't let him do this to her."

The cruiser stopped in front of the house.

"Let me talk, will ya?" Daws caught his eyes.

Giving in for the moment, he greeted the officer with a nod while his bodyguard explained they'd come a long way to visit his friend. And the front door opened.

Robert stepped out and pulled it closed enough Ryan couldn't see in. He greeted the officer by name, by first name.

"Is there a problem here, Robert? These gentleman say they're here to visit a friend."

"Not a friend. My daughter. And she doesn't want to see him."

"That's not true."

Daws nudged him.

"Are you calling me a liar, Mr. Reynauld?" Robert took a step closer. "This is my property and I want you off of it."

"She barely knows you and she doesn't want to be here. You can't hold her prisoner..."

"She is seventeen, which means, as her father, I have the right to decide what is best for her."

Daws halted Ryan's reaction with a firm grip on his lower arm. "With all due respect, we are only asking to speak with her. I see no harm in that."

"And who are you?"

"Fred Dawson. I work with Ryan."

"And that gives you what credentials to interfere with my family?"

"I've been around enough to see how comfortable Kaitlyn is with him and how she becomes more comfortable with people in general the longer she is."

"Yes well, I have a statement from her therapist stating otherwise, so unless you have professional credentials that will stand up to his, I'm afraid your opinion is invalid."

Ryan freed himself from the arm grip and pushed forward. "You are doing *nothing* but hurting her more and I *can't* allow it." He looked at the officer. "Tell him to bring her out here. You'll see. I have the right to..."

"You have no rights with her. Get off my property."

"Bring her out here and *ask* what she wants."

Robert's glance at the police officer made the man push between. He insisted they leave immediately.

"This isn't right..."

"You'll have to take it up with the judge if you think you have a legal leg to stand on. In the meantime, I don't expect you on this property again or you'll be arrested for trespassing."

"Are you kidding me?"

Daws pulled him away. "Come on. This is going nowhere." With a look that said it would be taken care of, the way Daws took care of everything, he put a hand on Ryan's back and half pushed him toward the car. He held the door and closed it behind him.

From behind the wheel, Daws looked up at the porch where the two men stood talking. "Call your brother and ask if he can come down as a witness, as many of them as can come. Nick, too."

Satisfied by Nick's anger when he heard what happened, Ryan thanked him for returning on the next available flight from England. Maybe Nick could sue for custody until Katie was eighteen. He had duel citizenship. Ryan couldn't imagine why it wouldn't be possible. By the time a kid was sixteen or so, he could choose which parent to live with. Maybe in this case, it would work with her uncle she adored over her father she didn't want to be around.

He couldn't eat, not even the bland garbage Daws ordered. His stomach was in knots. They were in the same little hotel Ryan stayed in during his last visit, but by now, his guard had called in a few of his best security crew and some local guards to handle any crowd that might appear. Ryan knew they were in the hotel somewhere, disguised as guests, but he hadn't left the room since Daws forced him in. Trying to avoid publicity. Good damn luck that would work for long. Especially if they had to fight her father as hard as Ryan expected.

Especially with Nick returning, and with a couple of journalists back in New York talking about how Nick Hollister visited *Riveting* Ryan. Ginny thought it might work in their favor, strengthen the rumor about Katie being his family, let everyone think he and Katie met through Nick somehow. None of that would hold up if they had to fight for her freedom. Daws asked if he was sure he wanted to risk his career for her. Ryan said yes. Without warning. Without thinking. Yes, he would risk his career for her. He'd promised. He wouldn't back out.

Staring out the fourth floor window, holding the dingy red and gold curtains back so they wouldn't bang against his face and arm, Ryan watched colored leaves blow along the building's parking lot. The end of September. Coolness in the air, emphasized more in Montana than in the central and barely southern states where he'd been touring, forecasted the loss of boating season. Soon it would be too cold in Vermont. Some days, it already was. If he wanted to take her on a boat, they would have to jump down south, maybe Key West, or before too much cold set in, South Carolina. Or Southern California. He had yet to go boating out there, no matter how often he'd been in the state.

Or somewhere more exotic. Australia would be warmer as the States grew colder. It would have to be beautiful out on the Australian coast. Not that he expected to be able to take her out of the country before she was eighteen. If he could even take her anywhere before then. It looked pretty unlikely. But he would. Eventually. There was so much he wanted to show her, so much he wanted her to experience...

"Hey sweetie." Deanna's voice wrapped around him at the same time as her arms. "Freddy says you won't eat. That won't help anything. Come on. Come sit with me."

Ryan gave in to the extent he would at least sit down and wondered when she'd come in. He hadn't heard the door. Or talking.

"Start with these." She set a package of plain crackers in front of him while he sank onto the hard chair.

Crackers. They made him think of the way Katie had carefully broken her Saltines into bits one at a time to drop into the chili she made instead of crushing a bunch of them between her palms as Ryan did. He'd found it enchanting. He found so much about her enchanting.

"Eat, Ryan. You know Freddy will help take care of this. Let him worry about it." Deanna pulled the bag open and set it down again, facing him, taunting him.

He got up and went back to the window.

17

His arms hurt. They'd been bent back and propped beneath his head too long as Ryan stared at the ceiling from the hotel bed. It was nothing compared his stomach. Or his brain.

Daws pulled a chair close. "I did some checking." He glanced up at Deanna and continued. "Her father's lawyer has been poking around. He had you watched while she was with you in New York and while you were on tour."

"He what?" Ryan bolted upright and cringed at the shooting pain from the sudden release of his arms. "That's invasion of privacy. He can't do that."

"Nothing illegal about private investigating as long as there's no wire tap and such, especially since you're a public figure and easy to keep track of. Thing is, no matter what they find out, or think they find out, he knows age of consent in New York is seventeen and it would be hard to say she wasn't a resident of New York. So on that end, we don't have an issue."

Seventeen? Should he have known that? At least Daws should have. "That's not the issue anyway. No one but you knows anything. And Dani, but she wouldn't..."

"Be that as it may, even if he tried, he couldn't use it as a reason to keep her away from you."

Ryan twisted his legs around until his feet hit the floor. "So he can't." A rush of victory washed over him and he stood, stretching his arms and back. He could go get her...

"Reynauld." Daws stood beside him. "It's not that simple."

"Why in the hell isn't it? If she's a New York resident and it's legal enough in New York..."

"She stopped being a New York resident when she moved back in with her father. Now she's his dependent, and in Montana, legal age is eighteen."

"Hell she did. She didn't move back..."

"She came of her own volition. She agreed."

"To prevent trouble."

"Doesn't matter."

"They can ask her. Simple. She still has stuff at my place. It shows she planned to return. She can tell them."

Daws grabbed a deep breath and set a hand on his shoulder.

"There's a problem with that."

"Yeah, she won't talk to them. But she will if I'm there, or if she knows it's the only thing keeping her..."

"He had her committed to the hospital, the psych ward."

The breath left him. It seeped out silently, taking all means of reacting with it. The psych ward. Where she said she couldn't go back. He'd lost her. She'd lost everything they'd done. She wasn't strong enough. He let her go too far too soon.

Deanna told him to sit down. He heard her but had no ability to listen. To move. To think. To fight Daws when he pushed Ryan into the chair.

"Nick will be here tomorrow night. Your brother in the morning. We'll fight this. I have Ned and a couple of others coming who saw her when she arrived and noticed how well she'd become..."

"It'll be too late." He heard the words come out of somewhere within. "She'll fall off before we have time to fight it, to get her out."

"Fall off?" Deanna set a hand on his back.

"Doesn't matter. It'll be too late."

"Of course it won't." She rubbed his shoulder as though the soothing motion would actually soothe him. "She's strong, Ryan. She knows you're here, that we're all here. Even if he won't let us see her, she knows."

He walked away from them. They didn't understand. She'd been there before. It was part of what hurt her. She couldn't handle more of it. "I have to get in to see her." He turned to Daws. "Get me in there. I don't care how."

"We're going through legal channels..."

"The *hell* with legal channels. Just get me in there. I have to tell her I'm here, that I'll get her out. I have to *tell* her."

"If you get caught, there's not a chance in hell a judge will rule in your favor."

"And you think they will, anyway? Here? Where the man knows everyone and calls cops by their first name?"

"I'm working on that."

"Well you know what, Daws? Maybe this one you *can't* fix. Maybe this time, *I'm* the only one who can fix it. I *have* to see her."

He was silent for some time, staring. "I imagine you're right. But you'll have to do it straight forward, no holds barred. Are you up to it?"

A chill ran through his spine. *Straight forward, no holds barred.* A phrase his dad used a lot. Those times Ryan tried to hide from what he didn't want to deal with – the moves, the bullies, the taunts from non-military kids who didn't understand. He'd turned his sarcastic attitude into a weapon to hide from it all. To make himself think it didn't matter. His dad used to tell him it wouldn't always work; some day he'd have to go straight forward through his problems instead of veering around them.

He supposed this was the time. "No holds barred. Let's do this."

Ryan forced himself to swallow most of the noodle vegetable watery whatever soup Deanna pushed at him, and paced around the suite. Legal channels. Daws was probably right; playing by the rules was his only real shot to get her out. Regardless of what most thought of him, Ryan did know how to play by the rules. He'd been raised with them, with the importance of knowing them and for the most part, following them. He'd also been taught to recognize when rules were more harmful than helpful and how sometimes breaking them was more right. Every instinct screamed this was one of those times, but not until the right time. He would know it when he found it.

Whatever else he did, he had to get a message to her. How he would, he didn't know.

Nick. Nick was on his way. Robert would never deny her uncle the right to see her. Nick would never allow him that denial. Ryan could send a note. Except it could be intercepted and he didn't know how to write what he wanted to say. He felt his eyes roll. He did it all the time – write what he wanted to say. It's what he did. This was different. But it could still work. With music. Any of his own would get intercepted, also. Someone else's music, then. Whose?

It hit him as he paced the room. But how would he get it? This bitty town wouldn't have it close by, he didn't guess. And he couldn't run around and search. He had to stay close.

No holds barred.

He returned to the table, grabbed his phone, and dialed Dani. Of course he got her damn voicemail but she'd check it soon. He asked her to express it. He needed it by Monday. He wanted it sooner but Monday would have to do.

Ryan wanted to swim, work out, walk ... something. Anything but pace the hotel suite. A knock on the door paused his course and he veered that direction, telling Daws he could look through the peep hole as well as his guard could.

Ryan tilted his head at his drummer. "You got here damn fast."

"Job got stalled since no one's there to sing. How is she?"

"Locked up like a lunatic. How do you think she is?"

"You've seen her?"

Ryan lightened his voice at Ned's obvious concern. "Nah. I'm the plague, apparently. The cause of all her evils."

"We know that's not true." He looked over at an older man Ryan recognized, barely. "And we're here to say we know it's not true."

Daws told them to come in. Ryan gathered the man worked for him, at least part time. Why the guy would want to help when Ryan had no idea who he was made no sense, unless Daws was paying him well, which meant Ryan was paying him well. Maybe it would be better to have a "witness" who wasn't close to Ryan – more impartial. Still, he couldn't guess any of the witnessing would matter. It was only Katie's reactions that would matter, and the longer it took to get in to see her, the less Ryan expected her reactions to be helpful. She would draw right back into herself.

Ryan listened to the plans until another knock gave him an excuse to answer the door: a couple of women he also barely recognized. Office help, he thought. No. The one he knew. The girl he'd asked to check on Katie when she'd stayed too long in the women's room, who'd offered Ryan "more" help if he wanted it. He'd seen her a few times since and acknowledged her with the slightest look. She had to work in the building. The other one ... did some kind of record keeping. He did his best to lodge their names into his brain when they were said. Next time they passed in the hall, he'd make sure they knew he remembered. Whether they were actual help or not.

He dozed in between the conversation in the suite and the droll of the inane television drama. The witnesses had gone on to their own rooms to wait until they were needed, or out to dinner, or somewhere. His stomach churned. It was dark, just after ten o'clock. Nothing would happen until Monday. The next day would be nothing but the torture of waiting. Ryan wondered how much Maalox he had left.

Getting up to grab a beer out of the mini-fridge, he stared at it and put it back. Katie would fuss at him if she knew he was adding fire to the flame in his stomach. He couldn't. She needed him. So he opened it again to grab ice and twisted a couple into a glass he hoped was clean. And he added water. It tasted like holy hell, but it would be easier on his stomach.

"Can someone grab cranberry juice from somewhere tomorrow?" He forced another swallow of the tap water and met the curious stares. "Katie says it's good for the stomach. Something's gotta be."

Deanna glanced at Daws and got up to grab the hotel phone.

Ned came over to him. "Don't put yourself in the hospital again from worrying. She'll feel bad."

"If she ever knows." Ryan pushed the free arm against a pain.

"She'll know. We're gonna get her out of this, Ryan."

"Glad someone seems positive. Hey. So tell me, what was with all the gifts? The ones you kept bringing her. Books. Plants. All the other stuff. Were you trying to hit on her?"

He laughed. "Hit on her. Funny." When Ryan didn't laugh, he shook his head. "I like her. She's good for you. Makes you easier to be around, for the most part. Guess they're thank you gifts."

"Thank you gifts." He eyed his drummer, not convinced.

"Okay. Just between us, they're meant as encouragement." He lowered his voice. "My aunt's a social worker. I've heard a lot about kids who need attention and what it does to them when they don't get it. How when the shy or not so pretty and perfect girls are always ignored, it gets in their heads they aren't good enough. She pushed me into taking one of the shy girls to a dance once. Incredible girl. We're still friends." He shrugged. "I kinda thought Kaitlyn might be one who didn't get enough of something. Thought it might help if more than only you paid attention."

Ryan studied him, this kid he barely knew although they'd been playing together for years. He barely knew any of his band, other than their musical capability. That had to change. "Thank you." He set a hand on Ned's shoulder. "You like boats?"

"Never been on one."

"Serious? Unbelievable. So when this is all settled, want to find out if you like boats? There's one I've been looking at, a big one with bunks and all. Plenty of room for a weekend out for a couple of couples. Interested in helping to break it in?"

"If I don't get seasick. But you don't have to return a favor or anything if that's what you're doing. I'm not asking for anything."

"Never crossed my mind you were." He forced another swallow of the vicious water and wandered over to the window. A few street lights threw a glaze over damp black roads, little two lane roads, or were they one lane? One lane each way was two lanes but some thought he meant two lanes each way when he said two lanes, which he figured would be four lanes. It never made sense to him. Either way, it was a small-ass road through the small-ass town he was starting to develop a hatred for. He shouldn't have ever brought her here. He should scream at Daws for finding her family and making her go through this.

Except she needed to know. She needed to find Nick. She adored Nick. Her uncle would help her. Even if Ryan couldn't.

"Want to trade me?"

He turned to find Deanna holding a glass of red liquid. The potent smell told him it was cranberry juice. "Where'd you get this?" As though he was famished and it was the only thing that would keep him from starvation, Ryan grabbed it and gave her take the water.

"Room service. It's not cold..."

"Don't care." He took a huge swallow and gave her a long hug.

~~~

Conversation pulled him from slumber and Ryan grimaced at a stomach pain. He was lying on top of the scratchy bedspread with an even more scratchy blanket thrown over top of his still-clothed body. The voices were familiar ... Will.

Sitting up, he stretched his shoulders and found his brother, and his sister-in-law and his mom. "Where are the kids?"

"Staying with Tracy's sister for a few days. How's the stomach?"

Ryan shoved a hand through his hair. "You didn't have to come. Not much you can do." With a weak attempt at disguising the pain, he shuffled out of bed. "I gotta shower. Aren't you early?"

"Honey." His mom came over and wrapped him in her strong arms, pulling his head down closer. "Of course we had to come. You know Kaitlyn's like family to us, as well." She moved back to find his face. "And you ... you're too tired and overwhelmed. You should have called us sooner. Maybe we could have come to talk to her father while you were on the road. She did well with us. We could have offered to let her come back."

"Wouldn't have worked. He wants her to have nothing to do with me. Have to figure that includes my family."

"But it doesn't make sense, Ryan. None of this makes sense. She looks up to you like you do with Will. Even if she has family, it doesn't hurt to have more."

Family. Ryan saw Deanna's expression at the term but he couldn't tell his mom. He couldn't admit more than that. Not now. Not until things were settled. "I have to shower. I've been in these since ... way too long."

Every time Daws hung up with whoever he was talking to throughout the morning, Ryan waited to hear something, anything. It was always nothing. She was still in the psych ward. They would still reveal nothing. Robert wouldn't take calls.

"I have to get out of here." Ryan headed to the door and pushed into his shoes.

Will stopped him. "You can't."

"The hell I can't. I can't keep sitting in this room doing nothing."

"Ry, the hotel is packed with fans, reporters. Everyone knows you're here."

He looked over at Daws.

"We're clearing them out as we can." He told someone on the other end of the line to hang on. "Hallways aren't too bad. The lobby is near impassable most of the time. It's a public hotel, impossible to keep them out."

"I'll pretend not to see them. I can't stay cooped up like this."

"Hold on. Let me get a few more guys up here. Where do you plan to go? Weight room?"

"Out."

"Reynauld…" His objection was interrupted by a knock. Apparently someone was able to get through.

Tracy checked but didn't recognize whoever she saw so Ryan looked out. A girl … a girl in disguise. Opening the door, he nearly yanked Dani inside and noticed last second it was Brian with her, also disguised. Daws was right. There was a crowd in the hallway. Several girls yelled his name when they saw him but his security blocked them from the door.

"Damn man, were ya going to leave me out there?" Brian punched him on the arm and pushed the door closed with his foot.

"Nearly didn't know you." Ryan pulled at the long-haired wig. "Oughtta keep this. It's better than normal."

Dani moved between and set a hand on Ryan's face. She peered into his eyes. "So tell me what's going on."

"You didn't get my message? I only asked for a CD."

She dug into a bag at her side and pulled it out: Sister Hazel's *Chasing Daylight*. "Yeah, so I brought it."

"Could've expressed it as I asked."

"You wanted it sooner than tomorrow. Nothing delivers on Sundays. Except me."

"You're insane."

"Yeah, and you look like death warmed over. What have you been eating?"

"Wanna take that thing off?" He eyed the curly wig and big hat. "Everyone here's safe."

Will greeted her by name while she and Brian pulled out of hiding, and Ryan lost her for a few minutes of introductions to his mom and Tracy. They knew she and Ryan were close, but had yet to meet her in person. Will met her the same night Ryan did, at a big party celebrating his record company's newest artists, although she was no longer with his company. They'd dropped her after the first album. It hadn't kept her down long. Nothing did.

He hung back and waited, allowing everyone more leeway with her time than he appreciated. He didn't get enough of it as it was. Ned came in and gave Dani a warm hello, Brian a friendly nod. Ned didn't like Brian much but if Dani ever gave him half a chance, he'd jump at it. She wouldn't. Even if he was her type, which he wasn't, she'd never even flirted back with any of Ryan's coworkers. Never mind that she flirted with most any other guy. Casually. With no real interest other than being friendly.

Ryan drifted back to the window as he waited, thoughts of escaping, out, anywhere, still in his head. Maybe he would borrow Brian's disguise. They could think it was the two visitors leaving. He'd take

Dani with him. Except Brian was a fair amount taller. They might notice that.

"Hey." Dani ran a hand up his back to his shoulder. "You didn't answer me. Will says your stomach's acting up. What have you been eating? And tell me you're not touching alcohol."

He turned enough to give her a light grin. "Cranberry juice. Straight up, on the rocks."

"Honestly?" Her blue eyes reflected concern.

"Katie insists. She reads a lot, even cookbooks. She loves to cook, especially all that green healthy stuff I used to detest."

"Used to?"

He shrugged. "It's not so bad the way she makes it."

"How is she, Ry? Is her father really that horrible?" Her voice was too low for anyone else to hear and she leaned in close, one hand circling his arm, the other on his stomach. "Or did he find out just how close you've become?"

"I can't talk out here." He grasped her fingers, led her to his room, and closed the door.

They were still talking, sitting on his bed, backs against the headboard, when someone knocked. He paid no attention. They could leave him alone until the next day when they could do something. He had no qualms admitting to Dani just how he'd fallen, how it scared him, how he was afraid he would never really get her back again.

She, in turn, told him her fears about losing her current relationship and eased into the increasing rumors about her and Ryan, that she hadn't confirmed anything but hadn't denied it, either. And she asked if he was still okay with that, if it made his situation with Kaitlyn's father worse.

Ryan ignored the second knock and denied it bothered anything. "Hell Dan, you never know. Maybe no one else is gonna want to deal with either of us long term and we'll be stuck with each other. Then they can all congratulate themselves for being right." He had to laugh.

She hugged him, her head against his.

With a third knock, different than the first two, the door opened and Nick barreled in with Will behind him. "Fall asleep in here?" He stopped when Dani raised her head and he stared at her, at the two of them cuddled on his bed.

"Not sleeping. Talking. This is Dani, a long-time friend." Ryan got up and held out a hand to help her up. "Nick, Katie's uncle. You just get in? Have you talked to Robert yet?"

"I've been talking to him since you called, other than when cell use was prohibited on the flight. The man's gone insane." He looked at Dani again, curious. "You seem familiar. Have we met?"

She nudged closer against Ryan. "You're Foresight's guitarist."

He tilted his head. "We have met."

"Long time ago." She found Ryan's gaze. "This is Kaitlyn's uncle and you didn't tell me?"

"Didn't know if I should. Guess you didn't catch the hype about it yet." She was annoyed but he would have to soothe it over later. He had to get answers from Nick. "Are you going to get me in to see her?"

"I don't know. Robert is dead-set against it and right now, he's holding all the cards."

"Why doesn't she tell them what he's doing? She can convince them she doesn't belong there. I know she can..."

"She's there ... is it safe to talk in front of your friend?" With the nod Ryan gave him, he continued. "She took a bunch of pills. Had to pump her stomach."

Will had to grab his arm to hold him up. He couldn't answer. He could hardly breathe. His stomach burned. His brother called out to someone. Ryan pulled out of his grasp, stumbling backward, away, until he hit the edge of the bed. No. She wouldn't. She wouldn't leave him that way.

Lowering, he barely touched the bed and continued to the floor. Will and Daws were beside him. He refused to answer when they spoke. There were too many voices talking to him and not the right one. He buried his head within his hands. She tried to leave him. He failed her.

"Ryan." Dani slid her hands over his arms and around his neck. "Ryan, don't do this. She needs you. More than anyone, she needs you. I know. Trust me, I know."

He forced his breath, forced the flame in his stomach to smolder into ashes, a hell of a lot of ashes. And he faced Nick. "Get me in to see her. Whatever it takes. Get me in there."

He nodded, extended a hand, and pulled him back to his feet. "This could be a hell of a fight. Are you up to it?"

"Yes. Whatever it takes."

"Then there's something you better know." His shoulders raised and lowered. "Her mom left us that way. With prescription meds. When she was alone so no one found her in time. Kaitlyn found her first. It changed her. She was little, but it changed her. She used to talk about how she was too bad and too hard on her mom until Robert argued enough she stopped. I don't know if she stopped believing she was. I hope she did. She was young. Five. Robert became crazy obsessed about keeping a close eye on her. And then she was gone. He won't let her go again easily. He won't take chances."

"Someone she doesn't hurt." Ryan mumbled to himself. She remembered. Even if she never talked about it.

"What?"

He shook his head and dropped onto a close chair, appreciating Dani at his side. "Nothing. Why did her mom do it? I can't believe it was because of Kaitlyn. Why did she?"

Nick rubbed the back of his neck, paced a couple of steps and returned. "She was caught between two lives she couldn't reconcile. She didn't want kids. She wanted Robert. She loved him. But she ... she had such a beautiful voice. And such spirit. I invited her to tour with me. She came once and loved it, for the most part, and she should have come back, but he made her choose. He wanted her home. The fight ended when she got pregnant, accidentally on her part. I'm not sure it was on his. He wanted kids." He noted Ryan's silent question. "Don't misunderstand. She loved Katie. She took good care of her and taught her music and read to her and played games with her and took her everywhere she went, even when Robert was home. She took her to the store ... everywhere. At the same time, she had the urge to run, to travel, to sing. He thinks I took her away by encouraging her wanderlust. I think he did by stifling it. And I think down deep he knows he did."

"And he's trying to do it Kaitlyn."

"No. He's trying to prevent it. He thinks he can do better, by keeping her away from you, from me."

Ryan dropped his head into his hands, eyes clenched. It wasn't the same. Katie knew what she wanted. Didn't she? She said she did. She said she wanted to be with him. Her mom wanted, or thought she wanted, Robert. Did she? Or did she get stuck with her choice, an escapist choice, maybe?

No. It wasn't the same. "Nick." He raised his head to meet her uncle's gaze. "This isn't about her mother. Katie isn't her mom. And I'm not asking him to let her go. I don't want to come between. I want what's best for her. I want her to be happy. Tell him that. Tell him we're on the same side, here. We both want her well and happy. If she wants to stay with him, I want her to stay with him. Tell him that. And get me in to see her. Tell him I can help. I'll play by his rules if it'll help her. Just get me in there."

"I'll try." He set a hand on Ryan's shoulder. "Rest. Take care of yourself. I'm heading to the hospital to see her. Rebecca's already there. I wanted to stop here first."

"Tell her I've been calling. He wouldn't let them through but I called every day, twice a day at least. She has to know." He remembered the CD. "And give her this." He returned to the main room with Dani at his side, and handed it to Nick. "Make him think it's from you if necessary. Tell her track seven."

Nick studied the album cover. "Don't recognize it, but will do." He gave the suite his goodbye and headed to the door. Before he opened it, his hand on the knob, he put his attention on Dani. "Ryan seems to have similar choices in friends as I did." He paused. "I know who you are. First time I met your mom she was expecting you."

Dani gripped Ryan's shirt against his lower back. "So she said. She also mentioned a lot of annoying phone calls."

Nick chuckled. "I was a huge pain in the ass when I was young. Not so much anymore. Are you going to be around a while? It'd be nice to catch up. I've been wondering..."

"Can't. Have to leave first thing tomorrow. Today's my only day off this month."

Ryan decided to ask more about the phone calls and her mom later. Her only day off. And she'd spent it running after him. The girl was a saint.

Nick glanced at Brian when he edged up, watching the conversation now that it turned to Dani. "Another time, maybe. Tell her I said hello when you talk to her, and anyone else you still talk to who might remember my name."

"I will." Dani was tense, rigid. "But do me a favor and don't mention me to anyone. I'm keeping a low profile."

"Of course." Nick studied her closer. "You look like her, by the way."

"Not much."

He frowned. "Then I suppose she's changed a fair bit in the last twenty years. You look like her when she was your age."

Dani turned in toward Ryan as though to say she was done talking.

Nick's expression suggested he thought the "friends" comment might not be very accurate, but he said nothing.

18

Caught between two worlds. Ryan repeated Nick's earlier words in his head. Caught ... between her husband and whoever she was inside. Her husband who wanted nothing to do with the entertainment business. Her brother who ignited her fascination with it. And now Kaitlyn was there.

She'd tried to get out of it the same way. Except she wasn't alone enough. Her father was there. Or Andrea was. Someone was. Ryan wondered who found her this time. And part of him was royally pissed off that there was a this time. She said she wouldn't. She'd told him she would be okay. Did she not give a damn about what he was going through, what he would have gone through if she'd succeeded? She had to remember how she felt when her mom did it to her. Why would she do that to him?

He made his way over to the couch and sank onto it, dropping his elbows to his knees, head on his hands. His mom sat beside him and pulled him in, covering him the best she could as she used to when he was small ... not nearly as small as he felt at the moment. He'd never in his life felt as small as he did now. Did he not matter to her more than that?

"So what do we do next?" Her voice was firm and strong. The words familiar, comforting.

"Wait till Nick gets me in. What else can I do?"

"Tell us about her father. If we're going into battle, we need to be fully prepared. From the beginning, tell us how he reacted to you, to both of you."

Ryan figured it was pointless but he knew her real goal – to get him to start moving toward action of some kind, any kind. It never helped to sit and wait. There was always something to be done. As well as he could remember, he started from their first meeting.

On his way to find something to eat, Ryan stopped beside Dani's chair and ran a hand over her head. "You should rest."

She grasped his fingers. "Pot calling the kettle." Her other hand tapped his stomach. "How's it doing?"

"Hm." Leaving a glance behind, he continued to the kitchenette and scrounged through cabinets and the mini-fridge. There was nothing interesting that wouldn't add to the pain.

"How about grilled cheese, low butter?" She pressed up against his back. "I'll make it."

"No you won't. It's late. Go to bed. Or at least sit down. Bad enough you're spending your only day off like this."

"Yeah well, that was a slight exaggeration. I might have one more."

Ryan turned. "You're going to have to slow down."

"When you do." She gripped his lower arm, her voice soft. "I wish I could stay. I hate to leave tomorrow when this is still so out of control. Maybe I can reschedule..."

"No. Dani, I'm glad you're here. You've made a hellish day a lot more bearable. But you have your own stuff to deal with and I know it's bothering you more than you'll admit. Go home and rest. Cancel things to rest if you need, but not to stay here."

"Are you going to be all right?" She touched his face. "Because you know how much that matters. You know you have to be."

"Then I will be. And same goes for me. Go sit down now."

"You go sit down." She grabbed stuff to make sandwiches and he argued. His mom took over and sent them both to sit down.

"Go shave."

Ryan looked up at Daws. He didn't want to move. He and Dani had stayed awake talking much too long, and then he got up early to see her off. She shared his bed so they didn't have to try to hide her in another room, despite a warning from Daws. It wasn't like they hadn't shared a room before, and Brian was happy enough with the couch.

"Reynauld. Now."

"Why?"

"You want her to see you like that?" He extended a hand.

Pulling himself up with it, he stared. "Robert agreed?"

"More or less. Shave. Let's go."

He started to go and turned. "Wait. What's the rush? What's going on?"

The expression softened as Ryan's family gathered to listen. "She's not doing well. She won't eat. She won't say a word. Her psychiatrist outruled her father and will allow you in on the off-chance it might actually..."

"They're destroying her instead of letting her out."

"Make it quick."

He rushed to get presentable, enough for Katie – she didn't like stubble – and pressed bits of tissue against the two spots he'd nicked.

"Been shaving long?" Tracy grinned, a forced grin, and put an arm around him. "Ryan, no matter what, you know you did what you could. You were good for her..."

"Don't." He pulled away, unable to listen to words of comfort. "What

I did won't matter if she won't come back again."

It took more time to get out of the hotel parking lot than it should have with all the bodies swarming. Ryan and Ned were with Daws and Deanna. Will and Tracy and his mom followed, as did Ryan's security.

He lost all patience with fans who meandered in front of the car to get a glimpse or more. "Run them the hell over."

Deanna swiveled to see him.

"Don't look at me like that. They'll be more where they came from. They're like flies. Lose one and you get five more." He dropped his head back against the seat and closed his eyes.

There were more at the hospital when they finally got there and he felt like a rag doll being pushed and pulled by those actually with him, protecting him ... from what? Losing more hair from grasping fingers? Losing another shirt to being torn? So there were questions being thrown by a myriad of reporters. He knew how to ignore them. As soon as he could get Katie out, they would go to the boat...

"They can't come inside." Will somehow got into the hospital before he did and met him in the entrance. "Are you all right?"

"Where is she?"

His brother motioned toward Tracy at the information desk. It didn't take long. They were waiting for them.

Escorted by white coats down sterile white hallways, he felt an urge to escape. It couldn't be as bad as Katie's. At least he hoped she still had the urge to escape.

Stopped by the entourage, he saw Robert. The eyes were still unfriendly, but also ... scared to death. He was scared for her. To his credit, he did approach instead of waiting to be approached.

"You know I think this is pointless." He didn't quite look at Ryan. "But by now..."

A man in a white coat with matching hair stepped in. "You're Ryan?"

"Yes."

"I'm Dr. Gentry, Kaitlyn's psychiatrist. Come with me."

Robert pushed a hand against his shoulder. "Be careful what you say."

"Why? I'm not the one who did this to her." Ryan knew it was wrong but he didn't care. He also knew her father followed him into the room.

He stopped; his eyes flooded. She was worse than when he'd met her although he wouldn't have thought it possible. She'd lost weight again, was more pale, or as pale as before but it looked worse to him now after seeing her grow so healthy. Her eyes were closed, her expression rigid. An IV and other tubes and wires ran from her body to machines.

"She's drowsing in and out. If you call her name, I imagine she'll wake." The white coat, Dr. Gentry, spoke with a low sympathetic tone that made Ryan think he might not be too hard to deal with. A nurse drifted around the bed, looking at monitors and checking whatever she was checking.

"Just a warning: don't get too close and don't touch her."

"Why?" Ryan finally looked at the doctor's face, noting her father close by, and his brother and Nick and....

"Physical contact upsets her."

His stomach twinged. "Not with me, it doesn't." He forced the same kind of control he always saw from her and moved to the side of the bed. Her hand stuck out from beneath the blanket and he entwined his fingers with hers. "Kaitlyn?"

She stirred, her eyes closed.

"Katie, I'm here. Look at me." Ryan brushed his other hand through her soft bangs.

She jumped, her eyes suddenly wide. The doctor told him to back up, but she recognized Ryan just as suddenly and tried to reach for him. Her movement was stopped and she looked toward the arm on her other side.

"Kaitlyn, you're fine." Dr. Gentry pulled her attention. "The straps, remember? So you don't hurt yourself."

Straps? Ryan moved the blanket off her arm. Straps. Holding her down. Anger surged through his body and he pulled at the closest one. "Get them *off.*"

"We can't do that. It's for her own protection." The doctor nodded toward a nurse beside Ryan who attempted to stop him.

He jerked away. "Get them *off* or *I will.*"

Nick kept Robert from closing in.

"Ryan." Doctor Gentry's voice remained calm. "I know it looks cruel, but she pulls away from us if she's not restrained so that we can't check on her and she won't stay in bed. We're afraid she'll do real damage to herself..."

He found her eyes. They were locked on his face, terrified. "It's okay." He ran fingers back through her hair, leaned in to help calm her. "Relax, Katie. It's going to be okay."

Still, she only stared.

"Talk to me. Tell them it's all right to take them off. I'll make them take them off. Just tell me..."

"She's not speaking. She hasn't said a word in days."

Ryan glanced at the nurse. "Because she's terrified of being here. Let her *go.* Take those things *off.*"

Will set a hand on his back and gave Kaitlyn a hello.

She looked over at him and returned her gaze to Ryan.

"Look." He forced a civility he didn't feel since he knew his brother was telling him to calm down. "I won't let her hurt herself. You have to take those things off. Being tied down is scaring the hell out of her. We're right here. What is she going to do?"

Robert ranted to ignore him, but the doctor looked down at where Ryan had hold of her fingers, caressing them. And he told the nurse to remove the restraint while he released the other.

Katie bolted to sitting and nearly melted into him, gripping his shirt with delicate fingers. She felt so frail, like she had at first. Ryan held her close, mindful of the IV. "I am so sorry. Katie, I am so sorry I let this happen. I shouldn't have let you come without me. I promised I wouldn't let you be alone, and I am so sorry."

"Take me home."

He drew back at her soft, trembling voice and nodded. "I'll try. You know I'll try. And I'll stay until I can. I've been calling you. I've been so worried." He ran a thumb down her face. "Tell me you'll come back to me again. Don't let them take away what we've done, how far you've come. Tell me you'll come back again."

"I belong with you. Take me home." She lay her head against his chest, clinging as though he was a buoy in the midst of a roaring sea.

Home. He had to take her home. She would be fine if he could. He wanted her to think about being home with him. "There's a boat I'm looking at, a big one, big enough we could stay out on the water for days. I want to show it to you to see what you think. We can dock it in Daytona for the winter, cruise down toward the Bahamas. Sit on the beach. The sand is white there, you know." He was rambling and he knew he was, but her frailty scared him, her paleness, her too-soft voice. "I invited Ned. Maybe Daws and Deanna will go with us, too."

"You haven't learned yet *not* to make promises you can't keep?" Robert's eyes narrowed and he moved closer. "She's not going anywhere with you."

"Why? Because you'd rather keep her locked up in here so you don't have to make her *want* to be with you?"

"Ryan." Will threw a warning and Katie held tighter.

"You're the only reason she doesn't." He turned his rant to Dr. Gentry. "I want them out of here."

"Robert..."

Catching Daws's expression from beside the door where he stood, arms crossed in front of his chest, Ryan interrupted the doctor. No holds barred. "*I'm* not the reason she doesn't." He stroked her back through the flimsy hospital gown. "You said she hasn't said a word in days or let anyone touch her." He shrugged, casting his eyes at where she held him. "I wasn't here to interfere. It had nothing to do with me. She talks to people she's comfortable with. Nick. Daws. Deanna. My brother. So what part of this are you *not* getting? Do you really care more about what *you* want than what *she* wants? You don't think she can *see* that? She was doing fine with me. With my family. Going to work with me. Shopping with Deanna. Playing with my niece. You can't think this is better?"

Robert stiffened. "And she was doing so *fine* with you and was taken care of so well that my *seventeen*-year-old daughter just had a *miscarriage*. You think I'll let her go back with you after that?"

Ready to fire an answer, Ryan froze. He felt Katie press closer into him. He felt the silence of the room and the eyes. Miscarriage. "No. Katie..." He tried to see her face but she wouldn't relax her grip enough. "Look at me." He heard his voice start to give. "Please."

"You didn't know." Nick's voice was half question, half relief. "You didn't know she was pregnant?"

Ryan managed to shake his head. He wouldn't say more than that. He had to talk to her alone.

"He's been guarding her well, hasn't he?" Robert moved closer until Will stepped in between. The blockade didn't stop the rant. "Was it you? Or was it one of your musicians or roadies or ... *security*?"

"My staff would never touch her." Daws came back at him just as icy, not bothering to move from his guard post. "I hire only the best, only who I can trust."

"If so, I suppose that narrows the field. She won't say."

Ryan stroked her head, felt her shake. "Let me talk to her alone."

"No chance in hell. If you have something to say, say it. Otherwise, get out."

"Fine."

She pulled back, her eyes touching his. "No."

"Kaitlyn..."

"I don't want them to know."

He had to get her alone, get everyone out so she would talk to him.

"I told you he knew." Robert was looking at Nick. "He's either protecting himself or someone else, but he knows."

Ryan had to force his temper back. He had to keep things from getting worse, if that was possible. "Please, give me a few minutes to talk to her. A few minutes..."

"No."

The psychiatrist focused on the way Kaitlyn clinged to him. "Robert, as her doctor, I have to insist you yield on this. The child has been through a lot. She is talking to him when she wouldn't to us. It would be best to let her talk to whomever she's willing..."

"I *don't* want him around her."

"I realize that. However, it's her interest I'm here to look after, not yours. And I insist. Don't make me call someone to have you taken out."

After a few seconds of enough silence Ryan could hear the buzz of the machines and someone's stomach growl, Robert bolted from the room, telling Ryan he would be watching. The window wouldn't allow much privacy.

Will touched his shoulder and followed the others out of the room. Daws gave him a sympathetic look and told Kaitlyn he was sorry for her loss. He was the last out the door. Ryan knew he would post himself just on the other side.

He leaned his head down against hers. "I'm so sorry, Katie. I'm so sorry. I was careful ... not enough. When...?"

She slid her fingers around to his stomach and her shoulders jumped with her quick breaths, turning into a firm shake. Her tears soaked through his shirt to his chest. He couldn't allow his own. He had to calm her, be strong for her. He'd done this. Her father was right to be so furious. He should have been more careful. He was careful, but not enough. And he couldn't begin to say anything to help, to make things better.

"Don't tell him." Her voice was weak, tired, scared.

"It'll be all right. He has to know." He reached over to the bed stand and grabbed tissue to offer.

"No." She wiped at her face but kept it from him. "He'll make you leave. He'll ... he wants him locked up, the father. So I didn't tell him. I won't let him hurt you."

Locked up. Except seventeen was legal in New York. She was a New York resident. He couldn't have Ryan locked up. He could cause trouble, though. The press would jump all over it. "Forget about your father for right now." He forced enough space to see her and ran fingers along her damp cheek. "You didn't tell me. I would have been here. I would've cancelled my shows if.... What happened? Why...?"

Tears welled again. She didn't try to hide them. "I got sick. I couldn't eat. I ... I tried ... I'm sorry."

"No. Oh, Katie, you have no reason to be." He wiped at both cheeks, conscious they were being watched. "They shouldn't have done this to you. You shouldn't be here. I tried to call you. Constantly. I tried..."

"He took my phone. He wouldn't let me talk. I ... I missed you. But I waited. Like you said. I held on."

Held on. Ryan remembered the pills. "You didn't, though. You took too many pills. You nearly..."

Her head shook. "Only enough. He wouldn't let me talk or see you. I knew..." She dropped her forehead back against his chest.

"You knew what?"

"You would know. If I was here, you would find out. You would come. You would make him let you in. I didn't mean to scare you. I'm sorry."

Clenching his eyes, Ryan held her tighter. "I could've lost you."

"No." Her voice was fading, her grip loosening. "I waited for you. Held on for you. I belong to you."

"Kaitlyn..."

"The pain was too bad. They were pain pills. It hurt. I lost your baby. It hurt..."

His stomach burned as though he'd just swallowed a bottle of tequila.

"You found me after the last time. I ... needed you ... to find me again."

He could barely hear her. She was sleepy. Ryan encouraged her to lie down with a promise he would stay and wouldn't allow the straps. Watching the IV to make sure he didn't bump it, Ryan pulled her blanket up around her and lowered the metal railing so he could sit on the side of her bed. They could watch. He didn't care.

Last time? Her words sank in while he brushed hair from her face. "What do you mean, after the last time?" Her eyes were mostly closed, but he had to know. "Katie, don't sleep yet. Talk to me. After last time what?"

"When you found me." Her eyes flickered to his and closed again.

"Yes, when I found you. After what?"

"After the baby, after I lost ... my baby. She ... she was three months. I tried to take care of her. They wanted ... to give her away and I ... she was mine ... so I left, and ... she got sick and I took her ... the hospital wouldn't look at her ... no money ... sent me to the clinic." She grabbed a deep breath. "I should have let her be adopted. But I wanted her and I was too afraid for her, where she might go. I didn't ... want him ... to be with him ... but she was mine ... so beautiful ... and I ... I couldn't help her."

Ryan barely noticed the moisture on his own face while he wiped the tears falling down hers. That's why she was on the ledge. The guy who'd forced her, raped her, had left her pregnant. And she couldn't care for her baby on her own with no help.

Trying to collect himself, he breathed as much air into his lungs as he could and leaned down to hold her. He kissed the side of her face, tasted the damp saltiness from her tears. "I am so sorry, Katie. For everything. Everything you've been through. Everything I did that added to your pain. I ... wanted to help you, but I made things worse. I'm so sorry."

"No. I wanted you. You are the only thing I'm not sorry about. The only thing I've had ... and Uncle Nick but he wasn't there when I needed him ... you ... always. I'm not sorry I had you."

Had. Ryan pulled up. Her eyes were closed, her breathing slower. "Katie." He picked up her hand. "Kaitlyn. Not had. You have me. Always. And you have to hang in there. I know you probably don't want to right now. I know. But please, let me try again. I'm here. I won't let you be anywhere you don't want to be again. Katie…"

"I need to sleep." Her voice was slurred. "Don't leave me. Don't let him … make you…"

"No. I'll be here." He leaned down. "Tell me you're going to be all right. Tell me we can go out on the boat. In Daytona or Tampa. Or anywhere you want. I want to spoil the holy hell out of you for the rest of your life. Give me the chance to do that."

"Does Will still have Chewy?"

Chewy? Ryan had to think a minute what she meant. The dog. "Chewy. Yes. He … I think he does."

"Can we go see her?"

"Yes." He ran a hand through her hair, smoothing it alongside her head. "Yes, we'll go see her." His lungs expanded, a sigh of relief. She was telling him she would be okay. "Sleep now."

"I can't stay here."

"No. Katie, you won't. I'll get you out. Sleep now. I'm here. I'll take care of everything. You sleep." He sat still until she was breathing deeply, until getting up didn't make her stir. Amazed they were left alone so long, Ryan knew he had to go face her father. And he had to get something for his stomach before it burned all the way through.

At the door, he looked back to be sure she was still asleep, still breathing deeply. Then he gritted his teeth and stepped into the hall. The first thing he did was ask a nurse if someone should stay with her. The girl smiled lightly and went in.

Robert descended, the rest of the crowd nearly plastered around his side, like a dust storm swooping in to suffocate the living breath out of him. "Daws." He looked past the rest to his friend. The one always there. "I gotta have Maalox. Or anything. Whatever they have."

"Here." Daws pulled a bottle from an inside pocket, opened it, and handed him a tablet along with a 7-Up. "Try this first."

"You carry it, do you?"

"Recently. Take it."

Ryan was glad to have his prescription he never thought to carry. Normally, he hated to take it. If Daws had handed him the bottle, though, he sure as hell would have popped more than one.

"Honey…" His mom felt his forehead. "You should rest."

"What did she tell you?" Robert pressed in. "Since she actually talked to *you*. What did she say?"

Ryan stared. Kaitlyn didn't want her father to know.

"You had your few minutes, and then some. What did she say?"

"She wants to go see Chewy."

"What?"

Ryan looked over at Will. "Please tell me you still have that dog."

"We still have her. That's what she said?"

"Yeah."

"A *dog*? My daughter is lying in there after a miscarriage and attempted suicide and you're talking about a *dog*? Are you completely *out* of your mind?"

"She wasn't attempting suicide." Ryan pressed a hand against his stomach and gave the 7-Up back to Daws.

"I suppose she told you that, too, along with wanting to see some dog."

"Yes."

"That's a lie. She downed a bunch of pills, just like her mother."

Ryan clenched his fists. "I don't know shit about her mother, Robert, but I *can* tell you that all *Katie* wanted was to get out from under your thumb so she could *breathe*."

Robert lunged. Daws and Nick stopped him. Ryan backed away, a hand pressed against his stomach. He had to find the toilet. Will took his side, directing him to the closest.

Once his stomach was settled enough to feel like he would survive, he rinsed his mouth and threw cold water over his face and head.

"You might want to see a doctor while we're here."

He started at Will's voice. "I didn't know you came in."

"I'm worried about you, Ry. Want to tell me what's going on?"

Scrubbing a brown paper towel over the dampness, he shrugged. "You heard it. What more do you want to know?"

"Tracy is worried about my coworker, the one you hit that night, but I swear she wasn't alone with him for anything to have happened."

"No."

"No? She told you who?"

"Will." The door opened and they were interrupted by someone in hospital attire. Ryan rinsed his mouth again, gargled, and accepted another towel his brother pushed toward him. Waiting until they were alone again. But he couldn't say. Katie didn't want them to know. Yet. He wouldn't hold it in forever.

"Deanna says five weeks ago when you were in London she disappeared for a while. By herself."

"So?"

"She was five weeks along."

His stomach buckled and he grabbed the sink. Five weeks. The specific time frame made it more real. Deanna was trying to throw them off track, protecting him.

Will pushed an arm around his back. "Come on. You've got to see someone."

"No."

"Ry..."

"Katie needs me. I can't be put back in the hospital. I have to be here for her."

"Hell of a lot of good you'll do her like this. Or worse."

"I gotta find Maalox. Pepto Bismal, even. Something more than that pill."

"All right. At least sit down. We'll keep Robert off your back. Don't answer him. Act like you don't hear him and let your stomach relax."

"Let go. I'm not going out there being held up. I do have a half a thread of dignity left." With Will reluctantly giving in, he straightened himself and went back out, to the window to look in at her. He heard Robert. Will didn't let him come close, telling Tracy to go find something for his stomach and something else Ryan couldn't quite hear. Daws told him Kaitlyn was still asleep and pushed him over to a chair to sit down. His guard – his friend – wanted to say something to him but there were too many people around. Too many people.

"Honey, now that you've seen her, you should go back to the hotel and rest. You don't look good. We'll get you something light..."

"I can't leave. I told her I wouldn't."

"You have to take care of yourself or you won't be any good for her. Deanna can stay. She said she would..."

"Mom, I can't."

The resignation in her face said she knew he was actually standing up to her and not budging, and she pulled him into a hug. "Then I'll find something and bring it to you here. You can't keep swallowing medicine without food."

"Okay." It was easier to give in, whether or not he'd actually eat it.

Tracy moved in front of him with a woman in a white uniform, introduced as a CNA. He didn't argue with her, either, while answering basic questions about his weight and height and ulcer history. Robert ranted in the background, Nick his victim, Andrea trying once to calm him. Daws and Ned kept him at a distance. Ned. Ryan only vaguely remembered his drummer was there, had been at the hotel. He wasn't sure why.

Taking whatever the nurse gave him, Ryan let his head fall back against the wall, hoping to hell it worked, and fast.

"Honey, if you could tell him something, anything that would help, he would relent more easily about letting you see her. She trusts you. He can see that. If you talk to him..."

"I can't." He didn't bother to open his eyes. "Have someone tell me if she starts to wake. I need to be there."

"He doesn't plan to let you back in."

Raising his head, Ryan stared at her.

"He said if you keep everything to yourself, there's no reason."

"The reason is she wants me there."

"I know. Ryan, I know. But we have to work with this. Tell him something..."

"I can't. She asked me not to and I can't go behind her back. Hell, it's his job to gain her trust, not mine to force her to give it to him."

"But the pain Kaitlyn has now from losing a child is what he's afraid to go through for the second time. He feels he's losing her again. He thinks you're the key to keep that from happening and nothing else will get in. I know he's being unreasonable, but when you have children, you'll understand better. Like Kaitlyn does now to an extent, when she gets through the grieving enough to see that he is, also."

When he had children. Except he did have. And it was gone before he even knew. Maybe he should rant. Maybe he should tell Robert he did understand more than he realized, maybe Katie understood more than he realized. It was her second time, as well. At least Kaitlyn was still around for Robert to see, to fight for. It was more than they had.

Whatever the nurse gave him must have had a numbing ingredient, something stupefying. Because he felt numb. He couldn't grieve. No one knew. She didn't want them to know. And he couldn't care less at the moment how Robert felt. He couldn't even care how he felt himself. He had to be there for Katie when she woke up.

Ryan pushed to his feet despite protest, and headed to her door.

Robert stopped him. "You're not going back in."

"She wants me there."

"I don't. And for another month, she's a minor so I'm making the decisions."

"And after that month, you'll lose her forever if you keep this up. Because she'll come back to me."

"To you. Or to the father you're protecting since everyone around says it's not you, says you're like her brother, according to your family. She has brothers already. She needs to get to know them..."

"I'm going in. I told her I would be there and I won't let her down again."

"Again. Like you did when you told her you'd protect her?"

"Robert, I'm not your enemy. I'm your biggest ally, or could be. If you don't let me be your ally, I could very well turn into your biggest enemy, although I don't want that. Your choice. Help me, I help you. Stand in the way..."

"Is that a threat?" He stepped closer.

Will was at his side, one side. His mom at the other. "I'm too tired for threats. Too tired for arguments. She trusts me. You need my help more than I need yours. I know what you want to know. If you work *with* me instead of against me, she might let me tell you. This is really all up to you. You could make this a hell of a lot easier."

"Tell me something. What are you to her? I don't buy the brother act."

"Never said I was trying to be."

"So what in the hell are you? Some black knight trying to find white armor through my daughter? Trying to look the hero as a publicity stunt?"

Ryan didn't answer. It was a stupid question.

"I know about you. I know what you are. I know any innocent young girl should never be within fifty feet of you or your kind…"

"Robert, that's enough." Nick tried to pull him away.

"Go stand with him. He's your kind, the kind that polluted my wife with your filthy lifestyle."

"Be careful. It's my sister you're talking about."

"And your activities when she visited you turned her into something she wasn't. I won't have that for my daughter. I won't have her dragged into the gutter with the other street slime…"

"*Don't* talk about my son that way."

Ryan couldn't react to the words, but his mom pressed forward, her sergeant stance returning.

"I understand you're upset about your daughter, but don't think you care more about her than I do about my son, and don't think I'm going to stand here and let you insult him. I won't hear another word about how your little girl is too good to be around my son, because I tell you you're wrong. There's not a girl in the world too good for my Ryan. You have no idea who he is."

"No? So the stories going around about him aren't true? All the girls? The raunchy parties? Different girl in every town, right? Maybe more than one? None of those stories are true?"

"Some are true, or used to be." Ryan interrupted his mom's coming attack. "Many aren't. But I'm hardly the worst she's been around."

"What are you implying?"

"I'm implying nothing. Only that I'm the least of your concerns. And if you knew what I do, you wouldn't be worried about me." Ryan was too satisfied at his stunned silence.

Robert clenched his jaw and stared in the distance before he threw the glare back again. "You know anything about the scars on her back?"

He had to force his breath. "You saw them?"

"So did you, apparently. I tried to ask her. The doctors found them while saving her life. Asked me what they were from. I had no idea what they meant. But you know. And her ears. She wouldn't tell me that, either."

Nodding, Ryan bit his lip. "Yes, I know. But I can't say. I can say that when I find out who it was, as we're trying to do, it'll be taken care of. I can say that it hurt me to find out about it as it did you. I can say the physical scars aren't the only ones she has and I've been doing all I can to help the rest heal." He grabbed a deep breath and pressed at his stomach, calming his tone.

"It took me time to win her trust. I won't lose it by talking behind her back. If you want her to open up to you, your *only* option is going to be through me, or at least not against me. Not by my choice. By hers." He grabbed the advantage of temporary empowerment and pushed around Robert back into Katie's room.

Settling in a chair facing her, Ryan watched her sleep. He would fight her father to the ends of the earth if needed. The man wouldn't win. He wouldn't destroy her by keeping her locked so far beneath his thumb. Part of him couldn't help wonder why his own father, such an incredible man, had been lost so early while Robert, who seemed bent to destroy all around him, still wandered the face of the earth. It was a horrible thought, and Ryan knew it was, but he wouldn't apologize for it, not even to himself. He rarely bothered anymore to wish his father was still around. Right now, he wished it vividly, obsessively. He would talk Robert down. Get him to back off. His mom was incredible at standing up for him, but his dad ... his dad could talk his way out of anything and, as the Irish saying went, could tell a man to go to hell and make him glad to be heading there. Or something like that.

Motion to his side pulled him from his thoughts. The doctor. Wonderful. Robert had sent in the professional, the one in charge of her care. Expecting to be told to get out or face security coming in to take him out, Ryan waited while the man pulled a chair beside him.

"You didn't answer about your relationship."

Ryan stared. No, and he wasn't about to now, either.

"I couldn't get her to talk to me."

"She doesn't talk to strangers, and never by force."

"I'm trying to help, Ryan."

"I'm not leaving."

"I don't think you should." Doctor Gentry pulled an ankle over his leg. "It would help if I understood your relationship."

Their relationship. Ryan wasn't enough of an idiot to tell him. "I care about her."

"I can see that. You know it's not what I meant." He pulled at the hem around his ankle, straightening it. "I'm a psychiatrist. Anything you say privately remains private."

"I'm not your patient."

"No, but you're the only one I've seen my patient willing to speak to. Is there anyone else?" Another pause through Ryan's silence. "Andrea says she talks to Nick."

"Yes."

"She hasn't since he came back."

Ryan shrugged and focused on Katie's fingers in his.

"Okay, let's try something else. If she didn't want to be at her father's, why did she choose to stay, without you?"

"We thought he'd relax if she spent time with him while I was touring. We thought it would ease his fears, make things less ... difficult."

"We?"

He returned his eyes.

"Whose idea? Hers? Or yours?"

"Both." He thought back. "Mine." Shoving a hand through his bangs, he inhaled deeply and held it to try to stop the fire. Then let it go slowly. "It was mine. I thought it would help. I did this to her."

"Did you?"

The question reached beyond whose idea. He wasn't answering.

"Tell me how you met."

"I don't think so."

"So Robert is right? She was one of your fans, meant to be a one night..."

"No. I don't think she even knew who I was."

"And that intrigued you. Raised your interest because she was different than most of the girls who try to get to you?"

"Don't try to turn me into your patient. I don't need therapy. I'm here for Katie."

"And yet you have nerve issues so badly they're leading to ulcers."

"Not your business."

"Sorry, trademark of the job to want to help when I see someone in pain."

"Is it? Then let me take her out of here. Let me take her home where she wants to be. That way, both of us will feel better and we can go on with things."

"With what things? You take her home and then what?"

Ryan waited, trying to understand what he was asking.

"If she tries again? If she succeeds next time?"

Bolting from the chair, he walked around to her other side and took her other hand. She wasn't trying to leave him. She said she wasn't.

"Ryan, I know you're trying to do what you think is best, but this is more than you can fix only by..."

"By what? Giving her what she wants? Giving her security? Safety? Comfort." He stopped before he mentioned love, but it flickered in his brain. "How do you know I can't? I know her history. I've seen how she's ... she's done so well. I'm not the only one she talks to anymore. Deanna. Daws. My family. Ned. She even talks to Ned now. She was doing so much better, every day. Until Robert. He's destroyed all the progress we made. You can't think it's better to leave her here with him, let him keep her locked up in a psych ward?"

"No, I don't think she should stay locked up here. I think she needs to get out as soon as her health allows. The question is to where?"

"Let her choose."

"You think she'll choose to stay with you."

"Yes, I think she will."

"If she doesn't?"

"Then I want her to be wherever she wants to be."

He frowned, studying him. "And you look like you're telling the truth. You would rather she be happy wherever she chooses, even if it's not with you?"

"Yes. And I always tell the truth, or I stay quiet. I can't lie worth a damn. I know, I've tried. Had to give up."

The doctor chuckled. "Gets frustrating at times, doesn't it?" He took a deep breath. "My inclination is to recommend she stay with someone else, not Robert since that hasn't worked well, not you since ... well, to be honest, I think her age makes it inappropriate, with all things in consideration..."

"You can't put her with a stranger. No foster home. Might as well leave her right here instead because this is where she'll end up again if you do."

"You sound sure of that."

"I am sure of that."

"Want to fill me in?"

Yes. Somehow, Ryan did want to fill him in. He wanted to tell this stranger everything and ask for advice and.... "I can't."

"Why can't you?"

"It's not for me to tell."

"You've told no one anything of what she's said to you?"

He couldn't say no. He told Will. And Dani. "Not much."

"And there's a lot."

Ryan didn't answer.

"That's another reason I'm not sure I should recommend she stay with you. The ulcer. The weight of it. A lot of responsibility on your part."

"I don't care. This is about her, not me."

"Nothing, Ryan, is ever only about one person. Everything is about everyone close to that person, as well. If it affects you, she can see that."

He had to pull away and wandered the small room, knowing at least someone watched through those damn windows. Robert. He would be watching.

"She's stayed with your brother and his family before? And she talks to them, you said?"

"Yes." He kept pacing, wanting to be outside, on his boat. "And Chewy's there." He explained when the doctor asked.

245 | Off The Moon

"Would you object if I recommend she stay with your brother's family, if they'll accept?"

He took Katie's fingers again. "They'll accept."

"And you would be fine with that?"

Ryan had to be careful how he answered, careful not to sound possessive. "Robert won't agree."

"I'm asking you."

"Why? I have no voice in this. You can't tell me my opinion actually matters."

"Your opinion matters to Kaitlyn. Therefore it matters to me."

Was it a trick? "What kind of restrictions would I have in visiting?"

Raised eyebrows questioned him. "No restrictions. I would encourage you to visit as you can. If you're the one person she trusts most, I don't want that taken from her."

"Okay, don't think I'm not appreciative, but aren't you Robert's friend? You'll have to forgive me if I'm suspicious about you siding with me."

"I'm Robert's friend. More than that, I'm a psychiatrist. More than that, I'm Kaitlyn's doctor. I don't take that lightly. I won't lie to you. Her situation is troubling. There is a hereditary issue that tends to come with suicide. Now that could be genetic or it could be imprinting. Either way, with this attempt ... that I realize you believe wasn't an attempt ... and the fight between you and her father, and the miscarriage, this is not something to take lightly. Wherever she goes, I want continued counseling..."

"She won't talk to a shrink."

"I think she might if you encourage her, which is why I'm making you a partner in this. I don't want it all on you and I won't allow it. Sacrificing one person for another is not part of my ethical code. There is, however, no way I can keep you out of it since she has you so firmly pulled in."

"I don't want out of it."

"What do you want, Ryan?"

"I want her to stay with me." He shouldn't have said it. But there it was. The truth.

They were at an impasse. He could see it. He could hear it in the quiet of the hospital room. Finally, the doctor dropped his head, his lips scrunched in thought.

"Tell me something. You want me to go all the way against her father's wishes and let her move in with you, a seventeen-year-old girl. Tell me what your relationship is with her and what you know about how she got pregnant."

Caught. He'd revealed too much. "I can't. Unless she tells me I can."

"Then I can't agree. The best I can do is your brother's family. Even that will be a fight, but Robert will have to accept my decision unless he decides to fire me and fight the Department of Children's Welfare. I don't think he'll be that unreasonable."

"No? I think he will be."

A light grin skimmed the doctor's lips. "That's fair, coming from your perspective, but as you realize there are things about you he doesn't know, you have to realize the same about him."

He put his attention on Kaitlyn. Her face. Her words as she told him she wanted to see her father. She'd wanted to. And the photo of her smiling, her hands alongside her dad's face. "I suppose that's true. I know Katie really wanted to see him. I know she was disappointed in what she found. She said he changed."

"Yes, as any of us would when we lose a child."

Ryan dropped his eyes and lowered onto the bed facing her. He ran his fingers from her forehead down her cheek to her neck. "Tell me what to do. Katie, tell me what you want." He touched the lobe of her ear, the scar she'd hidden from him for so long.

"I want to stay with you."

Startled at her voice, he had to think about what she said. "You're awake?"

Her eyes opened.

"Hey. How long have you been awake?"

"Thank you." She squeezed his fingers. "For fighting for me. For wanting me with you. Still, even after..."

"Oh Katie, you know I do." He brushed her cheek. "They're not going to allow it. In order to get you out of here..."

"You'll visit? At Will's?" She answered his silence. "It's okay. If they don't mind. I'll help ... as I can. I won't be in the way. I'll wait for you there."

Ryan wanted to kiss her. "You're never in the way. They love having you."

"You'll visit?"

"Always. Often. As much as I can be there. Are you sure?"

"I'll take care of Chewy. She needs someone who understands." She closed her eyes again.

Every part of Ryan wanted to take her in his arms, kiss her lips, her face, her neck. Someone who understands. The dog no one wanted until Will took him in. The one all of Will's neighbors wanted gone. Ryan couldn't let that happen.

Will and Tracy were more than happy to have her and promised to get a counselor for her. Robert exploded when the doctor told him his decision.

"*His* family? You can't think she should go with *his* family."

"Let me ask you something, Robert." Dr. Gentry was fully unbothered by the explosion. "If you had the decision to take a young child and put her with one of two families, one of which was mutually supportive and loving and accepting and the other of which was fractured and explosive and who rarely spoke to each other, which would you choose? Any child. Where would you place her?"

"We are not fractured." His tone dropped.

"Aren't you?"

Ryan was glad they'd found a private area, away from any prying ears. Regardless of how pissed off he was at Robert, he couldn't help but find a touch of pity at being told his family was fractured.

"Why in the hell do you think I'm trying to bring my daughter back into it? Yes, we're fractured. We have been since she left ... disappeared. Taking her away again..."

"You've had time to pull yourselves together. It hasn't happened. Robert, you tried having her there. This is where she ended up. I can't risk that again."

"It's her mother's genetics."

"As long as you believe that, nothing will change and she can't be there."

"I'm getting a second opinion. Thank you for your time. It's out of your hands now."

"I'm afraid not. She is a minor. If I report she's an endangered minor, the state will take it out of your hands."

"You wouldn't."

"To protect her? Yes. Don't push me that far. Being with people she knows who care about her who she's comfortable with will be better than the state shoving her into foster care."

Ryan got up. That wouldn't happen. He'd ... he'd kidnap her and escape first. Overseas. Anywhere. Daws held him back, motioned for him to stay quiet.

Robert paced the room. And stopped. "How do we know it wasn't someone in *his* family or one of their acquaintances who ... attacked her? How do we know it's safe? It apparently wasn't safe *somewhere* she's been."

"She never said she was attacked."

"She never said she wasn't." Robert threw a glare at Ryan. "He knows and he won't even say that much. He has no feeling about anyone but himself. No idea what it's like to be a parent and not..."

"The hell I don't." He met the stare but stayed beside his friend. "I can't tell you how much I wish you knew what I do, how I wish I could tell you. I can't. Because I care about how *she* feels. Because *she* asked me not to say."

"Which in this case makes you an accessory to the crime. Isn't there some legality where we can make him talk? For her protection?"

"This isn't a criminal investigation." The doctor tried again to calm him. "Let's keep things civil."

"It should be. And it will be. If you send my daughter to his family, I will press charges. He knows something. She's a minor. I have that right." Robert walked closer to him. "Check mate. You want this to stay out of the press? Take yourself out of it, away from her. Convince her she should be with her own family..."

"No."

"I'll press charges against you."

"For what?"

"She was under your care. You're protecting someone. And I will use everything I have to find out who it is."

Nick pushed in. "Robert, you'll do no such thing. You make it public, it affects her, also. You don't want that."

"I don't want to lose her again. I don't want some criminal to go loose just because he won't talk. I have spent long enough not knowing what was going on with her. I want answers. I don't care anymore how I get them."

"Robert..."

"If it was your kid, even your illegitimate kid you barely see, would you sit back knowing she may have been attacked and not insist on answers? On justice?"

"It was mine." Ryan heard his own voice. He felt Daws push at him. He saw everyone's eyes questioning. It didn't matter anymore. He would have to hope Kaitlyn would forgive him. Robert deserved at least the one answer that involved him. "The baby was mine. And I didn't attack her. I didn't force her. I would never force her. It was her decision."

Robert stared, and then lunged. It was fast enough Daws only partly stopped the attack. Ryan had to catch himself. He shoved Robert's hands away as others separated them.

At enough distance to have time to dodge another attempt if necessary, Ryan saw Robert's chest heave. He also saw Will's eyes questioning him. Surprised. Disbelieving.

"I want him arrested." Robert pushed out of Nick's grasp.

"Can't do it." Daws stayed one step in front of Ryan. "Legal age in New York is seventeen."

"That's a lie."

Daws inflated his chest, his back stiffened. "Look it up."

Robert withdrew. "Doesn't matter, either way. We're not in New York."

"They were." Daws crossed his arms in front of his chest. "She has a passport that shows her address as the same as his, proving not only her state residency at the time but that she was living with him of her own volition. Her choice. You have no grounds."

Ryan looked at his friend. That's why she had a passport already when they went overseas. He'd done it to establish residency. Expecting trouble.

"Honey?" His mom moved in, a hand on his arm. "Yours? The baby she lost..."

"Yes. We've been together for some time. But I didn't know..." He read disappointment in her face. It nearly killed him to see it. "It's not what you're thinking."

"She's ... so young, Ryan..."

"Defend him now." Robert's growl pulled his mom's head. "*This* is what you raised and you think you have the right to take my daughter from me? After he did *this*?"

She paused in her defense. Not quite able.

"He's good with her." Deanna took it up. "He's *good* for her. So she's seventeen. So what? It was her choice. She's ... she's become so much happier with him than she was. I know. I met her the day after he did. It was frightening how lost she was. Now she's not, or she wasn't until this."

Robert eyed her. "And I would expect that coming from one of you music people. You expect me to take *your* word?"

"Be careful." Daws matched Robert's earlier growl.

"My word." Deanna, undeterred, walked up to him, in his face. "Yes, take my word. Ryan is one of the best people I know or have ever known. Yes, he can be arrogant and self-centered at times. Hell, all of us can be. He has to be for his job. But I have known him for years and if I had a daughter, I'd be glad as hell if she found someone like him. I encouraged it. I encouraged him. Because he's good for her. Because they're good together. And let me tell you, my first time I was only sixteen and it was some business type like you who thought it was fine and dandy to act like I was everything in the world to him when the whole time he was looking down at me like something worthless to be used. Every man I ran into did the same until Freddy. One of the *music people*. He rescued me from the lies and the conniving. Just like Ryan rescued Kaitlyn. Take *my* word because *I* know."

Even Robert was silenced for the moment.

Ryan went over and hugged her. He knew her background, the only person other than Daws who knew. He knew how it embarrassed her. And he was eternally grateful someone was still able to defend him.

He knew, though, that he had to say something to Kaitlyn's father. Words wouldn't come. The look of disappointment in his mom's face lingered. Stalled him. Trying to pull out of it, he began to open his mouth and hoped something would come out.

"Don't speak to me." Robert stormed out the door.

Ryan's legs gave out. He sank to crouching position, sitting on his heels, hands sheltering his head.

Deanna lowered next to him. "Ryan, sweetie, it'll be all right. He'll realize as he sees you together how lucky she is to have you."

"Is she?" He kept his face hidden.

"Of course she is."

Someone took his other side and grasped his arm.

"Leave me alone." He kept his eyes clenched, resisting the pull.

"Stand up, Ryan." Will. Pissed off. He barely waited for Ryan to obey before he started in. "What in the hell were you thinking? And more, what are you going to do about it?"

What was he going to do? There was only one thing *to* do. "I'm fighting for her. Whatever anyone thinks." He raised his head to meet his brother's eyes. "She is not a fling. I didn't push her. I fell in love with her and I couldn't ... I *tried* to walk away from it. I *tried* to do what was right and the more I did the more she pulled away and I couldn't ... I couldn't lose her. I *won't* lose her. Whatever you think about it, I won't lose her. I'll keep fighting for her until ... until she is with me."

His mom intercepted whatever Will was going to argue. She set her hands alongside his face. "Fell in love?"

"Yes. She is everything to me. I won't lose her."

"Honey." Doubt reflected through her concern. "Sometimes ... things can feel like more than they are. When ... when someone needs you that much, depends on you that much, you can think..."

He backed away. He was having a hard enough time fighting her dad, the public, his manager and publicist. He didn't need his family to turn against him, also. Not when it mattered the most. Will called his name, but he shoved out the door and headed to her room. He'd been away too long. He had to check in. But Robert was there, and Nick. Standing outside her door. He couldn't deal with them.

Ryan turned the other direction, down some hallway, and walked along tan walls and swirled tan and white tiled shining floors, passing doorways, some open, some closed. There had to be somewhere he could sit. Alone. Not alone. He didn't want to be alone. He also didn't want to be with any of them.

He found an empty waiting room and grabbed his phone as he made his way to the back corner. Dani's number was the third on his contact list, after Daws and Will. He hadn't programmed Katie's number in. Just in case he lost it. It was in his head.

He got her voicemail. "*Damn* it." Waiting, he tried to decide whether or not to leave a message. At the beep, he started to ramble. "Hey. Where are you? Call me, okay? As soon as you get this. I gotta talk to you. It's important, Dan." He closed the phone and dropped his head on his hands. It could be hours before she got it. If she was working, recording, writing, promoting, it could be forever. Or feel like it. She would stand by him. If no one else did, Dani would. She always had.

The ring nearly made him jump out of the chair. Dani.

"Ryan? What's wrong?"

"Hey. I hoped it wouldn't be tomorrow before you got the message."

"Don't hey me. You scared the hell out of me. Are you okay?"

"What are you doing? Can you talk?"

"I'm ... of course. Answer me. What's going on?"

"Kaitlyn."

A pause. "Did he let you see her?"

"Yeah. She's..." He grabbed a deep breath and fisted his free hand in his hair. He told her what Kaitlyn said about the pills. And the straps. And the baby. His baby. And his mom's disappointment. Will's anger.

She was silent for some time when he stopped talking.

"Still there or are you ditching me, too?"

"You know I wouldn't ever ditch you. Tell me what you're thinking."

"What I'm thinking. I think ... maybe I should be as irresponsible and self-centered as they say I am and ... get her out. Take her somewhere they won't find us. Go hide somewhere away from everything. I can't, of course."

"No. You can't. Don't."

"Better suggestions?"

"Oh. I'm about the last person who should give relationship advice."

"But it's not about the relationship. We don't have a relationship problem. Everyone else has a problem with it, but we don't." He shoved fingers through his hair.

"Then that's your answer. Hold onto her. When you find something like that, you don't let it go."

"She's seventeen. And locked in the psych ward."

"Ryan, don't do this to yourself. If she wants this as much as you do, she'll help you fight for it. Let her. Don't try to be in charge. Work together. It can only work that way."

"She's ... so weak. Pale. She has no strength..."

"You'd be surprised what kind of strength a woman can find to fight for the man she loves. Don't underestimate it."

Ryan calmed with her words. The man she loves. But did she? She'd never said so. But then, neither had he.

"Still there?"

He straightened. "Yeah."

"So?"

"So I want her to meet you. I want ... when I get her out of here, when she's up to it, can I bring her out?"

"Of course. I'll make sure these guys are on their best behavior. And

I'm glad to hear you say when, not if."

"Not if." As he calmed, he began to hear something in her voice he wasn't used to hearing. "Dan, are you all right? You sound ... tired, or..."

"Tired. I'm always tired these days."

"Working too hard, as always. But what else?"

"I can't talk now. They're waiting on me. Can I call you later tonight?"

"Anytime. You should have told me you were busy."

"After a message like that?" He could hear the grin in her voice. "I've been worried about you. I'm glad you called. And Ry ... I'm so sorry, about the baby. I know how you hurt right now."

"I haven't had time ... I'm just trying to focus on Kaitlyn."

"Don't lie to me."

He grasped another breath and raised his eyes to the ceiling. "Yeah. It hurts like hell, even if I didn't know."

"I wish I was there with you. I would come out if I could. And if you need..."

"No. I'm not fit to be around anyway. We'll come see you. It's my turn."

"Make it soon. And I'll call you tonight. I have to go."

"Take care of yourself, Dani. Get some rest."

"Pot calling the kettle. Love you. Talk later." She didn't give him time to respond before he heard the click. Something was wrong.

Dropping his head onto his hands, elbows on knees, Ryan knew he had to go back, go to Katie before she woke. He had to guess she wasn't since her father was outside her room instead of inside with her. He also needed to find out when she'd be able to leave, how much time he had to make sure she did go to Will's instead of with Robert. Or worse. Anyway he figured foster care would be worse than Robert, as far as Katie would be concerned.

"Don't let him chase you away."

He jerked his head up at the soft voice and found Andrea barely inside the waiting area, watching him.

"I've been looking for you." She took a few timid steps closer. "Your security guard ... he's looking for you, too. Worried, I think."

Ryan couldn't respond. He wasn't sure Andrea had spoken to him since the day they met, although he often caught her staring. Nick said she was a fan. Ryan chalked it up to being star struck and paid no attention.

She came closer and settled two chairs away. "You care about her? Our Kaitlyn. Robert's Kaitlyn."

"More than anything in the world."

Her eyes touched his. "Then don't let him chase you away." Her face reddened, hands wrung together in her lap. "He'll try. He'll keep trying if there's a chance. He doesn't mean it the way it looks. He loves her, but he doesn't know how. To love. The way ... the way most of us do. He tries."

"He loves you. He must, since he married you, had kids with you."

She gave him a light half-grin. "He needed a mother for Kaitlyn. The girl was his whole world. More than her mom even, although ... he did love her. He still does. I thought I could help him. We did well together. We had good times and we laughed. Before. But he changed. Losing Kaitlyn and ... losing me the way I was." She swallowed hard and turned her head farther away. "That man destroyed us. All of us. He's in prison still but they'll let him out soon." She wrung her hands tighter. "Anyway, Robert hasn't been the same. He blames himself for not being there."

"I could help if he would let me." Ryan had to say something. It was too obviously a struggle for her to speak to him. "I could help them get closer, help Katie learn to trust him, if he would just stop..."

"It's too hard for him. To admit someone else matters more to his daughter than he does. He can't handle it. Not after all the years ... his guilt." She shook her head. Then found his eyes. "She's been hurt. Like I was. I see it in her."

Ryan felt the moisture in his eyes; the pain he saw in this woman he didn't even know was nearly as bad as the pain he felt for Katie. He nodded.

Andrea brushed at a tear, swallowing hard. "Was the baby really yours? Or were you covering for her so she didn't have to admit..."

"It's mine. Was mine. We ... I'm really uncomfortable saying too much to her ... her stepmom."

A sad grin highlighted the pale cheeks. "She's Robert's. Not mine. He wouldn't let her be mine like I wanted. I love her, you know. You can't tell maybe. But I took her in as mine and I love her as mine and we baked together and ... she was such a loving little thing, loved hugs and talking and singing and helping with the baby, with Paul. She adored him. Such a beautiful child. She's still beautiful. But she's lost so much of what she was. I know. I understand. If ... if he would let me talk to her..."

"Did you tell him what you see?"

She shook her head almost frantically. "I can't. He's already ... I can't. But I try to get time alone with her and he ... he's always there or the boys are."

Ryan couldn't help a touch of anger that crept in with his sympathy. If she knew, if she understood what Kaitlyn was dealing with, why couldn't she get up the nerve to stand with her, beside her, to stand up to her husband? Unless she was afraid of him. "Does he hurt you?"

Her eyes widened. "No." She twisted in her chair. "He wouldn't. He barely comes close enough to even touch me. At all. Ever. Not since....."

She reddened again.

"You have Curtis and Stephen."

"I thought having more kids would help fill some of his emptiness. And he was glad to have them. But he barely notices them. They're such good kids, all of them, and they need him and he...." A deep sigh overtook her frail body.

"He's too obsessed with her." Ryan rubbed his neck.

"You're not what I thought." She was staring again. "I see you in videos, on television. I have your music, but he ... I had to hide them so he wouldn't throw them out. But you're not ... you're very sweet. Kind. I'm glad you're the one she found. She ... she chooses ... to be with you?"

"Yes. I wouldn't push her. I would never hurt her."

Her lips curved, only a touch. "Robert can't ever get close to me without thinking about him. That man. Do you?"

The last thing Ryan wanted to do was talk with Andrea about his sex life with Katie. But he had the feeling it was more important to her than he could imagine. "I never think about that when I'm close to her. I think about ... how glad I am to be close to her, how she feels in my arms, how much I want her there." Embarrassed at where his thoughts went, he looked away.

"Dr. Gentry isn't Robert's friend. He's my therapist. He wants Robert to talk with us. He won't. Robert wants it to look like he comes for dinner as a friend so people won't know I'm seeing him. But he won't really help. He won't talk about it." She paused. "Don't let him push you away from her. He doesn't understand ... a woman's feelings, her needs. He can't see what I do when Kaitlyn looks at you. Her hero. Her ... her world. It's all over her face. Don't let him take you away from her."

"Rey*nauld*." Daws came toward him and Andrea pulled back. The guard's expression softened when he noticed. "Sorry to interrupt but Kaitlyn's awake. Her father's in with her, asking about you, trying to get her to admit you pushed her into..."

Ryan bolted to his feet, started to head out, then turned and went back to offer Andrea an arm.

She shook her head. "Robert can't know we talked. He can't know what I said."

"Okay. But walk back with me. At least most of the way, then we can separate." He waited impatiently while she agreed, shyly accepting his arm, and Ryan wished she would walk faster. He needed to be with Katie. Finally close to Katie's room, he thanked her and threw a glance at Daws to tell him to stay with her a minute.

Robert was talking at her, asking about their relationship, about how Ryan convinced her, pushed her, asking how much he pushed. His mom argued, insisting he would never in the world push any girl into anything. They all stopped and stared when they noticed he was in the room.

He looked only at Kaitlyn. "I'm sorry. I told them." She kept his eyes as he went to her side and grasped her fingers. "Are you mad? I know you asked me not to say anything, but..."

"No. Are you okay?"

She didn't look mad. She looked relieved to see him. And he knew it was wrong with Robert right there and fuming, but he couldn't hold back. He sat beside her, took her into his arms, and kissed her. A soft kiss, short, but with just enough passion to make his statement, his claim on her. He wasn't letting her go.

Kaitlyn held his eyes. "Don't let them hurt you. I'm waiting to go home with you." She brushed fingers up through his hair.

"I want that man out of here. I want him away from my daughter."

"Oh give it up, Robert." Nick sounded fully exasperated. "*Look* at her. Did you hear what she said? I don't know about you, but I'm damn glad to actually hear her voice again, to hear her want to go home, wherever home is for her. To hear her *tell* us what she wants. Doesn't that mean *anything* to you? What *she* wants?"

"She's a child."

Ryan threw his attention toward the stupid comment. "No, she's not. Yes, maybe she's only seventeen, but she has dealt with a hell of a lot more in her seventeen years than most people have to deal with in *forty*. And she deals with it better than most forty or fifty year olds."

"By swallowing pills."

"She was trying to get your attention. Taking control of the situation the only way she could figure out how. It was nothing more."

"You're insane, and even more naïve than I was if you truly believe that."

"No." Katie's voice shook, but she looked at her dad, fingers wrapped in the front of Ryan's shirt. "No. I didn't want to hurt you. I don't want to hurt you. I wanted him here. I needed him. I wasn't trying to leave. I told him I wouldn't. But I hurt too much. I lost his baby and I needed him and you wouldn't let me talk to him. You said you wouldn't let him come back."

Robert edged closer. "Are you telling me he's right? You did this to see him? To bring him here?"

Katie found Ryan's eyes. "Yes." She looked toward her dad again, not quite at him. "I knew you would be home then and I knew you would come check on me like you did every night. I knew it wouldn't do more than make me sick. I knew he would come. I hoped he would. If he didn't, nothing else would have mattered."

Ryan kissed her head. "You could have gone out for a walk and called me. I would've come immediately. You know I would have. And Katie..." He raised her face to his. "It would matter. If I'm here or if I'm not, you matter, you being here matters..."

She shook her head. "He would have arrested you. I didn't want you hurt. More than anyone, I don't want to hurt you."

"Kaitlyn." Her dad moved in, next to them, close enough Ryan could nearly feel the heat of his anger. "Why didn't you talk to me? I kept trying to talk to you..."

"No, you talked at me. You didn't want to listen. You wanted me to listen." Her fingers tightened. "I don't *want* any more orders. I don't want to be talked at. I don't want to be talked down to. I'm not stupid and I'm *not* crazy. I don't ... I don't want to be told how to do everything anymore. I don't want to be told what I want and what I don't want. I know. I'm smart enough to know. Not talking doesn't make me stupid. I've listened enough. I don't want to listen to everyone else all the time anymore. And I don't want everything that matters to me taken away again."

Ryan felt her tremble and wrapped his arms farther around her. He sheltered the side of her face with his hand, kissed the top of her head. Shoes scuffed, hospital equipment made noise, whispers floated around the room. He wondered if anyone else would realize just how much it mattered that she spoke up, that she said what she wanted and didn't want, that she would. Ryan's fear that he failed her dissipated. He hadn't. She stood up to her father, more than Ryan figured he appreciated about now. It was good, very good. Her progress wasn't lost. She was fighting for what she wanted.

She was fighting for him. As Dani said she would.

"All right." Robert's voice came at them softly. "I don't want you unhappy, Kaitlyn, I only want you safe. You have to know that. Come home with me and we'll work it out. He can visit and call, anytime. I'm not ordering you. I'm asking you. We can try this again."

She pressed into Ryan's chest.

"She's going to Will's. Doctor's recommendation." He rubbed her back. "She agreed. And she'll be fine there while I'm working. Until ... until she's ready to move back in with me."

"Back with you." Robert shook his head. "If you haven't gone off and found another roommate or road friends by then and she finds out..."

"I haven't been with anyone else since I met her and I don't want to be." He nearly held back, considering his family was in the room, his mom. But he couldn't. "You can look down on me all you want for what I've done in the past, but I was single, unattached, and no one gave a shit. I was hurting no one. Those girls you're so worried about? They came to me. They were everywhere. Pushing into my room. Hiding under food carts to get in. Climbing up fire escapes. Bribing security to let them backstage. I didn't go seek out innocent girls. Trust me, there was nothing innocent about any of them and I was nothing but a niche in their sticks. Hell, the ones who couldn't get to me settled for one of my musicians or roadies. I can't tell you how often I pushed them away." He swallowed hard as he'd seen Andrea do and calmed his tone. "I have no interest in any more of that. It was nothing. Empty. I'm sick of it. Sick of girls who don't even care if I know their names just so they can go brag to their friends. And I'm sick of the being alone, even in the midst of the crowd."

She looked up at him.

He touched her face. "You pulled me in more than the other way around. You don't have to worry about anyone else, about what I do while I'm away. I belong to you, Katie. Never doubt that I'll be here if you need me. And I'll wait for you."

She slid her hand up to his chest. "You're never alone anymore. Never."

"No. And you won't be, either."

With a light shake of her head, Katie leaned in to find his lips.

Robert swiveled and strode out of the room.

Ryan sat next to Kaitlyn as she settled onto the hotel bed. He wouldn't get up until sure she was asleep. He'd finally turned his phone off and would hear about it later, but he was tired of interference from work. They'd had to cancel shows and promotions. Ginny was furious until Ryan told her everything. Suddenly placating, his manager told him to take the time he needed and to keep her informed, but she kept calling about details. About a press release. About where he was and why they'd cancelled. She didn't quite accept his answer to tell them he had no comment and wouldn't have a comment. Giving in, he said to announce he had a sick friend and apologized and he'd make them up later. If he could help it at all, the truth would stay hidden. She'd been through enough without it all over the papers.

It took three days to get her out of the hospital, nearly three days. Her doctor wouldn't release her until she was eating well. Ryan sent people for carry out. He refused to let her put up with bland hospital food. Her father wouldn't speak to him but at least he stopped arguing about Ryan's presence. Daws took care of arrangements, on how to get her out and up to Vermont quietly the next morning. Nearly three days in the hospital and two more at the hotel where her doctor and social worker could stop and check on her made him more than ready to be free of it all, to take her away, to Will's.

Ginny wanted to know how soon he would be back in New York. The "whatever time he needed" comment lost from her memory, she'd hinted at him staying only a day or two at Will's to help Kaitlyn settle. Ryan couldn't imagine leaving her that soon. Katie said it was all right. She said she would be fine there and would keep her phone on so he could call any time. Robert had set it on her bedside during some point when Ryan was out of her room.

Even with Daws leaving two of his best guards in Vermont to keep watch, Ryan didn't want to leave her so soon. He didn't ever want to leave her. He wanted to surround her and make sure no one came near unless she wanted them near.

As he sat with her, she told him about her first baby, how an orderly at the mental home they'd stuck her in took advantage of her unwillingness to talk, how he went in to her at night for quite some time until he realized she was pregnant, and how he smuggled her out when he noticed so he wouldn't be discovered. He left her alone in the middle of the city in clothes he'd grabbed from someone being admitted. He expected she was actually crazy and even if she did talk, no one would believe her, and so he didn't consider it a threat to simply let her go. She didn't know where the home was but she described the place and the orderly. And she told him what last name she'd been using. One that was given to her somewhere along the line. Ryan would tell Daws to find him. However long it took.

The baby. Kaitlyn had been found and taken to a shelter for unwed mothers. But they were going to give her baby up for adoption so she'd fled with her and worked as kitchen help in a little restaurant. They'd lived in the frigid back room and she made barely enough to buy what the baby needed. Until they both got sick and she tried to get care for her daughter. The hospital wouldn't take her with no means to pay the bill. She left the clinic when they wanted too much information, afraid they would take her baby away. But the illness got worse and she gave in and returned to the clinic, determined to let her be adopted if they would help her. It was too late.

Kaitlyn sat at the baby's barely marked grave for days. And then she found the building.

Suppressing a hard shiver, Ryan touched her face to be sure she was asleep, and forced himself up. It was nearly five. They would have to eat soon but he would let her sleep a while first, for the second time that day.

On return to the sitting area, he plopped on the couch and dropped his elbows to his knees, head in his hands. His brain was spinning, fuzzy and overactive and ... and everything she told him rushed back in and swirled there. It wasn't the first time. She said the orderly wasn't the first time, but she wouldn't say more.

"Is she all right, honey?" His mom sat next to him. Will and Tracy were home with their kids. His mom refused to leave. She'd become a barricade for Robert, as though it was necessary. The man wanted nothing to do with him.

"Ryan?" She rubbed his back.

"She's asleep." It was all he could say.

"Good, it'll help her recover faster. We have food ordered. Freddy helped me find something nice without the fast food oil and so on. And ... I know you don't want to hear this, but her dad will be over to eat with us. I thought it would be good to start again on new ground, let him get to know you. He is her father and it will matter..."

His head dropped farther and he felt his body shake. His child. It had been his child she lost ... they lost. She'd asked if it didn't matter to him. He wasn't showing it. She thought it didn't matter. He hadn't been able to take the time to think about it. Of course it mattered. He would've been a father. As careful as he'd always been and with all the girls saying kids were his when he refused to acknowledge it because he'd been so careful and because they were only using him and ... and it never even got into his brain enough to think about it. And she'd lost the baby, when he wasn't there with her, when he didn't even know ... and for some reason, the loss dug sharply into his whole being anyway...

"Ryan, honey? What is it?" His mom pressed closer to try to wrap him in her arms.

He shook more, like she had been, the loss of her first child affecting him also, even though it shouldn't, except it hurt her and it had been hers ... a part of her that was lost...

"Here." Daws shoved a small glass of something under his nose. "I think you need this about now."

It smelled like whiskey. Ryan didn't care much what it was. With a shaky hand, he took a swallow. Straight whiskey. The burning made him cough. He took another good swallow and Daws took the glass.

"Go shower. You have an hour before company."

"I don't want him here. I can't deal with him tonight."

"Nick's coming, too. He said he'd keep him in line or kick him out."

"I don't *want* them here."

"Honey." His mom gripped his hand. "He's hurting, also. He feels as though he just lost her again..."

"It's his own damn fault. If he'd been nicer to her, if he hadn't been so damn overbearing, I would have been able to be there, to help while she was sick and maybe..."

"Maybe prevent the miscarriage?"

He grabbed a lungful of air and got up to grasp the glass Daws was still holding to refill.

"Not on an empty stomach that's already too uptight." His guard took the bottle from him. "Enough. Go shower. Stand under the hot water..."

"Call and tell them not to come."

His friend stared a minute. "I'll tell you what. I'll tell them to make it after dinner, to give you more time to unwind, so you can actually eat instead of..."

"Just tell them *not to come*. What is so fucking *hard* about that?"

"He can't, honey." A warm hand grasped his arm. "It was part of the release condition. He has a right to visit her, accompanied. Her doctor thinks it's important and tomorrow...."

"Important, hell. All he does is upset her."

"Ryan, you can't make this impossible. You can't block her away from everything."

"You *don't* understand. If you'd been through what she has, you *wouldn't* want to deal anyone, either. She has a right *not* to put with any more *shit.*" He paced. A right to visit. He had a right to visit. He didn't give a shit about Ryan's right to visit or to even talk to her. Why should anyone care about *his* right to visit?

"He may be misguided, honey, but he's still her father and he's doing what he thinks is best. I think he was wrong ... I *know* he was wrong, because I know you. He doesn't."

"He doesn't want to know me."

She grasped his arms to force his attention. "Well, he better start wanting to. Because the way I see it, she is part of our family now. He'll have to accept that."

He gave her his eyes. Part of the family.

"And if he's rude to you, Nick won't need to kick him out. I will. There has to be some benefit to having a ex sergeant for a mom."

Ryan knew he couldn't fight her. No matter how he thought he could when he was young, he quickly learned better.

He went to look out the window. There was a crowd below on the sidewalk. He let the curtain fall back. "Let them come for dinner if you've already ordered. But don't let them stay long. And I don't care how that sounds or how you have to make them leave. I just can't ... I can't." He grabbed clean clothes from his suitcase and headed toward the bathroom. "Daws, let me know if she wakes up. I don't think she will, but..."

"Go."

Ryan checked on Kaitlyn incessantly from the time he stepped out of the shower until the knock on the door. Daws pushed fans away while letting them in.

Although Robert gave his mom a polite greeting and otherwise held back, Nick walked straight up and set a hand on his shoulder. "How's she feeling?" His expression asked Ryan the same.

"She's been asleep a while. I'll get her up." He barely acknowledged Robert when he stopped him.

"Maybe we could talk first."

Ryan rubbed at a callous on his finger. "You know, I'm sure we should talk, but this isn't the right time. I can't do it tonight. I'll be polite, for Katie's sake, but I can't fight with you tonight."

"I didn't intend to fight. At this point, that would be useless."

At this point? As though it wasn't before? He felt his stomach twist.

"Will you sit a minute?"

Daws had moved only part-way into the room again. Ryan figured he was trying to decide whether to stay or go. His mom took over and told Ryan she would get him more cranberry juice so Kaitlyn could see he was following her orders. She offered Daws a coffee refill and asked Robert and Nick if they would like anything. Giving him time to settle.

Ryan knew she was.

With a deep breath, he pulled a chair from the table and planted himself on the edge, his feet propped against the legs, toes pressed into the floor. Nick grabbed one beside him, a show of support, maybe. Ryan couldn't help wonder why he still supported him.

Robert settled into one of the arm chairs. "Nick thinks it's unfair to judge you by your job, regardless of my feelings about it, so maybe we should get past that for the moment. I'd like to know if there's anything to you beyond what you do for a living."

"I don't have to listen to this shit." He stood again. His mom and Nick objected to Robert's statement. Ryan grabbed the back of the chair. "Maybe I should ask you the same. From what I've seen, your job and your obsession with Kaitlyn is all there is to you anymore. Kaitlyn says you aren't who you were, that she can't tell who you are. That scares her."

"I'm not obsessed. I'm concerned. And my daughter is not afraid of me."

"Okay." Ryan walked away. There was no talking to the man.

"And you're not obsessed with her?"

He pulled his shoulders back, stretched them, and considered the question. "No. I'm obsessed with keeping her safe, with helping her feel better about herself, with making sure what we've accomplished so far doesn't get undone..."

"Why?"

Turning back to stare, he couldn't imagine why Robert would ask such a stupid question.

"Why does it matter to you? Because it makes you feel better for doing more than prancing around on stage making yourself feel more important than you are...?"

"Don't talk to my son that way." His mom straightened, her chin raised. "I understand you have the right to visit your daughter, but you do not have the right to degrade my son."

"Understood." He dropped his gaze and returned it, to his mom, not to Ryan. "However, you have two sons, not a daughter. You can't understand how it feels to know your little girl has taken up with ... has ... become much more involved in an adult manner than she should have by now, that she's..."

"You think I can't understand? Try raising two boys mainly on your own as a woman and knowing one of them is out there in the midst of thousands of girls and that many of them would do nearly anything to try to trap him only because of his name, knowing how that could hurt him, and knowing there's nothing you can do to stop it."

"It's his choice. His job..."

"And he shouldn't do what he loves because of the mania involved?

It's not his fault they idolize him. He's doing what he loves. He can't even walk down a street without worrying about being mobbed. You think as a mother that doesn't worry me? I worry about him every day of my life, not because of his choice, because of what others are willing to do, because of the lies getting printed. Because they have no trouble treating him like property, like they own him, or ... like he doesn't deserve common courtesy and respect simply because he's up on that stage. And I can tell you right now that my son deserves a lot more respect than he gets, so don't think I'm going to sit here and let him take this from you, no matter who you are."

Ryan walked over to the window, trying to push it away, trying not to let any of it sink in. He knew his mom worried. He didn't realize she worried quite so much.

"Can I ask what happened to your husband?" Robert's voice pushed through to his consciousness, regardless of how he tried not to hear it. And he heard his mom answer, the training accident, no one's fault.

Robert softened. "It must have been a struggle at times."

"I was glad when it was no more than a struggle. Those were good days. It was hardest on Ryan. He was only fourteen at the time and try as I could, a mom can't quite be the father a boy needs."

"It wasn't hardest on me. I was just the biggest baby about it." Letting the curtain fall, he turned back. "If you have an objection about me personally, say so. My family history isn't your concern. What is it that you want from me? To change jobs? If I were an accountant, would that make a difference?"

Shifting, Robert sighed. "Honestly, I don't think it would. Fact still is that she's a minor and you're ... how old?"

"Twenty-four."

He glanced at Nick, surprise registering, and back to Ryan. "Twenty-four? Seven years older? You're *seven* years older than my daughter and you're surprised I have an issue with you?"

"You didn't think I was that old."

"No. Twenty-one, twenty-two..."

"Yeah, well, I know seven years sounds like a lot, and I guess it is, except ... that yeah, I've always been kinda young for my age, which I'm quite sure isn't impressing you at all, but then Katie is old for her age, so the difference isn't as extreme as it sounds."

"This is insane." He shut Ryan out and focused on his mom instead. "Is that what you would want? If you had a daughter, you'd want her giving herself to some guy seven years older, someone ... not nearly as innocent as she is, should be. She should be still." The calm anger in his face faded into desperation as he glared at Ryan. "She *should* be still. I resent the hell out of you that she isn't, and I will never in my lifetime forgive you for that."

Ryan couldn't even argue. He couldn't blame her dad for feeling that way, even if he wasn't the one, but he couldn't tell him. His mom argued it was only half his choice, he couldn't take full responsibility, which of course Robert wasn't buying since Kaitlyn was a "minor" as though that gave her no responsibility for anything, as though it meant she didn't know what she was doing, as though it made her brainless or...

"It wasn't him."

He swiveled toward Katie's voice. She was at the bedroom doorway, arms wrapped around herself as though she was cold. Ryan went to her and felt her arm. Warm. "How do you feel?"

"You weren't going to tell him it wasn't you."

"No."

"Why?"

He ducked his head closer to hers. "I wouldn't do that to you. You said you didn't want him to know."

Katie held him, her head against his shoulder.

"What do you mean it wasn't him?" Her father moved in. "He said the baby was his. Was that a lie?"

She raised her head. "No. Ryan doesn't lie. Ever. Most people do. He doesn't."

"Then how can you say it wasn't him?"

Her fingers wrapped into Ryan's shirt. "It's why I couldn't go back. Why I couldn't tell anyone. He ... the man ... the one who was in the house ... he followed me. He...." She dropped her head, breathing harder, fingers clenching.

The one who was in the house? She'd said the one at the mental home wasn't the first, but...

Robert stepped closer, barely inches from them. "He what?" His whole manner reflected fear at hearing the rest and he closed his eyes a moment when she pulled back at his touch. "Kaitlyn, he what?"

Her chest rose and fell roughly. She kept her head half hidden against Ryan's shoulder. "He ... attacked me too, like Andrea, when I saw him, yelled at him to stop, he..."

"No." Ryan pulled her face to his, ignoring her father, ignoring Nick closing in. "Kaitlyn..."

She pressed back in, hid in the curve of his neck.

"Hey, look at me." He knew his voice shook. The man who attacked Andrea ... she was seven then. Just a child. "Come here. Sit down, Katie. Sit with me." She didn't resist as he led her to the little couch. He kept her wrapped in his arms. And she told him. The man slowed her escape first by telling her he would kill her family if she didn't stop, and she did but then ran when he got close. She heard gunshots and stopped again, and he caught up with her, pushed her into his car and kept hold of her with one hand while he drove away, somewhere in the middle of the woods. Afterwards, he took her to a house with a couple of people who took her in and warned her never to say anything or he would come back and find her. They "adopted" her out. She saw the people who took her hand him money.

Ryan was nauseous. Furious. He kept her sheltered in his arms through her dad and uncle trying to talk to her. He didn't want them there. He didn't want them to speak to her. He didn't want anyone around her. Obsessed. Maybe he was. Obsessed about protecting her, not allowing anyone to harm her ever again. And he would find them. The man … the man was still in prison, so Andrea said. About to get out. No. He would make damn sure that wouldn't happen. And he would find the couple.

"Kaitlyn." Robert's voice was nearly a whisper from where he crouched on the floor in front of her.

"You don't have to see me again." She didn't look at him, firmly wrapped into Ryan. "I'm not the same. I'm not who you know. He wasn't the only one. Ryan knows. He knows I needed him. But you don't have to see me again."

"Baby." Robert reached for her hand and clenched his jaw when she drew away, but tried again, insisting on the contact. "My baby, you can't think I wouldn't want to see you because … because of anything. Nothing would make me not want to see you again. Why would you think I wouldn't?"

"I'm not…"

"You are. You're my daughter. Nothing in the world will change that. I'm sorry. I'm sorry I wasn't there to … to protect you. I'm sorry I didn't find you. I'm sorry … I'm so sorry you've been hurt, that you … Kaitlyn, I'm so sorry." He stroked her hand with his thumb, watching her, waiting for any kind of acknowledgement. "What can I do? What will make you give me another chance? Let me get to know you again and help you? What can I do?"

A knock at the door sent Daws to answer. He let them know dinner had arrived but would hold, then stepped outside with the caterer, escaping, Ryan figured.

"Was it your idea to be with Ryan?" Robert didn't seem to realize anyone was in the room other than himself and Kaitlyn. His attention was fully on her. "Just tell me that. Tell me that much."

She looked at him, at her father.

"Tell me honestly, Kaitlyn. Why? Why did you … after…"

"Stop fighting him." She glanced up at her uncle, at his mom, hesitated, then took a deep breath and faced her father again. "I need him. More than anyone. He didn't want to. But I needed him. He made me feel … like I'm … like I'm not ruined, like I still…"

"Oh Katie." Ryan kissed her head. "You are beautiful. Not ruined. You could never be. And don't think I didn't want to. I was so turned on by you. I still am. I always will be."

"That's unnecessary…"

Kaitlyn threw her gaze back at her father. "Don't fight him. No more. Don't fight him anymore. I need him." She found Ryan's eyes. "You matter more than anyone. You make me want to be here, just so I can be with you."

He cradled her in his arms, eyes closed, and pretended no one else was there. She would be all right. She wanted to be there. She *wanted* to be. Eventually, it would be more than him making her want to be.

"What do you mean by that?" Robert stood and pulled a chair up close. "Makes you want to be here? What do you mean by that?"

She slid her hand up to Ryan's neck, cuddled as close to him as she could get. Her face was calm, back in control. "I didn't want to be. I gave up. I kept trying. But it didn't matter to anyone if I did and … and it was too much, on my own, with no one who cared if I was around. I lost everything that mattered. No one…."

"You knew I was still around." Nick finally found his voice, standing close behind Robert's chair. "Even if you thought your father wasn't, you knew I was. Why didn't you come find me? I was doing shows … everywhere for a few years, small clubs but easy enough to find, no security to keep you away anymore. Why didn't you come find me?"

"I didn't know where. I didn't know you were playing. I heard nothing after…"

"After I dropped out of sight for a while." Nick rubbed the back of his neck.

"I tried to go home." She looked back at Ryan, gathering the will to keep talking, to finish telling them whatever she thought they should know.

"Do you want to eat first? The rest of this can wait. Daws is probably having a hell of a time fighting fans off from getting to the food cart."

"Will he be mad?"

Ryan chuckled. "Nah, not at you anyway. And I don't worry much about that. He gets over it." He ran a thumb down her cheek. "I just think you need to unwind. And eat. You've barely done that today."

"Why didn't you get there?" Robert seemed hesitant to interfere, cutting off Ryan's mom saying it was a good idea to relax and refresh. "If you tried, why didn't you get to us? You could have called. We moved but we kept the same number to be sure you could find us."

Ryan argued with him, said it would wait.

Katie touched his face with a look to say she was all right at the moment. She turned back to her dad. "They didn't have a phone. At the first place. I was never by myself. I was always watched. But I ran away, during the night. I … there was always money in a drawer, for emergencies. I wasn't supposed to know but I saw it. I grabbed it all one night and snuck out, quiet, walking ... I didn't know where, to find ... someone who might help, a phone...."

When she stopped, Robert carefully reached for her hand again. "What happened?"

She tensed and looked away.

"Kaitlyn, don't stop now. Tell me. I want to know what you've been dealing with. I want to know what I can do to help you. Please."

Silent, she studied him, for the first time actually meeting his eyes and holding them. Ryan figured she was trying to decide how much he meant it, whether to let him in that far, whether her needs would come before his as he knew she was waiting for and insisting on before she would let him in. She'd done the same to Ryan, tested him.

Finally, she tilted her head. "What if how I need you to help isn't what you want?"

Robert frowned a moment, then sighed. "All right, Kaitlyn. All right. As long as you'll let me try to be a father to you again, on your terms, if you don't shut me out. That is what I want most, after your safety, to *be* your father again."

In the time she took to consider his words, Ryan let his gaze move away from her, to his mom. He wanted to know what he should be doing, to ask if he should interfere and take her away from it, or stay silent. At least he agreed with Robert on one count: her protection came first. The return look and bare shift of the head from his mom gave her approval, and her support. Much of the weight slid away, the pressure of being unsure, of hoping he wasn't being selfish as Robert thought he was, as many who barely knew him always thought he was. This wasn't about him. It was about her. He would also do whatever she needed of him. Whatever that meant. And at least his mom was on his side. It was her opinion that mattered most, anyway.

"They found me." Katie's soft voice contrasted with the firmness of her grip on his hand. "He knew everyone around. Someone saw me and told him and ... and I tried again, two more times, but ... every time...." She lowered her head.

"Baby, every time, what?" Concern replaced all arrogance on Robert's face, in his mannerism. He even looked at Ryan, asking for help, or so it seemed.

He didn't want to push. He'd never pushed her, always letting her stop talking whenever she'd had enough. But her father wanted his help. It was a breakthrough, even if a small one.

He kissed her head. "It's all right, Katie. Finish this. You can't start to let go of it until you finish it. Until you get it out."

Her eyes questioned him and he touched his lips to hers. Briefly, enough to comfort her but hopefully not irritate her father too much.

Daws came back in with an apology that it was too hard to keep people away, that he would put the kitchen area and disappear again.

"You saw the scars, in the hospital. You saw them." Her voice trembled and she ducked her head into Ryan's shoulder.

She'd had enough. Her breathing was too fast, fingers gripping too tight. He finished it for her. "Every time she tried to get away, to get back to you, he added more while he told her you were all dead. She had to stop trying to find out for herself." He felt her shake. "Shh, Katie, it's all right now. It's over. You're safe." He nuzzled his head down against hers and held her as close as possible. "I won't let anyone hurt you again. You know I won't. It's over."

Before heading to his room across the hall, Daws set a hand on Katie's arm and told her he added his cell number to her phone, that she could call anytime she needed and even if Ryan got too tied up in work to get to Vermont, he could get there.

She shook her head. "Stay with him. Keep him safe for me."

Daws threw a grin. "Don't worry. My paycheck depends on him. I won't let anyone interfere with that." With a wink, he told her to sleep well, gave Ryan's mom a good night, and Ryan a quick nod of approval.

The sudden silence caught him off-guard. Robert and Nick left shortly after dinner with the admonition she should get plenty of rest, and a barely accepted kiss on the cheek from her father. They would visit her in Vermont before long, to check in, he said.

"I'm gonna take a quick shower. And yeah, I know I already did today." He pulled Kaitlyn's hand up and kissed her fingers. "Are you going to be all right sitting with Mom a while? I won't be long."

"Yes."

"Don't open the door to anyone but Daws. Call him if someone else…"

"I think I'm quite capable of managing." His mom pushed at him. "Go on. Wind down so you can sleep tonight."

Ryan closed the bathroom door and turned the water handle all the way to one side. He wanted it hot. Pulling out of his clothes, he stretched his shoulders and tilted his head back and forth to get the muscles to relax. It was all in the open. She'd told her dad everything, with less detail than she told Ryan, but it was good enough. And her dad saw that Ryan wanted her to tell him, pushed her to tell him. He hoped it was the right decision. She was so worn out, exhaustion set in fast after the talk. She ate, but not a lot. He would order a large breakfast, try to start fresh in the morning.

Under the hot water, he leaned back against the shower wall, something he never did in hotels since he was never convinced of how clean they were, but he lacked the strength to completely hold himself up. His own exhaustion set in. His own emotional release gushed out as the water washed down his bare skin and through the drain. He stood feeling the heat, the release, the muscle drain ... and then shoved his hands through his hair and pulled himself back up to full standing position. It wasn't quite over. She was to stay with his family, not with him. It wouldn't be over fully until she was with him.

He pulled sweats over skin that wouldn't dry well enough since steam filled the small room, but he couldn't make himself pull the shirt on until going out to fresh cool air. When Katie looked over from where she was snacking on ... something, he went to his room to find his deodorant and stood to finish drying for a couple of minutes. And to shove his emotions back in check.

Part Three

"Come sail, my love, the air is fine
the sand is white, we'll leave behind
the cold concrete and steel gray beams
for palm trees, beaches, and rolling seas..."

(from **The Palm Song**, ©2000 Ryan Reynauld)

With stories flying around due to his cancellations, Ryan had no choice but to work with his publicist to try to answer them. The official story. He wasn't sure it would matter if there was an official story, but some of the trash needed to at least be countered. Some tabloid reporter saw Dani arrive at his hotel while Katie was in the hospital. Rumors of a possible breakup between Dani and her long-time boyfriend mixed with her visit to Ryan translated to an affair. There were reports that Katie's "illness" was due to her finding out about it. Not that it was the first time the press made the assumption about him and Dani, and normally neither of them cared. This time, he did.

"So how about this?" Patricia glanced at notes, a pencil propped between her fingers. "We say she was a friend from long ago you heard needed help and you've been giving her a place to stay. Her hospital visit was an accidental overdose after a prolonged virus and that's that. You get on with things and with her at your brother's and you here, it'll look like it was nothing, just helping a friend..."

"She's coming back and I don't want it suggested it was nothing." Ryan leaned back in the chair and stared at the edge of the table. The edge was darker than the surface, although it was the same glass.

"Coming back? After what happened?"

He ran his finger along the cool smoothness of the edge. "Next month if all goes well, or soon after that. She's at Will's to give her time to recover. I'm only here long enough to do what I have to, to make whatever statements I need to make myself, then I'm going back up there."

Ginny straightened in her chair across the table. "Your job is *here* and you can't let that girl keep living with you, especially after..."

He raised his eyes. "Don't call her *that girl* and I'm not asking for your cohabitation advice or permission."

"It is my job to..."

"I know what you're trying to do for me and I appreciate it. You've done an incredible job through all my bullshit, like everyone else has. But this is the deal now: Katie is coming back with me as soon as I can manage; we don't hide that she is or that I'm spending so much time up there to be with her; we tell the truth but only as much as necessary while trying to protect her privacy; and if I lose fans because of it, screw them. That's what we're doing. It's only a question of how to say it and how much we can leave out based on what's already known, which I'm not sure about." He turned back to the publicist. "Patricia, what exactly is being said?"

She gave him a curious look. "What do you know? I didn't think you even knew my first name."

"I knew it. Sorry you couldn't tell I did. I have no excuse."

She was silent a moment. "Okay. So what's being said ... they know she's been staying with you and she was in the hospital. Rumor has it you're much more than friends and definitely not cousins. There are photos of the two of you quite close but not more than that. There's talk that she's still a minor and you were nearly arrested by her father, that she ran away from him to be with you, that she was locked in a pysch ward because you turned her away or because you were cheating on her, and there are some photos of you with Nick Hollister and talk about some kind of joint music project to pull him out of hiding and that you may have been using her to get to him. That's most of what I've heard and the rest is too ridiculous to bother about."

Ryan looked over at Daws and grabbed a deep breath. "So the parts we have to counter: I didn't turn away from her, she didn't leave her family for me, and I had no idea Nick Hollister was her uncle until I met him through her. Also there's no joint music project in the works, although I wouldn't argue if he was interested. Don't say that. I don't want to put him on the spot to answer."

Ginny leaned forward. "And the cheating on her bit. We need to counter that, too. It's time to make a statement about your relationship with Dani."

"No."

"Reynauld..."

"No. We say nothing about Dani. We've both agreed we say nothing. I won't go against that."

"You want your fans to keep thinking...?"

"They'll think what they want no matter what we say, and I don't think they'd actually care. Most won't. Hell, they know I haven't been particular. They know there's been one after another. Think the ones I've been with haven't talked? It's not like it's some kind of secret."

"They prefer it that way." Daws cut in and moved from where he usually stood or sat beside the door to pull a chair out at the table. "Counter the arrest issue. He was doing nothing illegal. That needs to be said, without detail. But as far as the rest, the more available he looks, the better. I agree with him on this one. Let them think he might."

"Available, yes, which is why that girl should stay in Vermont." Ginny caught Ryan's glance and backed up. "Which is why *Kaitlyn* should not live with him. Still, a statement to say Dani is only a friend and he wasn't messing around with her while ... while Kaitlyn was having such a struggle, would tell his more particular fans they have no reason to walk away. Some of them will care, Reynauld."

"Some might. That's why we say I didn't turn away from her. That's enough to tell them."

"Is it?" Ginny eyed him. "Just why do you refuse to say there's nothing going on with you and Dani? Because you can't lie or because you don't want to get caught in a lie?"

"Because we agreed from the beginning. The rest is between us. And I will not change my mind, so let it go."

Patricia stood and wandered around her office. As she did, she tapped her pencil against the palm of her other hand.

Against the palm ... tapping a rhythm.... "Can I use this?" Ryan picked up a notepad on the round glass table she used as a desk.

"Sure. But if you have ideas, say them out loud. I'll listen."

"No. Just ... unless you want a song idea, it won't do any good."

She grinned. "Sitting here talking about publicity matters gave you a song idea?"

"No, watching you pace the room tapping your pencil did."

Her eyebrows raised. "Well, by all means, go ahead."

He grabbed a pencil from the glass cup in the exact center of the glass table and returned to his thoughts. *Against my palm ... palm trees ... Florida ... Daytona ... white sand falling from a tanned palm...*

"So..." Patricia pulled him from his scribbles. "Sorry, should I wait?"

"No, go ahead." Ryan set the pencil down and rested his elbows on the table, fingers gripped in a tent shape. *Tent shape ... like a sailboat's sails.* He wrote that down, also, then gave her his attention.

"There is something I need to know before I suggest anything further." She walked over and set her hands on the chair beside him. "Where is this leading? This thing with Kaitlyn. Where is it going?"

Ryan dropped his eyes, not ready to discuss it. It was too soon to tell. As she healed and became more confident, less needy, she could very well move on. He wouldn't be able to stop her if it was what she wanted. He wouldn't hold her back.

"You don't know what it is you want from her?"

He met Patricia's gaze. "What I want isn't the issue."

Ginny threw a sarcastic chuckle. "Since when?"

Ryan forced himself to bite his tongue. Maybe he did deserve it, or at least he used to deserve it, but he sure as hell didn't need it right now.

"Since he found something that matters more." Daws crossed his arms on the table, addressing him, not Ginny or Patricia. "She would want you to do whatever you have to do to protect your career. Keep that in mind." When Ryan didn't answer, Daws turned to Ginny. "The thing to remember is that Kaitlyn matters to him, more than we do, and any decision has to work around that."

Ryan studied his friend. There was no derision or attitude in the statement, only truth. Yes, she mattered more.

"Okay." Ginny settled back in her chair. "So. How is she doing with it? How will she handle the attention and rumors, especially rumors you refuse to counter? What happens if the miscarriage is discovered and put out there? Can she cope with it? Because there's usually at least one hospital worker who will spill for money if it's offered."

His stomach tightened. "She doesn't care about the rumors. I warned her. She doesn't care. However ... I want ... as much as possible to keep anyone from hearing about the miscarriage. I don't want that out. It's no one's business."

"Pretty unlikely." Patricia seemed apologetic, watching his reaction. "But we'll try."

Ryan rubbed his neck as he stood. "So that's it. You know what I want said. Call me when you arrange however you want to do this. Make it soon. I'm heading to the studio, but I need to get back to Vermont as soon as I can, this weekend if possible."

"Reynauld, we have shows to reschedule and an album to finish."

"I know Ginny, and we will. But I have to ... she's not feeling well yet. Give me time."

Close to Will's, Ryan pulled into Dunkin' Donuts to grab a large coffee. After three p.m., Tracy would have the coffee pot washed out and empty until after dinner. He needed the caffeine. And sugar sounded good. Although Tracy would complain, he ordered two dozen donuts, also. It was his job to spoil his niece and nephew.

The radio blared *Careless Whisper* as Ryan approached the housing area with one hand on the wheel and the other holding one of the less messy doughnuts. He slowed when a sign in front of the house on the edge of Will's neighborhood caught his eye. For Sale. The house Katie had looked at as they drove past, at least a couple of times that Ryan noticed. A nice house, two stories with a big porch, painted light yellow with dark green accents. A large shade tree stood in one corner of the yard with a small table and chairs below. Rocking chairs adorned the ceilinged porch. A nice walk to his brother's house and as far as he could tell, a lot of open green space behind the house.

He stuffed the last bit of doughnut in his mouth, wiped his hand, and took a swallow of the steaming coffee as he crept through the housing area on the lookout for kids playing ball in the road or bicycling. He barely pulled onto Will's driveway before Bella ran outside. She jumped at him as soon as he stepped out. "Uncle Ryan! You're back soon!"

"Too soon? Should I go again?"

"Nooooo!" Her little arms coiled around his neck. "You can't go again. Your Katie is here."

He hugged her. *His Katie.* At least Bella wouldn't fight him on it. When Tracy stepped out the door, he threw her a smile and set Bella down to grab his coffee and the doughnuts. "Now don't badger your mom too much about these or you'll get me in trouble."

"You're silly, Uncle Ryan. You're too old to be in trouble."

"Hm. You have a lot to learn about being old."

Tracy sighed at sight of the box when they neared the porch.

Ryan crouched. "See. I'm in trouble already."

Bella frowned and looked up at her mom. "No mommy, I won't badger. I be good so Uncle Ryan isn't in trouble."

Standing again, he threw Tracy a wink and handed her the box.

"Isabelle, go tell Kaitlyn he's here, please, in case she didn't hear you yell it all the way through the house."

Ryan couldn't help a chuckle. "Where is she?"

"The backyard!" Bella tugged at his hand. "Come. I show you. She's playing with Chewy. Chewy likes your Katie."

He called a hello to his mom when he saw her and let Bella pull him through the house to the back door. Chewy was on a leash, sitting beside Kaitlyn on the grass outside the chain link fence.

Tracy pulled her daughter off his arm. "Come with me. Matt will be home from school in a few minutes. Let's get snacks ready."

"No, I want Uncle Ryan."

"Later. He'll be here ... a few days, right?"

Ryan turned to Tracy. "Depends what happens with work and the reaction to my little press conference this morning."

"How are things there?"

"Not great. I shouldn't have left."

"Then why did you?"

He moved his eyes out the door. "I wanted to be here."

"And she'll be glad you are, but she won't want you to mess up the career you've worked so hard on. She's okay here, Ryan." Tracy drew Bella away and said Will would be another hour or so.

He knew Tracy objected to his relations with Katie as much as Will did, but other than the edge in her voice she was less rude about it. Will had barely spoken to him since, with or without an edge.

Chewy gave his presence away when he stepped outside and Ryan stopped when the dog jumped to its feet. Katie stood, patted Chewy's head, pulled the leash up close to her, and came to him.

"She's not going to take my arm off if I hug you, is she?"

Kaitlyn set her hand on his stomach. "She knows I want you here."

"Does she?" He kissed the side of her head, and when she turned her face to him, he couldn't help brushing her lips also. They were alone. More or less. "How do you feel? You look good."

"I'm glad you're here. But is it okay? Your job..."

"It'll still be there when I get back. And you didn't answer me." He rubbed a hand down her arm. "You're getting too cold out here."

"It feels good. The open air."

"Yeah, it does. Much better than city air. Are you up to taking a walk?"

"Yes. Can we take her?"

"She won't pull at you?"

"No. I've been walking her. With Will. She pulls at him, not at me."

Ryan figured it wouldn't hurt to have the dog on her other side since no one would get close and they could walk undisturbed. He ran inside to tell Tracy where they were going, and grabbed Kaitlyn's sweater with Bella's help to find it. He couldn't quite refuse when the child asked to go with. Tracy warned him not to take Kaitlyn too far. She still grew tired fast.

Bella's chatter filled the air while Ryan and Kaitlyn viewed the surroundings: unpretentious but dignified houses, neat yards, flower beds with large mums taking over from faded summer growth, new mulch in preparation for winter casting a heavy, dirt-rich scent he was glad to get away from when they passed. A few kids here and there. Neighbors who waved and some who pretended not to see them.

At the edge of the housing area, Ryan noticed Kaitlyn look over at the house for sale that wasn't quite part of the area, barely on its border. "Nice place, isn't it?"

She touched his eyes and kept walking.

"Hey. Hold on." Ryan pulled out his phone, moved to where he could see the realtor's number, and added it to his contact list. Katie watched, curious, but she didn't ask. She did touch Chewy's head when the dog gave off a low grumble, standing stiff and facing the house.

"Hello."

Ryan found the frail voice from the front porch. "Sorry to bother you. We were only looking."

"Is that little Bella?"

Bella waved an excited greeting and headed to the house. Ryan tried to stop her but the woman said she was fine and knew she could visit. She beckoned him and Kaitlyn closer, as well. Checking the dog's reaction, Ryan figured it was okay to go at least close enough to talk without yelling, but he moved to her other side and grabbed the leash to add extra support. Bella introduced him and Chewy and her "friend" Kaitlyn. Nancy Stewart introduced herself.

"You're Will's brother? My goodness I've only seen you in the papers before now, although I think I've seen you drive by a few times. You are much more handsome than any of those mug shots they like to take." She studied him closer as she ambled out onto the sidewalk. "You're the spitting image of your father. Will takes after your mother more, but you ... you are Edward when he was your age.

Taken aback, Ryan had trouble responding. "You knew him?"

"Oh goodness yes. He was one of my first students. I taught fifth grade. He was the biggest troublemaker I had, but oh he delighted me. Such a vivid imagination. I had such trouble trying not to laugh when I was supposed to make him behave."

"Troublemaker?" Ryan had to wonder if she was confused. His father was a gentleman. Always. A rule follower.

The woman grinned. "He grew to be a wonderful adult, though. I would guess you are very much like him. And Kaitlyn, is it? Bella nearly talks my ear off about you. It's so nice to meet you, also. Please, won't you come in? Did you want to see the house?"

"Oh. No. Well, yes maybe, but I'll give your realtor a call. I don't want to impose and we have the dog."

"The realtor is my daughter. No need to call for this. Use the lead on the porch if she won't mind being on it. My daughter brings her Chow when she visits so I'm prepared for dogs." Turning, she didn't wait for agreement.

Ryan wasn't sure he should leave the dog out on the porch, but she let him hook her while Mrs. Stewart sent Bella to put water in the dog bowl. Chewy sniffed the area, accepted the water, and lay down at the top of the stairs as though she'd claimed the place.

Kaitlyn hesitated at the door but gave in to Ryan's hand on her back. It was as charming inside as it was out, and bigger than he expected, with the living room open to the second floor, lots of windows and lots of oak, including the oak mantle around the small corner fireplace flanked by bookcases.

"My husband built this for me, God rest his soul, just the way I wanted it. I hate to leave but my legs can't keep up anymore. I'm eighty-six, can you believe it?"

Ryan honestly said he never would have guessed she was.

"You're a sweet boy, like your brother. All of your family. I was so glad they decided to move back here to the old neighborhood. Your mother visits often, did she tell you?"

"No, she didn't know we were headed this way."

"Ah, well you tell her I said hello and she did a nice job with the second one, as well." She teased with a grin. "I tell her every time she comes she'll have to bring you so I can see how she did with her second boy. You're very busy, she says. Hard to keep still."

"Yes, I'm afraid that's true." He rubbed a thumb up and down Katie's hand as he held it.

"Not to pry." Mrs. Stewart lowered onto a straight chair while waving them at the couch. "But are you in the market or looking to build somewhere close to your work and wanting ideas? I don't mind either way. As I said, I'm glad to finally meet you. I'm too curious for my own good, my dear husband used to say."

"We uh … Katie looks at the house whenever we pass by so I thought we'd check it out when we saw the sign." He felt Kaitlyn's eyes on him.

"I'm glad you did. Take a look around. I can show you the main floor. If you don't mind, though, I'll let Bella show you the rest. I do avoid the stairs now as much as I can."

Ryan suggested again they could wait for her daughter to come show the house, but Mrs. Stewart insisted and Bella grabbed Katie's hand, so he had no choice but to follow. Ryan first checked on Chewy, still lazing on the front porch watching kids ride bicycles on the road. He imagined she would settle down fine once she had an actual place, a place that was hers, where she was free to run around and explore without people annoying her.

The stairs were hard on Kaitlyn also, after the walk to get there, and Ryan took her hand from Bella's to offer his arm. The top floor held a good-sized bedroom with master bath, two smaller bedrooms, and a full bath in the hallway. The basement was mostly finished with a full laundry room and a ton of open space, plus a bath, and the main floor had another decent sized bedroom as well as a huge kitchen. There was also an extension that curved around to make a wide V out of the backyard with a sun room that connected the two separate parts of the house.

Katie loved the sun room. He could see it in her face. The ceiling-to-floor windows on one side looked out over a shrub-lined patio with a glass door leading out. The opposite side, a narrow bit of wall, featured a small gas fireplace with bookshelves above. It would be a nice place for her to sit and read whatever the season.

They moved into the extension and found a large bedroom, bath, kitchenette, and living area. Mrs. Stewart said her sister had stayed there for some time until they lost her. She appreciated having both the company and her privacy, but now feared the house would be too large for most families. It didn't look nearly as large from the front, since the sun room barely showed and the extension was hidden behind trees.

She urged them to go out in the yard. Kaitlyn was tired and they still had to walk home but they stepped out onto the patio … and he was sold. The yard was huge, all bordered by a thick grove of trees, with a couple of well-placed shade trees inside the yard. One of them held a rope swing with a seat of white-washed wood.

"Are you all right? Too tired yet?" He touched Kaitlyn's cheek, glad Bella stayed inside with an offer of cookies.

"Why are we here?"

"Come on." He led her over to the swing and asked her to sit, persuading her after pushing down hard on the thing to be sure it was sturdy. Ryan haunched in front of her and gripped the ropes next to her hips. "What do you think of it?"

"It's beautiful. Why?"

"I think you should have it." Her eyes widened, the expression confused. "You should have your own place, Kaitlyn. Something that's yours. Not ... you shouldn't have to be shuffled from here to there anymore. It's not fair to you. Everyone needs somewhere to call home. That is, if you like it here. If you don't, we can find something else, away from the city, but ... this is nice, small, with the lake close by and Will just down the road and..."

Her eyes watered and she pulled them away.

Ryan moved his hands to her waist, letting his arms rest on her legs. "Don't misunderstand. I want you with me. And I'm going to fight to make them let you come to the city as often as possible. You could stay with Deanna and they might allow that for now, but until ... until your counselor clears you to make your own choices, the best I may be able to do is be here as much as I can."

She brushed a hand through his hair. "I don't want to be hard on you."

"Oh Katie." He claimed her hand and kissed her palm. "You aren't. The rest of the world is. I want you to have this. If you want it. Then when I am here, we ... maybe we can't be here alone, but it's big. We could have privacy. To talk. To sit out here in the yard. With Chewy. I want you to have her, too. I'll put a fence around the whole place, for security, for Chewy. If you want it."

Her eyes still watered. She tried to fight it, to find that control she always had. "It's too much. I can't..."

"Of course you can. I'll hire help. I'd never have you take care of it by yourself..."

"I mean it's too much for you to do for me."

"No, it's not." He leaned up to touch her lips. "Would you enjoy being here?"

"Not alone."

"No. Never alone. With me as much as possible when they'll allow it. And ... maybe Mom would move in. She could have the extension to herself and still be here. Will's had her long enough. Tracy doesn't need that much help anymore and I'm not sure she ever quite wanted it. I'd say it's my turn. If she's willing. If not, I'll find someone you're okay with when I can't be here. If you want it."

Katie fell into his arms. That was all the answer he needed.

He was afraid Mrs. Stewart was going to fall over in shock when he said he would take it and would have the cash to her within a couple of days to pay it in full. They stayed only long enough to agree on the purchase and he told her not to rush to move out, since Kaitlyn was recovering from an illness and needed more time to rest before she tried to set up a house. He also got an okay to put up a fence after the contract was drawn so it would be ready as soon as they moved in.

They collected Bella and Chewy from the front porch, and Ryan looked forward to when the dog would be able to run around the yard without being tied. Although she would stay in the same neighborhood, she would be safe from petitions with the way Ryan planned to have the fence done. He wanted a full row of tall hedges all the way around the inside, for privacy. He'd also have an electric gate installed so no one would get to the house without being buzzed in. It was overkill in the area, maybe, but he didn't want to worry about Kaitlyn when he wasn't there. And he didn't want neighbors to decide on their own to walk over and visit.

Tracy threw a fit when they returned and pulled Katie in to sit down and rest while he and Bella took Chewy to the back. As soon as Ryan walked into the house, she yelled at him for letting her walk so long.

"We weren't walking the whole time. We were visiting a neighbor."

"Oh?" She sent Matthew to get a glass of tea for Kaitlyn. "You visited who? You don't visit neighbors. You avoid them."

"Not this time." He didn't dare go sit with Kaitlyn while Tracy used the opportunity to vent her disapproval. "Mrs. Stewart saw Bella and asked us in. She insisted."

"You went all the way to the Stewart house? Ryan, the girl is still trying to recover. You should be more thoughtful."

"It's not that far."

"Will only goes up to the end of our street and back when they walk that dog. That's far enough."

"Oh, she's fine." His mom brought the tea in and handed it to Katie. "Fresh air and exercise will help her feel better faster. She would've told him if it was too far." She brushed a hand over Kaitlyn's forehead and into her hair, the way she used to do to Ryan when he wasn't feeling well. "Should we make your spinach lasagna tonight? That boy looks like he could use good food again instead of the fast food I'm sure he's had the whole time he was in the city. Think you can get him to eat it?"

"Yes."

Ryan grinned at the conspiracy, and the way Katie didn't pull away from his mom's caress. "You're getting along too well, I think. This isn't quite fair."

"It's fair enough since we both want what's best for you." She rested a hand on Kaitlyn's shoulder. "Rest a while and I'll get it going. I'll have to leave the seasoning to you to get it the way he'll eat it. Ryan, your brother will be home any minute. Why don't you help him out back when he gets here? He's put off fixing that wobbly table forever. Encourage him to do it before one of us falls off onto our rump."

Matthew jumped in and offered to help, but Tracy vetoed it before his mom could. There was an agenda to get him alone with his brother. Which meant Will was still pissed at him and his mom and sister-in-law wanted them to work it out, or maybe they thought Will would be able to talk sense into him. As though it ever worked before.

With everyone else scattering, he sat next to her and she moved in, her head against his shoulder.

Ryan stroked her hair. "I missed you."

She raised her head again; her eyes searched his.

"You know they're against this. Not ... not against you. They love having you here. Against how close we are. I hope they haven't said anything to you." She didn't answer. Waiting. "Are they right? Should I not have ... did I take unfair advantage? I've been wondering."

Chilly, small fingers touched the stubble on his chin. "You know." She slid them farther back, around to the side of his neck, her thumb against his ear. "They don't understand. You do."

Shivers ran through his frame. Her face grew closer. The cookie-like scent wafted around her mixed with the freshness of outdoors. Yes, he knew. She wanted it. She'd pushed it. She needed him. It didn't matter if no one else understood. "Think there's anywhere we could find a few minutes without interruption? They'd freak out if I took you to your room, just ... for a minute alone..."

She kissed him, leaning closer against his body. He gave in, with no choice but to give in. Ryan surrendered to her, caressed her back and shoulder. It was as close as they'd been since she left for her father's. He was relieved to know she still had feelings enough for him to kiss him the way she was.

"My kids are home."

Katie released him and pulled back at Will's voice.

Ryan took a second to gather himself. Irritated at the interruption. "What? They've never seen you kiss your wife?"

Will loosened his tie and left it hanging. "Not the same, Ryan. And not like that."

"Hell, relax. It's not like we were having sex on your couch."

Katie's eyes flashed toward him, a warning.

"Could I see you outside?" Will undid the button on his collar.

"It was my fault." Katie gripped his arm but spoke to Will. "I'm sorry."

"You don't need to apologize. You're fine. It's my brother..."

She tried to protest but Tracy and his mom returned. Will accepted a quick kiss from his wife and hugs from the kids who ran in behind her, and then looked back over at Ryan.

He got up. "Mom says we have a table to fix. Gonna change first?"

Will walked away, up the stairs. Tracy followed.

"The lasagna's probably ready to season. I won't be long." He saw worry in Katie's eyes. "Hey, we're only talking."

His mom claimed her with an arm around her back. "Don't worry, sweetie. They have a five foot rule. When they're angry with each other, they have to stay at least five feet apart until they aren't angry anymore." She threw Ryan a look. "That still applies."

He threw his hands up. He didn't plan to argue. While he waited, he walked with them to the kitchen and teased about how nasty the spinach smelled. "I can call for pizza."

"You like this."

With a grin, Ryan brushed a hand through her hair. "Yeah. But doesn't mean I won't give you a hard time about it."

"Coming?"

His brother was changed already, in the doorway. Not at all as inviting as Katie was. He kissed her aside the head. "It's fine. I promise. Don't stay on your feet long."

He followed Will to the backyard. It would be just as well to have it out. Much better than the mostly silent treatment. Ryan answered his phone on the way, listened to Ginny bitch at him about being out of town, and said he'd have to call back – there was a waiting list to yell at him and she wasn't at the top of it.

"Just how long is that list by now?" Will let the screen door close behind them and moved farther from the house.

Ryan wasn't sure his brother was at least five feet away when he stopped, but he let it go. "Long enough. Go ahead. I have people waiting for their chance."

"If you're trying to make me feel sorry for you so I'll hold back, it won't work."

"I've never in my life tried to make anyone feel sorry for me. You know that. So go ahead. I know you're pissed and if it makes you feel better to tell me off about being with her, then tell me off. It changes nothing, though."

"Ryan, you don't get it. I'm not only angry about you having sex with a seventeen-year-old girl, and unprotected at that..."

"I didn't know she was seventeen. They changed her birthday. She said she was nineteen."

"Seventeen. Nineteen. Big damn difference. You're nearly twenty-five. And you're..."

"I'm what? Just say it." His phone rang again. He saw Daws's number and ignored it. "I'm what?"

"Overly experienced in that department, to put it politely."

Ryan couldn't help but laugh. "Careful, sounds like you're jealous." By the way his brother's face darkened, he knew an explosion was on the way.

"Dad would have your ass on the ground for that remark. I'm thinking about it."

A big explosion and unfair. "You won't. And Dad's not here. And you're not him. Stop playing my father, Will, and go back to being my brother." He kept his face firm, his eyes intent.

"That's getting hard about now."

His stomach churned.

Will stepped closer.

"Five feet." Ryan raised his head, daring him.

"You think I'm going to hit you?"

"No, I'm not sure I trust myself and I promised Katie."

Will sighed but didn't back up. "I don't agree with what you're doing. Often, I haven't agreed with your decisions but I let it slide..."

"Like hell you did. Forget all the lectures? I haven't."

"They were apparently useless."

"Because they were condescending as hell. Yeah, I know. I'm the fuck up. You don't have to keep telling me. I know if I weren't your brother, you'd have nothing to do with me. Well, you know what? You don't have to have. I'm moving Katie out of here so we won't be a bother to you anymore. And we're taking the dog. She needs that dog..."

"You can't. Ryan, overlooking the rest of that bullshit for the moment, you can't take her to New York. Not at this age and..."

"I'm not taking her to New York. I don't even want her there right now. As much as I want her with me, I don't want her in the middle of that. The press is being even more accusing than you are, but then, I suppose I deserve it so it's all fair, right? She doesn't."

"Where do you plan for her to go?"

"Just down the road. I bought her a house. The Stewart house on the corner with the big yard. I just bought it, or agreed to buy it. I'll put a fence all the way around for the dog and I'll ask Mom if she wants to move in with her. If not, I'll hire someone to stay there."

"Ry. I'm not asking you to move her out. I have never once said I didn't want her here and I'm glad she is. We all are. It's not a problem."

"It is for me."

"Why?"

Ryan considered how to answer without invoking more anger. "One guard dog is enough." He met his brother's face. "I don't want to be watched every minute I'm around her. I'm not going to be able to be here a lot for a while and when I am ... maybe I'll hire someone to care for the house while I'm away and she can stay here with you when I can't be here, but when I am, I want to be with her without someone breathing down my neck and watching every move..."

"She doesn't need that kind of a relationship right now. If you're moving her out just so you can..."

"You have no fucking idea what she needs. She barely talks to you. And don't look at me like I'm a monster. She's trying to recover, you know. I'm not that much of a pig no matter what the press says. Honest. But hell, Will, we can't even sit outside and talk alone without someone hovering and keeping track. That's bullshit. She *lived* with me for months. Just the two of us..."

"And she ended up pregnant."

Ryan's whole body tensed. He could just say he wasn't the one who made the advance, then, or a few minutes before on the couch. He wouldn't. It would be disloyal to Kaitlyn. "You know what? Screw you. You're not my father. You're my brother. Accept me or don't." Wheeling away, he headed back to the house and nearly didn't bother to look at who was calling him this time.

On the fourth ring, he decided to check. Dani. Ryan answered and detoured to the living room. He needed to calm down before he went back to Kaitlyn.

"What's wrong? Bad time to call?"

Her voice soothed him. "No, never a bad time for you. What's up?"

"Don't give me that. Something's wrong."

"I'm at Will's. He's ... well, anyway, nothing to talk about."

"Fighting with your brother again? Aren't you getting too old for that?"

"And you still never fight with yours, right? Makes me sick."

She laughed. "I have a perfect, incredibly patient brother. What can I say? Hey, put him on the phone."

Ryan rubbed his neck. "Put who on the phone?"

"Will, of course. Let me yell at him a minute."

"Uh, not a good time for that."

"Yeah, which is why I want to yell at him."

"Dani..."

"Come on, Ry, don't try to tell me no. You know you can't."

Despite his lingering anger and cringing stomach, he had to chuckle. "Too bad I can't say the same to you."

"I don't know. If you were here right now, that could change."

"Don't tease." He thought he heard a serious tone in her voice. "Hey, what's going on with your asshole? Still being one?"

Silence came over the line while Ryan waited to be yelled at for calling her boyfriend what he always called him.

"Well, I won't even argue that count today."

Ryan lowered to the couch. "What's he done now?"

"You know, I ... not over the phone. If you have any free time, come keep me company. I could use advice..."

"Dump him. Easy. Your perfect brother is right, of course. Dump the asshole and move on."

"It's more complicated than that."

"Hell it is. Say no. You know how."

"Yeah well, you know the keyboardist I mentioned?" She sighed. "He's ... I'd like you to meet him. I really ... I've done something I never do. I ... do you have time to visit?"

Something she never does. Complicated. And another guy. He didn't have time to visit. He shouldn't even be in Vermont. He needed to be in New York. "Yeah. I'll ... give me a few days? Will that work?"

"You're an angel. Can't wait to see you."

"I'm a sucker for a beautiful woman who needs me." He grinned, figuring she'd hear it in his voice.

"Okay. Put Will on now. And don't argue with me."

Ryan considered arguing, but it would do no good. Dani had Will's number; she'd call him direct. "Let me find him. But hey, you know he has every right to be pissed at me, like usual."

"I'm sure he does. How's Kaitlyn?"

He filled her in on the way to the kitchen and wondered about taking Katie to Massachusetts to visit Dani.

They were all there, some cooking, some sitting around ... obviously talking about him since they stopped when he entered. "Here he is." He shoved the phone in his brother's direction. "Dani."

Will raised his eyebrows.

Ryan shrugged. "She wants to talk to you."

He knew his mom and Tracy wondered why Dani wanted to talk to him, but Ryan let them wonder since he wasn't sure himself. He went to where Kaitlyn stood cutting tomatoes. "Let me do that. You should rest."

"I have been resting. I just got up."

"Go rest more." His mom said they tried to suggest someone else could do it but she was tired of sitting. Ryan knew better. She wanted to help. But this wasn't the time and he didn't let her argue. Pulling her chair out with an ear on Will's conversation with Dani, although Will wasn't doing much of the talking, he kissed Katie's head and washed his hands. He hated cutting tomatoes. He would have hated more watching her do it.

"She had to go." Will moved up to him. "Said to call when you were on the way. You're going to see her?"

"Yeah." He picked up the knife, a good excuse to turn his back on his brother.

"Thought you were behind at work."

"This is my business. It isn't yours."

"Rumor has it she just broke up with the boyfriend, not a good break up. Might not be a good time to show your face considering..."

"She hasn't. Yet. She's hopefully about to. And it's still *not* your business."

Will dropped the phone on the counter and left the room.

A soft hand touched his back. "Is Dani all right?"

He set the knife down and turned to her. "She needs to talk. It's nothing more. I don't want you to worry about..."

"I'm not." She set her hand on his stomach. "It's hurting you again." When he didn't answer, she slid her arms all the way around him and rested her head on his shoulder.

His mom suggested they go out and play with the kids and let her finish up in the kitchen. She stopped him long enough to say Will was only concerned and wanted to protect him as he always had. It wasn't a scold. She wanted him to be less angry.

Kaitlyn took his hand and pulled him outside. He had to wonder if being around the kids didn't bother her, if it didn't make her think about what she lost, twice.

He realized when she touched his face that he'd stopped and was staring at Bella as she played with her baby doll. He took her in his arms again. He wouldn't kiss her. The kids were there. If Will had an issue with him hugging her in front of them, he'd have to get over it.

After dinner, Ryan took her plate with a hand on her shoulder to tell her she should sit still. He knew it made her uncomfortable to be waited on, to sit instead of helping, but she was darn well going to get used to it. When he came back to ask if she wanted more tea or coffee to go with the pound cake Tracy had for dessert, she tried to get up.

"Honey, let that boy wait on you hand and foot whenever he will. It'll do him good." His mom threw a teasing grin and took Kaitlyn's hand. "And it'll help keep his head level in between his pop star image. He always does chores when he's home. You can't let a man get too full of himself."

"Thank you." With a return grin, Ryan touched Katie's hair and continued helping Tracy and Will with the table. Thankfully, his mom stayed there, also. He was surprised, actually, how she didn't seem irritated with him. Not after her initial shock, anyway. Although Will and Tracy were legally responsible as long as Kaitlyn was under state supervision, which Ryan had to admit irked the hell out of him, his mom seemed to have taken over her care. She'd taken Katie under her wings beautifully and Ryan loved to see that the physical contact didn't bother her. The amount of it he'd already seen was strange, though, since ex-sergeant Marianne Reynauld had never been known to be highly demonstrative.

Bella helped get coffee cups and poured sugar and creamer while the coffee finished brewing, and Ryan easily enough avoided his brother going back and forth with Matt trailing him. It reminded Ryan of the way he used to trail Will and try to imitate everything he did. He hoped Matt had a better time of living up to his father than Ryan ever managed. Will was right about the comment. His dad would've knocked him down for sounding so competitive with his brother, especially over such a stupid thing. And since it sounded like a boast. He shouldn't have said it. And he didn't even mean it. It was ... a stupid, stupid way to try to be defensive. He would have to apologize. If his dad was watching over them as his mom always insisted, he would never be content until Ryan tried to make it right again. He didn't mind if his boys made mistakes as long as they righted them as soon as possible.

"Hey." He looked over at Will when he came back in. "Hold on a minute." Ryan set Bella down off her step stool and sent her to sit with Katie until coffee was ready.

Will leaned against the island counter.

"I was overboard." He leaned against the other. "I didn't mean it the way it came out."

"Didn't you? One thing about you, Ry, you always say what you mean."

"Okay, I did, but I don't. Look, I know you're trying to help like always, but ... I'm having a hard time trying to handle all of this and I know I've messed it up, but I'm trying. On top of everything else, with Ginny on my ass and all the shit in the papers I hope doesn't become more, I can't deal with you on my ass, too. No matter what you think."

"Tell Ginny to back off."

"Yeah, that'll work." He rolled his eyes.

"Come outside a minute."

With a sigh, Ryan followed him out the door and went to sit at the picnic table they were supposed to have fixed.

Will didn't bother to sit. "Truth is, I'm more angry that you didn't tell me what was going on than I am about anything else, although I did think you had more sense than to mess with someone so young."

"I'm not messing with her."

"Then what are you doing? Besides rescuing her. I get that. The rest I'm not sure about."

Ryan watched a beetle snake through the grass in front of his tennis shoe. Trying to go about its business. Ryan wondered how long it would be before someone or something interfered.

"Ry?"

"As I said, I fell in love with her." He felt his brother's stare but kept watching the beetle. They were often stepped on. Only because they were so unattractive. Or because someone was afraid of them. He wasn't sure he hadn't done it himself. Why had he? Because he was too self-involved to look at it from the beetle's perspective? What did it do to invoke such loathing? Searching for food? For shelter? Or a mate?

What else would it be doing? What was so wrong about that?

"So now what?"

Ryan was tired of talking, tired of trying to explain something that still didn't make enough sense to him. He set his foot in front of the beetle's path and watched it swerve around and keep going.

Will shuffled a couple of steps through the grass. "I am trying to be your brother." He turned, a thumb hooked in his pocket. "It's hard when you treat me like ... like more than that. I know the age difference and losing Dad made a normal brother relationship impossible for a while, but by this time, I thought it might work." He shook his head. "You know, I have kids, Ry. I'm not looking to try to raise you anymore. It was never what I wanted. I wanted to be the one you could trust to tell anything. And this ... you bring this girl into my house acting like you want to be family to her and you don't bother to tell me she's more to you than that? That's what I'm angriest about."

"All I meant to be was a friend, or family. That's all I wanted. No matter what everyone thinks of me about now, I only wanted to help. Because she desperately needed help."

"Then why did it become more?"

"Why did you and Tracy become more? Why did you marry her instead of one of the other girls you went out with?" He met Will's silent gaze. "And age beside the point, I know damn well you didn't wait until you got married. Hell, you didn't wait until you proposed. So why are you giving me all this shit about..."

"Age isn't beside the point, Ryan. It is the point. I never said anything about all those other girls. Hell, most were probably as experienced as you are, or close enough. As long as you protected yourself, I said nothing. Although I was afraid it would come back to bite you in the ass, as it nearly did several times. This is different. Not only her age, but also, she's ..."

"She came to me. Which I shouldn't tell you and I don't expect you to repeat it. But you don't understand..."

"So tell me."

Tell him. Ryan wanted to tell him, to let his brother know he didn't push her, he tried to avoid it. From inside, he could hear Bella laugh and Matt chime in as he could around his sister. He pushed off the table and walked farther into the yard.

Chewy barked enough to get his attention and Ryan called over to tell her to hush so she wouldn't bother the neighbors. Katie's dog. She belonged to Katie because she wanted to belong to her. Will was the one to rescue Chewy, but Katie ... it wasn't the rescue that made the most difference. It was ... what? The understanding? No, it was more. There was a connection. Unexplainable. The way Ryan couldn't explain why he went up to that window that day.

With a deep sigh, he lowered to the ground and tilted his head to the stars, arms tented behind him, the coldness of dew accenting the feathered grass pressed against his palms. Palms. Tents. He hadn't finished the song yet. He wasn't sure where it was leading. Wisps of clouds highlighted by the three quarter moon glowed like a beacon. Like a moving beacon. Washed along like a stick on the lake, with no control of its own.

Ryan wished for a radio, for his guitar in his hands, something besides the crickets and quiet and dusk-scented air and questions he couldn't answer.

"What's going on with Dani?" Will lowered at his side.

"Why?"

"I know you were interested in being more than her friend. Are you still?"

"No." He shrugged. "Wouldn't have worked. We're too similar."

"And if she's interested? If she does break up with the boyfriend?"

"She's not, even if she does."

"Doesn't answer my question."

"Will, I'm in love with Kaitlyn. She's what I want. And I won't cheat on her. I haven't since the day we met, and I won't."

"Not even for Dani."

"Not for anyone."

"And I figured all that messing around was just waiting for her."

"Nah. It wouldn't work. I love her. I won't deny that, but not the same. I haven't wanted that for a long time."

"Good." Will shifted positions, his face barely visible in the glow of the back door light. "So this is really it. With Kaitlyn. The real thing?"

"Yeah. Leave it to me to choose something so damn complicated."

Will chuckled. "Wouldn't do anything any other way, would you?" He tilted his head. "What do you mean she came to you?"

"Guess Mom didn't tell you any of the discussion from the hotel after you left."

"No. So you tell me."

Ryan told him. The basics. The way she'd been hurt. How much she needed not to be afraid. How she was the one who made the advances. Why he finally gave in to her.

Will shoved a hand through his hair, shaking his head. "How in the hell anyone could treat a child that way, I can't understand."

Ryan wouldn't let his thoughts return there. They'd been there too much, too often. "So what did Dani want to talk to you about?"

"Hm. Figured you knew."

"She wouldn't say."

"Then I would suppose she doesn't want you to know." He hushed Chewy when the dog started to whine. "You actually bought the Stewart house?"

"I'm in process. Oh, damn. I've gotta call and get money sent up here."

"And you think they're going to let you move Kaitlyn out of here into a house with you alone?"

"No. I hope they'll let her move into her own house with Mom as her guardian. Of course, I should ask Tracy if it'll bother her."

"I'm sure she'll be fine with it. Actually, I'm sure she'll be glad to have her house back again, not that she minds Mom being here. You know she doesn't, but..."

"But it's been long enough."

"It's fine..."

"My turn."

"It'll be good for you."

Ryan threw a sideways look. "Is that supposed to mean you think I still need to be raised?"

"It means ... you've refused her help too much since we lost Dad. It's good you're finally willing to accept it. She'll be glad, too. She's missed you, Ryan. We all have."

"I'll still be in New York much of the time. And I still want you to look after Kaitlyn for me, if you will, when I'm away."

"Glad to. And I'm sure Bella will ask to go over there a lot. She's pretty attached to her. *If* you can get the okay to let her move. When she's up to it. I think it's too soon, if you're still willing to listen to what I think."

"I always listen. I just don't always act like I do. And yes, it's too soon. I want her fully recovered first. And I want the fence up first, for security. You won't fight me about taking the dog?"

"Chewy belongs to Kaitlyn. Only reason I still have her." He stood. "I'm glad she'll have her own place, Ry. The dog, too."

"Hey." Ryan stood up beside him. "If it matters, you do good at being a big brother and I'm glad you care enough about her to bitch at me." With a light punch to Will's stomach, he jogged off toward the house.

21

"Someone at the hospital talked. Mentioned the pills she took. And a miscarriage."

"Holy hell." Ryan shoved a hand through his hair as Daws's words registered. He considered throwing his phone into the water.

"It's all over the news down here. Crowds are in front of the studio and worse in front of your building. They're even tracking me to try to get information. You didn't plan to bring her back here?"

"I can't. Even if I'd wanted to." He looked over at the pontoon where she waited on the dock. A few friends who learned he was in Vermont had driven from Sackets Harbor to catch up and were in the boat, yelling over at him to stop working and come drive the thing. He wasn't sure Kaitlyn would agree to go out with them, but she didn't argue. She apparently wasn't getting in the boat, though, not before he did.

"How is she?"

"Better. Emotional. Since she's started to let them out, they seem to overwhelm her at times. Of course she's still healing, too."

"And you have her out on that boat?"

"Her suggestion. She loves it. Didn't expect these clowns to show up but it seems to be okay."

"Reynauld, if this news isn't up there yet, it will be. You better warn her."

"Yeah." He watched her go sit at the edge where she could overlook the water, her back against a wide pole. "Hey, I bought a house. Already talked to my accountant but will you check and make sure he gets the money sent today? I want to sign for it tomorrow before I leave."

"You bought a house?"

"Well, I bought Katie a house. Mom's moving in with her as soon as she's up to it. When they'll let her. She's meeting with a counselor..."

"Damn, Reynauld. You had to do that now?"

"It was for sale now. Why?"

"Why." Exasperation flooded his voice. "You know it'll look like you're buying her off."

He ran the hand through his hair again. "You know I'm sick to death of what it looks like. I don't care, Daws. I bought it to give her a home, a real home, something that's hers. They can call it what they want. She knows why I did. What they think doesn't matter."

"Keep up that attitude and you'll be selling shoes for a living."

"Might be preferable at this point."

"Sure it would."

He grabbed a deep breath full of lake-smell air. "Thanks for letting me know. I'll be back in a couple of days. If Ginny calls and I don't answer and she throws a fit to you, tell her to back the hell off."

"Already did. She won't call." He waited through Ryan's stunned silence. "Tell Kaitlyn Deanna says hello. From me, too. And Ryan, make sure you rest and relax today and tomorrow. Get that stomach settled before you jump back into this. By the way, I reminded Ginny she works for you, not the other way around. You'd do well to remember that, also." He hung up before Ryan could answer.

Pushing it all away for now, he went to her. Yes, he would relax and enjoy hanging out with her and his old friends from school, from before he was a name, before his family moved away from the one town that had felt like home during their years of living here and there. He would have to take Katie. Some day, when they could just pick up and go anywhere together, he had so many places he wanted her to see.

She stayed still while he walked toward her telling the school mates he was the captain of the ship and would damn well take the time he pleased. Ryan ignored their return comments and gestures. He lowered next to her and asked if she was ready to go boating.

"What's wrong?" Her eyes picked up way too much. He couldn't hide anything.

"I'll tell you later. Let's forget everything else right now and..."

"Ryan?"

His name floating off her lips still got to him. And he told her.

She looked out at the water.

"I'll have to figure out what to say. Any ideas?"

She turned back. "What do you want, Ryan? What do you want to tell them?"

"Anything that won't hurt you more."

Katie took his hand and rubbed it with her fingers. "They can't. They can't hurt me more than it does already because I don't care what they think. It only matters for you, for your job. It only matters that I can't be there with you when you have to face them. And I'm sorry."

"No. It's my job causing it. You have no reason to be sorry."

"And my father."

"Well. That's at least understandable. At least he has reason to pry." He stood. "Come on, let's go get away from everything for a while." Helping her up, he kissed the bottom of her ear and took her aboard the pontoon. Some day he would buy the big boat he'd been looking at and take her way out into the ocean off the coast of Maine. Only the two of them. He didn't want it until she could go.

She didn't speak to any of his friends, not even to the one girlfriend who tagged along and flirted with Ryan at times. But then, the girl flirted with all of them. He only had to back one of the guys off from Katie once. Otherwise, they kept distance and studied her, trying to be sly about studying her. It didn't bother him. He could trust them to stay quiet, so it allowed Ryan to be close to her, away from his family, away from where her father would find out he kept a hand somewhere on her unless he was driving the boat. Or that he leaned her back against the cushions as the sun lowered and kissed her, softly, deeply, letting her know how much he didn't want to go back to New York. He loved that it didn't embarrass her to be kissed that way in front of his friends who acted like they weren't paying attention.

22

Taunts and questions flew and a few arms tried to grab at him while his guards shoved him through the crowd in front of his building. With Daws at his back, Ryan wasn't concerned, but he was tired. And he was glad Katie wasn't in the midst of it.

Over the past four days, he'd dealt with relentless reporters and irate fans, attended recording sessions and meetings, and did a photo shoot for a magazine Patricia set up to try to counter negative publicity. They somehow gave him a hell of a lot more sex appeal than he actually had – the wonders of artistic photography and the subliminal effect of gorgeous half-naked women at his side. At least they'd found shorter women this time instead of the normal model-tall girls who showed every lacking bit of his five-seven frame. According to Katie's hospital chart, he was still four inches taller than she was. He only had two inches on Dani.

While he dealt with his Grimms Fairy Tale world, Kaitlyn gathered enough strength to go with Will to meet contractors about the wrought-iron fence and gate, always taking Chewy and sometimes his mom. Will didn't expect it to get done nearly as fast as Ryan wanted, and wouldn't push, so Ryan called the contractor Katie chose and threw in extra incentive. He was guaranteed they'd get started within the next few days even if the company had to pay overtime. Occasionally some reporter showed up as Will and Kaitlyn walked to or from and Will had to grab the leash close to the dog's neck until the guy backed off. Ryan told Will he'd pay the costs if the dog happened to attack one of their asses. Word would spread. Others wouldn't get close.

He talked to her at least three times a day, or four. He also called Dani often. His visit to her lasted longer than it should have. Planning to stop only for a couple of hours, he ended up at Brian's for the night and hung out with Dani the next morning. The new keyboardist wasn't there. He was home visiting family, as he did much more than the rest of them did. Her asshole boyfriend was there, of course, and nearly smothered her the whole time Ryan was around, as usual. He knew damn well the jerk didn't normally pay that much attention to her.

"Complicated." She'd said again breaking up would be complicated. Ryan had a hard time seeing how it would be.

At the moment, he had to throw himself back into his own issues. They were nearly to the elevator. The clamor was worse inside the walls than it had been out in the open air. He continued to block it out as his publicist suggested.

Patricia did her best to keep him from answering reporters directly. Still, they were everywhere. So were fans. Outside work. Outside his building. Everywhere he stopped to eat. They asked about Kaitlyn, about Nick Hollister and if there would be a Foresight reunion or at least a song with Ryan. Daws refused him even a minute's privacy. He or another guard stayed at Ryan's or Ryan stayed at his place. Most of the band stopped coming over, except Ned. He pushed his way through from time to time to give him company other than Daws, he said, not bothered when Ryan withdrew into his guitar. He sometimes joined in by adding an impromptu drum beat.

The palm song he'd started in Patricia's office was coming along. Ned liked it and encouraged him to finish it. That's what he would do if he ever got out of the crowd and inside his loft. Even circled within the guards, it was taking forever to get from the car. He heard questions about just how crazy she was, if he had her under a doctor's care and who her doctor was, whether the baby was really his, and the one he most hated: how he felt about losing a child. He had to grit his teeth through it. Patricia warned him not to answer. He already had. They acknowledged the truth of the rumor and said he and Kaitlyn were both healing and would give no other comment. She'd hoped it would be enough. If he gave into the stalkers on the streets, it would only encourage them to push more. He couldn't deal with being pushed more and was incredibly glad Kaitlyn wasn't dealing with it.

But he wanted to be with her. His stomach told him he'd had enough. Four days felt like forty-four.

Shoved into the elevator while security kept everyone else out, Ryan took a deep breath, leaned back against the railing, and closed his eyes.

"Nearly there." His friend's voice was always calm. Always.

"I gotta get outta here. Tonight. Not in a couple of days."

"Reynauld, you have an album meeting tomorrow, to review..."

"I know. Push it back. I can't even think with all this." He pressed a hand against his stomach. "And I want to be there tomorrow, even if she doesn't care if I'm a day late."

"It's acting up again?"

He cringed at the jerking stop of the elevator and waited for the two guards to go first. The leeches were there, too, in his hallway. "How did they get up here?"

"I don't know, but I'll find out." Daws held the elevator open with one hand and put the other against Ryan's chest, making him stay until he checked the hall. "Come on, they've got it cleared enough."

Pulled out and down to his door, he didn't acknowledge anyone else. He put himself into a haze and allowed Daws to get him into the loft without knowing how he got there.

"Hey, I was getting worried." Deanna came to him and set a hand on his face. "You're not well."

Daws got on the phone to reschedule while Ryan plopped on his couch. Deanna went to find him something to eat. He closed his eyes and allowed the haze to return.

"Deanna and Enrico are going with you." Daws waited until his eyes were open again. "You'll leave early in the morning, once most of them have given up. Deanna wants to check in on Kaitlyn and I want Enrico to keep an eye out. But Reynauld, only a day or two. Go find some quiet and sleep at night, and get your ass back here."

Daws drove up part way with them, to be sure they got out of the city, with his most trusted team members following. As Ryan started to see open land and clear skies, he was startled by his phone. Will's number flashed at him.

"Did I wake you up? Wanted to catch you before work."

Ryan rolled his shoulders. "No. Actually I was about to call you..."

"Good, thought you ought to know ... are you all right? You sound..."

"Fine. Know what? How's Katie?"

"She had a bit of a relapse. Don't flip out. She's all right, tired. The doctor gave her pain pills and something to help her relax, but she won't take them..."

"Relapse? Why? What's going on?" He reached down to his bag to find his Maalox.

"Two things. Her family's here early. Her father and Nick. Visiting rights – I couldn't refuse."

"Hell, I could've been warned. How bad? She's still there, not ... Will, you didn't put her in a hospital?" His stomach burned and he grabbed a long swallow.

"No, it was a house call and she's right here. Asleep. I just checked. She'll be fine, Ry. We're taking care of her."

"He stressed her out again."

"He's being ... polite, actually. I think she's just not ready to deal with him. At least not without you here as a buffer. We're trying. Mom's playing bodyguard. Still..."

"Some reason I couldn't have been told he was coming early?"

"I didn't know. They called from a hotel nearby."

"That shit has to stop, visiting rights or not."

"Yeah well, that's not all of it, and I'm only telling you because I know you'll be mad as hell if I don't. But it's under control."

He shoved a hand through his hair. "What?"

"We uh ... have a bit of a crowd situation starting."

"You what?"

"One of those reporters spread it around that she was staying here. Attracted attention from people in surrounding areas. The police are patrolling, keeping them out of the yard and away from the house, but they can't keep them off the sidewalk."

Ryan cursed in between telling Daws and Deanna, and went back to his brother's voice.

"It'll likely blow over in a few days. They've been here before. You don't stay interesting very long up in these parts."

Ryan knew Will was trying to be funny, but he saw no humor in it. If the story was picked up, it would spread and there would be no peace for them there, either.

"I don't want you to worry yourself sick about this. We'll take care of it. I have Chewy tied close to the back door at night instead of in the fence. No one gets close."

"I'm on my way."

A pause. "It's not necessary. Concentrate on work while you can…"

"No, Will, I was already on my way. We've left the city. Deanna is coming, also, so if you can make room…"

"Why?" He paused again through Ryan's silence. "Why are you on your way? You planned…"

"Had to get out of here, hoped for a bit of quiet. Guess that won't happen…"

"You're ill again."

"Getting that way. I just … I don't know. I don't know if this is worth it anymore. I'm so sick of the whole business, the bullshit that comes with the business. I've had enough." He peered out the window into the dark. "I want quiet. I want her to be able to recover without the press in her face and fans and questions."

"Ryan. You're not driving?"

"No."

"Good. Don't think about it all now. We'll talk more when you're here. Call when you're close and I'll try to have things cleared out."

Hanging up, Ryan kept the phone in his hand and stared out the window, his head dropped back against the head rest. Her father. And a crowd. Vultures. He was so sick of the damn vultures. He was sick of all of it, of everything but the actual music itself. All the rest was too much bullshit. Maybe that was why Nick pulled out, stopped everything so suddenly at the height of his career. Maybe he couldn't deal with the bullshit either.

He woke to a nudge and Daws calling his name. With a quick rub of his eyes, he saw Will's neighborhood up ahead.

"You drove all the way. You should have told me to wake up and take over." Ryan sat up and stretched his stiffened neck, then looked at his friend. "Wait. You weren't going all the way. You were supposed to go back."

"After I talked to your brother, I changed my mind. Ned will take care of things in New York. I want to see what's going on up here with the crowd."

"Talked to my brother? When?"

"Just after you crashed. You take something to knock you out flat?"

"What?"

"We stopped in between."

"No." He hadn't slept for nearly a week. He didn't say that much. "Look." As Daws turned the corner, Ryan pointed toward the SOLD sign. "That's Katie's house. Stop in front."

"Reynauld, it's early. No one's there now."

"I know. I just want to look." When the car stopped, he tried to get out and reached back to undo the seat belt. Standing and staring at it, he felt the same kind of gratification that came with the first time he held a new album in his hands.

"Katie's house?" Deanna took his side.

"I put it in her name. I had to be on as a co-owner because of her age, but it's her house."

"It's beautiful."

"Even more so inside. I'll see about taking you in later today, if you want."

"I'd love to see it, Ryan." She put an arm around him. "She's a lucky girl to have found you, to have you so wrapped around her."

He found her face, questioning.

"Don't lose yourself, though, okay? We kind of like you for you, as you are."

"What? Self-centered and arrogant?"

She grinned. "Well, you have to take the bad with the good, I suppose. I mean full of spirit and sure of where you're heading. Not willing to let anyone or anything stop you. You're on a path that is touching a lot of people. More than you see. Side-stepping now and then is all well and fine, but keep your eye on that path. Don't get so settled you can't see it."

He turned his gaze back to the house. *Settled.* Settled sounded incredibly luxurious. Settled into a house with a yard, a girlfriend, and a dog, eventually ... eventually more than that. With a sigh, he held the door for Deanna, the front passenger door, and crawled in the back of the car. "Hell, I forgot to call Will when we got close..."

"Already did. Shut the door." Daws flicked his eyes back at him through the mirror. "And we're not staying. As soon as you're in, we're heading to the hotel to crash a while. Stay in until we come back."

He didn't bother to answer, noting the police cruiser go by them and grabbing his own bag when they got to Will's. He saw no sign of anyone around, but Daws walked up to the door with him, waited only long enough for Will to unlock it and ask if they all wanted to come in for coffee, and refused with thanks, repeating instructions to stay inside.

Glad his brother was the only one up, he headed first to relieve himself then accepted a coffee mug. He breathed its thick aroma before he sipped at it. "I'm gonna go up and see her."

"She's asleep. You might as well wait."

"I'm not gonna wake her."

"You okay?"

"Stomach burns like holy hell. I'll be right back." He took the coffee with and sipped it on his way up the stairs. Afraid to knock and risk waking her, Ryan nudged the mostly closed door until he could pass through. The soft hall light cast a glow over her face but she didn't stir. She looked ... uncomfortable. But asleep, at least mostly, fighting to stay that way. He wanted to sit next to her, to hold her in his arms. There was no way she wouldn't wake if he did. And if she was in pain already, he didn't want to startle her.

She would be awake soon enough. At least he would be there when she was.

Back downstairs, he found plain toast and a glass of cranberry juice on the coffee table beside where he always sat. "So how bad have the crowds been?"

"Get something in your stomach. Mostly, they haven't been bad. Off and on. You're going to end up back in the hospital if you don't stop this, Ryan."

"Can't. No time for that."

"Besides the point."

He bit off a chunk of toast. "What happened with her dad? Where is he?"

"Hotel. He'll be back this morning." Will took a swallow of his coffee. "I don't know that he did much of anything. Like I said, he was fairly polite. She was on edge the whole time, though. Rarely sat for more than a few minutes. I think she made herself too tired. That, on top of the stress of him being here, and ... since strangers are floating around all over I insisted she not go outside without either me or her father or uncle, although she wouldn't go anywhere with her father alone. She went outside with Nick once. I hated to act so restrictive but..."

"No, I'm glad. I'm sure most are only hoping for a glimpse, sightseeing, but you never know. Daws is taking it seriously when he doesn't always."

"Are you getting threats?"

"Nah. Well, maybe, but hell that's part of the territory. Not serious threats – stupid stuff like I want you for my own and no one else can have you. Crazy. Nothing new."

"But you've never had an actual ... girlfriend before."

Ryan grinned. "Was girlfriend hard to say?"

"Still trying to get used to that."

He cringed at a stomach pain and downed some of the juice. "Yeah well, as soon as it settles into everyone else still trying to get used to it, I'm sure they'll back off again."

"Hope that's true. You're going to be okay here if I go in to work? With her dad? I have to go for a while since I took yesterday off. Didn't want to leave Tracy in charge with that man here, but..."

"Go to work. I'll handle things." He bit off more toast.

"Ry." Will leaned forward in the chair. "Remember, we're on your side, however it's seemed recently. You're not in this alone."

"Good to know."

"You should see a doctor. That stomach's worrying me."

"It'll settle now that I'm here. Does every time. The only reason Daws didn't push me to stay in New York when I'm so behind."

"There are worse things than being behind." Will stood and touched his shoulder. "I need to get dressed. You might lie down a while when you're done eating. I'll try not to be late, but call if you need."

Switching the television on low, Ryan shoved the rest of the toast in his mouth, washed it down with the juice and a coffee shooter, and reclined onto the pillows Tracy always kept at each end of the couch.

Despite having slept all the way there, he was drowsing when Matthew's voice in front of his face roused him.

"Hey little man." He tousled the boy's mussed hair.

"I didn't know you were coming."

"No, I didn't either until last night. Thought I'd drop in. That all right?"

"Yes, silly. Are you moving in the new house now?"

"Not quite yet. Soon."

"There are people all over, trying to look at Kaitlyn."

"I know. It's 'cause she's so pretty." Ryan threw a wink.

"Dad says it's because you're a pop star. It makes them curious."

"Got them fooled, don't I? You know I'm just plain Uncle Ryan, huh?" He pushed himself up, just in time for Bella to jump on top of him.

Tracy apologized but Ryan threw her a grin and returned Bella's hug. "Hey, it's nice to wake up to this kind of attention. Worlds better than Daws poking me with that face he makes and telling me I'm late."

Bella giggled at his imitation.

"Hm. Will said you had toast. Feel like pancakes, too?"

"Sounds good. Want help?"

"No, relax. Mom already has them started. Matthew, go dress for school."

"But I want to stay home with Uncle Ryan."

"Nothing doing. Go get dressed. He'll be here later."

Ryan promised he would be. "Hey, and you study hard so you can get a better job than me. Trust me on this."

Making a silly face, Matt jogged away up the stairs.

Whether Robert timed his arrival to coincide with Katie's counselor's visit, Ryan wasn't sure, but he bitched at himself for sleeping so long his mom had to come wake him. Not only was Katie downstairs, but Robert, Nick, and the counselor had arrived. He'd only meant to relax a few minutes in the quiet of Matthew's room and let the pancakes finish absorbing his excess stomach acid before having to face her father.

He had to run through the shower after the three hour drive and then sleeping in his clothes. It was even disgusting to him, and it wasn't the appearance he wanted to present to her counselor he hadn't met. As far as he knew, Katie didn't speak to the woman at all, although Tracy said she didn't seem uncomfortable around her.

Kaitlyn was sitting in the little easy chair she liked, her dad talking to her, when Ryan made his way down the stairs. He couldn't hear the conversation. One-sided conversation, as Katie didn't answer. An older woman with reddish brown hair in a short casual style and a flowing brown dress chatted with Bella. She reminded Ryan of a flower child except more professional. Most of her attention was on the interaction between father and daughter.

"There he is." Tracy got up to meet him; relief covered her face.

"Sorry, you should've whacked me on the head and told me to get up."

"Oh sweetie, I'm sure you needed your sleep." She led him toward the group, a hand looped around his arm. "Sit. I'll get you some coffee since you barely touched what you had earlier."

She ignored him when he said he'd get his own, using the hostess duty as an escape, and Ryan threw a hello to Robert and Nick. His mom introduced the counselor, Ms. Myers – Jeanette, as she corrected. Ryan made a point to remember her first name. Her smile and friendly eyes put him more at ease than he expected. He could see why Kaitlyn wasn't bothered by her.

"*Uncle Ryan.*" Bella yanked his hand to get his attention. "Are you moving here now so I can see you every day and every day?"

"My Bella." He scooped her up for a hug. "You know I can't work from here. It's too far to drive to the studio. I guess I'll just have to take you back with me if you won't get sick of seeing me every day."

"Yes! I go to New City with you and I help you work. I'm learning piano. I do Twinkle Twinkle."

"You mean New York City."

"Yes, New York City to play piano."

"Well, I tell you what. You keep practicing Twinkle Twinkle and some day we'll do a duet, okay?" He noticed Tracy approach with the coffee. "But your mom would be really mad at me if I took you to New York so she couldn't see you every day."

"No, my mommy needs 'cation from me. She said so."

"*Isabelle.*"

Ryan laughed. "I'm sure she does, but that would be way too long. Maybe Katie and I will take you out on the boat and give her a break. What do you think?"

"*Yes.* Today? I get ready."

"Maybe not today. And don't pout or I'll change my mind." Setting her down with a playful pat, he went to Kaitlyn and kissed her head. "Happy Birthday."

She reached for the hand he set on her shoulder. "Thank you. You weren't supposed to be here yet."

"Didn't want to miss it, even if you don't care. How are you feeling?"

"Better now."

"Yeah?" She looked pale and he took the other hand from where Bella was still pulling at him to feel Katie's forehead. "You're warm."

"Bella, stop badgering your uncle." Tracy pulled the girl away and told Kaitlyn they would get her more juice.

Ryan focused on her eyes. "How long have you had a temperature?"

Ms. Myers – Jeanette, answered instead. "She had a slight setback yesterday, but her doctor said she'll be fine with rest and liquids."

"I should have been here. I didn't know..."

"Our fault." Nick cut off whatever Robert started to say. "She was fine when we got here. We should have told you of our last-minute change. But I hear you should be in New York. Isn't work backing up?"

"So far I'll be circling myself soon, but it'll be there." He brushed fingers along Kaitlyn's face, checking the warmth of her cheeks. "Ned says hello. He sent a book he said you'd like. It's in my bag."

"Are you okay?"

"Yes." He wanted to take her to the backyard, away from the stares so they could really talk.

"You look like you're not."

He couldn't stop a sigh. "I hoped you'd be recovering better. Will said you wore yourself out. They shouldn't have let you. So I'm ... annoyed, and..."

"It was my fault. They told me to sit. I was tired of sitting."

Tracy returned with the juice and Ryan again bit his tongue. He wanted to blame her father for agitating her enough she wouldn't sit and rest, even if Will said he'd been polite. Katie's hand shook when she took the glass. He grabbed it when she began to set it on the table and did it for her, retrieving the coffee Tracy had set there for him.

"Your work must be exciting." The counselor watched him more than she watched Kaitlyn, or it felt like she was.

He shrugged and lowered to the floor in front of Katie, keeping hold of her fingers so he could judge her reactions. "At times."

"I don't listen to a lot of pop, but my nieces are fans of your music."

He threw a light grin in answer and grabbed a swallow of too-bitter coffee. It needed more sugar.

"And you're working on a new album?"

"Supposed to be. Pretty slow right now. I've had other things on my mind." He rubbed Katie's fingers when he felt them tense. "So is there something about me you want to know that we could get out in the air directly instead of hedging?"

"You don't like small talk?"

"Depends. Not at work."

"But you're not at work now."

"You are." He shrugged again. "Don't misunderstand, I appreciate what you're trying to do. But it's making her nervous so if we could get it out and be done with it, I think she'd be just as glad."

"Because you know what she wants." Robert's sarcasm shined through amazingly well. "Being hostile to her counselor won't help anything."

"I'm not being hostile. I'm being straight-forward. And yes, I know talking to counselors, shrinks, whatever, makes her nervous."

"Well." Jeanette reclaimed control. "As Kaitlyn hasn't decided to talk to me yet, I thought it might be helpful if we got to know each other since you're here. Robert says she only talks to those you okay."

"No. That's not true." He looked up at Katie. She was turned away from it, from all of them. "Am I saying too much? Tell me if I am."

She gave him her eyes. "Did you see the house?"

The house? Was she telling him to change the subject? "Yes, the outside. Deanna wants to see it while she's here."

"She's here?"

"Oh. Yes. They're at the Four Chimneys. Drove up with me. Think you'll be up to showing it off later today?"

"Yes. Mrs. Stewart moved out. It's empty."

"Is it? What do you think of the fence design? He sent me drawings and it looks good, I think. Is it what you want?"

"It looks strong. Safe."

Strong and safe. She wanted to be within it, shutting everyone else out. It's what she had to be saying. "Yes. And when the shrubs go up around the inside, it'll be more private, too. Did you pick them out yet?"

Her head shook lightly. "I was waiting for you."

"The house rumor is true?"

Ryan glanced at Nick and back at her. "You didn't tell them?"

Another shake, then she looked at her uncle. "Yes. I have a house. Ryan bought it for me. It's ours."

Robert stiffened. "You actually bought her a house? The child is seventeen years old. Eighteen. What does she need with a house?"

"Stability." He met Robert's stare. "A place that feels like home. Just like everyone needs. Thought it was about time she had it."

"She has a home. And she would be there if you didn't make her not want to be."

He felt her fingers tighten and caressed her hand. "You can't tell someone where their home is. Trust me, I know. I lived in lots of houses. Lots of towns. It's only home if it feels like it to you, not because someone says it's supposed to be. This one was her choice. She looked at it every time we drove past. So I offered it to her when it went up for sale. Her choice. She would've said no if she didn't want it."

"And does she tell you no?"

Ryan tilted his head at Jeanette Myers. "Yes."

"Honestly?"

"Ask her. She's right here."

When Ryan turned to see her face, Katie met her counselor's gaze for the first time that Ryan noticed.

"Kaitlyn, if Ryan asked you to do something you didn't want to do, would you tell him no?"

She slid her free hand down his shoulder, leaning forward to be closer.

Robert stood, walked around behind the chair where he'd been sitting. "You think she's going to admit she wouldn't in front of him? It's like buying a kid an ice cream cone. What kid is going to try to anger you if she thinks she'll get another one? He's buying her off. Even the press knows he is. It's everywhere. So much for being only a rumor, right Nick? You think it's all right for her to be made a laughing stock all over the papers because of him?"

Ryan nearly jumped all over that but Nick jumped faster, arguing. Ryan's mom said he would absolutely never try to buy her off, or anyone else. Jeanette Myers tried to pull the conversation back to Kaitlyn, not to theories, and asked if Robert had noticed any actual coercion on Ryan's part, noting she seemed comfortable with him and that she was talking, which Jeanette hadn't yet heard.

"You can't see how controlled he has her?" Robert paced a few steps then returned to hold the back of the chair. "You saw that she said nothing to any of us, that she hasn't said anything to you in all the times you've been here, but she's talking to him. Why else do you think that is?"

"There are many reasons for silence. It's not something I can answer..."

"She spoke to me." Nick leaned back, pulling an ankle over his leg. "I don't intimidate her. That's your problem, Robert."

"My problem?" He jerked his chin up. "I am not intimidating. She knows me too well to be intimidated..."

"I don't know you." Kaitlyn tensed with the sudden attention at her words. She leaned closer to Ryan and caught his eyes. But she kept talking. "You're not the same. I'm not the same. Ryan knows me. He doesn't see me like the little child I was before. He sees me now. I tell him no." She turned her gaze to Jeanette. "I tell him no. I'm not afraid to. I trust who Ryan trusts because I know I can. And I'm not crazy. I have reason. I don't talk because I don't want to. No one listened when I did. But Ryan does. He listens. He knows why when I don't talk and he doesn't care."

She trembled and he stood to lower onto the arm of her chair to pull her closer.

The doorbell made her jump and he kissed her head. While his mom went to check it, he whispered into her ear, told her they would go look at the house, take Deanna and Daws and get away from everyone, like they were in New York again, only the two of them and the city and...

"Sweetie, are you okay?" Deanna knelt in front of her. "Ryan, she's shaking. What's going on? Do we need to get her out of here?"

Before he could answer, he looked up at Daws and tried not to laugh finding his friend in his don't-mess-with-me bodyguard stance, ready to do whatever needed to guard Katie. Tracy took care of introductions with the counselor and offered something to drink, which they refused.

"We don't want to interrupt." Daws watched Ryan's expression for reason they should. "You're getting quite a crowd out there. I just called in for more assistance..."

"A crowd?" He got up while Deanna stayed with Katie and peered around the edge of the curtains out the window. Not a large crowd. Nothing to be concerned about. "Don't bring them up from New York for this. They're just..."

"No, local crew. Should only be a half hour or so. If you plan to go out, you need to wait until then."

"They're only curious. Not a big deal. When we go to the house, we'll drive. She doesn't need to do much walking today."

"Ryan. You'll wait until they're here."

The use of his first name instead of last, along with the direct order, backed him down. There was something he wasn't saying, and Ryan didn't expect he wanted Daws to say in front of her father. Or the counselor. "Fine. I didn't plan to go that soon, anyway." With a glance at his guard, he returned to Katie. Deanna was still sitting with her. The counselor was still studying her. Robert was still glaring at him. Ryan changed the subject. "Maybe tomorrow we can go look at shrubs to find what you want?"

"Yes. Or today?"

He started to ask if she was up to it yet, not at all sure she was, but her father jumped in and insisted she should stay in the house, or she could stay at the hotel with him while Ryan ran around with fans and security following.

"Robert." Ms. Myers, in her soothing but firm voice, cut him off. "Kaitlyn is under guardianship of Will and Tracy. She will stay here until I recommend otherwise. Please do me a favor and stop talking about her going home with you. It makes her uncomfortable and it won't help what we're trying to do."

"She is my daughter."

"Then you'll want whatever is best for her, as any parent should." Her direct gaze silenced him and she turned back to Kaitlyn. "Deanna is a friend of yours?" She got a light nod. "How about if we talk somewhere alone, the three of us? Is that okay?"

Katie pulled Ryan's hand closer.

"I know, you prefer to have Ryan beside you and I'm not trying to discourage that. I only want a few minutes. Maybe in the kitchen so he's still close by?" She looked toward Tracy.

"Of course. Deanna, don't let her clean up from breakfast. I'll do that. I have a hard time getting her not to help when she should be resting."

Ryan made himself not interfere, not tell her to go to the kitchen or not go. He stayed still and stayed out of it, and Deanna convinced her it was fine.

He took the time to pull Daws off alone, to a far window, careful not to show himself.

"It's not you they're trying to get to." Daws eyed him. "It's Kaitlyn. Most are only curious. But we've had ... rather threatening letters, fans angry that she's stopping your shows and holding up your album, worried it might pull you out of your music, away from them. Some of course who think she'll keep you from finding and marrying them."

"Morons."

"Fans. Very passionate fans."

"They're threatening Katie?"

"A few."

He grabbed a deep breath and cast his eyes back out the window. "Raucous all over again." He wondered if he could tell Dani about this, if it would bother her too much to tell her.

"No. I don't intend to let it get that far." Daws insisted on his full attention. "You need to get back to work, get the album finished, get back on the road. Reassure them. If you won't do it for yourself, do it so they'll relax about her. Get to work, Ryan. Give her time to recover. Give your fans time to adjust and see nothing is changing. It'll settle down."

"Will it? Doesn't seem to have worked well before."

"Their management didn't handle it right. We will. Ask Nick. He knows what they did wrong."

Ask Nick. Ryan wanted to talk to Nick about it, but he had to be careful. "Management? Is that what you are now?"

Daws raised his eyebrows. "You think I insist on being paid what you pay me only to be your bodyguard?"

"You've never been only that. And I pay you what I do for the hell of putting up with me."

"Reynauld, I don't think even you have enough to cover that. I'm a masochist. Be that as it may, when you do go back to work, I'll leave Enrico here and a few others. I don't want her out and about without them. She'll have to meet them, make sure she's comfortable..."

"That could be a problem."

"I've handpicked each one. If she disagrees, you tell me and we'll try again. Not a lot of time, though..."

"Or we could just take a long-ass trip out of the country, Katie and I, until they all go on with their own lives and stop worrying about us."

"You don't want to do that."

Ryan turned at Nick's voice.

"Sorry for intruding but I had a feeling your thoughts were going there."

"They're threatening her. Fans. You still think I shouldn't get her out of here?"

Nick scratched his stubbled chin. "I think you should go back to work. Maybe we can convince Ms. Myers to let her come to London with me. No one will pay attention to her there. She'll be away from it. You can go on with business..."

"She won't go with you." The last thing Ryan wanted to do was tick off her uncle, but facts were facts. "Never mind London would be a hell of a commute from here to visit her, she won't go. Not if I don't."

He threw an appeasing grin. "She does talk to me. We get along well. Always have. I think..."

"She won't go with you. And don't think I'm saying she shouldn't. I'm saying she won't."

"If you encourage her, she might."

"No."

"No, you won't try?"

"Nick, you left her alone at her father's when she only agreed to go because you were there. She won't try again."

The grin faded. "She was doing well when I left. She didn't argue. This isn't because of anything I've done..."

"It's because of everything *every*one has done. Why is this so hard for everyone to understand? She has huge trust issues for good damn reason and everyone keeps making that worse. Look, I know you had things to do in London. I understand, and this isn't about what I think. I'm telling you what she said. She won't go with you."

He'd raised his voice too much. It brought Robert over to join the conversation.

Nick, to his credit, didn't explode in return. "You leave her here."

"She's comfortable here. I wouldn't have otherwise."

"Go where?" Robert planted himself between Ryan and his brother-in-law.

"To London, to get her away from it all. Thought it might be a good idea."

"No way in hell."

"Robert..."

"It wasn't a good idea for Marlisse. What makes you think it would be for Kaitlyn?"

"It wouldn't be the same."

"Wouldn't it?"

Ryan was too worn out to listen to Robert and Nick argue about old history, especially the way they always circled it around him so he was never quite sure what they meant. "Okay, so what was the big deal with her mom hanging around Nick's band? I don't get how that would be as bad as you're saying. Hell, Deanna's around it all the time. So are hundreds of others..."

They were interrupted when the counselor stepped out of the kitchen. She asked Ryan's mom to join them. He wanted to go check on her. Why did she want his mom there and not him?

"The problem with her hanging with me..." Nick walked around Robert and to Ryan's other side, "had nothing to do with my job. She always thought I was more than I was. She had me on a pedestal because I was living my dream, showing her only the big brother image I wanted her to see. But on the road, that gets impossible. I was seeing Becca then, pretty much together. Well, we were together. But she worked and wasn't with me much. And I ... let my head get too swallowed up in the girls falling all over us. Becca knew. I kept saying it would stop, that it was a mistake, and why she took me back, I'll never know, but she dealt with it by having her own life and doing her own thing. Not in the same way. She's a far better person than I am or ever was. Still...."

"Katie's mom found out."

"Yes. Some people don't know when to shut up." He shrugged. "She left the next day. Didn't talk to me for weeks. I said a really stupid thing when I went to see her because I was upset that she wouldn't even take the phone when I called." His voice lowered. "I told her she was overreacting, that it was just something men did and it didn't mean anything and if she believed any man was that faithful, she was a naïve, silly child ... and as soon as I said it...." His chest rose deeply and fell again. "It was only to cover my own guilt, my embarrassment, but I could never tell her otherwise."

"Okay, so?"

"So, between that and Robert's refusal when she wanted to go the same route, to do shows of her own, and having a kid she didn't want, I guess..."

"She was a good mother even if she didn't want to be." Robert took over. "She loved Kaitlyn. Never even left her with a sitter. Wouldn't do it, until I pushed her to go visit her brother because I thought it would get it out of her system. I shouldn't have."

"You were trying." Nick threw a grudging acknowledgment. "I know you were trying and I shouldn't have messed around when she was there – okay, at all, but I don't think any of it mattered. She thought she couldn't find herself because she never got to go live the young single life she used to want and follow her music dreams, and then I had to tell her I was never sure I knew who I was because I was so lost in the circus of the show, and she finally saw ... too much. That it wasn't the answer she thought it would be." He shrugged. "Maybe none of us really know who we are and what we do or don't do is an excuse."

Suddenly drained all the way to his bones, Ryan walked over to the couch and plopped down. His head dropped against the back.

"Stomach all right?"

He opened his eyes again to Daws standing over him. "Yeah."

"Ryan, the thing is...." Nick sat on his other side. "None of it should have gotten to her enough to make her react the way she did. She'd fought depression off and on for years. They gave her drugs and sent her home and ... she took too much of it one night when Robert was working late, after Katie had been sick and kept her up for several days straight."

Robert stood watching, his arms crossed in front. "They blamed depression and fatigue. But she was stronger than that. There was more to it, more she would never say. I don't want that to happen again."

Nick shook his head. "But you can't smother Katie the way you did Marlisse. I kept telling you..."

"I'm smothering my daughter? You're doing the same now as you did then – letting her get closer to you because you don't have to be the parent and make the decisions. You can be the fun uncle who makes her laugh while I take care of everything and again she gets more attached to you than she is to me."

"No, she isn't. And she wasn't." Nick argued as though he'd never heard the statement before. "You were afraid of her, of trying to decide what to say or not to say, and you worried so damn much about her that's all she felt from you. It was easier for her to be around me. She wasn't more attached to me. She was worried about you. She still is."

Ryan stood again. "Look. It's all well and fine to share your family history, her history, but it has nothing to do with who she is or what she needs now and frankly, I'm more concerned about here and now."

Silence overcame them until Robert found his voice. "And I'm telling you why I'm so concerned. Her silence combined with her mother's history and the kind of life you lead..."

"Has changed. I no longer lead the life I was, not since I met her. I don't mess around on her and she knows..."

"And the rumors about you and that singer..."

"Are rumors. Whichever singer you mean, it's all rumors and promotion and people assuming they know what they don't. She knows I wouldn't."

"And you're sure you won't?" Robert stepped closer.

"Yes, I'm sure I won't."

"How do you know?"

"Do you?" At the confused look, Ryan pressed the issue. "You cheat on your wife?"

"No. Not that it's your concern."

"How do you know you won't?"

"I gave her a ring and vowed I wouldn't."

"Because that always works." He moved farther away. "The ring isn't what matters as to whether you're committed, you know. Sometimes you are just because you are, not because you think you have to be. Being committed only because of the ring is kinda sad, the way I see it."

"Committed?" Robert's snippy, unbelieving tone matched his near laugh that was close to a sneer. "You want me to think you're committed to her just because you got her pregnant?"

"You know...." Ryan clenched his jaw long enough to control the anger he felt swelling. "I know it was stupid. I didn't protect myself the way I always have before, although I was careful. Because I don't feel the same need for protection against her. But it wasn't on purpose as you make it sound. I would never hurt her..."

"And yet you did. Losing that baby hurt her a lot more than she'll say..."

"Yeah, me too. Even if I didn't know and didn't want it, not so soon anyway. It hurt me, too. Both ... losing the baby and knowing how it hurts her. Both. It's my child you're talking about. I lost him, too." He turned half away and gathered himself with a long, deep breath.

"Not so soon?"

Nick's teasing made him realize what he'd said and Ryan tried to move around it. "I knew she was young, not that young, but still, I understand why you're upset and I'm sure I would be too, but you have to understand that she ... she was already much too hurt. I didn't want her to think she had to stay that way. I didn't want her to think ... after she told me what she did, that I would turn away from her because of it, when she knew.... She could see my interest no matter how I tried to hide it. If I turned away...." He shook his head. "I'm not the one who hurt her. Maybe we should work together to find the people who did. Because trust me, I want that as much as you do."

Ryan heard Bella playing upstairs. From the way the sound had increased with an occasional stomp or clatter, he figured she was tired of being cooped up in her room to stay out of the way. He wondered what they were talking about so long in the kitchen, if she was upset, if he should interfere. But Deanna would let him know. She'd get Kaitlyn away from the counselor without hesitation if she thought it was necessary.

"One's about to get out of jail." Robert's face tightened. "I'm going to fight it. It might help if..."

"If they know the rest of what happened." Ryan nodded. "It has to be up to her. I'm not sure she can handle it."

"Andrea is terrified he might get out since she testified against him."

"I can imagine. And I'm sure Katie won't want him out, either. But we'll have to work together on this. She can't be afraid you'll..."

"Try to keep her away from you."

Ryan waited. It didn't need to be answered.

"I'm pretty well locked in a corner here." Robert dropped his head, stretched his shoulders, and returned the wary gaze. "I don't trust you. I haven't seen any reason I should. But she does. And she barely speaks to me. I don't want her to not speak at all. I don't want her to take the path her mother did. I can't..."

"She won't." Ryan went all the way out on the limb since he was already making it shake. "She promised me she wouldn't. You can stop worrying about that. And I get it. The not trusting thing. Understood. But you don't have to trust me. Trust her."

"I'm not sure I can do that, either. I tried that the last time."

Ryan took another step, a big one. He felt for Robert, could see his fear, the loss still all over his face. "I'll bring her to visit you." A spark of interest in Robert's expression kept him going. "I'll have to stay. I won't leave her, but I'm not trying to take her away from you. We can visit if I can get permission to travel with her alone. You might have to help with that since, because of everything, even though she is eighteen, she may still be restricted, watched. I may need your help to get them to let me take her on trips."

"You're bargaining with her?"

"No." He straightened. "I'm trying to help her. She'll be wary of you until we stop being enemies. I don't want her to deal with that."

No holds barred. "To be honest, your opinion of what I am doesn't mean shit to me except how it affects her. It bothers her for us to argue, to know how much you disapprove. So okay, I'll do what I can to help her be willing to talk to you. We'll visit as much as my schedule allows. You want to know something about me, I'll tell you. If you want to see exactly what I do at work, you're welcome to come along on a tour or to the studio. Meet the people I work with, the people she's around." He threw a shrug with his hands. "It's all I can do. But if I'm going to make that kind of time and effort, I at least want you consider working with me instead of against me. For her sake."

Through Robert's silent perusal, Ryan could hear the tick of the clock and more noise from Bella. He'd have to make it up to her, give her extra time. Why had he invited the man to tour with him? Not that the offer would ever be accepted, but how would he work that way?

"So you mentioned commitment." Robert crossed his arms in front of his chest. "Have you ever had a committed relationship?"

Ryan grabbed a breath. He'd said he would answer whatever he wanted to know. "Yes. Once. I screwed it up. It was a long time ago. Six years, before I got into all this."

"You wouldn't want to say how you screwed it up?"

"No. But I didn't cheat on her if that's what you're wondering." He knew that wasn't a good enough answer. "It was a misunderstanding and I didn't try hard enough to fix it."

"Didn't try hard enough. No relationship will work if you're not willing to try hard enough. So just how committed are you to this one?"

How committed? Ryan nearly laughed. After all he'd been through already, he couldn't imagine how anyone could wonder. It was easy enough to tell him, though. "I'm on the ledge with her, and as long as she's there, so am I."

He let Robert try to figure out his meaning. There was one more thing he had to say. Although he knew he probably shouldn't.

And he didn't have time. He followed Nick's nod toward the kitchen where the counselor stood, close enough to hear. He wondered how long she had been there.

She came to them. "Kaitlyn was afraid you might be at each others' throats so I thought I'd check. It's good to see you talking." She focused on Ryan. "I know what you mean by the ledge. She told me. I wish more of my patients had someone they trusted the way she trusts you."

"Is she all right?"

She gave him a grin. "We're done. I didn't want to bring her out to hostility if there was any. Working together is exactly what has to be done for her to finish healing. She does need you to get along." Jeanette threw Robert a glance and returned to the kitchen.

"What did she mean by the ledge?"

Ryan figured it was safe enough to tell him if her counselor already knew. "That's how we met. She was on a seventh floor window ledge. I went out and convinced her to come back in with me. Never mind I'm petrified of heights and I think she actually had to push me back in..."

"Wait." Robert moved up in front of him. "You met ... when she was contemplating..."

"I don't think she was. I think she was waiting to be found. So I found her. And I'm not letting her go, however you want to take that." He had him. Ryan knew from her father's look, from his knowledge she may not have been around for him to find if Ryan hadn't, that he finally had the upper hand. A safety net. There was no reason not to say what he needed to say. "Honestly, I think you have more to be concerned about with Andrea than with Kaitlyn. Not that it's my business, but Katie knows how much I want her around, how much I need to be with her."

The light slump of Robert's shoulders turned sharp. "And you think my wife doesn't? Andrea knows..."

"No, she doesn't." Tracy's voice surprised him. He hadn't even seen her come back in the room. "She doesn't. While you were hovering over Kaitlyn in the hospital, I talked with her." Taking Ryan's side, she first studied him, then steeled herself to finish, to help him. "Mr. Murray, she understands why you haven't been able to concentrate on her or the kids because you were so wrapped up in where Kaitlyn was, in what happened, but she doesn't know if you really want her there. She hasn't known for a long time. Kaitlyn's going to be fine. We all care about her and she knows we do." Tracy set a hand on Ryan's arm. "You didn't tell us you met that way. You went out on the ledge? You were tied or something, I hope."

"There wasn't time." He was saved from further explanation when they came out of the kitchen. The counselor had a hand on Katie's back, and she didn't pull away. She looked calm. Relieved. She came to him and slid her arms up over his shoulders.

"Everything okay?" He caressed her lower back.

"Yes. She said I can stay at our house when it's ready. With your mom. With you when you can."

"With me?"

"Yes. Not alone. Your mom has to stay..."

He caught her up in a hug. A tight hug, but careful. With him. They could stay at their house. He wanted to be there now.

~~~

More satisfied than Ryan should have let himself be about Robert's grudging approval of the house, he sat on the back step and watched

Kaitlyn walk Chewy around the yard. Will was at her side to take over with the dog if necessary and Deanna talked with her about the shrubs in pots waiting for the fence to be finished. Most would be delivered later but Ryan had the nursery go ahead and bring one of each kind he and Katie chose. He figured it would be a nice reminder of what was to come and help make it more real.

He'd never paid much attention to the things before, but he enjoyed wandering the nursery comparing colors and textures and sizes. His favorite was the Mountain Fire shrub with its light green delicate-type leaves and the tips of red here and there that made it look not quite as delicate as it would seem. The touches of "fire" reminded him of what he could see inside Kaitlyn every now and then. He knew it was there. It excited him to know how it bloom more with time.

Ryan found it amusing to see Daws pace the perimeter of the yard along with the crew he hired. Now and then he introduced one, and only one at a time, to Kaitlyn. He did a good job handpicking. She hadn't once objected, although Ryan told him it was probably more because Daws trusted them than whatever she thought personally.

Robert spent a fair amount of time talking with Ryan's mom. He wasn't sure he appreciated it but supposed it was better than Robert hanging on Kaitlyn too much. Her father and Daws exchanged numbers so they could compare notes and work together to trace the guilty. Ryan had yet to relinquish his own cell number to the man. Very few people had it and he wanted it to stay that way. He would leave them to the investigation. If they needed more information from Kaitlyn, he would ask her. Otherwise, he had to shove it from his mind.

There was a scent of pollen in the cool breeze, of leaves turned red and orange and brown and yellow. Fall leaves smelled different than spring and summer leaves. He'd said that once out loud, but because of the raised eyebrows and laughter he received, hadn't again. Still, they did. It smelled heavily of fall.

The day-late birthday party he threw for her with Will's help wouldn't have been as nice anywhere but at their own house. Katie's house. It was empty, except for folding chairs borrowed from Will and the table in the living room that held a large cake. Ryan also had a ton of balloons floating around the ceiling and as her gift, had ordered a huge set of classic books that were set up in the bookshelves around the fireplace, along with several blank journals for her own use. He nearly felt guilty at her reaction. The tears she couldn't control in front of everyone embarrassed her. But he'd warned her. He told her in the hospital he planned to spoil the holy hell out of her, and he meant it.

Glad the majority of his most valued people were there for Katie's eighteenth birthday celebration, he wished Dani could have been. He wanted them to meet. She was the only one missing Ryan ever missed.

He thought about pushing the right to take Kaitlyn to New York with him, since she was legal age in every state now, but she would be better off in Vermont until things settled. Until fans and reporters backed up to their normal off and on coverage instead of the current onslaught. Until she had more time to heal.

As Bella interrupted Kaitlyn's walk by throwing a ball for Chewy, making the poor dog look at the ball then up at Katie since she wouldn't release her to run after it, Nick lowered beside Ryan. He stretched out on the step, feet reaching out into the grass and hands propped at his sides. Her uncle was always relaxed wherever he was. Ryan couldn't help but be envious of his calm, unrushed, unexcitable nature.

"I've been hoping to grab time alone before we leave tomorrow."

Ryan stretched a leg out in imitation of the natural ease, but he kept an eye on Katie, afraid she was getting tired. "Why?"

"I've been thinking about what you said yesterday. You're not serious about walking away from the business?"

"I don't know. Maybe for a while. Depending..."

"You don't want to do that. Trust me." Nick pulled a long blade of grass from where it had been curling up over the cement step. "If you need a break, fine. But get going again first. Get it revved up. Get your album out and make it a kick ass album that will stay in people's minds, tour it, then back off for creative recovery. They'll understand that."

He tied the blade into careful loose knots, with half his attention on Ryan, the rest on his niece. "In the meantime, Kaitlyn has your family and the house for company, and later when things settle down, you'll both be more ready for ... whatever comes of it at that point. But don't walk out on your music. You're one of the few still in it for the sake of the music itself, for the passion of the art. You can't step back and lose that. We need more like you, not less."

The passion of the art. Ryan figured he'd lost most of that long ago, when they started changing it for him. Took control away. He wasn't walking out on it. It was walking out on him.

"Your friend. Dani. Have you told her your thoughts?"

Ryan eyed him. He'd expected Nick to try for more information. "No, she'd be a lot more pissed off about my thinking about it than I wanna deal with right now."

Nick nodded. "Because she's another one. Still in there fighting against the tides. I've been checking her work."

He didn't know half of it. But Dani was a fighter. It was innate. It gave her strength. Fighting wasn't in Ryan's spirit. That much, he didn't get from his father. Or from his mother. He figured he should have gotten even a touch of it from one of them. "Why did you walk away? You're telling me not to. Why did you?"

Nick dropped his eyes while his chest expanded and released. "Saw too much. The thing with Marlisse was only the topper. Couldn't do it anymore. But I was wrong. If I could go back, I'd do it different. You have too much going for you..."

"There are rumors we're working on a project together."

Nick laughed. "Are there? I'm surprised anyone would care. About what I'm doing, that is."

"Yeah, I think you might be surprised. Maybe we should talk about it. Could be interesting."

"You don't want to waste your time with someone who disappeared from the scene thirteen years ago." He threw the mangled blade to rest atop the unpicked, unmangled grass.

"I've wasted my time on lesser things. And as you said, we need more."

Nick stared, possibly considering. Then he shrugged. "Tell you what, you hang in there and get yourself moving again and we'll talk."

"That was a sucker punch."

"Whatever works."

He couldn't help grinning. "Just so you know, this thing with Katie you seem to think will wear off? Don't count on that."

"Guess if it doesn't, it's not meant to. Just be good to her. As long as you are, you'll have no problems with me." Nick pulled his feet in closer. "Hell, Becca wasn't even seventeen yet when we got together and I knew she wasn't. Not smart, and it caused a lot of trouble, like both of us having kids with someone else in between and separating for quite some time, plus more reason for Robert to object to me. But it worked out in time because through everything, there was nothing I wanted more than I wanted her. And because she gave me more chances than she should have along with allowing space to do what I needed to do." He glanced over at Robert now talking with Tracy. "He'll come around. He may be a royal pain in the arse at times, but underneath it, he's alright. I shouldn't have complained about him to Marlisse as I did."

Ryan wasn't fully convinced Robert would come around, but he wouldn't argue. "So you have a kid?"

"Yes, a beautiful daughter. Don't see her a lot, but now and then. She lives in Winchester, outside London, with her mum."

"How old is she?"

"Oh. Three years older than Katie. Twenty-one. Good kid. A lot like her mom, thank the Lord. Has a good stepfather. She considers him her dad and that's fair."

"Has to be hard."

Nick sighed and looked over at Will playing with his kids since Deanna and Daws were now walking with Kaitlyn. "The hardest thing is wishing I'd had one with Becca. The one I had caused so much trouble when it was found out, I made sure I wouldn't have more, when I thought she would never take me back. Stupid thing to do. She wishes I hadn't. My bass player is her kid, if you couldn't tell. We get along well, which is nice but not quite the same."

"I've heard they can reverse it."

"Tried. Hasn't worked." He stood. "Katie will be a good mom. But she should wait a few years."

"No argument. On either count." Ryan stood beside him. "And she's tired." Without excusing himself, he went to her, claimed Chewy's leash, and took her over to a chair.

Robert and Nick left on a late flight the next day, and Daws and Deanna went out to explore the restaurant recommendation Tracy gave them, so by dinner it was down to his family. He had to leave in the morning. Whether or not the album was going the way he liked, it had to be finished. He had to show his fans everything was still a go.

He figured things were as wrapped up with the house as he could manage and the plan to draw attention away from Vermont seemed to be working. Friday – was that only two days ago? – Patricia had launched full steam into arranging appearances. She announced tour dates would be out soon after the album which they had a rough date for, and Ned and the rest of the band did a last-minute appearance to talk about how it was coming along. Which, at the moment, it wasn't. But they made it sound like it was, enough that New York fans and reporters weren't sure he wasn't there, despite local reports.

Kaitlyn stood at the counter in Tracy's kitchen to cut up cauliflower for the salad. Maybe they would put a garden in their yard. She so loved fresh vegetables, and fruit. They could add an apple tree. The things were all over Vermont but having her own would be nice, one of the short ones that would be easy to pick. Maybe apricots, also. They were his favorite, although they made a mess of the ground below.

"Quit staring at the girl and take these to the table." Tracy tried to hand him plates but Katie turned to find his eyes.

"Can't help it. I'm awe struck." Before she turned back, he thought he caught a touch of a grin. It froze him where he stood.

"Ryan, that's very sweet and all, but dinner will be ready in a minute. Here."

He passed the dishes on to Matt, went to Katie's side, and stared at her profile. She paid no attention, acting like she didn't see him except for a quick flick of the eyes. Teasing. The girl was actually teasing him.

When she still didn't pay attention as he pressed closer, he took the knife from her hand to set aside and circled an arm around her waist.

"I'm not done."

"I know. I want your attention."

She faced him fully and wrapped her arms over his shoulders.

"What?" Her eyes still teased.

"You're beautiful."

"No, I'm not."

He laughed. "What makes you think you're not?"

"I have a mirror."

"Oh, well, it doesn't work right, then, because you are. You are incredibly, amazingly beautiful. And I don't want you to pick up other guys when I'm in New York. Tell me you won't. Tell me they don't have a chance."

She played with his hair, running it through her fingers. "I don't want anyone else. I never want anyone else to ... be this close."

Ryan felt his lungs expand and his head swell to triple the size even from what it was at his most arrogant. "Then I'll make sure that never happens." He rubbed his thumb over her cheek. "I don't want to leave you tomorrow."

Katie ducked her head into his shoulder. "I'll be here when you come back. I'll have the house ready to live in."

He nodded and held her. His family moved around them until his mom stepped in to ask what still needed to be done and shepherded the others out to the dining room. Giving them space.

The oven buzzed. Ryan called out to say he'd get it so they wouldn't come back in, and he kissed her.

With no answer to his knock, Ryan opened the door slowly enough she could warn him to stop if needed. Not that she was ever embarrassed if he caught her in between dressing, as he had a couple of times.

She sat on the bed, her back supported by a pillow against the headboard, writing in her notebook, one of the small nicely bound journals he'd picked up for her birthday. When he moved into the room, she looked startled and closed the journal.

"Sorry. I knocked. Not loud enough?"

"I was..." She glanced at it.

He walked up to the edge of the bed. "Don't worry, I won't ask to read your diary." With a grin, he brushed fingers against her arm.

"It's not."

"No?" He sat facing her. "Can I ask what it is?"

The hazel-brown eyes peered into his. "Nothing. Thoughts."

"Isn't that a diary? Nothing but thoughts?"

"Your songs are thoughts. Not a diary."

"Yes ... you're writing songs?"

"No."

He raised his fingers to her cheek. "You don't have to tell me. I was only curious. And I'll go so you can finish your thoughts."

"No." She set it aside and shifted closer. Her warmth penetrated the chill that still blanketed his clothes and skin from wandering Will's backyard looking at the stars. "It'll wait."

Closing his eyes when her body pressed into his, her hand on his chest, her lips touching his shoulder, Ryan had to remind himself they were in his brother's house, and she was still recovering. By the time she was fully recovered, he would be in New York – probably talking to her on the phone every spare minute and taking cold showers at night. In his apartment alone.

"Kaitlyn." He had to pull his head back. "I have something for you." He reached into his jeans pocket and pulled out a little box. As Ryan handed it to her, he hoped she wouldn't misinterpret what was inside.

Her fingers ran across the pendant. She didn't look disappointed.

"You know fans are always giving me wolves since they found out I like them. But they don't know why I do. No one does." He pulled it from the box, the silver chain draped over his fingers. It came out better than he expected, the crescent moon with a howling wolf perched atop. "The moon is made of moonstone, which is supposed to be healing and protective. I had it made for you, but I have to tell you why."

She found his eyes.

"We used to camp a lot, us boys, when Dad was still here." He noted the nod of her head that said she remembered. "Well, one of the first trips when I was still pretty young, I wouldn't sleep because a wolf kept howling in the distance. It was scary, even though Dad said he wouldn't come close to the fire and we weren't in their path. That didn't work, so he finally told me I shouldn't be afraid of the wolf's howl; he was only calling for his mate because he didn't know where she was and he was lonely. He didn't want to bother us. He wanted not to be lonely."

He paused, not sure if it was to check her reaction or to control his own. "So then I wouldn't sleep because I wondered what he would do if he never found her. Dad said I needn't worry. Any wolf that howled that well and for that long was determined enough to find just the right mate." He shrugged. "I guess he was right."

Her eyes watered and she turned, raising her hair so he could clasp it around her neck. He watched as she straightened the pendant. The necklace was the right length; the wolf dangled at the center of her chest, showing nicely just below where her collarbones nearly met.

She leaned in to kiss him and he knew he would stay with her. The kids were in bed. He would be up early. And they couldn't do anything, but he didn't care. He only needed to be beside her for the night before he had to go back to work.

Taking the pendant in his fingers, his hand rested against her bare skin, and he had to tell her the rest. "This ... this was me before we found each other. It belongs to you always. So do I. I love you, Kaitlyn."

Heat from the mug penetrated his fingers as Ryan sat on the back steps with his first coffee of the morning. Chewy lay beside him. Her thick body warmed his leg. Ryan scratched behind the dog's ear and couldn't resist running his hand over her smooth black coat.

A chilled breeze brushed his face and he closed his eyes to allow it to wash through. Late October already. Winter was trying to set in. Matthew and Bella had, again, asked him to be there for Halloween, to walk around town with them as he did when they were younger, before he was so well known. He couldn't. Besides the fact he needed to work, it wouldn't be safe for them if anyone found out who he was, unless they included a squadron of guards. That was no way for them to spend their trick-or-treating night. Ryan would make it well known he was in New York and they would hint Katie was there with him.

He had only a couple more hours before Daws would yank him back to the city. Once he went back, he'd have to stay. For some time. Long enough to finish the album. Long enough to make appearances. Long enough to convince fans he was sticking around. His stomach cringed at the thought of being away from her for so long. But it was for the best. He wanted her to be left alone.

"Take care of her for me, Chewy."

The dog raised her head and settled it atop Ryan's leg.

"So much for not liking dogs."

Ryan looked back at his brother as he came out through the screen door. "Hard not to when she means so much to Katie."

Will sat on Chewy's other side. "Careful. It becomes an addiction."

"Well, better than most of my addictions, I suppose." He swallowed a large, warm gulp of too-sweet coffee. Katie would have argued if she'd seen him add so much sugar.

The dog bolted to her feet and headed out into the yard toward someone Ryan hadn't seen. Someone with a camera. Luckily for the photographer, she couldn't get far from the porch. The intruder didn't realize she couldn't and dashed off again.

Ryan sighed. "I'm really sorry about this."

"Not your fault." Will called the dog back and stroked her to help her calm.

"How is it not my fault?"

His brother shrugged as though photographers hanging around his backyard was an everyday occurrence. "It's your right to do the job you love. Not your fault the country is star crazy."

"Not like I haven't tried to feed into it, though. You know how much time and energy goes into feeding it? To grab as much limelight as possible to help sales? Part of me gets really pissed off when they badger me like this, but then, I've never minded when it pay the bills."

"Part of the job. We all have the right to support our careers. And don't think I've always felt that way. I've had my share of being ticked off at the invasion into our lives because of it, but it's not like we're not used to being affected so much by a career. We grew up that way. More than most can understand."

Ryan couldn't argue that. Growing up a military brat and having to move every couple of years to wherever the Army said, like it or not, leaving friends behind, never with extended family around, hearing all of the political ramblers argue whether their parents were heroes or villains without knowing them and with no idea why they chose that life or what it was actually like on the inside ... they were both well used to living on the outskirts of regular society instead of within it.

"You escaped it, though, decided to blend in. My choice shouldn't affect you and your family." He kept his eyes in the distance, in case the photographer decided to return.

"It's not ever possible to not affect those around you with your choices. You know that. And you balance it well – your need with ours. I know how careful you are to hide when you're here. I know you're going to make a big promo scene in New York the day before Halloween even though you want to be left alone to work, as you have often, just so they know you're not here." He sipped his coffee. "I'm proud of Mom and Dad for what they were willing to do and for how well they managed to balance it." Will turned from studying the yard to face him. "I'm proud of you, too, Ryan. I always have been."

He knew his mouth must have gaped while he stared at his brother, but he was trying too hard not to drop his cup to worry about it.

"Don't look shocked. You know I am."

"Uh, no, I gotta say proud is not what I would guess you were ever thinking of me. Stubborn. Arrogant. Jackass. Determined, maybe. Annoying. How much more do you want?"

Will chuckled. "Okay, maybe all those things, too. But along with all that, I'm also proud of everything you've accomplished, how you found what you really wanted and went after it with all you had. And ... I'm glad to see what you've grown into. You've had me worried. I was especially afraid of the kind of girls you seemed attracted to. I worried about that a lot, about where it would lead."

"Kept telling you not to." Ryan stretched his back and shoulders. "Short term attracted and long term attracted are usually two different things. Guess it wasn't for you, though."

"No, and I can't say I understand that."

"I don't know why not. You know the only other girl I was serious about was sweet and patient, a real lady. Someone I could respect, not...." And he hadn't even thought of her in some time. After years of the breakup hurting like hell.

Will studied him. "Still miss her?"

"Nah. I still resent that Veronica made her think I cheated on her. She didn't deserve that even if I did." He grabbed a swallow of the coffee when Will raised his eyebrows. "Got too damn drunk and she had someone take photos of us. Nothing happened. Sure looked like it did. Never told you because I didn't want to admit how stupid I was." He shrugged. "But I never felt for her as much as I do for Katie. I wouldn't mind clearing the air, but nothing more."

"Maybe you should."

"She'd never believe me. She didn't then, has no reason to now."

"She's married, has a kid a few months old. Wasn't sure I should mention it."

Married. He took another swallow of now cool coffee. "Hope he's good enough for her."

"He's a good guy. Works with me. She asks about you when I see her, glad you're doing well."

Ryan stared into his cup. Maybe she wasn't still mad. Maybe she'd realized Veronica made more of it than it was. He'd just as soon she wasn't mad at him, or worse, still hurt.

"You two are up early." Tracy told Chewy to relax when the dog jerked her head up to see who was there. "Am I interrupting?"

Ryan assured her she wasn't, that he was about to go see if Kaitlyn was awake yet. Tracy said her door was still closed as she lowered beside Will with a soft caress to his back. He kissed the top of his sister-in-law's head when he got up, not answering what it was for.

"Let's go, Reynauld. I'm leaving my girl here, too, but you don't see me acting like a two year old with separation anxiety."

Ryan threw Daws a gesture no one else would see ... except Katie did and she pulled his hand down. "Be nice to him. He's taking care of you for me." She kept hold of his fingers and ran her other hand into his hair. "Be careful."

"Don't have to be. That's what I pay him for."

"Ryan..."

"I'm kidding. You know I will. Damn, I'm going to miss you. Feels like I just got here."

"You did. But it's okay. I'll get the house ready, so next time..."

"Yes. Next time, we'll stay there. At our place." He pulled her in close, clenching his eyes. "You be careful, too. I know Deanna and the team will be watching out, but if Will gets protective it's only because he cares. Let him be, okay?"

She nodded against his shoulder.

"And hey, I got something for you. Will has it and he'll show you how to use it: a laptop, with email he'll set up so you can write to me, and a word program so if there's anything you want to save in your notebooks, just extra backup or whatever, there's plenty of space on it." He brushed his thumb against her cheek when she returned her gaze. "If you happen to see stuff about me on the net, don't believe it's true unless it's on my site. Ask if you want. I'm not on it a lot. Someone's gotta run it for me although Dani uses the things like they're part of her brain. I'm sure you'll get the hang of it fast, too..."

She kissed him. A soft, quick kiss. There were people around. His family since he was supposed to be leaving. Daws and Deanna. A few guards. "Don't worry. Don't let your stomach get bad again."

"I'll stay stocked with cranberry juice."

A light expression that couldn't quite be called a grin touched her face. It was close to that. Someday it would be. "I have to go." He started to pull back. Then he pushed closer again and gave her a longer kiss. It didn't matter who was around. The kids could look the other way.

He rested his forehead against hers, knowing Daws would come drag him away if he didn't go on his own. "I love you, Kaitlyn. Don't ever forget that. You be okay for me."

Her fingers slid from his shoulders down his chest, resting on his stomach. "If I can have even one year with you, it'll be worth the last ten years of ... of howling ... silently, and waiting."

"Oh Katie, I plan to give you so many more years than that. Good years. Traveling. Boating. Whatever you want. It may have to be in between my job for a while, but..."

She brushed his lips. "I love you, Ryan. I'm always beside you."

He felt the sharp intake of air. The shock of the words. The deep touch of his soul. And he wrapped her in, holding as tight as he dared, planting kisses on her neck, her face, again on her lips.

"Last thing you need is to be harassed for too much public affection." Daws tapped on his back, although his voice held an apology.

"Okay." His own voice was breathless. "I'm coming." His eyes were on Kaitlyn while he backed away and their fingers slipped apart. "Keep your phone on." She nodded with a quick brush at moist eyes. He gave in to Daws pushing him toward the car and it sank in that his family was still there; they'd seen him get too carried away. Ryan already gave them his goodbyes but threw a wave as Deanna wrapped an arm around Kaitlyn.

She stayed outside until he couldn't see her from the car.

Make it a kick ass album.

Nick's words buzzed Ryan's head as he listened to the most recent playback. It wasn't. They'd toned it down too much, took out the edge. "No." He waved his hand at the producer to tell him to stop.

Ginny eyed him. "What was wrong with that? It sounds good..."

"It sounds like crap – mushy crap. That's not what I wrote. It's not what I want."

"We've been over this." Mac leaned back in his cushy black swivel chair. "It's commercial. What you wrote..."

"What I wrote is what I want. The way Ned played it is what I want. And I mean the way he played it before all the changes I don't want. Still have that version?"

"I have the adapted version."

"Not good enough." He looked over at his band. "Gonna walk out if I ask you to try it again? The way it was?" They glanced at each other, at the producer, at Ginny.

"You don't have to ask them for permission. We do this right or it doesn't go out." Ryan stood, trying to imitate the stance he'd seen Daws take so often, the don't-mess-with-me stance. He supposed his imitation was pathetic without the build to back it up, but at least it was an attempt.

"Then let's do it right." Ned stood with him. The others groaned.

"I know, it's late and we're tired and we all want this done, but..."

"Reynauld, you do the one song over to make it more raw the way you want and it throws the album. It won't work, unless you do it as a bonus at the end and call it a demo or..."

"The whole album. I want the whole thing changed. It's not going out like this." He saw the glances suggesting he'd lost his mind. Maybe he had. But he was done being walked on. It was his album.

"Not happening." The producer leaned forward again. "The thing is pretty much done. No way we're starting again."

"You've got most of the original cuts, or the less edited cuts. We won't be starting over, only backtracking."

"You can't ask your band, who aren't even studio musicians and do this reluctantly as it is, to start over. Not to mention the cost."

Ryan knew they expected him to back down, as always. Not this time. "If you won't do it, I'll find someone who will."

"Hey." Mac threw his hands in the air. "I'm gonna be here if it's with you or the next in line. No skin off my nose. But try getting your label to fund it. And get your band to agree. Unless you plan to replace them, too, maybe with studio musicians."

"No. If the band doesn't agree we use whatever early cuts you have and work around that. But money isn't the issue, even if it costs more than it'll make. It's *not* going out like this." He maintained his pose during the silence.

With a sly grin, Mac shifted backward. "IF you get an agreement, it'll take a hell of a lot more work. Late nights. Early mornings. Unless we push the date back again."

"We can't do that." Ginny nearly jumped out of her chair.

"No. I don't want it pushed back. So it'll mean long days. Not the first time."

"Gonna get these guys to agree?"

Ryan wasn't sure about that one. He knew he didn't deserve quite that much loyalty from them. Figuring he might as well find out, he walked closer, with a shrug. "Anyone in or am I hanging myself here?"

"I'm in." Ned took his side with a slap on the back. "About time you found your gonads. Been waitin' for that."

"Had to be sucker punched often enough, I guess. Kind of tired of it."

Ned grinned and turned to the others. "Come on. Let's do this thing right."

Sam rolled his shoulders. "Yeah, easy for you to say. You have no life. My girl's getting fed up never seeing me as it is."

"Have her come in." Ryan understood their sideways glances. He never allowed girlfriends at the studio, or on tours, not wanting the distraction. Daws was right; he was a moron. If Katie could be there, he sure as hell would have her there. "Bring her to the shows, too, if she wants. Same with any of your girls. As long as the work still gets done. I don't mean girls off the street, though. I mean ones that matter if you lose them."

"Damn Ginny, where'd you find the body double to play Reynauld? 'Cause this isn't him."

He ducked his head in acknowledgement to his keyboardist. "All right, I know. And I don't deserve for you to put more into this than you already have, but I'm asking anyway. If you won't do it, Ned and I will do what we can to spice this thing up."

"Gonna fire us, too, if we refuse?"

"No way in hell. We've been through too much together. And I've been thinking...." He rubbed the back of his neck. They would be certain he'd lost his mind if he continued. Maybe, though, that's what he'd needed, to lose his mind at least to an extent. "Since we are all doing this together, studio and touring like we're a whole band, might as well

call ourselves a band. Change things around. Not sure we can do it for
this one with the time limit, but..."

"Wait." Thomas held up a hand. "A band? Not Ryan Reynauld's
backup musicians?"

"Hell, that's what we are. Might as well make it official."

"Reynauld." Ginny moved over to him and pushed him back away
from the others. "You do that and the whole cut changes."

"Yeah. And it's about time. These guys work as hard as I do."

"It's your name selling it. Your songs."

"Yeah well, maybe I'm not so interested in being a lone ranger
anymore. And I'll still get my cut for songwriting." He moved around
her and went back. "If you're interested."

"What are we going to call it?"

Ryan figured Carl was testing him to see if he was serious. He hadn't
thought far enough to consider names. "We'll come up with something.
Won't be my decision alone."

"Reynauld." Ned nudged him. "Just drop the first name. You know,
like Bon Jovi or ... Santana. Van Halen. Ramones ... Hanson. We call it
Reynauld and you're still easy to find that way."

Thomas stood. "So let's go fix this thing. I'm in."

Melded onto the couch in the control booth, Ryan allowed his eyes to
close while he listened to the track. The touch-ups didn't work as well
as he hoped. There was still so much to do on it. Monday. It was mid-
November and he'd barely been out of the studio since he left Vermont.
His tour manager kept him updated on show dates scheduled, not that
he would remember, and Patricia reported on how well they were
getting the word out about the album progress, saying it was on track
(a touch of a lie, but Ryan said nothing since it would eventually be on
track). Daws let him know it was working, fans had calmed down. He'd
kept in touch with Will and security was hardly necessary up there.
Deanna was back in New York. Enrico and a couple of local guards were
staying there.

Ryan often woke Kaitlyn up when he finally got home since it was
the only time he could talk to her without others around. She always
insisted she didn't mind. At times, he wished he hadn't invited the
girlfriends into the studio. Not that it bothered anything. When they did
come, they were respectful of work time and standoffish enough of
Ryan he wouldn't have had to speak to them if he decided not to. He
did, out of respect for his band. But it was hard to have them there
when he was trying so hard not to miss Katie.

"Still awake?"

"Yeah." He opened his eyes to Mac handing him coffee. "Thanks."

The producer lowered beside him. "So what do you think about this?"

"I like some of it better than the rest. This one..." He nodded toward the panel. "Needs something but I can't figure what and I don't want it out like this."

"Yeah, I'm thinking the same. Problem is ... how fast are we going to be able to figure it out?"

Ryan sipped the too-strong black coffee and shrugged. "Maybe we replace it and think about it later. Are we out of sugar?"

One of the girls who worked for Mac offered to get it for him.

"Replace it with what? You have no energy to write another song..."

"I have a ton that would fit better."

Mac bent his head with the frown that said he was interested but doubtful.

"What do you say I give them to the guys and see what they think? Might be faster than fixing the mess. Keep the ones that are done and right and fill in the rest."

"You have lost your mind."

He accepted sugar with thanks, holding the cup while the girl poured it in and stirred it. "Probably. But I want the raw sound and it's easier to keep it in the first place than to return to it."

"You have them with you?"

"Daws has them." He closed his eyes again.

"You're doing what?"

Ryan heard the disbelief in Dani's voice even through her irritation. "Hey, it's working out great. May lose all the newer fans but the older ones will like it better. I like it better."

A pause came across the line. "Well, that's what matters most. But don't sink yourself, Ry. If you lose too many with this one you might have to balance it more with the next and pull them back."

"Yeah, we'll see. I'm kinda enjoying just throwing them out there and letting them be as they are, for the most part. Hell of a lot faster, too. We might actually finish this thing before the month's out."

"Release it for Christmas?"

He laughed. "Well, maybe for the new year instead. Not something most are gonna think of to buy for Christmas, I don't guess, but they can save their gift money for it. It's kind of a new start thing, anyway, so..."

"What are you calling it?"

Ryan nearly told her, for her reaction, but decided against it. "Can't say. Top secret."

"Are you kidding? You can't tell me?"

"Could. I'd rather wait till I give it to you. Have any time coming up you could get out here?"

"I don't know. Things are ... with going home for the holiday and all,

I'm not sure. Can't wait to hear it, though."

"Yeah, I'm doing a working holiday."

"Ryan, you can't skip out on your first Thanksgiving with Kaitlyn. Even if she understands..."

"Nah, I'm not. Got a show in Bennington day after Thanksgiving, so I'll do the family day and then do the town duty thing afterwards so I'll have some time there with her. Hey, so we're hosting dinner at our house. I'd invite you but your parents wouldn't appreciate it."

A chuckle came across, barely. "I don't imagine. Wish I could, though. Hold on ... Brian wants to know when you're coming out here."

"Tell the freak he can come this way just as well. I was there last."

"Yeah, but they all want you to bring Kaitlyn so they can check her out."

Bring Kaitlyn. They'd never before asked him to bring anyone. Rarely was an outsider allowed to visit their private domain. But she wasn't an outsider. They'd accepted it already. "I don't know when I'll be able to take her anywhere, but I know you two need to meet."

"Damn right we do. You know you better not get too awfully serious until I approve."

"Hm. Guess you'll have to approve since it's kinda late for that." He looked over when Daws called his name. "I gotta go. I'll try to call on Thanksgiving but if I don't..."

"If you don't, I'll call you. And I'll make time soon. Promise."

Hanging up, Ryan considered the meeting between his two favorite women. They had to get along. He couldn't imagine otherwise.

25

Ryan took Katie's hand and walked up the sidewalk to their house. He'd been frustrated about not being able to leave New York until that morning, especially when they were hosting Thanksgiving dinner later in the day, in the house he hadn't seen since his last visit to Vermont. And Katie's family was coming to share the holiday, all of them: Robert, Andrea and the kids, and Nick and Rebecca and Rebecca's son, the bassist, whose name Ryan couldn't remember. They were there, in the hotel, for another hour or so when they would descend on the house. He was glad it wasn't horribly cold for November and they could spill into the backyard.

But, the album was done, his part of it, and his band would join him in the morning to rehearse for the show the next night. And the gate was up. He knew there was some furniture in the house but wasn't sure how much or what it looked like. When Katie asked about colors or styles, he told her to get what she liked. He was interested to see her style. Especially in her room. For the moment, they would maintain separate rooms.

She handed him the house key when they got to the door, his family behind them, playing security in the guise of carrying bags of things for dinner since Ryan insisted Daws take Thanksgiving off. He opened the door only a crack, dropped the key into his pocket, and bent to swoop her up into his arms.

"I know this is typically for married couples, but I figure it's close to the same, a new start to our lives. Right?"

She nodded, her eyes shining. And she was as radiant as any bride. The new fullness in her face and the tan showing she'd spent a fair amount of time outside gave a beautiful healthy look that helped her sparkle. Matthew and Bella heckled him as he carried her to the middle of their living room and turned a slow circle, looking at the place, unable to hide his surprise at how much she'd done already.

"Is it okay?"

"I figured it would still be nearly empty." He almost felt like he was out on the boat with all the blues and greens and teals and the nice, but casual furnishings, earthy and ... calming. The heavy curtains that had covered the big windows overlooking the backyard were replaced by soft white curtains looped and draped around a silver curtain rod. Behind them were narrow light green vertical blinds. It made the windows look bigger, the house even more open.

"You don't like it." Her voice sounded wary, concerned.

"It's incredible. I never imagined ... Katie, it's beautiful. It's you. I hope you didn't wear yourself out doing all this." The walls had even been painted, the color of the sky at its lightest blue.

His mom hushed Matthew and Bella's teasing by sending them to take their bags to the kitchen. "We didn't let her get too tired. A few of Will and Tracy's friends helped out. You owe them a barbeque."

"At least one, I think."

"Most of it isn't done yet." Katie brushed fingers through the hair at his nape. "Just this. And parts of the rest."

Ryan kissed her. It was perfect. Comfortable. Relaxing. It was her.

"You've got company coming soon." Will, amused. "Maybe put her down and check out the rest, then get in here and help out since you are the host of this thing."

"Yeah." But he didn't want to put her down. He focused on her face next to his, her arms wrapped around his neck, her scent. Reluctantly, he set her on her feet. His family moved into the kitchen but Ryan stood holding her there.

"You're sure you like it?" Her eyes reminded him of half-muddy water.

"It's perfect. Almost like being out on the boat."

A light grin skimmed her face.

He ran his fingers up to her forehead, down the side of her cheek, back behind her ear. "You have a beautiful smile. It's incredible to finally see part of it."

Katie pressed in, hands against his back, her breasts against his rib cage. The kiss held him planted, grounded. At voices returning too close, he made himself release her, or allowed her to release him – he wasn't sure which. "Show me the rest."

She started with the extension, which was furnished, barely, in neutrals so far, tans and whites. Ryan could see his mom's influence there. Every room was barely furnished, with nothing yet in what would be the music room, except for a daybed with pull-out trundle. She said it could be moved if he didn't want it. He saw no reason to move it. At least it would look like he planned to use it as his room for the moment while their guests used the others. She showed him the bedroom last. Her room, that eventually would be theirs.

"I expected you would have done something with this one." He moved his eyes around the blank room with only a large bed and basic furniture. It was nice furniture, traditional wood, but there was no decoration anywhere. No curtains, even, only the shade for privacy and a basic white comforter, the kind he had in New York.

"I'm waiting for you." She moved in against him. "I want us to choose together."

"Katie, I don't care…"

"I do."

He held her gaze until she kissed him. Ryan picked her up again and took her over to the bed, laid her down gently, and sat next to her. "Be happy here. I just want you to be happy here."

Sliding her hand up to his chest, she gripped his shirt and pulled him down. And she touched her lips to his. Teasing. "I missed you."

Ryan deepened the kiss, the weeks of being too far away dissolving into her lips, her body beneath his, her arms pulling at him to get even closer. He lowered to the bed and drew her to his side, her head cradled between his arm and shoulder. "I'm going to ask to take you back to New York, at least part of the time. Do you want to go? Or … if you'd rather be here…."

"I want to be where you are." She kissed his chest through his T-shirt. "But only when it's okay for you."

He wanted to pull the shirt off, to get it out from between them. But his family was there. And hers would be there soon.

With the turkey dinner, which he ate too much of, adding to his fatigue, Ryan pushed out his back door and headed to the bonfire most of their family was huddled around, on chairs or standing, or on a cut up log. It took him a moment to find where Kaitlyn was, on the ground with an old blanket underneath and Chewy at her side, her head on Katie's leg.

Taking her other side, he was careful not to spill the mug he'd overfilled as much as he'd overfilled himself. He'd snapped a lid on it but it still splashed from the drinking hole as he walked.

"You're tired." She grasped his free hand.

"Long day. Actually, very long five weeks."

Nick chuckled. "I'm sure that drink isn't helping out, either."

"I'm hoping it will." Ryan took a swallow. "Coffee. Anyone want any? It's just made."

"Coffee." Nick wasn't buying it. "With what?"

"Sugar, probably too much."

Katie released his hand and took the mug with his warning that it was still hot. She tasted it carefully and made a face. "Too much." Still, she took another swallow.

"Yeah well, I ate some of the cucumbers you pushed at me so I deserve sugar tonight."

A slight grin curved her lips while Tracy harassed him that it was good someone watched how he ate.

To change the conversation, Ryan called over to Curtis to ask him to bring a sausage. Katie had been right, of course, and the sausage wasn't necessary with as much turkey as they still had left, along with the potatoes, vegetables, and pies. Still, they planned a bonfire and Ryan couldn't imagine not offering sausage and hot dogs at a bonfire. He'd cooked too many.

"Thank you, little man."

"You eat a lot."

Ryan laughed through Andrea correcting the boy. "Yeah, sometimes, but this isn't for me."

"Kaitlyn doesn't eat sausage."

"No, but Chewy does." At her name, the dog raised her head. "Here you go." Tearing off bits, he handed it to her, careful to pull his fingers back quickly.

"She won't bite you." Katie scratched the dog's head.

"Just don't want her mistaking it for my fingers."

"She won't. She's smarter than that."

"You'll spoil her feeding her sausage."

He shrugged toward Rebecca. "Yeah well, I figure she needs it. Will said she was nearly starved to death when he found her." He gave Chewy another and stroked her head.

"So your brother's in the animal saving business?" This time it was Robert. He sank into a chair beside Nick.

Ryan looked over to where Will and his mom and the older boys were playing horseshoes under the big yard light. "Not exactly. He just can't resist stepping in when he finds an animal in need and they tend to get dumped out there by the plant. But he's been doing this since we were kids. Used to drive Mom crazy. At one point, we had four puppies that had been dumped at the side of the road, a large cat with a limp whose hair was falling out, and a skinny-ass skunk that was half dead when he brought it home."

"A skunk?" Robert pulled one leg atop the other. "And how long did it take him to wash the smell off?"

"Oh, he never got sprayed by the thing, but it took me three or four days every time I did."

Rebecca laughed. "Every time?"

"Yeah, that thing and I did not like each other. I think I got it three times before Mom made him take it back to the woods. Two times earlier would have suited me better." Rolling his eyes, Ryan took a bite of the sausage and saw Chewy looking, waiting for her turn. "Here." He handed her the rest of it. "Hey Curtis, wanna bring me another sausage while you're on your feet?"

"Another one?" The boy put his hands on his hips.

"*Curtis.*"

Ryan grinned at Andrea's scold and set a hand on his hip in imitation. "It's for Chewy."

"No it isn't. I saw you eat it."

"One bite. Now she wants it back. Do I have to arm wrestle you for it?"

"That's not fair. My arms are little."

Ryan shrugged.

"Okay." Curtis faked a big sigh and went to grab another, licking his fingers off after handing it to him. "Dad said I can get a doggy, too, like Chewy but smaller 'cause I'm not so big yet."

Robert raised his eyebrows. "I said I would think about it. You need to learn to pick up after yourself before you can care for something else."

"But Ryan doesn't. He makes me get his sausage."

Andrea took the boy's arm, embarrassed. "He doesn't make you. Don't exaggerate. And he's your host. Be polite."

"Yeah." Ryan acted insulted. "And besides, Chewy isn't mine. She's Katie's, and Katie does pick up after herself." He glanced over at her, thinking again he saw a partial smile or at least a thought of one.

Rebecca nudged one of her feet into his. "You're as bad as the kids."

"I've been told that more than once." Ryan looked back at Curtis. "How 'bout we make S'mores after Chewy and I finish this?"

"Yeah!"

Ryan found it hard to believe Katie had never had a S'more. He convinced her the marshmallows weren't done until they were black and crispy, and laughed at her catching parts of the dripping stuff with her hands. She had three, surprising him, and then toasted another marshmallow just to have the marshmallow, crisping it black. Paul handed her a disposable cloth in between, apparently sharing her penchant for tidyness. He occasionally tried to talk to her, but mostly, he watched her, like there was something he wanted to know but didn't want to ask. Ryan talked to him as he got close enough. Mainly, the boy kept to himself.

Restless as it got later and afraid he would fall asleep if he didn't move around, he went to put stuff away. Katie started to get up to help, but Nick suggested all the ladies sit and visit while the rest of them took care of the mess. Curtis rushed over to be door boy.

With things cleaned up and Robert playing horseshoes with his boys under light of the big security lamp that nearly matched the one at Robert's, Ryan sent his mom back out to relax. She'd finished details he wouldn't do as well as she said Katie would want. But Nick lingered, waiting her out.

He leaned back against the kitchen counter as soon as they were alone. "So you finished the album."

"Done with my part. Producer's finishing it up. We're doing shows all next week and getting an album tour planned." He swallowed the last of his now cold coffee and washed out the mug.

"Gonna give me a call when you're ready to do something together? If you were serious, that is."

Ryan turned back to him. "Yeah I was. You're interested?"

"Maybe. It'd be nice to get my feet wet on this side of the ocean again."

"Sounds great. We'll work something out." Not sure what else to say, he looked through the window at the dark.

"I hear you're being harassed about Kaitlyn. Don't let it get to you."

"Not letting it get to me isn't something I do well. Gets me in trouble on a regular basis." He shrugged. "I nearly decked a guy the other day for a nasty comment. Would have if Daws hadn't stopped me. Still wish he hadn't."

"Then you're the bad guy instead of the asshole who started it."

"I'm plenty used to being the bad guy."

"Acting the bad guy, not being it."

"Little difference."

Nick studied him a moment. "It matters to those close to you, even if it doesn't to anyone else." He paused when Ryan didn't answer. "I've seen it, you know. I saw it as bad as it gets."

Ryan tensed, telling himself to be careful, and offered Nick a beer.

"Whole different lifetime ago." He pulled the cap off and sipped at the bottle. "Raucous was a damn good bunch of guys. I miss hanging with them. We were never of their caliber, of course, but they let us open for them now and then. I made a real pain in the ass of myself with their lead guitarist. Still don't know why he didn't tell me to back the hell off."

The lead guitarist. Dani's father.

"I know you prefer directness to beating around the bush, so I'll just say I would love to be in touch with them again. Whoever might be interested."

"Yeah well, I can't say I wouldn't either, but I'm not. Haven't met them, except for Stuart Lowe. I've talked to him now and then."

"Stu. Quite a character." Nick grabbed another swallow, his eyes still on Ryan. "I know he still plays at times. Hard to find where."

"You've tried to find out?"

"For years. They're all keeping a pretty low profile. Hard to find anything."

Ryan studied the floor. Helping Nick find one of Stu's shows wouldn't be using Dani. He could do that much. But he would ask her first. "I'd love to take Katie to one of his shows, too. When I find out where he's playing that it'll work, I'll let you know."

"I'd appreciate it. Your friend's still in touch with him, then?"

"Nick, I'm glad to connect you to one of Stu's shows, but Dani and I don't share each other's personal business. Ever. I can't tell you anything."

"Got it, and I didn't mean to intrude. Just do me a favor and try to give me plenty of notice in case I'm in England. He's not playing there, is he?"

"Not that I've heard." Ryan edged toward the door. He wanted to return to Kaitlyn.

She was on the blanket again, Chewy at her side with Bella and Curtis petting the dog's head and scratching her ears. Bella had been following Curtis around like a puppy. Although he rolled his eyes with an exaggerated sigh at times, he didn't actually seem to mind. Matthew was relieved to have his sister not follow him as usual, and spent time with Stephen kicking the soccer ball around.

Katie leaned against Ryan when he lowered beside her. "They're going to your show tomorrow."

"Yeah?" He looked over at Robert.

"We figured we might as well see what you do since we're out here."

~~~

Propped on the daybed with dawn's light filtered through the blinds, Ryan fingered his guitar strings playing with sounds, the idea of a song at the cusp of his mind. A few words added themselves now and then. It was about Katie. He had enough of a grasp on it to know that, although he didn't quite know where it was heading.

She was asleep. Her family was staying with them the rest of their trip instead of at the hotel, with his mom back at Will's for the time being. Still, he'd gone to her room the night before. He only meant to tell her good night, to talk with her alone, but they'd stayed up late, holding onto each other, lying quietly with bare skin pressed together. He'd refused her advances since he didn't have protection with him, until she told him she was protected. Tracy took her to pick up her prescription just after he'd returned to New York. Her doctor wanted no chances. Ryan wondered if her dad knew.

He thought of her eyes, her emotions that rushed to the surface when they were together, how she'd fallen asleep on top of him then wanted him again when she woke at his movement. He wanted her again at the thought of it and grabbed a deep breath, returning to the music.

"It's there ... in the air when we're together ... under wraps when they're around... It's there ... hiding deeply in their vision ... seeping gently in my ... in my...." He went to humming, not able to think of what he wanted to say. It would come later. The music came together much easier, building ... intense and powerful, echoing the emotion he saw in her no one else did. "It's there ... hiding deeply in their vision ... resting peacefully ... on my skin..." That didn't make sense. Resting ... no ...

hiding meekly in their vision, *"resting deeply on our touch..."* He wasn't sure that made sense, either, but he jotted it down and went back to the music.

Until he noticed Paul peek in the door.

"I'm sorry." The boy ducked away.

"Hey." Ryan waited until he poked his head back in. "It's all right. Come on in."

Carefully, like he was waiting for a reprisal, Paul took a step inside the room. "I didn't mean to bother you."

"You're not." Ryan moved to one end and motioned for him to sit down. "Best I can do since we don't have much furniture yet."

"You're busy."

"I'm stuck, anyway." He again nodded to him to sit and waited until he did. "You play music?"

"No. Well, I played violin for a while. Guess that sounds kind of lame, huh?"

"Not at all. It's a beautiful instrument. My friend's brother is a hell of a violinist. Impressive. I keep thinking I'd like him to play on one of my songs sometime since none of my band can do it. Why'd you stop?"

The boy shrugged. "Dad wanted me to do something more social, like sports. Said I stayed to myself too much."

"You don't like sports?"

"They're okay but I'm not good at it. With music I only mess myself up, not a whole team."

Ryan set the guitar down. "That may be true while you're practicing but not once you start actually playing."

"No, I don't want to play in front of anyone, just for myself."

Ryan flashed back in time enough to remember the fear of playing in front of others. Not that he had to go back too far. He'd been frightened in front of crowds for some time after he started. "Ever think about trying guitar? It's a chick magnet, you know."

Paul blushed. "I don't have one to try. Dad would never agree. He doesn't want us to go into music."

"Because of your mom." Ryan wasn't sure he should mention it, but he figured Paul opened the door to talk.

"You mean Kaitlyn's mom. She wasn't mine."

"Sorry. Yes." Feeling every bit the moron, he picked up the guitar again. "Here." He handed it to the startled boy and stood beside him. "Three chords are all you need to start playing. Easy enough I can do it."

Paul exuded nervousness but Ryan wasn't backing down. If he was that into music, he should have a chance to play. He picked up the chords quickly and Ryan started to show him individual notes, which he also had no trouble learning.

Movement at the doorway took his attention and he found Kaitlyn leaned against the frame. "Good morning." He told Paul to keep at it and went to meet her, forcing himself to keep enough distance. She was in her pajamas with her robe wrapped around, the hair on one side of her face pushed back behind her ear. Completely bewitching. And smelling that fresh from bed smell he loved. "Did we wake you?"

She touched his arm and peered around him at her brother. "I didn't know he played."

"He didn't until now, not guitar."

Her eyes returned to his. "Be careful."

"Why? Will I make your dad mad at me again?"

She moved her fingers to his face. "Because Paul won't want to leave here, either. He needs someone to pay more attention to him. Because they don't."

Ryan felt his lungs expand, releasing the breath slowly. "Maybe he could come for a visit sometime when I'm off work. If your dad will allow."

"Thank you."

"For what?"

She leaned in and rested her head on his shoulder.

After the late morning rehearsal, Ryan gave in to Ned's request to see the house and invited the rest of the band and the two girlfriends with an offer to order pizza. He was unsure about having them there along with Katie's dad who was opposed to the whole business, but they were his band. And Katie said it was fine.

Ryan didn't think about getting Nick's okay, but he didn't appear to mind attention from the younger musicians, and the respect Nick showed Ryan in front of his band didn't hurt his credentials. Ned let it slip that Ryan was going from a solo artist to humble, or not-so-humble in his case, lead singer of Reynauld. It wouldn't be until after the album tour and wouldn't be announced until after then, but wheels had started turning that direction behind the scenes.

Paul was in awe of the group of musicians and Ryan made a point to draw him in. Now and then he set an arm over the boy's shoulders and dragged him over to talk with the guys. They'd been warned to watch their language in front of her family and painted courtesy on their behavior more than normal. Stephen, for some odd reason, attached himself to Daws and followed him around despite Andrea's plea to leave the man alone. Ryan found it hilarious, especially since Curtis avoided the guard, walking all the way around several people instead of in a straight line past him.

"It's not funny." Kaitlyn looked at Ryan when he laughed about it. "Curtis shouldn't be afraid of him."

"Yeah well, he has that kinda look, you know? He's used to it."

With a glance to say she didn't approve, Katie went over and spoke to him. Curtis shook his head hard enough his brown hair flopped back and forth across his neck. But she took his hand and walked over to Daws, who immediately turned her direction away from Nick. Curtis pulled at her, backing up, until Nick said something to make him stop. The boy stole glances at Daws while he and Kaitlyn talked.

Ryan loved that she would go up to his friend to start conversation. Other than her brothers, Daws was the only one he'd seen her do so with. Even Deanna went to her instead.

As he refilled his glass, he looked over at Robert. The man was sitting alone, fully out of place, and fully resigned as he kept attention on his daughter, on how comfortable she was among his musicians, his friends. She had yet to speak to any of them other than Ned, but at least she didn't jump if they got close or accidentally brushed against her in passing. They, in turn, relaxed around her.

Ryan gathered his nerve and went to sit next to her father.

"She's opened up a lot." Robert didn't look at him, but he did sound at least civil. "She still sees her counselor?"

"Yes. They get along well. Doing some kind of creative therapy with her journal and so on. I don't think it's forbidden to repeat that much." He took a swallow of his Coke, and had a sudden longing to add Jack.

"Her journal. Is that what it is?" He continued at Ryan's silence, his eyes still on her. "She used to fill notebooks with scribbles of things she saw, and then words as she learned them. Called them her diaries but wouldn't let us see much of them. Not sure where she got the idea so young. We knew she was writing something while she was home with us recently. Andrea figured it was a diary."

"She says it isn't. I don't know more than that. Haven't pushed the issue." He leaned forward, elbows on his knees.

"You don't push anything with her."

Ryan tried to figure out whether that was a question or an insult. He tended to think the latter, considering their history. "Not my place."

Finally, Robert turned to him. "If you don't mind my asking, and with full realization that's it somewhat late to ask, what exactly do you think *is* your place with her?"

He shouldn't have come over. Ryan considered saying as much, that he'd come over ... why had he? To make peace? Not that he believed it would be that easy. "My place." He shrugged. "Whatever she wants it to be, I suppose."

"And you want me to believe it's all up to her?"

"It is." He swallowed more Coke, as a distraction.

"You always fall to the whims of whoever you're dating so easily?"

"Never." Ryan straightened and pulled an ankle across the other leg. "Honestly, I've never cared too damn much what they thought, with one exception a long time ago. I was in charge. Pretty detached from the whole thing, to be honest. Music has always come first, before any girl."

"I'm sure she'd love to hear that."

"She knows. And she knows it's not true anymore."

"Isn't it?"

"Nah. Close second. Not first."

"Interesting. I don't think my brother-in-law ever caught the idea of music not coming before everything else."

Ryan wouldn't touch that comment. He turned his eyes back to Kaitlyn where she stood with Daws and Nick ... and Ned, again trying to get her to talk. Ryan figured he should be happy enough with the few words she did say to him now and then. He wasn't.

"What's going on with that one?" Robert eyed the drummer.

Ryan had to chuckle. "He's a stubborn ass. Determined to get her to talk to him."

"And you're not worried about it?"

"No. I know him too well and he knows he'd be out the door if I ever half thought I had reason to worry. Plus, Katie doesn't mind. I think she purposely doesn't say more than a few words to him just because he's trying so hard. She has a hell of a teasing streak once she relaxes."

Robert was silent a moment. Then nodded. "She always used to. I was afraid it was gone."

"Think it was. But it's coming back."

She caught his stare and gave him a light grin, flirting with her eyes, as he sat next to her dad. Ryan threw her a wink.

"That was as close to a smile as I've seen yet."

Ryan grabbed a swallow of the soda, his gaze on her even though she'd turned back to the conversation and acted as though she didn't know he was still staring. "Got a better one yesterday. Wow she has a gorgeous smile. And yeah, it's incredible to finally see it."

While things were civil between them, Ryan considered mentioning he wanted to take her to New York, but he decided to wait. They would be there one more day. He had time.

It felt strange to have his security team guard him against his own town. Although it wasn't his town as much as it was Will's and his mom's since he'd barely been there before he took off on his own. They'd visited his mom's friends and a few relatives now and then through their military years, but it was always only a place he visited as far as Ryan was concerned. Until he bought the house. Now, apparently, he was one of them. So was Kaitlyn. Many knew her better than they knew Ryan, with his mom and Tracy taking her out shopping so often. Katie appeared more comfortable being one of them than Ryan was. He didn't feel one of anything other than his job. He never had. For her sake, he'd make the effort, though. She needed it more than he did, to be a real part of a place. He could sense it from her, see it in the way she tried to make herself more friendly than normal. He could also see it still made her nervous. Maybe it always would.

As he left the stage, a cold breeze slapped his sweaty forehead. A closed canopy covered the stage and much of the seating area, and large portable heaters ran within. He first appreciated their warmth and then wished they'd turn off. He and the band gave in to two encores although they were all bone-tired, and sweat dripped down his back and matted the front of his shirt by the time they gave up. Nearly five weeks of daily studio work, very long days, and then early morning travel to Vermont, hosting Thanksgiving, staying up too late with Kaitlyn and getting up early to be sure he was back in his own room before anyone noticed, had worn him down.

Still, he stopped to sign autographs around the bodies and arms of security until Daws pushed him into the performer's tent and handed him a rag to wipe his face. Katie slid her arms around his shoulders and kissed him, undeterred by whistles and comments from the band.

"Damn, I wish you could be here like this after every show. Hell of an encore." He threw a grin, and saw her dad nearby.

"Come look." She took his hand and led him away, to the far end of the tent where a guard stood blocking entrance. "It's snowing."

"Great." From her glance, Ryan figured it wasn't the reaction she wanted. "You like the snow?"

"Yes. It's beautiful. Especially over the water. Did you see it?"

"No, couldn't see much of anything besides heads."

"Can you walk out there?"

"Sure." He asked the guard to let them through.

"Reynauld." Daws grabbed his arm. "Sorry, if you're going out, we're following. And put this on." He shoved Ryan's coat at him.

"I'm soaked in sweat. This is the last thing I want."

"Just put it on so you don't end up with pneumonia. You have a hell of a lot of shows coming up."

Draping it over an arm, he gave Katie the other ... and they were flanked by people asking for autographs. Not people he recognized. Not that he would recognize many of his neighbors yet, but he supposed they weren't. He gave in for several minutes so he wouldn't look ungrateful until more security showed up and edged them through.

Finally, they were in the open. He could see the dry dock where his pontoon awaited better weather. His security stood close by, but not too close, and he decided not to notice. Instead, he turned his attention to the sparkling snowflakes tumbling out of the black sky with lights dancing in the water beyond. When he shivered, Kaitlyn told him to put his coat on. He didn't argue. And he never used the zipper, but he didn't stop her when she moved close and pulled it up nearly to his neck.

Ryan took her hands. They were cold against his. Her eyes were bright, though, her cheeks flushed with the winter air. Snowflakes fell into her hair, covering her like stardust, and he wiped one from her face. "You're right. It's beautiful. I haven't bothered to notice since I was a kid."

She kissed him, helping him unwind so much faster than he normally did after shows. He was ready to go home.

Someone grasped his hand and pulled at his arm.

"C'mon, man. You'll sleep better lying down." Nick stood over him.

Ryan hardly remembered sitting on the carpet beside Katie's legs but was now vividly aware of the crick in his neck and her fingers running through his hair. He straightened his head from where it rested against her leg and rubbed his neck with the hand Nick wasn't pulling. "Damn. I'm sorry. Hell of a host I make."

Katie touched his shoulder. "You got too tired. You're working too hard."

"Part of the job. Come on, Ryan. Go sleep. Don't worry about us."

He gave in to Nick and stretched his shoulders once he was on his feet. "Nah, I'm okay. Anyone need anything?"

"If we do, we'll find it or ask Kaitlyn. Go to bed."

"I gotta shower."

"Then go shower."

"Just don't fall asleep in there." Daws moved in. "I don't want to have to go in and drag your ass out."

"Not like it'd be the first time." Ryan scratched his head. He really needed to shower.

"Could've lived without you sharing that detail. Go on."

"Hey. Why are you here?"

Daws raised his eyebrows. "Why do I always get you back home after a show? You pay me."

"Yeah, I mean ... hell, whatever. If you're staying, there's..."

"Kaitlyn has everything handled. Go shower and get some sleep. You have an appearance in the morning."

"Wait. I what? Why?"

"To keep them from hounding you for autographs tonight. Ten a.m. at the dock. Dress warm."

"Hell, Daws. I was supposed to have the next two days off."

"You do. Except for this."

About to argue, he let it go when Kaitlyn took his arm and said she would walk up with him.

~~~

He heard noise downstairs and checked his watch. Or tried to. It was still half dark and his eyes didn't want to open. But he definitely heard noise. Pulling into his jeans, Ryan stopped at Katie's room and opened the door only enough to see she was still asleep, cuddled beneath the comforter. He fought the notion to crawl in next to her and closed the door again. As he treaded down the stairs, he listened.

With no idea what he would do if there was a prowler, he rounded the corner into the dimly lit kitchen. Coffee scented the air and Robert and Nick looked over at him. And Daws.

"Did we wake you?" Nick pulled out a chair.

"I sleep light."

"In your line of work?"

"Yeah, it sucks at times."

"I would imagine. Glad you're here, though. Want coffee?"

Ryan wished he'd pulled a shirt on. "Shouldn't I be asking you? Are you always up this early? 'Cause I'm trying to be a good host, but I gotta say I generally sleep in longer." He scratched at the back of his head.

Nick chuckled. "Don't worry about it. Sit down."

Daws poured a mug of coffee, added sugar, and set it in front of him. "We were comparing notes on what we've found so far. On Kaitlyn's past."

He should have stayed in bed.

"Want us to outline?"

"I don't know." He rubbed his face with a deep sigh. "Yeah. I mean, it's early and I'm..."

"So let's wait on that." Nick leaned toward him. "Got a question we've been trying to figure out and haven't found records. They changed her age, along with using a different last name to make her harder to find. We know she didn't go through legal foster channels, at least not at first."

"Yeah, I figured." He sipped at the coffee and got up to make it sweeter.

"She shouldn't be out of school yet, but she said something about getting out early. Do you know if she finished or...?" Robert this time.

Ryan leaned back against the counter while he stirred. "She got her diploma a semester early, in December."

"Early? She would've been ... sixteen still." He stared through Ryan's silence. "Did she say how she did?"

He couldn't help a grin. "Top of her class. Out of ... about two hundred kids. And they had her in a special program because she wouldn't talk to anyone but one teacher she liked. Had a hard time with a lot of the others making remarks. Saying she cheated and so on. She didn't, of course. She's unbelievably smart, never mind she chooses to hang out with me when she could do better. Reads all the time, the big books most of us would only use as paperweights."

Nick glanced at Robert. "Sounds like her father."

Robert ignored it. "She should go to college."

Ryan took a sip of the coffee that was now too sweet. Actually, he didn't want it. He wanted to sleep. He set it on the counter and again took the chair beside Nick. "Don't know if she's up to that yet."

"But if she wants to go?"

He shrugged. "Then she should go, but there's no harm in her waiting until she's more ready since she's already ahead. Not that I'm an expert on college since I never went but yeah if she ever wants to, I agree she should. Hasn't been high on my priority list to think about."

"Didn't like school much?"

"Me? I was voted least likely to succeed, unofficially. Grades were okay 'cause Mom woulda been all over me otherwise." He got up to retrieve the coffee and sat again. "But you know, the 'right crowd' bullshit irked my ass and I did what I could not to be in it. Still ended up in the fuckin' top ten, against my protests not to put me there. Wasn't as high up as Will since he just did his work without hassle and of course I had to hear about that one from teachers who thought I could be doing better and should keep my nose cleaner considering who my parents were."

He sipped at the coffee he still didn't want. "I almost kept from telling them the *right crowd* did a hell of a lot more partying than I ever did. Didn't quite keep from saying it and it didn't buy me any goodwill when it got around. Still, I think they were wrong about my not succeeding, though I guess that depends how you look at it. They figured no one would want to hire me because of my attitude. Guess they didn't stop to think maybe I didn't want to be exactly *hired*." He took another sip and propped an elbow on the table. "Sorry, I ramble way too much when I'm tired. Daws is usually telling me to shut up about now. Not sure why he isn't."

"Ramble away." Nick grinned. "He's a good man, Daws. You're lucky to have found him."

"You have no idea. He found me, though. In a bar fight during a show before I was anyone. A drunk-ass moron in the crowd was heckling me and I got sick of it. Stupid thing to do, but I went after him. The guy was built like an ox, but I was tired and frustrated and ... next thing I know I'm on the floor with my head feeling totally split open and this even bigger guy standing over me shoving people away. He got me on my feet, more or less, and sat me at a table. Had someone bring a cold towel for my face. Damn, I looked like something a truck ran over for weeks. But he said I should stop wasting time playing to drunks who weren't really listening. Shoved me in the right direction. So really, I owe it all to him. The man's a fuckin' genius and can get anything done. He may be smart enough to give Katie a run for her money..."

"He exaggerates when he's tired, also." Daws threw a look over his coffee cup.

"Hell I am. Seriously. Don't know why he's wasting time on me when he could be ... hell, anything."

"Told you. Masochist." Daws grabbed the mug from his hand. "Go back to bed or you'll never get to your appearance today."

"You'll get me there. But you should've told me to shut up long ago." He looked at Robert. "I just gave you even more reason why I should have nothing to do with her, right? But I don't do that anymore. Pick fights at bars. Or anywhere else. Not often. Sometimes it's just unavoidable and I don't walk away from it, either, although my security team is liable to step in too fast to accomplish anything. And I don't drink much anymore, if you're worried about the partying. The stomach can't deal with it. I feel like an old man already at times..."

"What's the deal with your stomach?" Nick grew serious. "I know Katie worries about it."

"Oh, mostly it's okay. Just now and then. Ulcers. Had them since I was ... since my dad's funeral. Damn I was sick that day. Not an ulcer yet but it started then. Everyone had enough on their minds and I'm being a fuckin' baby with my stomachache. Pathetic."

"You were fourteen, according to your mother. It's not pathetic." Robert grabbed a deep breath. "We all have our weaknesses. There's no shame in that." He continued while Ryan was trying to figure out how to answer. "Go get some sleep. We'll talk more later."

"You haven't told me what you've found out. About Katie. Getting anywhere?"

Robert and Daws exchanged glances. Her father answered. "We're getting somewhere. Your help would be good, if you can. But it'll wait."

"I don't want to talk about her behind her back."

"Well, understood, but how much will she want to be involved?"

"I don't know. But I can't say anything without her okay. Although I don't think I know anything you don't that will help."

"I need her to testify against that man, to keep him in jail." Robert watched his reaction. "I'll need your help. I know she won't do it without you."

Rubbing his hand over his face, Ryan didn't even want to think about dragging her back into it. She was smiling now, relaxing, teasing. He didn't want that to stop. "How soon does it have to be?"

"Soon. A few weeks."

Ryan nodded. "Okay. But let me bring it up. There's something I want, too. This isn't a bargain. I'll ask her anyway because I don't want that monster out more than you do, but..."

"What is it, Ryan? You're already living with her again and don't think I don't know where that'll lead despite my objections. What else is there you want?"

Where it'll lead. He figured it wouldn't help matters to say it already had. "I want her to be able to travel with me. When she wants to. Not always. She's comfortable here and it's relaxing for her, but..."

"It's not in my hands. You took it out of my hands getting the state involved."

"Yeah, and Will and Tracy are her guardians now, I know, but ... I won't even ask her counselor unless you okay it. I don't want to be your enemy. I want us to be on the same side."

Robert drummed fingers against his cup. "Why were you teaching my son how to play guitar yesterday?"

Hell. Ryan hadn't expected Paul to say anything. "He was interested. And he learned fast. Quite a knack for it."

"Knowing how I feel?"

"I wasn't ... he walked in while I was playing. Looked interested. I think kids should learn music whether or not they use it. It's good for them."

"Got that right." Nick scooted back from the table. "It doesn't mean he'll want to get in the business, Robert. I can't see him doing that."

"And if he does, it doesn't turn him into a bad guy." Ryan reclaimed his mug. "Being a musician doesn't change who you are, it only amplifies it, makes it public. There are some really great people out there on the road. Loyal people who would do anything for you."

"And some not so great."

Ryan nodded. "A lot of not so great. But that's everywhere. In every business. You don't work with any?" Figuring he'd pushed that too far, he tried to backtrack, looking at Nick. "Yeah, never tell me to keep rambling."

"No, you're right. I'm not sure what this has to do with Kaitlyn going to New York, though." Nick tilted his hands toward Robert. "What difference does it make now that they'll be living together whenever he's here? She wants to go with him. She told you she does."

"What?" Ryan focused on Nick. "She said so? I mean, she told me she does but I didn't know..."

"Yeah, she told her dad, too, while you were on stage last night. Said she was most comfortable wherever you are."

She told him. It was a huge step. He was glad to know.

Robert leaned back in his chair. "Still plan to bring her to visit?"

"Yes. When she's ready. Around my schedule." He could feel his eyes try to close and his head grow fuzzier the longer he sat.

"How about we take one trip at a time and let me know what you have planned before she goes? Sound fair?"

"Of course."

"And you'll keep her safe?"

Ryan and Daws affirmed that at the same time and he threw his friend a grin. "I've got the world's best security. She'll be safer with me than anywhere else."

"All right. Just make sure Montana is on the list every now and then and I'll talk with her counselor to suggest it might be a good idea to give her what she wants most. Even if that is you."

If he wasn't mistaken, Ryan figured it was at least partially a joke. "She'll be grateful. So will I." He rubbed at his eyes. He was going to look like holy hell at his appearance with bags bigger than his luggage.

"Go to bed, Ryan. We've kept you up long enough." Robert stood.

Unable to argue, he got up and set the cup in the sink, dumping it but not bothering to rinse it. Katie could fuss at him when he was more awake.

"One thing." Robert stopped him. "You make sure, when you need to, that she's protected. She is too young for that, no matter what anyone else says."

"Agreed."

"I'm holding you to it. And selfishly, I'm glad we woke you. You're easier to talk to when you're not trying to be defensive."

"Uh, well, this isn't ... I have no idea what I've been saying, you know. You should probably ignore all of it."

"That's generally when people are most honest." He backed away.

Saying good night, or at least that's what Ryan thought he was saying although it was a stupid thing to say since it was actually early morning, he grabbed the railing on the way up the stairs and stumbled to the daybed. He paused there, and went back to Katie's room. Careful not to thump the door as he closed it, he shoved his jeans off and crawled in beside her. She turned to cuddle in as close as she could get and kissed his chest. He stayed awake only long enough to feel her breath become deeper.

26

Running lines of poetry Katie sent him through his head while he watched her sleep, in his bed at his loft, Ryan had to force himself not to wake her. She filled her journals with poetry. She'd been writing it since she was able to write, earlier than most kids learned English, using diaries that locked and hiding the keys in a glass jar hidden in a hollow of a tree in her backyard. The yard she was taken away from. She supposed the keys were still there but hadn't looked at the diaries her dad moved into "her" room with her other things except to see they were still locked. No one had bothered them.

She was both relieved and saddened to think if she hadn't ever gone back, her dad would maybe never care enough to look into who she was inside. She wrote all this to Ryan through email during his short tour. She couldn't admit it out loud. With his urging, she sent one of her recent poems. When he praised it, honestly, telling her – also through email – how it literally moved him to have to wipe moisture from his eyes, she continued to send them.

He was the only one who knew. The only one to ever read them. He'd yet to suggest she share them further, that they were good enough to put out there. As far as he knew. He never read poetry other than the section they were forced through at school. But he knew beautiful wording when he saw it. And he understood hers far more easily than any others he'd read. For now, he enjoyed being the only one who could see her so deeply through her words.

When she wrote to him, her sentences were flowing, full, detailed – opposite when she spoke although she said more when they talked directly, also. It was easy to see why her counselor had better luck having her journal than getting her to talk. It seemed to open whatever valve she normally kept closed.

Unable to resist any longer, he ran fingers through her hair and down beneath the blanket. She opened her eyes but remained still as he caressed her shoulder, slid his fingers down her arm, to her stomach, up ... and she moved in, arm around his waist, face against his chest. "I didn't mean to wake you. I just...."

She moved back to see his eyes. "It's okay. It's nice to wake up to you."

He stroked her hair. "How about omelets this morning? I'll cook."

"It's early."

"Yeah, but I'm starving. Your fault. Worked me out too much last night."

"No I didn't." Katie ran her fingers from his stomach up to his chest.

"No?"

She slid her hand to his shoulder, and down his arm, pushing the blanket out of her way, uncovering him nearly to the waist. And she kissed his chest. "You work out more on stage."

"Ohhh, damn, that was a low blow." He turned her onto her back and leaned in over her. "You know I have to redeem myself now."

"Your friend will be here soon."

"Not for a couple of hours. She can eat breakfast with us."

"She won't before she gets here?"

"Probably, but the girl never eats enough for as active as she is. She can do with more. And um..." He kissed her shoulder. "I don't want to talk about Dani right now. Kinda have other things on my mind."

Glad Nick, who accompanied Kaitlyn to New York since Ryan couldn't get away, had decided to stay with Daws instead of with him, Ryan wouldn't leave her side long enough to let her shower alone. He jumped in with her, enjoying the free space they had while he could. Dani and Brian would stay with him while in town a few days. Ryan warned his friend Nick would be there but she shrugged it off. She was as good as Katie at simply not saying what she didn't want to say, at avoiding certain conversations.

They were all going to Stu's show on Friday night. The Bitter End, a small club in mid Manhattan, was one of Ryan's favorite hangouts when he first moved to New York, when he could sit there and be left alone to listen to whoever was playing. He'd gone back to do a couple of shows as his name grew and signed the wall full of names much bigger than his own along with a bunch he didn't recognize. So the owner was more than happy to set up the show for Stu when he suggested it, as a gift for Katie and a thank you to Nick for standing by him the way he had.

When the doorbell rang, earlier than he expected, they were in the kitchen finishing the omelets she insisted on throwing vegetables into, tons of red and green stuff. He complained but knew it would do him no good, especially since his complaints accompanied kisses to the back of her neck while his hands ran along her waist and hips.

Dani's eyes ran along his chest. "Trying to turn me on answering the door like this?"

He greeted Brian first. "How was the trip? Get bothered at all?"

"Nah, it's amazing how long wigs keep people from looking at your face. Damn uncomfortable, though." Brian pulled his off and tossed it onto a side table.

"Got you through without security. Gotta be worth that. I might have to consider it so I can run around alone."

"Like you'd go anywhere without Daws. Big baby." Brian scratched at his head and smoothed his hair down.

"Hey, trust me, I try."

"Yeah, okay. Don't rub it in that you're stalked more than we are. Be a good winner."

"Hell. Just different fans. Different music."

"Uh huh."

Dani punched his arm. "Hey asshole, don't ignore me."

He barely glanced at her. "Take the wig off. I don't like redheads."

"No?" She shrugged out of her coat and handed it to Brian, then slid her arms around Ryan's waist and pressed into him. Her warmth mingled with his own and the skimpy baby-doll tee didn't hide any of her incredible shape. "Never saw you that particular before, and I can get your attention, you know." She ran fingers up his back.

He laughed and returned the hug. "Okay, you got it."

"Don't mess with me. You know you won't win." Dani released him with a grin and looked around him toward the kitchen.

Ryan turned and went to Katie, grasping her fingers while Dani pulled out of the wig and readjusted her own dark hair into the ponytail she always wore.

His friend didn't wait to be introduced; a quick stride brought her face-to-face. "You're Kaitlyn. It's wonderful to meet you." Instead of a handshake, she gave Katie a quick hug.

It surprised her but she accepted and met Dani's face. "You too. You've been Ryan's friend a long time?"

"Forever. At least it seems that way. About ... what? Six years or almost?" Dani didn't bother getting his answer. "Doesn't sound like a long time but it is for us since neither of us do friendships that well. Part of the job, really. It gets hard when you don't know who wants to be an actual friend and who's trying to be only for the name and image, but I suppose you've seen that by now." She studied Kaitlyn, not long enough to make her uncomfortable, but long enough.

Brian introduced himself and settled for a handshake. Dani nearly interrupted. "Damn Ry, she's way too pretty for you. I think you're out of your league."

"Yeah, no kidding, but you don't have to tell her."

Dani smiled and gave him a quick half hug, leaving her arm around him as she returned focus to Katie. "He knows I'm joking. I've chased girls away from him plenty when they weren't good enough. Wasn't sure he'd find one who was." She patted Ryan's stomach. "Go put some clothes on and at least try to be polite, would you?"

He shrugged. "Like you haven't seen me in less? Doesn't seem to be bothering you."

"Not doing anything for me, either."

"Ouch. Thank you."

She glanced at his chest. "What can I say? I like my guys bigger than me, and that's not really very hard to find...."

"Stop there. And don't tell secrets while I'm not listening. I've been emasculated enough for today." He threw Brian a gesture at his 'need to workout with more than a beer bottle' comment and surrendered the battle of wits to go grab a shirt.

Ryan enjoyed the interaction through the morning. Kaitlyn seemed both intrigued and overwhelmed, a typical reaction when someone met Dani, and his friend ignored his warnings and acted like she and Kaitlyn had been best friends forever.

Dani became quieter, though, when Daws brought Nick over, other than giving Daws a big hug and teasing him throughout conversation. She spoke to Nick enough to be polite, but as Ryan expected, she avoided any personal talk.

As soon as he could, he grabbed a moment to draw Daws off alone and asked how the show plans were going, glad to know it wasn't out that Ryan had anything to do with setting it up. They would get there early and have the small dark side section reserved so maybe they could go unnoticed. If not, there would be plenty of security around acting like customers unless needed.

Arms wrapped around him from behind. "Hey you can talk to him any time. I'm only here for a few days."

He turned his head to half see Dani's face. "Well hell, you're more interested in talking to Kaitlyn, anyway. What do you need me for?"

She laughed and moved around to his front, still with an arm around him. "Wow, she's adorable, Ry. And sweet as can be. Sure she can handle you?"

"She can handle him." Daws took a swallow of his water with a glance over to where Katie talked with Nick and Brian. "Don't be fooled. He'll have his hands full as she keeps getting more comfortable."

"No kidding." Ryan threw her a grin when she looked over.

"Yeah? So she seems good for you. You're..." Dani searched his face. "More relaxed. And her dad's okay with it by now?"

"I don't know that he is, but he's given up fighting it."

"Want me to talk to him? I can tell him how great you are, how much I adore you, not that my opinion would count for anything..."

Ryan hugged her. "It matters to me. And I'm glad you're getting along with her. That matters to me, too."

Dani pulled back. "I can't imagine how anyone wouldn't be nice to her. It's impossible to imagine."

"Yeah. And hey, there's something I want to do, that I started already, but I want your opinion before I tell her. Come talk to me a minute." Ryan pulled her into the kitchen.

Deanna and Dani decided to take Kaitlyn for a girl's afternoon the next day while Ryan took care of business. Deanna took a couple of friends along, as well, one of whom was on his security team. Brian went to visit other friends in the city and Nick decided to hang out with Ryan. When he mentioned Nick's deal to do something with him musically in front of his band and manager, plans began to form.

Ryan had a great time hanging with Nick at work, but he was more than ready to see the girls when they all met up for dinner. He stared finding Kaitlyn. She'd had her hair styled and highlighted. It was partly pulled back and showed her ears. Opal pierced earrings matched the moonstone necklace he'd given her and some kind of twisting things clamped along the outside of her ears. Dark green gems embedded in them highlighted both her eyes and the shiny emerald blouse.

Dani nudged against him. "We were playing with makeup. Worked well, didn't it?"

Makeup. The dark red scars weren't even noticeable around the earrings. He nodded and took Katie's hands. "Have a good day?"

"Yes. Can I keep her?"

Ryan laughed. "Good luck. She's hard to hold down."

Dani gave her a hug. "We'll get together. Promise." Then she smacked Ryan on the chest. "Let's eat. We've nearly worn her out walking all over the city."

With Dani in the guest room and Brian on his couch, Ryan was content enough to lay beside Katie and just hold her. Besides, Dani was right. She was tired from the girls' day out, and likely from the emotions of dealing with her ears.

He brushed hair from the side of her face. "So I've been talking with a plastic surgeon." Her eyes shot to his, waiting. "She thinks she can help with the scars on your back and maybe your ears, if you want to try. It might not be perfect, she said, but better. And by summer, if you got started soon, you'd be able to swim without..."

"It would be expensive."

"Doesn't matter."

"Ryan..."

"Katie, the expense doesn't matter. It only matters if you want to go through that, because she said it would be painful and I nearly didn't mention it because the idea of you going through more pain..."

"The pain doesn't matter."

He could feel his eyes widen. "No? How could you not care about going through more pain?"

"It's not as bad as staying covered, never being able ... but it's too much, with the house and..."

He rolled her to face the other direction and traced the scar lines with his fingers while he kissed her shoulder. "The expense doesn't matter. Don't even think about it. But..." He trailed a line of kisses along them, as he did the first time he'd seen her back. "You wouldn't have to cover them. You could know it doesn't make you less beautiful, doesn't make you less anything. You know it doesn't change anything. You're okay as you are; you shouldn't have to hide."

"People stare."

"Ignore them. They'll stare anyway because you're beautiful and you're sweet and you're smart and it shows all over you."

"But they won't see me. They'll see what happened and they'll avoid me or they'll ask and I ... I'd rather keep it covered." She turned onto her back and found his eyes.

"Do you want to at least talk to her? Let her tell you more about it?" He saw her consider, maybe still worrying about the money. "I'll make an appointment. Just to talk. But at any time, if you want to try, you stop if it's too much. I don't want you to be in pain."

She pulled his face closer and touched his lips. "It hurts a lot to have a baby, too, but someday ... someday I want to try again."

A baby. It was still in her thoughts. He wondered how constantly it was. Ryan nodded. "I hoped you would. Someday."

~~~

So much for staying in the background. Stu made a production out of Ryan being at the show, teasing that he was honored such a pop superstar would make time for a washed up musician. He looked glad to see Nick and chatted freely about the old days, with a hand on Dani's back now and then.

When he went on stage, though, he was more careful. Ryan had a hard time watching Kaitlyn as much as he wanted since Dani's gaze pulled so much attention. Her adoration for Stu was impossible not to see. And while Stu did point "Riveting Ryan" and his drummer out to the crowd while he was at the bar, making too much of it that he was there, he said nothing about the others.

Deanna worried that it would insult Dani and Brian. Ryan assured her it absolutely wouldn't. Stu kept her hidden by her own preference and Brian went along with what she wanted, whether or not he agreed.

"Hey." Outside The Bitter End under glow of city lights, Stu set a hand on his shoulder. "Hope you don't mind my outing you like that. Gotta forgive a guy for doing what he can to get his name back out there enough to get a show or two as he can."

"Hell, we both know it looks better for me than it does for you. And you know attention doesn't bother me. Most of the time." Ryan looked over at the girls checking out posters tacked up in front of the building. Some advertised coming acts and some bragged about acts that had already been there. Daws and Nick watched over them, their eyes on anyone who walked by. Brian and Ned were of course flirting with a couple of girls from the club.

"Gonna be around the next couple of nights? I have other shows set up while I'm here."

"Sure. Tell me where and I'll drop by. Katie and Nick are going back to Vermont on Sunday, though, and Dani's leaving in the morning...."

"No, she's not." Stu glanced over at her. "She's heading back with me on Monday. Her dad's request. Don't know why, but she agreed when I talked to her before I went on so I guess she does."

Monday. So much for free time with Kaitlyn before she had to go. Her counselor okayed short visits to New York, but wanted her mainly in Vermont for a while yet.

Stu insisted they all find something open late to grab food. Daws wasn't happy about the group of them wandering around New York City at night but no one paid much attention other than when Dani and Brian and Deanna got to laughing. And they were only barely curious glances. That's what Ryan liked about the place. People were too concerned with their own business to worry much about anyone else's, for the most part.

The best they could do was a bar where they found an open corner. Deanna sat on Kaitlyn's other side until Dani got tired of Ned and traded her places with the excuse of wanting to "chat with Katie." Ryan grinned at her use of Kaitlyn's nickname instead of her full name.

Sipping his beer, he mainly sat back and kept an eye on the whole scene, and especially on Kaitlyn's reaction to it. She wasn't bothered. She'd purposely moved back against a wall so no one would be behind her and when Dani ordered two grasshoppers and handed her one, she gave no reaction to show she was too young to have it. Ryan knew the bartender was watching, but he also knew the guy recognized both him and Stu and would say nothing if it wasn't necessary. They would be sure to tip him well.

Since conversation around the table didn't include him at the moment, he moved closer to Katie and raised her hand to kiss her fingers. "Are you having fun tonight?"

She smiled at him, a light, soft smile. "Yes."

"Seriously? This is okay?"

"You have good friends."

"Yeah, they're pretty cool. I'm glad you're enjoying yourself. Interested in going to another show tomorrow night? Stu's playing again."

She nodded.

"You know you can tell me if you don't. He won't be offended."

"I love to watch music. I always wanted to. I saw local bands sometimes at fairs when I was little but not since. I always wished I could like other kids did when I heard them talk about it."

"Katie, if you want to go out and see live music, any time, just say so. I'll find someone playing somewhere. Any night I'm not working." He shrugged. "That is, whenever you can be here. Or when I can take you anywhere."

Her hand slid around to his waist and she pressed her face against his neck. Then she raised her mouth close to his ear. "You don't have to keep trying to fix everything. It's okay now. I want to be here. With you. Even without you if you get tired of me. It's okay. You don't have to worry anymore."

Ryan clenched his eyes through forced breath and moved to touch his forehead to hers. She wanted to be there ... to be. If he was there or if he wasn't.

He couldn't wait for privacy. He had to give it to her now. Moving back to unzip the inner pocket of his jacket, he pulled out the ring that matched her necklace – moonstone, shaped the way the moon had been when she mentioned being able to sit up there on it.

Ryan grasped her fingers and raised the ring to where she could see it. Silence grew as the noise shifted from around his table to farther out into the bar as though a wave rushed to shore and hushed out again. He let the effect refresh him, strengthen him, his attention on the gem left in its wake. "I had this made a while ago and I've been waiting for the right time. It's a promise ring, my promise to you that I want to be here, that I want to be with you and only with you. Everything I do for you is because I want to do it, because I want to give you everything I can give you." Caressing her fingers with his thumb, he leaned closer. "Will you accept it? It means I don't want you to date other guys although I'm sure there are so many who would be better..."

"No one else." Her eyes watered. "I don't want anyone else."

"I hope that doesn't ever change." He slipped the ring onto her right ring finger, not the left, it wasn't an engagement ring. "I love you, Kaitlyn. You will never have to worry about what I'm doing when I'm not with you. I promise." He heard the comments and congratulations while he kissed her, blocking it as well as he could from their view with a hand against her face.

Dani grabbed his arm and pulled him back as they strolled the sidewalk waiting for the taxis and admiring strands of lights wrapped around windows of businesses. "So I have to ask. Why didn't you just propose to her? Not that sure yet?"

Ryan grabbed a deep breath of nippy winterish air and checked to make sure no one was close enough to hear. "Because she's eighteen. And because she still has a ways to go before she can really stand on her own. She may change her mind at that point and I don't want her to feel too locked in if she does."

"She won't, Ryan. I can see it in the way she looks at you."

"I can only hope." With a wink, he locked his arm around hers. "By the way, I have her Christmas gift already. Part of it."

"Yeah? After buying her a house, how do you plan to top that?"

He laughed. "Well, probably won't. Told you I changed the album last minute. Mac thought I was nuts but damn, you gotta hear it. It's me again. My songs, the way I meant them to be. And most are about her."

Dani stopped walking. "Serious?"

"Very. I have a demo for you but you can't let anyone else hear it or know you have it. The cover matches her necklace. I dedicated it to her."

"Well. I take it back." Dani held his gaze. "You outdid the house."

"Think so?"

She threw a half grin. "You know what I'd give to have a guy do something that sweet and insane for me? She's a lucky girl, Ryan. There isn't one of us who wouldn't want that." Grabbing his shirt in front of his stomach underneath the unzipped jacket, she pulled him closer. "Can I make one suggestion?"

"Of course."

"Don't be too careful. Don't treat her like anything's wrong with her. It'll just make things harder."

"I don't think I am..."

"You warned me before I came not to push too close to her. Why?"

"Because she ... it bothers her, close contact. Usually. Apparently not with you. Maybe she knows already how much I trust you."

"And maybe you're being too careful. There's a fine line between being protective and being possessive. Watch that. Let her handle her own situations as much as possible. She needs to be able."

He looked over to where the rest had stopped down the sidewalk to wait for them. Katie was talking with Stu, actually speaking to him, Daws at her side. "She reminds me of you in a lot of ways. Should I tell you that?"

Dani set her chilled hands alongside his face. "I'm flattered. Just be good to her or you know I'll come after you. No matter how much I love you." With a light kiss, she lowered her hands to take his arm and catch up with the group.

27

Nick and Rebecca's "cabin" in Montana turned out to be an old ski lodge they'd redesigned into a private residence. When he told Ryan he had plenty of space to host whoever he wanted there for Christmas, Ryan expected to be crowded. He gave in, though. Katie had agreed to testify against the man who attacked her and Andrea. It was scheduled for a few days before Christmas and Robert wanted them to stay. Ryan couldn't blame him for wanting her around for a few days afterward to be sure she got through it all right.

He'd yet to spend a Christmas away from his family and couldn't imagine doing it this year, either, so he flew them out to be there. Matthew and Isabelle had a grand time building snowmen and playing with Katie's brothers on the bunny slope using sleds Nick always had on hand for his nephews.

Katie got through the ordeal better than Ryan, or anyone else, expected. Because of the circumstances, she was able to testify in a small, private way without it being publicized. He stayed at her side as her condition of agreeing to testify, with no one in either family allowed in the room. She didn't want them there. And it worked. The man was sentenced to another fifteen years. Ryan stayed in her room that night although Robert was in the house. She was shaken. He didn't want her to be alone. Her dad didn't argue.

Ryan admired her now from across the room as she sat beside the crackling fire, legs curled up on the big chair, a book in hand. Bella and Curtis were lying on the floor in front of her, also with a book they talked about together. Every chance she got, Bella imitated Kaitlyn. Tracy worried it would annoy her but Ryan knew she was too flattered to be annoyed. And he expected it reminded her at least somewhat of her own child she missed. She didn't hide from the reminder. She embraced it, and often held Bella in her lap to enjoy her company.

"Can I tell you how beautiful it is to see you watch her with that expression?"

Ryan turned to Andrea. And she glanced over at Kaitlyn. "I'm so glad she found someone who loves and respects her as you do. We should all have that."

He tried to figure out how to answer, hearing Dani's near exact words echoed in Andrea's thoughts. He couldn't, though. Robert was just behind her.

"Yes, we should." He walked around to his startled wife and sat next to her. "I was just talking to Nick and Rebecca about babysitting for us." She stared at him. "Why?"

"Because you've always wanted to go to Egypt to see the pyramids. I thought we could go alone, for the honeymoon I promised you and never got around to doing."

"Robert ... are you ... you mean it?"

"Merry Christmas, Andrea. This is only the beginning of what I should have been for you. Thank you for waiting it out."

Katie looked over. She saw Andrea hold onto Robert and listened to Nick's chatter about the fulfilled promise, long overdue.

"Dad!" Stephen interrupted. "Come snowball fight with us! You said later and it's later now."

"Yes, it is." Robert gave his wife's face a caress and turned to the boy. "Go get ready."

Kaitlyn closed her book. Before Robert got up, she walked over beside her brother.

"Are you going to snowball fight with us?" Stephen tilted his head at her. "Come on, it'll be fun. We'll be easy on you because you're a girl."

Matthew pushed at him. "She's bigger than you."

"But she's a girl."

"So? My grandma is a girl, but she's scarier than most boys."

Ryan chuckled at Matt and at his mom saying he better remember that, too. But he kept his attention on Katie. She moved in front of her dad. Will shooed the boys and Bella over to find their coats and hats and gloves.

"You never liked snowball fights." Robert studied her as she stood silent. "Don't let them push you into it."

"You promised to teach me to ski. You haven't yet."

Robert's chest rose sharply. "Yes, I did. Go get your coat."

"The boys..."

"They'll be fine with the rest of us." Ryan jumped up from the chair. "Go ski. Just be careful, okay? Don't break anything." He kissed the side of her head and went off to join the noisy garble of adding winter gear to the excitement of choosing teams.

With the snowball fight arena close to the bunny hill, Ryan was hit several times while he kept track of how she was doing.

Nick laughed at the newest hit. "Gotta keep your head in the game."

"It is." Ryan ducked an incoming. "More than ever before." He held up a hand as a sign for time out, and looked over again. Mastering a quick, graceful run down the hill, Katie waited for her dad to take her side and gave him a long, tight hug.

Ryan and Nick agreed to play for the cold-tired group as they sat around the fireplace. They did some Christmas carol sing-a-longs and then a few of his songs and a few from Foresight and Raucous, as well as others they both knew well enough to fake being able to play. Rebecca requested *Baby I'm A Want You* from Nick, and Ryan sat out to let him have full attention.

Tracy threw a wink as Nick finished. "I think it's Kaitlyn's turn. Tell him what he should play for you."

He wasn't sure she wanted to make a request, until she found his eyes and asked for the one he'd started to sing on the ledge. *Open Shores*. His own. He finally finished it, with plenty of rewriting, during her hospital stay.

As it ended, she moved up against him and cuddled into his side.

Ryan was done playing. He handed the guitar to Paul and told him to go practice. Robert suggested his son ask Nick to help him with chords.

As they exchanged gifts, Kaitlyn said the emerald and ruby jewelry set he gave her was too much. Her dad gave him the impression he thought it was too much. Ryan didn't care if it was. It was gorgeous on her.

She, in turn, handed him three journals he didn't recognize. They were filled with her poetry, handwritten. Enscribed to him. It was worlds better than jewelry. Especially when she admitted in front of everyone what it was and that they were only for him.

He saved the CD for later in the evening when the kids were in bed and the fire had waned nearly to ashes. The cover sported a wolf howling in front of a crescent moon, with the album title in bold swirled letters: *Off The Moon*. Her eyes watered as they touched his. And then he opened it to the dedication.

> *To Kaitlyn, my star*
> *This one is for you*
> *and for me*
> *and I'll always be*
> *at your side*
> *off the moon.*

Katie held him for the longest time as the CD was passed around. He didn't tell her the last song on the album, also the title track, was about her child, and theirs, and those yet to be. Not yet. He would tell her when he took her to the headstone he'd had added to the nearly unmarked grave of her child, where Kaitlyn sat for days before walking away, to find him.

Find lyrics for Ryan's songs and a discussion guide
on the author's website,
plus photo album, guest book, and information
about LK Hunsaker's other works.

www.LKHunsaker.com

*and everyone's
in love and flowers pick themselves*

EE Cummings

I've Waited For You
Vicki Blankenship

Time sometimes slips away
And time sometimes just stands still
Time builds upon our memories
And time washes away the thrills

I looked to the future to find brighter days
I looked to the future to change my silly ways
I looked to the future hoping for you
To see what was deep inside my mind.

I've waited to hold you deep in the night
I've needed to feel you with all of my might
I've ached to feel your breath in my ears
And I've wasted away too many years.

Love sometimes gets away
And love sometimes leaves at will.
Love sometimes carries on
And love sometimes is simply reborn.

I've waited for you to look straight in my eyes
I've waited for you to finally realize
I've waited for you to be by my side
And I'm not gonna go without a fight.

Oh… come here to me

From *Blue Flame Trance* by Vicki Blankenship
©2008 Vicki Blankenship. Reprinted with permission.
www.SpottedKivaProductions.com